The Silvered Heart

Katherine Clements

headline
review

First published in Great Britain in 2015 by HEADLINE REVIEW
An imprint of HEADLINE PUBLISHING GROUP

First published in paperback in 2016 by HEADLINE REVIEW

1

Cataloguing in Publication Data is available from the British Library

ISBN 978 1 4722 0426 4

Typeset in Aldine 401 BT by Avon DataSet Ltd, Bidford-on-Avon, Warwickshire

Printed and bound in Great Britain by Clays Ltd, St Ives plc

MIX
Paper from
responsible sources
FSC® C104740

HEADLINE PUBLISHING GROUP
An Hachette UK Company
Carmelite House
50 Victoria Embankment
London EC4Y 0DZ

www.headline.co.uk
www.hachette.co.uk

For Ian and Paula

'Near the Cell there is a well
Near the well there is a tree
And under the tree the treasure be'

Old Hertfordshire rhyme identifying the whereabouts
of the spoils of highway robbery, buried by the
Wicked Lady of Markyate Cell

1648

Chapter 1

The distant drum of galloping hoofs conjures nothing but doubt and fear, these days. I am the first to hear it – a far-off rumble, creeping to the fore, pushing other thoughts aside.

My maidservant, Rachel, nods on the bench opposite, head bobbing and swaying with the motion of the carriage. I don't know how she can sleep. My own mind is so busy I've barely rested in the two days since we left Markyate Cell.

Our journey has become a slow crawl across England's lead-pocked, battle-churned land. In my stepfather's coach the seats are hard, the hangings plain, and the cushions have long since shed their down. My bones ache, bump and bruise with every jolt of the wheels.

We cannot travel in comfort, for that would attract the attention of thieves and brigands, but Sir Simon insists that his stepdaughter must arrive in the manner most fitting, despite the danger on the roads; the cramped, heavily armed and escorted carrier might be safer, but it's no transport for a Fanshawe. Nor can they spare arms to protect us, for any honourable man is gathering his strength and his guns and preparing to fight the Roundheads once again. With the King imprisoned at Carisbrooke, and his men turning traitor every day, not a single steadfast soul can be spared, and certainly not for me. We must all take risks for the sake of King Charles.

I hear the sharp swipe of the whip as Master Coleman, our driver, spurs the horses on. The pair of greys we switched to at Bedford do not have the strength of Sir Simon's own, but the coach bounces in the ruts as we gain a little speed.

Rachel wakes, rubs her eyes and wipes the corner of her mouth where drool has crusted. 'Is it evening so soon?'

I pull back the leather flap at the window to show her dusk creeping through the trees. The sun is low and fiery orange, dazzling through the branches to play tricks on my eyes. The sky is turning red. The thrum of horses' hoofs draws closer.

'They said we'd reach Hamerton before dark,' she says, frowning. 'Lady Alice will fret if we don't arrive by nightfall.'

The riders are clearly ahead of us, the rolling thunder suggesting a number of men on the road. Rachel registers the noise, forehead creasing. 'Who could that be?'

I say nothing, but she must read the fear in my eyes, because she reaches across and circles my fingers with hers. 'I'm sure they'll pass us by.'

There is movement above – George, the coachman's boy, turning back along the roof to fasten the straps on my trunks. Master Coleman cracks the whip and the horses break into a reluctant canter. Rachel is thrust forward into my lap.

Both of us let out a cry of surprise, but before I can call out to Coleman, there is a sudden blast and a *whump* as something hits the rear of the carriage. A small round hole appears in the back panel, just to the right of my head, sending a shaft of golden sunset streaking across the gloom.

Rachel clutches my arm, panic-eyed. 'What, in God's name—'

There are voices up ahead, the echo of men's shouts amid the trees. Then, one voice raised above the others: 'Hold your horses or pay with your lives!'

My heart climbs into my throat.

We judder to a stop, the horses whinnying their protest, harnesses jangling, like discordant bells.

Coleman's voice calls urgently from above. 'Keep inside, Lady Katherine . . . and stay silent.'

I can guess what is coming. It is the thing that all travellers must risk in these days of misrule, when men make opportunity from misfortune. The lucky charm that Lady Anne pressed upon me will do nothing to protect us from bandits and outlaws. A swarm of them infects the roads like a plague, plundering at will, with no one able to prevent it. We have a musket, tied between the chests on the roof of the carriage – a better hope than any trinket, but poor protection against the ruthless demands of the lawless, and at this moment, out of reach.

I see the barrel of a pistol before I see the man, its round, black mouth no bigger than a penny. Then the leather flap at the window is torn aside and a face appears in its place. A filthy brown kerchief covers the man's nose, mouth and chin. His hat is pulled low, leaving only squinting dark eyes and heavy brows in view. He stares at me. Rachel pulls herself onto the seat, positioned between us. Her expression is defiant but her hand, settled protectively on my knee, trembles.

The man tugs the door open.

The pistol twitches. Once. Twice. 'Get out.'

My legs are weak and my heartbeat rapid as I step down from the carriage. I stumble, clumsy and tripping in the mud. Rachel follows and puts her arm around me.

'Be strong, Kate,' she whispers, close in my ear. 'Don't show your fear.' But there are no tears in my eyes: terror is trapped in my chest, squeezing my lungs, binding my breath. She grips my hand tight.

I can smell them: three men stinking of rot, liquor and the latrine – the stench of scum. One, still mounted and holding the reins of two other scrawny nags, nervously watches the road. A second stands by our coach horses, pistol trained on Master Coleman, who sits on the driver's seat with George, hands surrendered to the sky. His face quivers, the spark of fury in his eyes. For an older man, I know he still has some fight in him – among Sir Simon's stable lads, he is known for boxing ears.

The man who turned us out of the carriage lowers the pistol. 'Do not think to tarry with me,' he says. 'I've no patience for weeping women.' His voice is gruff, as though he has swallowed flint.

He searches inside the coach and pulls out my travelling pack. He upturns it, emptying it into the mud. My discarded needlework, a book and the doll, Henrietta, which I could not leave behind, tumble out. Henrietta's dark curls splay on the ground, yellow-white painted pearls matching her teeth, her smile serene as always. Lady Anne was wise when she bade me leave behind my mother's jewels.

The man is not satisfied with this girlish plunder and steps back to scan the coach, his eyes narrow and searching, like those of a rat seeking scraps.

'The trunks . . .' he says, indicating the luggage tied atop the carriage. 'You, boy, throw them down.'

George looks to Master Coleman, who gives a grim nod. He stands, swaying slightly, giving away an uncharacteristic lack of deftness, and starts to untie the straps.

The man turns his attention to me. He levels the pistol at my chest.

'Take off your cloak.'

I lower my hood and unfasten the cord at my neck with fat-witted fingers. The heavy grey wool drops to the floor.

'I knew it,' he says. 'Ripe for the taking.'

Although I cannot see his leer, I sense the stirring in him. I have heard that cracking thickness in a man's voice before.

'Come closer,' he says.

I back away, still clinging to Rachel's hand. She stands before me. 'Leave her be.'

'Move aside, girl. Unless you want the same.'

'If you touch them, you'll regret it,' Master Coleman says, voice full of threat, but one of the others raises a pistol and demands silence.

The man grips my arm and drags me away from the roadside, taking me down a steep bank, through bracken and brambles, thorns tearing at my skirts, the pistol dug hard against my ribs.

Rachel cries out, 'Please, no! She's barely more than a child . . .'

I twist to look back over my shoulder just in time to see the second man go towards her, while the third trains his gun on George, now lowering the luggage from the roof.

My captor's fingertips dig into my flesh, even through the thick layers of my winter travelling gown. My arm feels as though it might snap like a twig. My heart patters, a bitter tang rising on my tongue. I cannot tell whether the sound in my ears is the rushing of blood or the wind in the trees.

I can no longer see the road or the carriage, though the echo of Rachel's pleading winds eerily through the canopy like birdcall. The man pushes me up against the wide trunk of an old, dead sycamore and brings the barrel of the pistol level with my chest.

'Your jewels. Where are they?' His fingernails scratch my neck. He finds the thin chain of silver that is always fastened there and slowly draws the pendant up and out from beneath my bodice. 'Here's a fine treasure.' With a swift, hard tug he breaks the chain and dangles it to take a better look. The polished silver heart gleams in the fading light, brilliant as the rising moon. 'A pretty trinket. Where's the rest?'

'I have no other.'

'Don't lie to me, girl.' He slides the barrel of the gun up my neck to rest against my cheek. I try to turn my face away but he catches hold of my chin, digs his nails into my jaw and forces the maw of the pistol between my lips. It clashes against my clenched teeth. I taste smoke and iron. His eyes follow the path of the gun and I see their dark points widen. He holds me there for a few seconds. I dare not move, nor even breathe. I close my eyes, too afraid even to pray.

'Money, then.' He releases me slightly, slides the barrel from my mouth so I can reply.

'In the trunks, what little I have.'

His free hand moves over my waist, my bodice.

'Your pocket?'

I fumble for the small pouch, hidden always in my petticoats. My fingers are clumsy as I untie the knot and offer it to him. He snatches it away, the paltry contents spilling into his palm. He snorts. 'There must be something else worth having in those skirts.'

'I swear, I have nothing of value.'

He bends and places the pistol on the forest floor, never taking his eyes from mine, and then, before I have the wit to run, his hands are on me, tearing at my lacings.

'Please, no . . .'

He bats my hands away and lands a stinging slap across my cheek. Sharp, bright pain explodes across my jaw, making stars before my eyes. He tugs at my stays until he can slide his fingers beneath. He makes a low growl, like a hound, as he finds flesh. He squeezes my breast hard.

I try to fight, finding strength in my panic, but he pushes up against me with such force that the air is squeezed from my lungs, and I am crushed against the bark. The stink of him, like a long-dead carcass, makes me retch. As his face comes close to mine I catch the stench of rotting teeth beneath the kerchief, and rank traces of sulphur. In the struggle I knock his hat to the ground. Rat-brown hair is shorn close to his scalp, a few longer strands plastered against his neck, but there is a patch where there is no hair at all and the skin is red and scabbed: a wound of some sort that oozes, slick and yellow. His eyes are dark, flat, without depth, without even a haze of lust. They are the eyes of a dead man, the eyes of a ghost.

His hand searches beneath my petticoats until he finds skin.

No man has ever touched me there. I begin to sob and plead. Strength deserts me as my body begins to quake. He is forceful, moving towards my centre. I shut my eyes and beg: Please, God, do not let this happen. Not here. Not now. Not this man.

From the road comes the sharp retort of gunshot. Once. Twice. Rachel's scream echoes through the trees, like a fox's cry. My heart plunges and tilts. The man hesitates for the briefest moment. I think that he means to rip off the kerchief and kiss me with that foul mouth, but instead he finds the place between my legs.

Fear gets the better of me then. My body rebels. A stream of hot wetness gushes over his hand. It does not stop him. He seems to like it. He enjoys my terror.

'You dirty whore,' he says, leaning up against me. I feel him harden against my thigh as his fingers stab inside. I sense it then – a breaking apart deep in my chest, as something shatters like a dropped looking glass. The silvered shards protecting my soul crack and cloud with black, broiling smoke. The choking stink of charcoal and scorched bone fills my nostrils. I cry out; part pain, part despair. Above me, the ancient, twisted boughs of the sycamore tree stretch away like the Devil's claws. Amid the flaming red sunset, a single star blinks bright.

The air cracks and there is a rushing, whooshing sound. I feel the sudden impact as something hits the man, forcing the weight of him further against me. Then he arches backwards, making a strangled cry. He twists away, hands leaving my body, clutching at air instead. My gaze finds George standing atop the ridge at the roadside, smoking musket at his shoulder, face curd-white against orange hair, the gun heavy in his hands.

My captor slumps to his knees, face twisted in a grimace of angry shock. I slide away from the trunk as he falls at my feet with a strange burbling moan. There is a small red hole in the leather of his coat where the bullet pierced him.

There is another shot and George is tossed backwards with a yell. I see the man on horseback, struggling to reload his pistol, as his mount bucks and dances.

I grab the flintlock from the leaf-strewn floor. It's loaded and cocked. All I need do is pull the trigger. Suddenly I'm five years old, back in the parklands at Markyate Cell, watching my brothers at their marksman practice. My father's voice comes to me: 'Use both hands, and steady yourself before the shot.'

I take aim. I pull the trigger. My hands are shaking and the bullet goes wide, but it's enough to cause the horse to fright, almost dumping the man on the road. He struggles to keep his seat, then holsters his pistol, wheels about, dragging on the reins, and takes flight away to the south.

I drop the gun. It lies smoking at my feet. My chest heaves. The man is still and silent, no breath left for him. Quickly, I reach into the pocket of his coat and take back my necklace, then push my way through the bracken to George.

He is awake, eyes rolling like those of a wounded deer. The shot has grazed his arm, taking the flesh with it. I see pale bone amid the mess of gore. His face is grey, sheened with sweat, and his teeth are chattering.

I shout for Rachel. Searching for her in the gathering dusk, I find her standing by the carriage, staring at something on the ground, perfectly still, fixed by what she sees.

George is bleeding fast. I recall something I once saw done by my father's groom, who nursed a dog hit by shot, mistaken for a hare. I tear at my petticoats, now damp with my own waters, ripping away a strip of fabric and knotting it tight around George's arm, above the wound. He cries out and tries to push me away.

'You must stand it, George,' I say. 'It'll slow the bleeding. You must stand the pain.'

He grits his teeth, fixing me with a determined stare. Although he is taller than I, I manage to help him to his feet. He loops his good arm around my shoulders and we struggle towards the carriage. Thank God, the horses have not bolted, but they are twitching and stamping, ears flattened and eyes showing white.

As we reach Rachel, she turns her face to us, eyes dark with horror. There are two bodies on the road. One of the robbers, the man who held our horses, lies in a puddle of blood. His throat is slit. His mouth gapes, tongue lolling, fat and dripping red. The second is Master Coleman's, but I know so only by the little Fanshawe crest sewn upon his coat. His face is a ruin, a mess of flesh and bone, one eyeball dangling above the crescent moon of his teeth. There is a bloodied dagger, still clutched in his hand. George emits a low whimper. My stomach heaves. I swallow down the rising sickness.

There is no time for grieving. The light is fading fast and we must be away from here before it is dark. I dare not guess what fate awaits us in the woods after nightfall. The sound of shots will surely draw ruffians from miles around. The sense of urgent danger seems to clear my mind rather than cloud it. I'm determined to reach Hamerton before it is too late.

'Rachel, take George inside the coach,' I say. She pulls her eyes from the grisly scene to find mine. 'Do as I say.'

She falters as she sees George's injury, but she takes my place at his side and helps him into the carriage.

I cannot rescue the trunks, or save my belongings that lie strewn about the place, but I snatch up my woollen cloak, and the doll, Henrietta, now lying face down in the dirt, and toss them both inside the carriage.

Climbing up to the driver's seat, I gather the reins. I'm not sure the horses will answer to my voice but I urge them on, as I have seen others do so many times. They prick their ears and start to move. The coach lilts, like a boat at sea, and it takes a few faltering attempts but finally the suck of mud releases the wheels and the coach moves ahead.

I twist in my seat to make sure we are not followed.

Then, I see it, glowing ghostly blue in the twilight – my wedding gown, lying in the dirt, torn and spattered with blood.

Chapter 2

I have not seen Thomas Fanshawe, the man who is to become my husband, in five years. Five years of war.

Our only meeting was at Oxford, the King's court, in those days before the Roundheads stormed the field at Naseby, when we all believed our exile was temporary, our time in Oxford a happy inconvenience. The college cloisters were brilliant with silks and ribbons, the glitter of sapphires and emeralds, the heavenly chorus of lute and viola.

Thomas Fanshawe was a short, round boy, made up of coddled cream puddings and too many sweetmeats, not far beyond his tenth birthday. He was two years my elder, with a child's pre-occupations and a child's temper. When I first saw him he was sprawled on his belly, next to a fountain in the gardens of Merton College, where the Queen had her rooms, and her women gathered to escape the fetid air of the city proper. The most fashionable ladies of the court were drawn there, to wander the gravel paths, smell the summer roses, or idle away time in gossip.

My mother had found a shady spot for us to sit, her hand, as usual, in mine. Thomas was floating a wooden ship on the circle of water – a finely carved thing, with silk sails and tiny flags, embroidered with the colours of the Fanshawe crest. His play-mate, a scrap of a boy from the cellars, who should have known better, sent specks of gravel, like cannon fire, against the little boat. The boy, exuberant in his new-found freedom, unleashed one stone too hard. It caught a sail, tearing it, knocking the ship onto its side. The wreck bobbed sadly, waterlogged, adrift and out of reach.

Thomas attacked the boy before he had time to atone, barrelling into him, knocking him to the ground, fat fists pummelling. Their shouts echoed in the cloisters. A bevy of doves flapped skywards. Ladies looked up from their sewing, squinting against the sun to see what the fuss was about. But it was my mother who called Thomas to order. She clapped her hands for a page, and two appeared, wraithlike, from the shadows. They separated the scrapping boys, boxed the servant lad about the ears and dragged him off, protesting.

'Bring Master Fanshawe to me,' my mother said. Thomas, near to exploding with indignation, slumped towards us.

I studied this boy, my new-made cousin, from beneath lowered lashes, as my mother reprimanded him. His skin was pink, like fresh-carved ham, his full lips drawn into a sneer, his cheeks mottled. His eyes were brown and heavy-lidded. I noted the Fanshawe nose, the very likeness of Sir Simon – my mother's new husband and my new father, who was not my father at all.

Thomas was still a boy then, on the brink of manhood, burdened with the awkwardness of not yet fitting into the body that God had given him. He did not seem to notice me, his small, young cousin by his new aunt's side, except to glance at me, just the once, and I looked away quickly. When my mother had finished with him, he went, pouting and strutting, back across the garden to find some other scrape, the ship left bobbing, alone and forgotten on its small sea.

Five years have passed since that day. The court is no longer at Oxford because Oxford has fallen to Parliament's army and there is no longer any court at all. Those rosy, glittering ladies, who circled the Queen, like bees to blossom, are scattered as petals in the breeze, husbands and lovers all dead, exiled or battle-broken. The sun-soaked idyll of Merton ended for me on the day my mother died, but it was not long before it ended for all the others too.

I know my betrothed has arrived because I hear the clatter of hoofs in the yard, the yelp of hounds, the echo of men calling for stable lads.

Rachel is at the casement, the torn petticoat she is mending cast aside. 'They're here,' she says.

The chamber that George has been granted for the length of his recovery looks over the inner yard. Though my own room is much finer, with a view over the gardens to the orchards, it is from here that we can better see the comings and goings at Hamerton Manor.

In the three weeks since that awful night in the woods, we've spent almost every day in this room, keeping vigil over George. My aunt Alice, mistress of Hamerton, hears the story of George's valour and names him the saviour of the Fanshawe family, as if all hope of that great dynasty lies with me. He is lavished with strong caudle, meat pies and good beer from the brewhouse. Rachel insists on dressing his wound herself, packing it with salve to stop the rot, making sure he gets good food from the kitchens, not the scraps usually kept by for servants. After a week of fevered sleep, he overcomes the sickness, his wound begins to heal and he is gaining strength.

But I have not had a moment alone with him to ask what I must. Only George knows the truth of what I suffered at the hands of the robber in the woods. Only he witnessed the devil's touch upon my flesh, the fingers at work beneath my skirts. Only he knows that a musket shot saved me from worse. I've told no one, not even Rachel, swearing, when she asked, that the man did not dishonour me. I've swallowed the foul queasiness that rises when the memories come and I've kept my bruises well hidden as they yellow. They are almost healed now. When they are gone, that must be the end of it. George must keep my secret, because I fear Thomas Fanshawe would not take so tainted a wife.

I join Rachel at the window. There are six of them, young men, filling the yard with shouts and laughter, back-slapping, calling for ale, dogs yapping at their feet, stable boys scurrying around the horses, like vermin. They shed their travelling cloaks, revealing a rainbow of silk and velvet, the glint of gold buttons, the shine of silver swords, the lightning strike of white smiles. Capes whirl and hats are doffed as Aunt Alice bustles, hands clasped, thanking God for the safe arrival of her guests.

'Which one is he?' Rachel is impatient.

I cannot recognise the fat-faced boy with the sinking ship.

'I don't know,' I say. But there is another I have noticed, who keeps himself apart from the others and is taller than the rest, older too – too old to be my husband. He has dark glossy curls and a serious, handsome face with a neat black beard.

'They're all sporting swords. Are they all soldiers? Have they all fought for the King?' Rachel's cheeks grow flushed. 'Imagine . . . to be married to a hero.'

I shrug, but I know my future husband is considered too young, yet, for the King's army, just as I am too young to take up the Ferrers' estates. There has been no battlefield glory for him.

'They're all dressed very fine,' Rachel goes on. 'See the tall, dark one? Is that him?'

'No, I think not.' A glut has risen in my throat and my stomach feels alive with worms.

'Ah, well, that's good. You don't want a husband so handsome that other ladies are always in love with him.' She glances at me, waiting for a laugh that does not come. 'What's wrong?'

I have never been good at concealing my feelings – my mother used to say she could read the truth in my eyes as if she were reading scripture – but even so, Rachel has grown more attuned to my moods than most.

'Don't be afraid,' she says, taking up my hands. 'Thomas Fanshawe will not help but fall in love with you. You could have the pick of them, I'm sure.'

'As could you,' I say, in an echo of her faith in me.

She drops my hands and flaps her own in dismissal. 'What would I want with a fine gentleman like that?'

She turns back to the scene in the yard, watching as the men follow Aunt Alice inside, taking the glamour and light with them, like a band of players. I notice that she bites her lower lip to bring up the colour, eyes sidling to the bed. She knows she has her fair share of charms.

Rachel is every bit my equal, in everything but breeding. Three years ago, when she first sought work at Markyate Cell, it was our mirrored looks first caught my attention. I do not need a glass to see how a bolt of cloth brings out the hue of my eyes, or how a new stomacher flatters my slim waist; I need only look to her. I soon realised that we are alike in other ways too. She is similar in nature, but with a steadier temper and a capacity for obedience I could never match. And we share a mirrored history, both understanding what it means to be orphaned too young and to find ourselves in circumstances we were not born to. I need no other companion to laugh at my follies, or cheer me when the grief returns. We are a matching pair, sisters, in everything but blood.

I look to George, laid back against the bolster. He is pale still, a rash of freckles across his cheek lending some colour. He looks like a child compared to the men in the yard, though he is certainly their equal in years. He has a peculiar, haunted look in his eye.

Rachel goes to him and rests her hand on his forehead. 'Are you unwell, George?'

He pushes her wrist away and frowns.

She laughs nervously. 'Pay us no heed. I'm sure none of them is as brave as you.'

But George fixes his eyes on mine and they are full of questions.

Chapter 3

I marry Thomas Fanshawe in a borrowed gown and worn travelling shoes.

Master Maybury, Aunt Alice's steward, sent out a party to recover my things, but they tell me there was nothing to be found on the road, not even a bloodstain to mark poor Coleman's passing. Whoever those men were, somebody made sure to cover their tracks.

The dress, belonging to Lady Anne – another Fanshawe aunt – is made of red damask so stiff it could stand alone to meet the priest. There are petticoats of fine cambric, intricately embroidered with a rainbow of flowers, vines and tiny insects. 'Like the Garden of Eden,' Anne says, stroking the shimmering threads as she hands them over. 'Paradise beneath your skirts.'

Rachel gasps when she first sees it, whispering, 'Red is bad luck for a bride . . .' but she soon falls dumb under the weight of Anne's glare.

As I am dressed and primped by a giggling flock of Fanshawe women, I feel like a doll, trussed up in someone else's costume. Catching sight of myself in the glass, I barely recognise the girl looking back at me. I think of Henrietta, cleaned and mended now, face scrubbed of woodland mulch, sky blue silks puffed upon my pillow. If only I could scrub away my feelings so easily.

When I am ready, Anne shoos everyone but Rachel and me from the room. Anne's own gown hangs loose and flowing over the mound of her belly, her stays barely laced. Her hair is sugared into tight little coils, glistening with the syrup that binds them. She hauls herself onto the bed, leans back against the bolster. 'Ah, blessed relief. My feet are so sore.' She pats the mattress. I cross the room and perch beside her.

'Are you prepared, dear one?' she says.

I need not answer for Anne reads the trepidation in my eyes. She takes up my hand. 'I was a little older than you when I married my Richard, but I was a maid nonetheless and I know how you must feel. There's no need to be afraid. We are all slaves to Nature and there's nothing any of us can do about it.' She cradles her belly. 'This will be my fourth in as many years.'

I know that bedding is expected on a wedding night. I've watched enough newly-weds, drunken and laughing, borne away to their chambers. I've heard the bawdy comments of the groomsmen and watched the older women exchange know-it-all glances. But to imagine Thomas Fanshawe in my bed sends cold dread coursing through me.

I think of the man in the woods, the stab of his fingers, the stink of his breath, and the shame of the gushing wetness between my legs when I could not master my fear. Will my husband be able to tell that I have been touched in such a way?

'Thomas will make a fine father, in time,' Anne goes on. 'And until then, Alice will look after you.'

'What about the journey home? Will Thomas accompany me this time?'

'My dear, given your youth, it's wise to postpone your new life until you're both ready.' She twists towards me, hampered by her own weight. 'You'll stay here at Hamerton, out of harm's way, until the time is right.'

'But I thought to return to Markyate Cell . . .'

'We cannot risk another misadventure on the roads. My Richard is sure there'll be more fighting soon. You cannot go running about the country at whim. It's far too dangerous.'

'But Markyate Cell is the Ferrers' house. It's my home. It's where I belong.'

'I understand, Katherine, I do. As last of your bloodline the responsibility you carry is a great one, and it does you much credit that you wish to honour it. But by tonight you will be a Fanshawe. And Markyate Cell will belong to Thomas. You know this.'

'My mother always promised I would be mistress there one day. Sir Simon promised . . .'

Anne sighs. 'Times have changed and we are forced to change with them. We must be cautious. You must be patient and bide your time.'

The coiled temper that snakes about my heart begins to stir. 'But I—'

She holds up a hand to hush me, irritation barely concealed. 'There's no point in arguing with me, Katherine. I have little say in these matters. These things are up to our men. Believe me, yours is not the only life touched by the times. There are others have lost everything – their homes, their fortunes, their sons. Some of the old families are in tatters now, with no hope of recovery. We're lucky that we have not yet joined their number, but it is only a matter of chance. Count your blessings – be thankful for what little you have left and do not trouble Thomas with petty inconveniences. We must trust our king, trust our husbands, and trust that God will see our way clear through this.' She fixes me with such a determined, meaningful stare that I fall silent. 'Now, tell me, do you yet have your monthly courses?'

'For more than a year now.'

'Then there is no shame in doing your duty on your wedding night. The family expects to see the thing done, so there cannot be any doubt that the contract is binding. But after that you will be given some time. We cannot risk so precious a vessel.' She manages a smile. 'Now, is there anything you wish to ask me?'

I shake my head.

'Good girl.' She strokes my cheek. 'Such a pretty face. Thomas is quite the envy of his men. I'm sure you will be a great success together.' She draws out a little leather pouch. 'Here are the things I promised to keep safe for you.' She spills the contents into her palm. Diamonds sparkle like stars, pearls gleam like moonbeams.

I take the necklace and hold it up, remembering it glimmering at my mother's throat. I place it at my own. Rachel's eyes pop. 'Beautiful . . .' she whispers.

'Your girl is right,' Anne says. 'Make sure you look your best. Thomas is your future happiness. Make sure you secure him. The family expects much from your union.' Again she fixes me with her many-layered stare. 'And, Katherine, remember – there is no joy to be found in fighting our fate.'

And so I do not fight. I bend my knee before the priest and I say the words required of me. I hold Thomas's plump, damp fingers as we are bound together before God. I watch his face as we are made man and wife, studying the pinkish flush to his cheek, the fleshy downturned lips, and the drooping, haughty eyes that give nothing away. Although he is no longer the child from that day in Merton College, there are remnants of him in the young man at my side. He does not look at me once. And, perhaps because of this, I feel nothing – none of the joy or hope that I expected to feel on my wedding day. Instead, my hollow stomach aches and I am filled again with a dull sense of dread. As I make my vows, I cannot look the priest in the eye.

Afterwards, the guests gather in the hall. Wine is flowing. Aunt Alice has paid for minstrels, and as daylight fades, they set to work. A few couples are already merry enough to take to the floor. Fire flares bright in the hearth. Beams are garlanded with apple blossom from the orchards, white petals wilting in torch heat, falling in pretty flurries of springtime snow. A young man rushes past, balancing three plates of sweetmeats, face creased in concentration. I can smell the sprigs of tansy and rosemary that the maids have strewn about, the cloying scent of fat in the roasting tray, the tang of so many bodies.

Thomas guides me to a table where his groomsmen sit. I feel pricked all over with their stares. They take it in turns to kiss my hand and offer compliments. Each one bears a good family name and the confidence that comes with a few cups of wine. But there is no sign of Sir Richard Willis – the dark-haired man I first noticed in the yard. It was Anne who gave me his name, with a hitched brow and a knowing smile. 'A finer gentleman, I never knew,' was her only comment.

The young men's talk is all of hunting and horses. They speak over and around me, calling for more wine, easy in each other's company. No one addresses me. Every so often Thomas casts a sly little glance in my direction, checking that I'm still wearing my practised smile. I take the chance to observe him.

He is pleased with himself – that is clear. He talks a lot, and loudly, trying to outman his friends with a long tale of a stag slain in the King's park at Oatlands. He makes free with the wine and is quick to laugh, which is a promising sign, but I can find nothing to admire in his looks. He is too fleshy, too pallid, his stature yet unmoulded.

I feel the eyes of his friends slide towards me, settling on my body, my hair, my lips. They are judging me, I think, as I am judging Thomas. They are wondering what he will find beneath this suffocating scarlet cloth.

This is far from how I'd thought my marriage would be. When I was very young, and my mother first spoke of such things, she made marriage sound full of promise and sparkle. I know I am a prize for any man – the Ferrers name is still worth something, even though the estate will not bring the wealth it did in my father's day – and I always thought that I would have my choice of husband, in the end. But when my father died, my mother found no interest in the yields of our land or the prices at the Exchange. She had no head for account books and Parliament's taxes. Her solution to the great burden fallen upon her shoulders was to find another husband to take it all away again. And Sir Simon Fanshawe was pleased to do so. Now she is gone, my marriage to Thomas will bind the two families closer still, and strength is what is needed now, when the very roots upon which such things grow have been spliced and hacked about by Oliver Cromwell's army. Anne is right: the future is uncertain and we must all do what we can to secure it. Women cannot take up arms and ride into battle, but we must play our part all the same. Our role is more subtle, but no less important. We must use what talents we have to ensure the continuance of a family line. Family is what matters, especially in these days when our place in the world is turned upside down. Our hopes for the future must depend upon our courage and our children. We make our victories, and our legacies, in blood.

I understand all this. I have been taught well. I must do what is required by duty. Love does not come into it.

I become aware of a presence behind me, and turn to find Richard Willis standing there, one palm unfurled.

'My lady Katherine . . .' he says. 'Will you dance?' His voice is deep, measured, a hint of a smile behind it.

Thomas looks up.

Willis nods an acknowledgement. 'Fanshawe.'

'Ah, Willis, there you are. My bride would be honoured to dance with such a distinguished servant of the King,' Thomas says.

'I did not ask you, Fanshawe.'

Thomas raises an eyebrow and looks at me. 'Wife?'

'I'd like to dance,' I say, grateful that someone has thought of me.

Willis takes my hand and we join the couples close to the hearth. My body finds the rhythm quickly and my feet know the steps. For a while we mirror each other in silence. I know that, around the room, faces are turned in our direction. He makes a fine sight, after all. His black velvet doublet is rich and soft, trimmed with delicate lace. His boots have a high shine. He is neat and proud, not ostentatious like the others. Everything about him seems properly arranged and considered. Next to him I feel small, witless and unpolished. I long to break the silence between us, but cannot find the right words.

When, at last, he speaks, his voice is low, his words meant only for me. 'We've met before, though you won't remember. You were very young. It was at Markyate Cell. I knew your father a little, when I was a young man, schooled at Hertford.'

'You were a friend of my father?'

'Of sorts. He was a good, generous man. I was sorry when he passed.'

The pattern of the dance parts us for a few moments. When we come back together, he continues: 'I remember you well too. You cannot have been more than four or five years old. There was one afternoon in particular, when your father and I watched over you at play in the gardens. It was hot, summer, I think, and you had made up a song.' He pauses. 'Yes, I recall it now. You were dancing to your own tune in the sunshine.'

He conjures seductive memories. 'It was always sunny at Markyate Cell,' I say.

'Mm. They were happier times.'

Again, we are parted. It frustrates me. I want to hear more. I'm distracted until the music reunites us.

'And now my lady Ferrers has married a Fanshawe,' he says, his arm encircling me this time, as the dance requires. 'Your father would have been proud of you, Kate, if he could see the young woman you've become. Any man would be proud of you.'

I falter to hear my pet name upon his tongue. Only those closest to me call me Kate.

He fixes me with his dark eyes until I have to look away.

'Are you married, sir?'

'I am not. The King's business has kept me occupied these last few years. Besides, why wed when there is so much pleasure to be had elsewhere?'

I feel his hand gently squeeze my waist and my body tenses a little. There is a glint of amusement in his eye. Is he mocking me, or testing me? 'I don't know what you mean. I've always been taught that marriage is a duty, one of God's highest sacraments. It's what we are meant for and, as good Christians, we should aspire to it. Though . . . perhaps it's not the same for men.'

He laughs. 'You're very young, Kate, and yet untouched. You will learn, soon enough.'

His words make an uncomfortable curl in my innards. Untouched. He is wrong about that. The dance ends and he leads me back to the table.

Thomas looks relieved. 'Will you sit, Willis?' he says. 'Take a drink with us.'

Willis picks up my own cup of wine and drains it in one. 'Sorry, Fanshawe, but I've had some bad news. There's a messenger waiting for my reply.'

'Not bad news of the King, I hope?'

Willis makes an ambiguous gesture.

'You'll forgive me, Lady Katherine.' He retreats with a low bow.

Before he leaves the room he makes his way over to Sir Simon and bends to whisper in his ear. A cloud passes over Sir Simon's face. He excuses himself from Aunt Alice's company and follows Willis to the door.

'We're honoured to have Willis here at all,' Thomas says to me, and I realise he has been watching me, watching Willis. 'He's an intimate of Prince Rupert, and close to the King. There are few have proved themselves so brave, or so loyal, in these last years. Do not take offence if he is too busy, or too distracted, to notice you.'

But I see how Willis, reaching the threshold of the hall, turns back and holds my gaze, just for a few seconds, before he walks away.

Chapter 4

When the clock strikes midnight, a ribald cheer goes up from the men. They gather around Thomas, pawing his arms, pulling him up to standing. One man takes Thomas's fist, punches it into the air and makes a drunken, animal howl. In their midst, Thomas raises his eyes to find mine. He is not smiling.

Anne is behind me. She puts a hand on my shoulder, belly brushing against my back like a warning. 'It's time to prepare.'

Despite the warmth in the hall, and the heat from the good wine I've drunk, I shiver at her touch. As I stand, my legs are weak.

Surrounded by the Fanshawe women, Anne, Aunt Alice, her two daughters, and several others whose names I cannot remember, I'm escorted to my chamber. Rachel twines her fingers with mine and holds on tight. The younger girls are full of laughter, giddy with dancing and flirtation. Only my aunts stay silent as we climb the staircase.

The fire has been banked up and someone has prepared the bed. Hangings have been loosed and bedding drawn back so that the rich velvet coverlet and crisp clean linen look warm and inviting – the doorway to my new life.

Rachel stays close by as the women help me undress, a grim little smile fixed. We are not free to talk as we may, but her expression says everything. It is a night of transformation, and not just for me. This will be the first night in years that someone other than Rachel will share my bed. Tonight she has been given berth in the servants' quarters. Tomorrow she will take up her new place on a pallet bed in the little anteroom next to my chamber. It is no longer proper for her to take the place that now belongs to my husband. I am not a child any more: I am a married woman.

The women fuss around me, releasing the row of tiny pearl buttons on my bodice, unlacing the ribbons in my stays, combing out my hair. I hear the echo of song and the metallic clatter of something dropped on stone steps as the men bring Thomas to join me. My head swims and the beat of my heart feels too strong in my chest.

When I'm in nothing but my nightgown they lead me to the bed. Anne and Aunt Alice take it in turns to kiss me on the forehead. As she does, Anne whispers, 'Just this once, my dear, and then your future will be secured.'

Rachel stays with me for as long as she can, holding my hand as I climb beneath the coverlet.

'Stay,' I whisper, as she leans in to kiss me.

'You know I cannot.' There is a low cabinet next to the bed. She stoops, opens it and brings out Henrietta. 'She'll watch over you in my stead.' She slips the doll beneath the bolster, out of sight.

Just then the door bursts open and men spill into the room. Sudden colour and noise send a sharp pain shooting at my temples. Thomas stands mute and sweating while they undress him, roughly pulling away his doublet, his breeches, his ribboned garters, his polished shoes. His cheeks are even more flushed than usual, high spots of pink where the drink has heated him. He does not look at me but stares, bleary-eyed, at the floorboards.

I wait, knees and sheets pulled up to my chest. They lead him to the bed with calls of 'Go to it!' and 'Make us proud!' He climbs up beside me, naked except for the shirt that dangles to his knees, splashed and stained with claret wine.

The men cheer as he reaches out and puts a hand upon my arm. Over his shoulder, my eyes meet Willis's. He's laughing along with the rest, but his smile fades then and he lowers his gaze. His is the last face I see as the women draw the hangings, plunging Thomas and me into darkness.

Thomas's hand remains, unmoving, on my upper arm. He is still and silent as the others leave, waiting until we hear the fall of the latch. He stays that way while footsteps echo back down the corridor and laughter fades, the men heading back to their cups in the hall, the women to their beds and some to secret couplings in dark corners. Still he does not move, his palm our only meeting point – hot and damp, I can feel it through my gown. Then there is just the crackle of the fire and the sound of our breath. I can smell him, sweet and slightly acrid, like sour milk.

At last he moves, reaching to draw back the curtains to let in the light and heat of the flames. It's the first time that we have ever been alone together. We are man and wife.

He sits facing me, legs folded, limbs pale and skinny, with a sparse sprouting of hairs. I'm reminded of a plucked chicken.

'Wife. Let me see you a little.' He tugs at the coverlet. I'm aware that the stuff of my nightgown is fine, almost transparent. My skin rises into goose bumps as his stare moves from my face, down over my body. I'm terrified he will see the evidence: the faded remains of yellow bruising, the marks of the devil's hands upon my skin.

He comes closer, on all fours, and puts a finger beneath my chin, tilting my face. I'm not sure if I'm meant to respond in some way, to open my arms and invite his touch, but I'm bound by uncertainty, so I do nothing.

'It's true you have a pretty face,' he says, slurring slightly. 'But there is not much of you.' He sounds disappointed, accusing almost, as if I am at fault. He runs a finger down to my throat, making me swallow hard, and pulls at the dangling thread fastening my gown. My body stiffens. He loosens the drawstring and tugs the linen down roughly over my chest.

I'm pinned by his gaze on my skin, frozen by fear of his judgement.

'They say you'll fill out in time. They tell me you'll be good for breeding. That's why we're here, after all – breeding.' He manages a stiff smile and I suddenly realise – he is nervous too.

He fingers the charm that hangs, as always, around my neck, the glinting silver heart sitting between my breasts.

'What's this?'

'I . . . It was a gift. It's important to me.'

He looks a little closer, dangles the heart to shine in the firelight. 'A pretty thing,' he says, echoing the words of the robber in the woods, the memory causing my body to tense further.

He drops the pendant and shifts, kneeling before me. He frowns, taking on a determined look. He puts an unsteady hand on each knee and slowly parts my legs, shuffling between them. Tentatively, he begins to push my nightgown higher. It gathers in pale folds around my hips.

As he catches first sight of the place between my legs, his lips part and his eyes glaze. He hesitates. He stares. My heart trips. Is there something wrong with me? Is there some sign, as I have feared, that he is not the first man to touch me there? If he knows the truth, he will not take me. No man of any worth will accept sullied goods, and there is no contract without consummation.

But then he leans forward and puts his mouth to mine.

It is not how I imagined a kiss to be. I thought it would be a gentle thing, lips meeting and knowing how to mould to each other. His lips are soft at first but then he opens his mouth and slicks his tongue between my own, licking my teeth. He mumbles something that I cannot hear because his face is pressed against mine. I open my jaw a little, sensing this is what he wants. His tongue seems to fill my mouth. I think of the ox, served this evening on a silver platter, shivering in aspic, congealed and slimy. A wave of nausea rises and I pull away.

He seems taken aback, embarrassed even, and will not meet my eye again. Instead, he fixes upon my breasts, but he does not try to touch me there, and I am glad.

'Lie back,' he says, voice thick. 'Lie back and open your legs.'

I do as he says. He pulls his shirt up and places himself on top of me, balancing his weight on his elbows, hair falling into my face. I feel a soft fleshiness dangling against my thigh. Then he lowers himself onto me, crushing me so much I can barely breathe. He cups one breast and starts to move, rubbing himself slowly back and forth, face buried in the bolster at my shoulder. Breath is pushed out of me in gasps. Strands of hair catch in my mouth. He shifts a little so that he is brushing up against my navel and begins a slow panting. I remember the man in the woods, the urgent solidity of him, butting against me as though made of iron. I remember the hot gush as my body betrayed me. Pray God don't let that happen now.

Then, Thomas freezes. He pulls himself up on one elbow and, with his other hand, draws Henrietta out from beneath the bolster. He stares at her and something passes behind his eyes. He looks at me then, really looks at me, searching my face as though he does not know who I am. His own is a picture of frustration. He flings Henrietta across the room and rolls away. I flinch, thinking he will hit me, remembering the Oxford kitchen boy who spoiled the ship, but Thomas simply pulls his shirt down over the shrinking swell between his legs.

'Cover yourself,' he says, strangled.

I do as he says and wait for the anger that will come next, but instead he lies down beneath the coverlet and turns his back.

My mind is reeling and I'm full of shame. Anne's words come back to me: 'You must secure him.' But I don't know how. I don't understand what I've done wrong. I'm not practised, not schooled in this. When I told her I was prepared, it was a lie. I always assumed I would know what to do when the time came, that Nature would take her course, but now I see how naïve I have been. There are things a wife should know that I do not. I've been married only a few hours and already I have failed my husband. I watch the rise and fall of Thomas's shoulders as his breathing calms.

'Husband . . . what can I do?'

He is silent for a long time. The fire crackles and spits. From somewhere in the house laughter resounds. Then, without turning to look at me, he says, 'You will tell them all that our union is complete. There cannot be any doubt.'

'But—'

'That is my wish. Do you understand me, wife?'

'Yes. I understand.' Inside, my belly squirms.

I lie awake while the fire dims and, in time, I can tell by the sound of his breathing that the drink has sent Thomas to sleep. I dare not move because I do not want to wake him. Henrietta lies across the room, a jumble of wooden limbs, skirts raised, legs splayed. There is nothing at all between her thighs.

I do not expect to sleep, but I must, for I wake with the dawn, slivers of spring sunshine creeping through the panes. Next to me, the bed is empty. Instead of my husband, Henrietta lies against the bolster, tucked primly beneath the coverlet, eyes staring, wide and innocent as before.

Chapter 5

August 1648, London

My dear wife,
You will forgive my long silence when you understand the deep distress that has overcome us all, here in London. The King's cause has suffered a terrible blow. The army is defeated at Preston and the fleet, so recently harboured in Kent, and raising such hope in our hearts, has fled back to its Dutch hideaway, taking Prince Charles with it. Uncle Richard Fanshawe is put under house arrest. Leventhorpe and I are known as the King's men and dare not walk in the streets for fear of reprisals.

There is little chance, now, that Ware Park will be returned to us until this sorry business is settled. It is a sad truth that it may be settled soon, but not as we would wish it. Such speculation is written every day in the newsbooks, and is on the tongue of every gentleman I meet in St Paul's churchyard and Covent Garden. But I must say no more. Spymaster Thurloe and his agents capture the correspondence of His Majesty's friends to look for evidence of treachery and treason. They find it where there is none. Three of Uncle Richard's acquaintance are taken to the Tower this last week and we cannot get any news of them.

You will understand, then, that I must disappoint you. London is no place for a lady. And I must decline your request for coin. We suffer like beggars in our sorry state. The penalties and fines imposed upon us are harsh. I comfort myself that our good aunt Alice will ensure you do not go without.

But here is happier news. The man who carries this letter is commissioned to paint your portrait. It will be a wedding gift, much delayed. He is a pleasant enough fellow and good company. I hope you will make good use of him.

Your husband,
Thomas Fanshawe

Rachel wrinkles her nose, Thomas's letter in hand. 'Well, at least he calls you his "dear wife".' She knows this is no real consolation.

'But he refuses me.'

'He says London is not safe.'

'Nowhere is safe any more.'

'He means only to protect you.'

'Do not take his side against mine.'

'It's not a matter of sides. It is a matter of safety.' She looks to George, but he stays silent, declining to offer the support she seeks.

'But the money too? Does he wish me to stay in these borrowed gowns for ever? Am I to live on nothing but bread and pottage? Aunt Alice will never admit it, but our presence here is a burden she cannot afford.'

Rachel says nothing but raises an eyebrow and looks pointedly at our new companion.

I can feel the red heat of anger rising. I turn to the man sitting opposite, half hidden by canvas and easel. 'How much longer must I sit like this?'

Cornelis Van Keppel raises the one blond eyebrow that I can

see. 'Some time to come, I'm afraid, Lady Katherine,' he says, in his angular, seesaw accent.

'I've been sitting for hours and you have not even mixed your paint.'

'Today I take your image in charcoal.' He shows me the black stump between his fingers. 'Tomorrow . . . the paint.'

'It's not been long, Kate.' Rachel wanders over to the window and peers out at the sky. 'It just feels like it.'

It's a grey day, but humid, the heat of summer trapped by a sheet of flat, low cloud. I'm wearing heavy green satin that is too hot for August, and my mother's pearls. Dampness gathers in the creases of my stays.

George's gaze follows Rachel, settles on the pale slice of flesh at the nape of her neck. 'Read the bit about the battle again,' he says, frowning. He sits cross-legged on a low, cushioned bench before the hearth. Although it is hot, the fire is lit, and George, still weak in his recovery, likes the warmth.

'No. I cannot bear it,' I say. I'm still reeling from the crushing blow I felt when I first read Thomas's letter.

'Do you really think all hope of a victory for the King is lost?' Rachel's voice is small. 'Because there may be reprisals, or soldiers fleeing after the battle. Where is Preston? Is it far from here?'

'Very far, I think.' George nods. 'Though it'd be wise to mount a guard at nights.'

I notice Van Keppel smirk behind his canvas. 'What is so amusing, Master Van Keppel?'

'Please, madam, you must be still.'

'What do you find to smile about in this news?'

'You have moved your arm a little . . .'

I give him a cold stare and twist back into the pose that he says is most flattering and most fashionable. 'You must have an opinion on these matters. Were you ever at court?'

'I was at Blackfriars for a time, at the studio of Van Dyck. But that was a long time ago. Now, I prefer to find my own way.'

'And did you find favour with His Majesty's friends? I'm sure many of your patrons are loyal subjects.'

'Indeed, that is true.'

'So you support His Majesty's cause?'

'I take my bread where I can find it. Sometimes here, sometimes there.'

'But you are loyal to your king, of course.'

Van Keppel shrugs. 'I am not an Englishman and your king is not my king. God is my master and my mistress is Art. I do what I must to serve both.'

He has a cup of burgundy wine on a table next to him – the last of the vats that Aunt Alice had bought for the wedding – and he pauses in his work to take a draught of it. His fingers are black; he leaves sooty prints.

I am not surprised that Thomas could not afford a more famous artist to make my image. Most of them are gone away to find a less troublesome living in Paris or Antwerp, following the Queen and those members of King Charles's court who still have the coin for fripperies. But this does not stop me feeling the slight in his choice of Cornelis Van Keppel, a man I have never heard of.

'Where did you meet my husband?'

He looks thoughtful. 'In a tavern house, I think, close to the Strand.'

'So, Thomas is not too frightened to frequent the taverns.' I cannot hide the bitterness in my tone. 'Or St Paul's churchyard, or Covent Garden.'

Rachel shoots me a warning glance.

Van Keppel waves his hand in a dismissive gesture. 'It was some time ago, when things were not so difficult for men like your husband. Long before this battle you speak of.'

'How I long to see the King again,' I say.

'You have seen him before?'

'We are not so unworldly as you would have us, Master Van Keppel. I saw the King several times. My mother and I were quartered with the Queen at Oxford.'

'Ah, but you were younger then, I think, with a child's understanding.' He turns his attention from the canvas. 'If you wish to see your king again, you must pray for him. I do not think these men of blood will have mercy now. I have seen it before, in the European wars. Once a man has shown that his word cannot be trusted, then blood is always spilled. If a fighting man is betrayed, he will do anything to take his vengeance. It is the way with your king, I think, and it will be the way with these Englishmen, Cromwell and Fairfax and Lambert.'

'What do you know of them?'

'Only what any man can hear in the taverns and read in the news-sheets. They hold the King like a prisoner, yes? They will not let him go free again. He has lied to them once, so why not once more? While he lives, the English people will always look to him, will always follow blindly, like dogs. If they want a republic, they must clear the way. The people in my own country have learned this lesson. If these Parliament men are wise and godly, as they claim, they will look to the Low Countries and see what must be done.'

George snorts. 'This is England, sir, and we do not kill our kings.'

Van Keppel swivels in his seat to face George. 'I think you do not know your history.'

George hesitates. 'I . . . I know more than any foreigner. It is against all reason, and against God to say it.'

Van Keppel tilts his head and looks George up and down. 'Have a care, Mister George, for the tide runs against your king. England is changing. You do not want to be left behind.'

I see the flush of anger on George's pale skin. 'No God-fearing man would dare to think such blasphemy. Even the rebels would not go so far – not if they want any hope of peace. The people would never support an action so plainly wrong.'

'In a war where both sides claim to fight for God, it is no longer a matter of right or wrong – it is a question of which side is most determined. The men who will win this war are those willing to go to the greatest lengths.'

'You have strong opinions for a man who claims not to take sides,' I say. 'And I think you are a Royalist at heart, sir, or you would not work for the likes of my husband.'

He turns back to me. 'I say only what I see. Just as I draw only what is before my eyes. I do not nail my colours to any cross.' He lifts his hand to the canvas. 'I make a better living that way.' I feel his sharp focus on me, the intensity of his gaze. It is not a comfortable feeling. 'But your husband is right to keep you here, my lady. London is not safe for a young woman who loves her king.'

'My husband means to keep me under lock and key.'

'He tries only to care for you, I think. Please, you must be still.'

'He's right, Kate,' Rachel says, coming back from the window and sitting down next to George. 'We are all safer here. Don't you agree?' She looks to George for an answer.

'I think Lady Katherine can look after herself,' he says, raking his hand through his hair, clearly discomfited by Van Keppel's words.

'But not without your help.' Rachel rests her fingers on George's forearm.

I cannot meet George's eyes. I'm sure he is remembering the same thing as I – that day in the woods when he was the one to save me and, in turn, I saved him. These sudden flashes of memory return again and again, like a bad dream my mind is destined to repeat on waking. But something else has stirred in me too: an ever-present spark of foreboding, now fanned into flames.

I am not so innocent that I do not understand how my own fate is tied to that of the King. Families like mine have already suffered the loss of their blood, property and land. All we have left is hope; the hope that, one day, balance will be rightfully restored and things will be as they once were. That hope burns fierce in me. But, if Van Keppel is right, we are headed towards a different end. Shut away at Hamerton, we are like autumn leaves caught in a whirlwind, tossed about by forces beyond our control, utterly helpless to stop it.

Chapter 6

I leave my candle burning into the small hours. I doze at times, disturbed by unsettling dreams of soldiers and swords, the thunder of cavalry and the beat of battlefield drums. I have never been witness to these things but my mind makes such convincing images that each time I jolt awake I am sweating and anxious. Rachel lies next to me, making little snuffling snores, like a pig rooting for truffles. She has abandoned the pallet in the cold chamber next to mine to share my bed like she used to, but she did not undress this evening and her skirts are bunched around her knees.

Eventually I rise and sit by the window, waiting for the first signs of dawn light on the horizon. When it comes, I wake Rachel with a whisper. She helps me dress in common servants' clothes: a skirt and bodice of brown worsted that scratches and itches through my shift, and a plain cap to hide my hair. I see myself reflected in the windowpanes, my image jumbled in the glass. I do not look like myself. I look like Rachel, or one of Aunt Alice's maids. When we are ready, we snuff the candle and creep through the dim-lit passages to George's room.

He is awake and dressed, sitting on the edge of his cot, good hand rubbing the site of his healing wound.

'Are you fit?' Rachel whispers, but George stands and nods.

This was his idea and nothing will keep him from it.

We tiptoe down the servants' stairs, George pointing out the steps that creak, and into the yard. George leads the way. If he is seen by any of the household's early risers, he will be taken for a stable boy. Glancing up at the blank face of the house I see no candlelight, no glow of fresh-kindled fires, and no watching eyes at the panes.

We are lucky that the groom does not sleep in the hayloft above the stalls but in the bakehouse, where the ovens make for a warmer bed. So, when we reach the stables we have nothing to fear except the noisy welcome of the horses, surprised to be disturbed so early.

Aunt Alice keeps two good steeds: a grey gelding named Applejack for the steward, Master Maybury, and a bay mare named Glory, which was her husband's mount. Though her master has been dead these five years, Glory is still cared for with great attention. Aunt Alice insists upon this, making sure that Glory is always ready for the return of a man who will never come. But, as was the case when Sir Capel was alive, no other soul is allowed to ride her. I know because I have often asked to take her out, and seen the stricken pain behind Aunt Alice's eyes as she refuses me.

I go to Glory now. She snuffles into my hand, velvet-soft nose warm in my palm.

George comes up beside me and runs a hand down Glory's neck. 'She's a fine horse, Lady Katherine, but you know how Lady Alice is about her. I'd take another.'

I glance at the two stumpy, muscular farm horses, used to pull everything from Aunt Alice's carriage to the dairy cart, then back at Glory, with her powerful dark flanks and lively eyes. 'She's mine,' I say. 'You two will take Applejack.'

'She's not been rid in years.' There is a warning in George's voice that I'm determined not to heed.

'All the more reason, poor thing.' Glory is eyeing me, ears pricked. She shifts her weight and makes a little whicker.

'Kate, is this wise?' Rachel says. 'It'll hurt Lady Alice that you've not heeded her wishes.'

'It's unfair to keep such an animal confined. It will not bring Sir Capel back, and he would not wish it.'

George exchanges a look with Rachel and shrugs. Neither of them can argue with me. He disappears into a room at the end of the stalls, feeling his way in the darkness.

'Rachel, go and make friends with Applejack,' I say. 'You'll ride behind George. You'll be safe with him.'

This seems to mollify her and she does as I say, tentatively reaching out to pet the other horse. Applejack is jumpy and shies away at first, rolling his eyes and making Rachel snatch back her hand. But when George returns with two leather bridles, he slips one on to Applejack with no trouble.

'See? You'll be safe with George,' I say. Rachel smiles, as George takes her hand and brings it up to the horse's neck.

'He likes you,' he says, and she flushes, fingers tangling with his.

We take a mud track to avoid the cobbled yard and the ring of iron on stone. I glance back to the house, afraid I will see lanterns aglow, or hear the shouts of a raised alarm, but there is nothing. How easy it would be for a thief to slip through the shadows and creep into Hamerton. How simple to take the horses, as we have done, to raid the larders, to slit throats as we sleep. I have heard tales of such things, done at other private houses by savage Parliament troops, turned wild by battlefield bloodlust. The thought makes me shudder, or perhaps it is just the dawn chill prickling my skin beneath my clothes.

I climb onto Glory's back, skirts swaddling my legs. I have not ridden without a saddle since the day my father lifted me on to my brother's pony and led me round the yard at Markyate Cell. I still recall the roughness of the animal's coat, the solid muscle of its body, my little legs stuck out before me, not yet long enough to reach the pony's flank. The memory is with me as I feel the dip and sway of Glory between my thighs. I gather the reins, childhood instruction coming back to me.

The day is dawning with a dove-grey sky and the birds have begun their chorus. The land behind Hamerton Manor rises and we follow a drovers' track across a wide common. When we have been walking for some time, I glance back to the house and see a thin twine of smoke rising from the bakehouse chimneys. I know it will not be long before our disappearance is discovered.

George twists in his seat, sees what I see. He looks back at me, eyes alight, and spurs Applejack into a canter. Rachel squeals and grabs George around the waist, presses her face against his shoulder and screws her eyes tight shut.

Glory needs no encouragement and we take off after them as though I have a whip to her rump. I almost lose my seat, but as she settles into a steady rhythm, I grip hard with my knees, find my balance and lean forward, into the breeze that rushes past, until her dark mane tickles my face. Sheep scatter away from her hoofs. My body is awakened, limbs alive to every movement, blood thrumming. The wind snatches my breath. The chance that I may fall and be trampled makes my heart clamour.

The sun clears the horizon just as we reach the brow of the hill and we pull up the horses. Before us, the land falls away into a flat plain, fields and common land stretching for miles in a patchwork of greens, browns and yellows. Far off, the River Nene loops and sparkles, like a bracelet of gold. We circle the horses, their breath steaming in the morning air, mingling with our own. I feel a surge of pleasure. I have not felt the like in a long time.

Around noon, when the sun is high and the heat of the day makes the horses' coats glisten with sweat, we stop by a woodland stream. George leads Glory and Applejack to drink while Rachel and I find a shady place beneath the trees. We have begged a loaf from a lone cottager some miles back and we sit, dividing the still oven-warm bread into portions. I lean back against a tree trunk and watch George tending the horses. He is good with them, gentle and natural, and they respond to him. He leaves them to forage, snatching at the long grass by the water's edge. Then he strips off his shirt and kneels to splash water over his face and chest.

He has his back to us, his pale skin milk-white, the scar on his arm a puckered patch of angry purplish red. As he bends to cup the water in his hands, I see muscles glide, sinew over bone. Then he stands, kicks off his boots and rolls his breeches up over his knees. He takes tentative steps into the water, arms outstretched for balance. He emits a yelp as the coldness bites, then twists to look back at us, grinning. There is a rash of freckles across his shoulder, and down one side, a deep red birthmark, like spilled ink, rising from his navel to a scattering of tight-curled hair on his chest.

I have a strange thick feeling in my throat. I look at Rachel. She is staring too, lips parted, a hunk of bread hovering halfway to her mouth. As I watch, she licks her lips.

'Come, Lady Katherine,' George says, beckoning. 'The water's good.'

As I kneel to stand, Rachel catches at my sleeve. 'Don't,' she whispers.

'Why ever not?'

She hesitates. 'It's not proper.'

'And when has that ever mattered to you?'

Her eyes plead. 'Just . . . don't.'

I shake her off. 'No one will know. There's no one for miles, and you won't tell.'

At the water's edge I take off my shoes and stockings. I dip a toe into the flow. It is icy cold. My whole body tingles, cheeks sunshine hot. George holds out a palm to me, smiling. With one hand gathering my skirts and the other in his, I step into the water. It eddies around my ankles, fresh and cooling. He's right: it does feel good. The bed of the stream is strewn with pebbles, hard and slippery, and I need George's hand to steady me. I make my way further in, taking little gasps, until the water runs up my calves and my toes begin to numb. George does not let go, not once. There is a quickening in the pit of my stomach – a rushing, flooding feeling that matches the stream's flow.

I look back over my shoulder. 'Come in, Rachel. Why not? There's no one here to see.' But she does not move, and she does not match my smile.

When we return, at twilight, Hamerton Manor is in uproar. At the shouting and commotion, Aunt Alice comes into the yard. She will not upbraid me before the servants – she will save that for later – but her reservation on my quarter does not apply to George. Master Maybury takes him by the collar the moment his feet touch the ground, leaving Rachel to dismount and scurry to my side. I swing my leg across Glory's back and drop to the cobbles, knees buckling, body aching.

Aunt Alice's eyes flash. 'Master Maybury, see to it that the boy is locked up tonight, no food or water. Tomorrow we will send for the constable.'

'Aunt Alice, I—'

She silences me with a knife-edged glare.

George is led away, his desperate, pleading eyes finding mine. He knows his fate is in my hands.

Inside, Aunt Alice beckons me wordlessly into her chamber. When the door is closed, the two of us alone, she paces up and down on the bare boards before the hearth.

'Do you realise what you have done?' She does not wait for an answer. 'All this day I have been in terror, waiting to hear news of your injury, your kidnap, or much worse.'

'I'm sorry, Aunt—'

She holds up a hand and speaks over me. 'Master Maybury sent out all the lads to search the lanes. We sent word to the farm and the village. The whole of Hamerton knows you were missing. I feared you were taken.' She spreads her fingers on her chest as if to catch her breath. 'Have you no thought for others?'

'I meant no harm,' I say.

'Half of Hamerton has been out looking for you. And now you come riding back into the yard as if nothing in the world is wrong. How do you think that looks to those who have lost a day's wages in searching for you?'

'I did not expect anyone to look for me.'

She makes a splutter of disbelief. 'You are second only to me as their mistress. The whole parish would search for you, if I asked it.'

'Surely riding out is not such a dangerous thing.'

She gives me an incredulous look. 'There is a garrison of Parliament troops not ten miles from here. What if you had encountered them? A young woman of breeding, with no chaperone and no protection. I cannot imagine what might have befallen you at the hands of such men.'

'But nothing happened.'

'By God, Katherine, there are rules that govern how you must behave. I know you are young, but that is no longer an excuse. Your mother was a fine gentlewoman and she would have had no truck with such wildness. The good Lord knows I was willing to take you into my care, but I did not know what a trial it would prove.'

'I do not mean to shame you, Aunt.'

'You spend your days cooped up with that boy, or flirting and talking sedition with that painter Van Keppel – yes, I know the nature of your conversations with him – you gallivant about the gardens, giggling and gossiping with your girl, like a pair of butter maids. And now you present me with this outrage. I am at my wit's end with you.'

'I'm truly sorry if I have caused you distress, Aunt. It's just that the days here are so very long and quiet. I merely wanted—'

'You think you are alone in your boredom and frustration? Believe it or not, there was a time when I was young and pretty like you. There was a time when I flirted and gossiped and thought that the world and all its delights were made for me to enjoy. You will soon learn the world is full of small disappointments, none more so than the day-to-day resentments of a woman's life. You must accept your fate. You are here to learn how to run a household. You are here to learn how to be a wife.'

'A wife without a husband,' I say, under my breath.

She gives me a hurt look; I have touched upon the rawness in her. She sighs and perches on a seat by the window, silent for some moments. When she speaks again, she sounds weary. 'I am put in charge of protecting you, for my sins, of delivering you whole and unsullied to your husband, when that blessed time comes. By your actions today you have made my task impossible. If Thomas hears of this, I will be blamed. Tell me, how do I know what truly occurred today? How can I promise that my duty is fulfilled?'

'I say again, nothing happened, Aunt.'

'I have lived many years more than you, Kate, and I have seen the importance of a clean conscience and a clean reputation. I have seen the damage that a woman's self-will can do. Trust me, you must give up the wild ways of your childhood. There is some freedom here, away from London, away from watchful eyes, but propriety and duty still count for much. Your duty now is to your husband and your family. It is my task to keep you safe and prepare you for that. I hope there will come a time when you understand.'

'I understand my duty.'

'You do?'

'Yes. I must be ready to give Thomas an heir.'

She lowers her voice. 'And that child must be untainted by any blood but your husband's. I say this only for your own good, for I know what passions a girl can fall prey to. Any hint of impurity would be your downfall. You must guard against it. Will you promise me that at least?'

'Yes, Aunt,' I say. 'I promise I will try my best.'

But her words make me think of one thing: George's hand in mine, the pale skin of his chest glistening with droplets of water, and the way that something stirred in the very depths of me.

It takes a good deal more pleading and many promises to secure George's place. It takes much more to persuade Aunt Alice that the fault is my own. George is turned out of his chamber in the house and banned from my presence. He is given a job as a labourer at Rectory Farm, and allowed to sleep in the barn there. As Master Maybury says, if he is recovered enough to ride a horse all day, then he is well enough to work for his keep.

Rachel is unscathed. After all, as I persuade Aunt Alice, Rachel is under my command and must do as I say. Still, I notice that in the days that follow she is cowed and quiet. The dairymaids give her suspicious glances and whisper behind her back. They all saw the way she was holding on to George when we rode back into the yard and the way her eyes filled with tears when he was led away. We do not speak about it, and I'm glad, because I could not tell her the truth.

No doubt there are whispers about me, too, but I care very little for servants' gossip. I do care that George is gone, and we never see him, save snatched moments in church on Sundays, or when he delivers churns to the buttery. Every time I catch a glimpse of him my heart flutters and my stomach turns, for I cannot forget the secret ways in which I am bound to him.

Chapter 7

It takes Cornelis Van Keppel two weeks to complete the portrait. The day after he is finished, he packs up his oils and pigments, his brushes and mixing pestle, and leaves Hamerton as suddenly as he had arrived, gone back to London, seeking a new commission. The house feels empty without him. I found the sittings irksome, but days without his conversation are even more lacking by comparison.

I have never met a man who professes no loyalty but that due to God, except the friars who come begging for alms. In these last years of war, I have not heard a man speak so freely without fear of the consequences. Two weeks in his company have opened my eyes to a world quite different from mine.

The painting is carried to my bedchamber and propped up against a wall where, in time, when the paint is dry, it will be hung.

Rachel and I sit on the bed, staring at it. I'm disturbed by the sensation that there is a third person in the room. I wonder what my husband will make of her.

Van Keppel has made her forehead high, her brows neatly arched, her eyes large and glittering. Her cheeks are blushed with just enough rouge to be fashionable but not whorish. Her lips are blood-bitten rose, her skin milky as fresh cream. She is doll-like in her finery, the shimmering green satin dress mirrored in her eyes.

Her hair is curled in perfect shining ringlets. Breasts bud beneath her bodice; an alluring pillow for a husband's head. She is everything that Thomas could wish her to be.

'A very good likeness,' Rachel says, eventually.

'But it's not truthful,' I say, hands running over my shabby gown, thinking that the picture reflects a life of wealth and luxury that is no longer my lot. 'And what use is it, when we're shut up here, with no one to see it?'

'It's a thoughtful gift.'

'Thomas has sent no money since the wedding – he says there is none to send – but then he pays a man to paint my picture. I would rather have a new gown, or my own horse to ride. He does not consult me, or seem to care what I think at all.'

Rachel's brow furrows. 'I'm sure that's not true.'

'Then why does he leave me to fester here? Admit it, you long to go home, to Markyate Cell, just as much as I do.'

She considers her reply, twisting her fingers in a fretful gesture I've come to recognise. 'It's true . . . I do wish to see my brother again. I had no chance to say goodbye. I worry about him. I would like to know he's safe.'

'Have you any word of him?'

She shakes her head. 'I've a feeling that things are not well. It's silly but . . . it's been so hard for him since . . .' She trails off for a moment, thinking. 'With the fighting, there'll be no men to work the land, and no coin to pay even if there were. Some of the local men are set against him. He does not say so, but Rafe blames himself for the failure of the farm. I wish I could help . . . but he's too proud.'

I know that the Chaplin farm lies on the borders of the Ferrers estates in Hertfordshire, not far from Markyate Cell. Rachel has told me the tale of her childhood, cut short, like so many others, by the outbreak of war and the loss of her parents. Raised to a comfortable life as a yeoman's daughter, she was suddenly forced to seek a living elsewhere. I still see flashes of stubborn pride behind her demure resignation. Her disappointed expectations resonate with me, but my heart has always hardened against this faceless, feckless brother, who does not have the strength or guile to provide for his kin. I find no sympathy for a man who fails to support his own sister.

'Some people bring their fate down upon their heads,' I say.

Rachel turns away. 'It's not all his fault. Without money . . . it's impossible . . . I worry what he might do, all alone there, with no one to look out for him . . .'

I did not mean to upset her. I reach out and squeeze her hand. 'You must pray for him,' I say. 'And I shall too.'

'You will?'

'Of course. God will look after your brother until you can do so yourself.'

She sighs. 'I think you have more faith than I.'

I look back at the portrait. I cannot tell her that, these days, my prayers have taken on a selfish bent. Sometimes I do not pray at all. I bow my head, steeple my hands and say the words, but my mind runs away with itself. On Sundays, as I sit in the front pew, I sense George's gaze upon me. It makes the pit of my stomach swim. When I close my eyes, sinful images flood in and I cannot cast them out. They are not images of my husband, but of him, and of other men, and they plague me like a cloud of midges.

The girl in the portrait is beautiful, I suppose, made perfect by an artist's imagination. But there is something in her gaze that is too familiar and unsettling. There is something more behind the upturned lips and the points of light dancing in her eyes, something shadowy and complex.

And then it strikes me, in a sudden realisation that is almost physical in strength. There is something inside me that causes these ungodly imaginings, some wildness that is beyond my control, and Van Keppel has seen it. I have read it in the hand glass every day since my encounter with the robber in the woods but until now I have not understood it: there is a darkness in me, a corruption, an unholy taint that can never be undone. I think of the man's filthy, blighted fingers. What poison lay upon his skin? What devil's wickedness did he put inside me?

The understanding takes my breath. I remember Van Keppel feeding me a slow, knowing smile. How is it that this man has looked deep into my soul and shown me something I did not know about myself? With horror, I wonder, will others see it too?

Chapter 8

Rachel and I are breakfasting on thin, mealy pottage. The dish is bland and unsalted, tasting of nothing but long-boiled carrots. It has been weeks since we last had meat and even longer since my stomach was full. I push away my bowl and pick up a piece of maslin bread – yesterday's leftovers turned stale and hard. Though my stomach growls, I cannot bring myself to eat.

Master Maybury says the harvest has been poor again this year and we must make a meagre yield of grain last through the dead months ahead. I see concern in the creases at his brow and notice the tense, whispered conversations between him and Aunt Alice. I see the way my aunt's worried eyes flit about the table at mealtimes, as if she is waiting for the day when the sparse offerings are not enough to go around. I understand there is nothing to be done, and that what little we have must be stored away and portioned out over the winter, but I am already weary of this hardship.

There are sudden shouts from the yard and the clatter of iron on the cobbles. My first thought is that my husband has returned, the echo of voices reminding me of that April day when Thomas and his men arrived to make a young, hopeful bride into a penniless, abandoned wife. Rachel's spoon hovers halfway to her mouth, then finds its way back to her bowl, contents untouched. I strain for familiar voices and the sounds of welcome.

Instead, a scruffy boy I recognise as the lad who scrubs the turnips outside the kitchens comes hurtling into the hall.

'Soldiers . . .' he says, catching his breath. 'Soldiers are come. Master Maybury said to fetch the mistress.'

My stomach tightens into knots. Aunt Alice appears from the kitchen stairs, wiping floured hands on her apron.

'The King's men?' she asks hopefully, but she knows the answer, for there is fear in the boy's eyes.

'No, mistress, not the King's men.'

We have been lucky at Hamerton. So far from the centre of things, we have been ignored. The manor is not a great, rich house like Thomas's Ware Park, the place where I should now be mistress, currently given into the hands of some Parliament lackey. Aunt Alice has already forfeited a portion of her estates to Parliament's coffers – the pottage in my bowl is proof enough that our days of comfort and wealth are over – but until now we have escaped the unwelcome attentions of the local militia.

It is no secret that, with no rule in England, the army men make their own laws. The garrisons stationed about the country to keep the peace are the worst of their kind. Away from their commanders, turned savage by years on the battlefield, they have consciences as black as their souls, and no respect for their betters, no matter what their godly colonels may claim. They steal and plunder without fear of retribution, because no one has the courage to challenge them now the King's army is broken and fled. I have heard how they raid houses that were once loyal to His Majesty, taking whatever they choose. I have hoped, against all reason, that Hamerton will escape their notice. I suppose I have been blind: it was only a matter of time before we came under their gaze.

There are about a dozen of them. Soldiers in filthy buff coats and muddy boots, some with battered, tarnished breastplates. Two men are mounted, the rest travelling in a dilapidated cart. Several carry muskets. The fizzling spark of matchlight is bright in the weak November sun.

As we step into the yard, one of the men dismounts and strides towards Aunt Alice. He is a big man, made broader by a thick, padded coat and a wide-brimmed hat. He tips it to her while making a low bow, pretending a show of respect.

'Madam,' he says loudly, so that all the gaping servants now gathered in the yard can hear. 'My name is Captain James. Forgive our trespass here this morning, but I have my orders . . .'

Aunt Alice's face belies the fear she must feel. 'What is it that you want?'

'We must make free with your larder. I have a warrant from my colonel.'

He hands her a document, scrawled with script and stamped with a black wax seal. She passes it to Master Maybury without a glance. 'We have little to spare.'

'You are bound to do your duty, as the army and the law require. We must have a defending force in this land, to protect the citizens against rebels and traitors, and that force must be fed.' He fixes her with a surly stare.

She does not reply. She knows she has no choice but to submit to these men. Even though we outnumber them – surely at least a score of us are gathered now – we are without weapons or protection, save the crude blades of farmyard and kitchen. I notice a group of labourers near the gate, arrived in the soldiers' wake, the orange blaze of George's hair among them.

'We've heard reports of some fine animals here,' Captain James goes on. He indicates the stables, giving the nod to two of his men, who set off towards them.

'Just the nags required for working the land,' Master Maybury says, stepping up to Aunt Alice's side.

'My men will be the judge of that.'

It takes only moments for the soldiers to lead Glory and

Applejack into the yard. The groom has already been at his work this morning and both horses look healthier and better fed than many of us.

'There are two others, Captain – two old dray horses – not much use. But these two will suit our purpose,' one of the soldiers says.

Captain James goes to Glory and runs a hand down her neck. She tosses her head, eyes rolling. He raises his gaze to Aunt Alice. 'Past her prime, but still spirited,' he says.

'Sir, please, that was my husband's horse.' Aunt Alice's composure is beginning to crumble. I see her hand trembling as she clasps it to her heart.

'Your husband who fought for the traitor Charles Stuart? Well, this beast will work for both sides before her day is done. Is that not sign of a world turned?' His men snigger. 'Even God's creatures must bend to the times, madam.'

My anger starts to rise. I cannot bear the thought of this man upon Glory's back. How can the others stand by and allow it?

Before I can think better of it, I step forward. 'You cannot take them,' I say.

Aunt Alice puts a steadying hand on my arm.

I shake her off and take a few more steps towards Captain James. He is sliding a palm down Glory's legs, checking her over.

'Do you hear me? You will not take them.'

He straightens, looks me up and down, frowning, taking in my threadbare dress. 'And who are you to give commands?' he says.

'You have no right to come here and demand what is not yours.'

'Katherine . . . be silent.' There is fear in Aunt Alice's voice. 'You will make it worse.'

'I do not care about your orders, or what your piece of paper says. It means nothing. You are no better than a thief and should be hanged for what you do.'

Captain James squares up to me. 'You will stop your mouth, girl, if you know what's good for you.'

There is outraged protestation among the servants. None of them would dare to address me in such a way. But his dismissal only makes me more determined. My fists curl. 'I will not let you take those horses.'

He comes closer so that we are standing face to face, though I barely reach his chest. When he speaks his voice is threatening. 'What do you mean to do about it?'

I hesitate. I have not thought this through. 'I will . . . I will strike a bargain with you.'

The muscles in his jaw twitch. 'What are your terms?' He is humouring me, I know, laughing at me, but I cannot stop now.

'I cannot offer food. We have nothing to spare.'

The corner of his mouth curls. 'This is not how bargains are struck, girl.'

'Then . . . take the other horse, the grey, but not this one.' I indicate Glory.

He smiles then, a creeping, greedy smile. 'I see . . . what will you do to keep her?'

My anger is keen but tempered by a sense that, if I say the right thing now, I may get my way.

I tilt my chin to level with him. 'What is it that you want?'

His gaze slides over my body and I see the flash behind his eyes that I'm beginning to recognise. 'To begin, you will bend your knee to me,' he says. 'And you will beg.'

There is a ripple of approval among his men.

'Katherine, come back to my side at once,' Aunt Alice says.

I ignore her. I want him to think I am colluding in his game. 'And if I do what you want, will you give your word that you will not take that horse?'

He shrugs.

'And more, will you give your word that you will leave this house untouched and never return?'

He turns to his soldiers, palms upturned. 'What do you think, men? Is it a fair offer – to leave empty-handed for the satisfaction of this one upon her knees?'

'On her back and I might be tempted,' one says.

James takes a step towards me and fingers the ragged lace collar at my neck. I will myself to stand tall and hold his gaze. I will not let this man see how he frightens me.

There is a sudden commotion in the yard as George breaks away from his friends and runs towards us. No one moves to stop him and he is by my side in seconds. With a great roar he swings a single punch, catching the captain's jaw with full force. James reels backwards but steadies himself quickly – clearly the man is used to taking hits.

'You'll not touch her!' George yells, but two of the soldiers are upon him before he can attempt another blow. He curses and kicks as they grapple, pinning his arms behind his back, forcing him to his knees. One of them draws a sword and holds it to George's throat so he cannot escape. George's face twists in rage. The last time I saw him look like that he was holding a smoking musket, and a man lay dead at my feet.

'You dare to challenge me, boy?' Captain James is like a ravening dog. He snarls, rushes the few paces between them and lands a boot hard between George's thighs.

The sharp gasp of horror from the onlookers does nothing to cover the sound of George's pain. The poor boy howls as the captain repeats his torture. James bares his teeth in a wicked grin: he is enjoying himself. He pulls off his riding glove and strikes George's chin with a shattering blow, then another and another, until George spits blood.

'Stop!' I fall to my knees in the dirt. 'I'll beg if that's what you want.'

Master Maybury is by my side, dragging on my arm, trying to pull me up, but I cannot leave George at the mercy of this monster. I shake Maybury off and half stumble, half crawl a few paces towards James. 'Please, stop . . . Have pity.'

James gathers himself. He wipes spittle-flecked lips on his sleeve, knuckles dripping blood. George crumples to the ground. He puts his hands to his face, where his brow and lips are cut and bleeding. At the flick of James's wrist, the soldiers drag him up onto his knees again, sword back at his throat. George's eyes turn wild and darting. One of the soldiers aims a musket at anyone who dares come close.

James swings about to face me. 'You beg for mercy? There is none. I'll show you what happens to those who defy us.'

He nods to his men and the one holding George grabs a hank of hair and wrenches George's head back, exposing his neck. I can see a thin red line where the blade has caught the pale skin and blood beads.

'Please! I'll do anything you say!'

'What will you do to save him?'

'Anything.'

His gaze settles on my mouth as I speak. He licks his lips. 'You will lie down,' he says. 'Lie down and lick my boots.'

Never in all my years have I been spoken to in this way.

I look about me for help and find none. Everyone in the yard has fallen silent, waiting to see what I will do. A couple of the labourers, fists flexing and spitting fury, are held at bay by the musketeer. Aunt Alice has turned ghostly white. Rachel is on her knees, hands covering her face as though she cannot bear to watch. The cook's little boy sets up a high, thin wailing.

I have no choice. Slowly, I put my hands on the ground and lower myself until I am flat in the dirt, prostrated like a papist before a priest. Captain James puts one filth-spattered boot to the fore. The leather creaks. I can smell the damp scent of mud and grass, the pungent reek of horse muck.

I press my lips to Captain James's boot.

'Lick it,' he says.

Tears of fury and shame sting my eyes but I do as I'm told. Dirt grits my tongue. The taste is earthy and strangely sweet but the stench makes my stomach heave.

'Again. Lick it clean.'

I hesitate, swallowing the sour bile that rises.

'Do it, or he dies.'

'What kind of man are you?' Master Maybury says, finding his courage. 'Have you no respect?'

James's attention turns. 'Respect? For what? For some spoilt whore who has never known hunger, or lain down to pass the night in a cold, wet field, or watched her fellows die in blood and pain?'

I take the chance to sit back on my heels. 'I have done as you asked,' I say. 'Now let him go.'

Captain James gives a cold, humourless laugh. 'By God, girl, you still think to bargain with me? It's you and your sort have brought us to this sorry place. You may feel yourself shamed, but that is not one half of the retribution I would have visited upon you and your kind. It's time to pay for your years of privilege. Now you'll know what it means to starve. You'll know what it means to suffer.'

He turns and barks orders to his men. 'Search the kitchens, the storerooms, the brewhouse. Take a good portion of what you find.'

'Sir.' Aunt Alice breaks her silence. 'I have the care of at least twenty souls, all dependent upon this household and what we have gleaned from a hard year. If you take our stores we will not last through the winter. Please, have pity. Have some understanding.'

'I'm following orders. Perhaps your husband should have considered your future plight before joining with the King.' He spits the word 'king' as if it's a curse.

'But the horses,' I try again, unable to give up. 'Please, at least leave the bay mare.'

He swivels on his heel, kicking up a cloud of dust.

'Those horses belong to Parliament now,' he says. 'If you have any grievance, you may lodge it with the Sequestration Committee.' He knows this means nothing to us. He knows that this will never happen. We do not need an argument: we need horses in our stables and food in our larders.

We stand by, helpless, as the soldiers drag sacks of grain, all that day's bread, crates of fruit and casks of beer from the still house. They take churns of milk and butter as the dairymaids cling to each other and weep. They pile their stolen goods into the cart; Glory and Applejack are tethered to it. George is left in a groaning, wretched heap, a gun to his head preventing any further outburst. Rachel braves the musket's dead eye, fetching a cup of water and helping him drink, her arms offering poor protection.

When their work is done, Captain James climbs back onto his horse. It has taken less than an hour to undo all the good work of the past summer.

I tremble with fury at the injustice of it all. If I were a man I would challenge him with my sword – I would fight with my bare hands if I had to. I cannot understand why no one, not even Master Maybury, who watches with horror as all his carefully planned stocks and stores are taken away, will argue against him. But none of our men dares go up against these seasoned swords, not after what the captain has done to George. Aunt Alice has tears in her eyes. Her last bit of hope has crumbled.

Later, when the soldiers have gone, Master Maybury goes from cold room to still room, from buttery to bakehouse, from dairy to pantry, noting down what is left. Servants huddle together in the yard, in the kitchens, at the gateposts, talking quietly. Those with children about their feet watch their broods with worried eyes.

Master Maybury and Aunt Alice disappear into the study and shut themselves up with account books and ledgers. From behind the door, I hear raised voices. Suddenly this morning's thin, tasteless pottage does not seem such a bad thing.

In the late afternoon, Aunt Alice goes to the hall and sits in front of the big chimney, staring into the space where a blaze should be. Nobody has thought to tend the fire and it has almost gone out, just a few embers glowing in the hearth. I sit with her. Her brow is furrowed and there is black despair in her eyes.

'At least we have wood to keep us warm,' she says. 'They did not touch that. We will not freeze to death.' She does not say, of course, that we might starve instead.

Chapter 9

In the end Thomas relents. He has no choice when he hears of our plight. He sends a man, all the way from London, to deliver a pouch of coin and a blunt-worded order that I give up my mother's jewels in return. Aunt Alice's eyes swim when I put the money into her hands; it will not solve our problems, but it gives some temporary relief. At least there will be bread tomorrow.

With it comes the news from London: the army has marched into Westminster Hall and purged Parliament of any man who would still treat with the King. They are determined to try Charles Stuart for crimes against his own people.

That evening, when we sit down to eat, stomachs growling as we wait for our portion of watery broth, it is all we speak of.

Aunt Alice is determined not to believe it. 'Surely it's a joke,' she says. 'Or a rumour, put about to frighten the King's supporters.'

'There was no jest in Thomas's letter,' I say.

'But who can try a king for treason? There is no one in the land with higher authority than him.'

Master Maybury pulls a doubtful face. 'Things have come to pass in these last years I never thought to see. Why not this?'

'But what can they hope to achieve? What possible good can it do?'

I remember Van Keppel's warning. 'They want rid of him,'

I say. 'To clear the way for their new government. Some people think they will stop at nothing to get what they want.'

'Then let them go ahead,' Aunt Alice says, exasperated. 'They will never be able to convict him. Who will sit as jurymen? Who would condemn their own king? Surely that is treason in itself. The idea is a sham.'

'But if they do it, and he is found guilty, what then?' I ask. 'Will they lock him up for ever?'

'That or exile would be my guess,' Master Maybury says. 'I expect they'd prefer to keep a close watch on him. It'll be a sad day for us all either way.' He nods his thanks to the girl who serves the broth as she spoons a portion into his bowl. 'This country won't be the same without a king. It's not right.'

'It's an outrage,' Aunt Alice replies. 'They may as well claim judgment against God Himself. They are the traitors, not him, and they deserve to burn for it.'

But no one dares say the thing we are all thinking: in this life there is only one punishment for traitors.

Later, when Rachel and I are alone, we fetch the diamonds and pearls from their secret hiding place and wear them with our nightgowns one last time. In the golden glow of firelight, wrapped in such beauty, it is easier to forget our hollow bellies. But the thought of giving up the jewels makes my heart ache. Like everything else that was once mine, they belong to my husband now, but they are all I have left of my mother, and serve as proof of a time that is fading in my memory.

Rachel understands what this means to me. When we climb into bed and snuff the candle, she twines her fingers with mine and strokes my hair, but I know I will not sleep. My mind is too busy clinging to fragments of the past.

I close my eyes and remember the apple trees in the orchards at Markyate Cell, boughs of fat, ripe fruit, windfalls crawling with beetles, the sickly sweet cider smell of rot. I picture dragonflies dancing among the foxgloves, bees from the skeps feeding on the roses, my own small world filled with sunshine, lace-winged insects and ladybirds crawling on red brick. I can almost feel my mother's arms, warm and safe, a kiss after tears, my balm after a scrape. Her hair smelt like roses, the subtle scent of warm skin beneath like comfort.

Next to me, Rachel's breathing has slowed and deepened. Her fingers are relaxed in mine. I slip my hand away and turn onto my side, gently so as not to wake her. I long for the oblivion of sleep. But as I begin to drift, the pictures come, vivid as always. My heart clenches. I'm told that time heals all wounds, but I've been waiting long years for a respite that still does not come.

I am back in the garden, sitting next to my mother while she sews. Her needle is glittering silver between her fingers. I'm leaning against her side, sucking my thumb, making slurping sounds. I can still taste the sugar cake we had this morning and I suck harder, relishing the sweetness beneath my fingernail. There are shouts and whoops from the orchards. On the bench, next to my leg, there is a red silk pincushion, prickled all over with silver pins. I'm engrossed in my own little game, pushing the tiny forest of pins into the cushion one by one to make sure they are all sitting level.

My eldest brother, Knighton, comes panting across the garden and sits down, a tangle of limbs at Mother's feet, legs splayed, boots making tracks in the gravel. He's hot and flushed, hair plastered against his forehead. He leans back against her skirts, sighs and closes his eyes.

She frowns. 'What is it, my love?' She puts her hand to his cheek.

'I'm so tired,' Knighton says. It's not even noon and I don't see how he can be tired yet.

'Let's go inside, where it's cooler,' Mother says. She stands and takes Knighton's hand. He scrambles to his feet, swaying, unsteady. His eyes are strangely unfocused, as though he will fall asleep where he stands.

My mother abandons her sewing and marches him towards the house. I trail behind, not knowing what else to do, until I spy two butterflies, in flight over the hollyhocks. They are performing some dance, outstripping each other in a battle to reach the clouds. They whirl and flutter, climbing higher and higher, pale spotted wings flickering. They keep rising up and up into the sky, swirling about until they are so high that they disappear into the bright, ceaseless sun. I shade my eyes but I cannot see where they have gone.

When I look back down, Mother and Knighton have gone too.

I never see Knighton again.

I am shut up in my room. Days go by when I seem to exist half in and half out of sleep. The sleep is the deepest I can remember – blackness pulling me down and down, sinking to a place where nothing else matters. Then there are other times when the air is flame hot and burns in my chest, or freezes and needles like frost, and I dream of ugly, twisted creatures, writhing in agony amid Hell's flames.

I wake one day to find God has spared me my nightmares, but I have no brothers any more, and a long, dark winter has come to Markyate Cell.

I lie awake, staring into darkness, no hope of sleep. Next to me, Rachel snores softly. I rise, throw a warm shawl over my nightdress and quietly leave the room. I pad barefoot along corridors and down staircases until I reach the yard and pull on a pair of old dancing shoes that will be silent on the cobbles. The dirt will ruin them, but I don't care. I have not danced since my wedding.

The night is chill, my breath making clouds as I cross the yard.

The moon is fat and luminous in a clear, velvet sky. I hurry to the stables, keeping to the shadows so I'm not seen.

Slipping through the stable door, I find a candlestick on the sill with a half-burned stump of tallow. Although it no longer smokes, there is a sickly, charred scent in the air, as though it has just been snuffed. The groom must have been here late, checking on the horses.

I linger by the empty stalls where Glory and Applejack were kept. The dark spaces are swept clear of hay, but rats have made a nest in one corner, a trail of droppings showing where they like to run. It has been weeks since the horses were taken but the wound is still raw in me and news of the King's trial opens it afresh. It took days for the taste of Captain James's filthy boot to leave my tongue, and now the smell of horse dung makes it surface once more. But, somehow, I like to look at the deserted stalls and feel the swell of fury. My rage has a purpose and direction that makes it sharp and keen. If it were a blade it would be made by the finest smith, and I would use it to slice apart the heart of every loathsome, thieving Roundhead I could find.

The two carthorses that the soldiers did not take are wakeful. One of them, a piebald gelding, is nosing in a pail, where someone has left a few kitchen scraps. My own stomach grumbles. I click my tongue to call him over. He comes and nudges my hand, expecting treats.

'There's nothing for you here,' I whisper, running my palm down his neck. His coat is rough, and the solid warmth of him is welcome.

I stay there for long, slow minutes, stroking his ears and whispering secrets, telling him how, if I were a man, I would find Captain James and make him pay for what he did.

I hear a noise. At the end of the row of stalls is a small room where the tack is kept. It is only big enough to hold the equipment, a small table and stool, where the groom sits to shine the saddles and clean the bits. From that room there comes a soft shuffling. I fall silent and listen, but the noise stops with me, and there is nothing but the muffled thud of hoofs upon the straw-strewn floor. The tack room is in blackness.

A rat, perhaps, looking to poach a few scraps from the horses' feed.

The other horse is inquisitive now and hooks his head over the door of his stall. I put a hand to his nose, pat his neck and soothe him.

The shuffling noise comes again, louder this time and unmistakable. I think of the candle on the sill.

'Is someone there?' I say, voice unnaturally loud in the stillness of night. There is no reply save the snort of horses' breath.

I stay silent and, after a few moments more, it comes again, a soft, regular rustling. It is too purposeful, too repetitive to be an animal. The hairs on my neck and arms bristle. I'm suddenly chilled beneath my nightdress. I shiver. I'm convinced there are eyes on me. I think of the diamonds, still fastened about my neck – a thief would slash my throat for less.

'Is somebody in here?'

I take a few careful steps towards the dark space. From here I can see nothing inside the room but shadow, a slice of moonlight falling on an empty dirt floor.

And then I hear the gentle rhythm of human breath. There is someone in that room, watching me.

I should run. I should go to the house and raise the alarm. Instead, I stand there frozen, holding my own breath while I listen to the steady pant of whoever, or whatever, is in that room. I am wide-eyed with fear, alert to every sound, every movement. But if I run now, I will never know who, or what, it is.

I summon all my courage and rush the last few steps to the door.

There, in the cast of moonlight, is George. His face is pressed against the adjoining wall, and as I make my sudden move, he jumps back. I see straight away that there is a small hole where the daub has crumbled, just big enough to spy, unnoticed, into the stalls. As he backs away I see that his breeches are unlaced, his shirt pulled up and pushed aside. He holds himself brazenly in one hand.

He says nothing.

I say nothing.

He does not flinch. He does not hide himself. He does not drop his hand but keeps it fixed there. His eyes meet mine. Even in the pale blue moonlight I see a challenge in them. An invitation. A dare.

I do not move. My gaze is drawn. I cannot help it. I know I should call for help, or leave, or at least demand the show of respect due to me, but I do none of these things. He stares at me, so shameless, eyes moving down over my nightdress. A wicked thrill moves within me.

For a moment I hesitate. My fleeting thought: I could go to him. I could flout every rule, every promise by which I am bound. George could do the one thing that my husband could not. But then my shame, my sin, my damnation would be complete.

Instead, I turn and walk away.

When I get back to my chamber I climb back under the coverlet. My heart thumps so heavily I'm sure it will wake Rachel, but she does not stir.

I should be disgusted. I should be offended. But I am not. And I already know why not. I have known it since George was sent away but continued to haunt my daydreams. I knew it when he took my hand and helped me into the cool flow of the woodland stream. Even before that, I knew it in those days spent at his bedside when we first arrived at Hamerton, while Rachel tended and fussed over him, but his eyes would linger on mine.

There is something unspoken between us. He knows my

secret. He knows that I am tainted. He can see the devilment in me. Of course he can: he witnessed the very moment of my fall. It is this knowledge that allows him to take such a risk. He knows I can never tell anyone of his secrets without exposing my own.

I wonder if he stayed in the stables to complete his task. Wickedness gets the better of me and I cannot clear the image of him from my mind, no matter how I try. I long to quell the heat that rises, but dare not. Instead I pray – I pray that God turn my mind from these sinful thoughts. But the prayers are half-hearted. The Devil is sharpening his claws.

After this, I take to visiting the stables at night, whenever I cannot sleep. I do not let myself dwell on the fact that I always wait until I know Rachel is sleeping. I start leaving my cloak on a nail by the stable door, even when the nights grow icy cold. And sometimes I tie the fastenings on my nightgown so loose that it slips down over my shoulders and I shiver at the prickle of the chill night air on my breasts.

I tell myself that there is no real sin in these things, for I am alone, even on those nights when the silence is broken by the sound of fast, panting breath from that small, dark room at the end of the stalls.

1649

Chapter 10

Winter is long and bitter.

Christmas passes without feasting or Twelfth Night revels. Though the servants make some attempt to dress the hall with holly berries and mistletoe, we are a small party, lacking in cheer.

The money that Thomas sent in exchange for my mother's jewels does not last long. I'm angry that I'm forced to give up something so precious for so little. Aunt Alice collects promises of help from Fanshawe relatives, but the family is scattered, fortunes broken, and empty promises are of no use to us. We are left to fend for ourselves.

We eat like gypsies, our meals collected from woodland and riverbank. Traps are set to catch coneys, but we cannot afford to be too fussy, and other, unnamed, creatures find their way into the pot. As a child I had a talent for marksmanship, evidenced whenever I could persuade my father to include me in my brother's instruction. Now I prove my worth with a pistol and shot, persuading Master Maybury to lend me a gun and matching his paltry brace of partridge and pigeon within days. But no matter how hard we try, we go to bed hungry more often than not.

At the very tail of January, I am in my bedchamber with Rachel, wiling away another pale, grey day. There has been a heavy frost in the night. The timid blaze in the hearth is not enough to warm me. It is well after noon when I put my stitching aside, pull my shawl tight and begin to doze.

I am jolted by a sudden loud noise – a crack like a musket shot.

'What on God's earth?' Rachel is already on her feet. She goes to the casement and peers out, but I see it before she does. One of the panes is splintered into a tracery of lines. I think, at first, that the ice has warped it, but looking closer I notice a waxy smear on the outside of the glass. Imprinted in the frost, there is a perfect impression of a bird's feathered wing. I lift the catch and open the frame. Leaning out I see a large black raven on the terrace below, sleek, still and lifeless, a mess of oily dark feathers.

I think nothing of it until two days later when the news reaches us. The sound of the messenger's horse, clattering on the icy cobbles, brings us all out from our firesides. We are wary of strangers, these days, and the men appear with hunting knives and makeshift clubs at the first sign of unexpected visitors.

The rider, face hidden by thick woollen wrappings, will not give the letter to anyone but Aunt Alice. She comes out of the hall, shivering, winding another shawl around her shoulders. Rachel and I watch from the doorway as the household gathers.

Aunt Alice breaks the seal, cold fingers fumbling as she unfolds the paper and reads. One palm goes up to cover her mouth. She drops to her knees, letting out a cry.

I run to her, slipping on the ice in my indoor shoes, but Master Maybury gets there first, crouching with his arm about her shoulders.

He takes the letter and reads. I see his face change, as hers had done, shifting to shock and horror. He stands, shakily, and tries to help Aunt Alice to her feet, but she is wailing, rocking back and forth on her knees. She pushes him away.

He looks around at the aghast, questioning faces. He clears his throat. 'The King is dead,' he says.

I think I must have misheard him, but the cold, sliding knowledge begins to creep.

'The King was executed, two days since, in London. Beheaded on Parliament's order, as a traitor against England's people.'

There are gasps from a few of the servants and one of the kitchen lads mutters, 'Not one half of England's people,' but most maintain a stunned silence. I feel we are awaiting some further explanation, some means of understanding this impossible thing.

Master Maybury takes off his hat. 'God rest his soul. And God save our royal princes.' His voice breaks. He kneels and puts a palm on Aunt Alice's shoulder. Slowly, he takes her hands and pulls her to her feet. She turns her face to his chest, allowing his arms to shelter her as he leads her back inside.

A few of the men are muttering in low voices. One of the dairymaids is crying. A man I recognise from Rectory Farm is on his knees in the dirt, offering up prayers. I should say something, I should offer some message of comfort to these people, but I am as shocked and wordless as they. More so, perhaps, because I have seen the King, and he is more than an ideal to me: he is flesh and blood. My head begins to spin. Rachel takes my hand and leads me away.

Back in my room I feel otherworldly. How is it that this room looks exactly the same as before, my sewing cast aside where I left it, hot caudle still steaming? How can these things be unaltered when the rest of the world has changed so essentially? I sit and stare at the flames in the hearth. Rachel added a fresh log only moments before we heard the messenger's arrival. It is not yet ablaze. It balances between two others, beginning to blacken and smoke, a bright orange glow licking its underbelly.

The echo of Aunt Alice's grief resounds.

Rachel sits opposite, rubbing her hands to warm them. The colour has drained from her cheeks. 'I cannot believe it,' she says.

'Van Keppel was right.'

She nods slowly. 'And we laughed at him. We said they would never go so far.'

We are silent a while, both lost in thought.

Rachel watches me. Her eyes brim and she pushes the tears away with the back of her hand. Then she says, 'Will you tell me the story again?'

I know which story she means. It has always been one of her favourites, recounted several times in the years we have been together. I shake my head. It seems futile and inappropriate. How can I weave my tales of the King and his magnificent court, when it is all crushed to dust?

But I do remember, and somehow the brightness of those days makes this one seem all the darker.

After the death of my brothers, we were all still in our blacks when Papa went to join them. All the light was gone from my mother and she seemed shrunken and old. Even a new husband could not cheer her. She still dressed her hair every day and dabbed rosewater on her cheeks, and, after the wedding, returned to her coloured silks and wore pearls, but something in her eyes was for ever gone.

And then the King raised his standard at Nottingham and there was a skirmish not two miles from our gates between the King's guard and the men of the local trained band. My new father, Sir Simon Fanshawe, decided that Markyate Cell was not safe. We joined the court at Oxford.

At first Oxford was a haven for us. Away from Markyate Cell, the finery of the court distracted my mother from her grief. Sir Simon was lodged with the King at Christchurch, but we never saw him; all the men were preoccupied with the business of war. I began to forget what it was to have my brothers about me always, and we were never alone, for we shared our small chamber with Betsy, my nursemaid, and Hester, my mother's woman. Others slept in the storerooms, or camped in the cloisters on cold, hard stone. Oxford was the King's new castle and it was under siege.

Despite his worries, Charles Stuart brought the best of his kingdom with him. Sometimes there was feasting, dancing and even plays, though I was too young to be a part of it. I lived for the stories my mother would bring, when she came home long after midnight, wafting in a scented cloud of sweet sack, lavender smoke and beeswax.

One night, Mother had gone to see the King, taking Hester with her. Betsy excited me with tales of the entertainments to be enjoyed at Christchurch. She preened and blushed as she spoke of a new friend, one of the King's players, who had flirted with her in the marketplace that afternoon. I wanted to see it all for myself and Betsy was an eager conspirator.

Swaddled in dark cloaks, we sneaked from our chamber to pad our way through the corridors and cloisters to the street. Outside Merton's walls, Oxford was a different place. There were soldiers everywhere, with swords and muskets, horses trampling the streets into mud, messengers scurrying between the colleges, servants running errands and losing their way in the dark. Betsy found a boy to carry a rush light. As we followed the winding street, it cast a dim glow on bodies huddled in doorways. In nooks and crannies, filthy, starveling children made their beds. Hollow-eyed beggars held out their palms. A band of raucous, ragged men gathered outside a tavern house, frightening me. This was not the Oxford I had come to know.

Betsy's friend might have been handsome beneath the white lead and cochineal. He took us into a room where the King's players were preparing. The chamber was bright with rainbow costumes, jewelled doublets, striped hose and the flash of polished swords.

The men laughed and joked, drinking from green glass bottles, helping each other into feathered hats, applying patches and combing out periwigs. One by one they shed themselves and each became someone entirely new: a sprite in silvered feathers; a prince with a golden crown; a painted tart with a bosom made of oranges; a highway robber with a greedy grin and a glinting dagger, spilling rubies from his pockets. I was enraptured. They barely noticed Betsy and me as we stood, astonished and gaping, in a corner.

One slim young man, lips and cheeks red as a ladybird, suddenly slipped off his breeches and shirt. I caught a glimpse of the darkening fur running in a line from his chest over his belly and down to the fleshy thing hanging between his legs. I could not help but stare as he stretched naked, this intriguing, oddly beautiful creature. Betsy saw him too, hesitated a moment, then pulled me away.

We were given a hiding place among the hangings at one side of the stage. Peeping at the crowd, it seemed to me that all the ladies were dressed in costumes even finer than those of the players. The gentlemen were the most handsome I had ever seen, wearing silk, velvets and white lace collars like snowfall. Torches flickered in the sconces, casting a golden glow on bright smiles and the gleam of fine glassware.

A hush fell as the King entered. It was the first time I had ever seen him and a shiver of awe tingled up and down my spine.

He was small and slight, dressed more simply than many of his retinue but, somehow, he looked more splendid than all the rest. The finery of his courtiers was not necessary for him. The only sign of royal riches lay in the delicate lace collar and cuffs, glinting with just a hint of silver filigree.

A step behind him came a short, dark lady with bouncing ringlets, smiling and nodding in a puff of pale blue silk. I had caught glimpses of her before, in the quadrangle at Merton College.

Betsy clasped my hand. 'The Queen . . .' she whispered, and I could see by her face that she was as grateful as I for this chance to be so close to the royal couple.

The King looked tired, bestowing the barest of smiles as he took the seat marked out for him. Servants scurried, offering sack and dishes of sweetmeats.

I sensed an alteration in the room, a shift in feeling, the easy gaiety giving way to a quieter reverence. To me, it seemed as though something ethereal had entered our midst, something sacred that made all the other wonders of the evening less magical by comparison. I understood then why so many people clamoured to be near him. I recall the strong sense that everything would be all right – that I would be protected, safe. I knew that this man would find a way to right all the wrongs done against him, and against us all, because how could he possibly fail? How could anyone argue against such glorious, God-given power? It radiated from him, the divine blessing of our Lord here on earth. It was who and what he was. I was too young, then, to realise that this power was at the very root of his problem.

I caught a glimpse of my mother, leaning heavily against Sir Simon, goblet in one hand, the other on the mound of her belly. She was smiling, sleepy-eyed. She looked beautiful. She looked happy. I knew then that I would never forget this night and the charm that had been cast, over the players, over Betsy, over my mother and me. All the sadness of our days was gone, cast out of the shadows by the bright flickering lights, the shimmer of diamonds, and the spell of the King's smile.

I think of the raven, dead on the terrace beneath my window, its limp body scraped up and taken away by the gardener, discarded without a thought. I remember the sudden splintering of the pane, the jolt of shock awakening me, two days since, in the pale light of a cold January afternoon. The raven is a proud bird, the King's creature. I have a strange feeling that it was not a coincidence.

I know what this news means for me. While the King lived, there was still hope – hope that God would punish those evil, hateful Parliament men and restore all deserving, loyal subjects to their rightful place. I have lived these last years, holding that hope inside, like a brilliant candle, because I could not bear the thought of a world without its light.

Now they have snuffed it out. They have won. They have done this to crush us, once and for all. They might as well have cut off all our heads.

I draw out the silvered heart from beneath my stays and cradle it in my palms. If the King is dead, then the promise it holds is all the more important. How can such a small thing carry the weight of all my hopes and dreams?

1655

Chapter 11

London, April 1655

My dear wife,

I have news at last. My father has compounded for Ware Park. The house and a portion of the grounds are to be returned to us. The estate will be signed over to me and I expect to be installed there soon. I will be ready to receive you by midsummer. But you must prepare yourself for our reduced circumstances. The heavy fines imposed by the Compounding Committee have greatly injured our prospects and the house has suffered the ravages of war as sorely as our fortunes. I trust that under the guiding hand of my wife, it may be restored to an acceptable level of comfort.

Here in London there is determination that Parliament will not tolerate open supporters of the King so we must learn to live quietly, or not at all.

Your husband,
Thomas Fanshawe

I visited Ware Park in the days when Sir Simon courted my mother. Those were the dark days, after the death of my father, when my mother believed herself alone and friendless in an uncertain world. I was a child, with the easy pleasure of an innocent eye. I was awed, and a little cowed, by the splendour of the place.

By then the house was already a century old, but the patterned brickwork was free of moss and ivy, clear glass gleamed in the casements and clusters of red-brick chimneys stretched towards Heaven. The gardens were ordered and formal, the clean, perfect lines of the knot a particular pride of old Sir Thomas, the man who would, in time, become my father-in-law.

Inside it was so very different from Markyate Cell, with its patchy sections of ancient flint walls, dark cobwebbed corners and rickety staircases; all the peculiarities of a house built upon a house. Ware Park had ceilings the height of two men, polished and painted panelling in all of the big rooms, every corner bright and sunlit, like a palace for a princess. I did not suspect, though others did even then, that one day I would return as its queen.

When, after three days' travelling from Hamerton, we turn the final bend in the track and see Ware Park, what greets me is a sight so at odds with my memory that I think we must have taken the wrong road.

The walls are covered with creepers, one section of the building is blackened by tell-tale smoke stains and there are gaping dark holes where there should be glittering glass. A chimneystack is collapsed in a mound of rubble. There are cracked panes in the remaining casements and tiles missing from the roof. Swifts dart from under the eaves. In front of the main entrance the track turns to mud, where other carriages have turned. Fresh horse muck waits to seep into my shoes. It seems that, even years after the fighting has ended, Ware Park still suffers war wounds.

Despite Thomas's warning, this is not what I have been imagining since I received his note. During my long years at Hamerton, I have grown accustomed to hardship. I have toiled in the kitchens, alongside Rachel and Aunt Alice, scalded my fingers and blistered my palms because, one by one, we had to let the kitchen lads go. I have planted the vegetables and picked slugs from the crops. I have pricked my thumbs a hundred times mending my time-worn gowns and ragged petticoats. I have learned what it means to go hungry for days on end. I have experienced the dull despair of sleepless nights, plagued by an empty belly and aching limbs. But when Thomas's letter arrived, a new hope grew inside me, as quick and wild as weeds in the kitchen beds. The images I've conjured of my life as Thomas's wife have kept my spirits up ever since. I shall be mistress of my own house, have food in my larders, servants at my command, and one day, God willing, a brood of sweet children about my feet. Most of all, I shall be closer to Markyate Cell. I am beckoned home at last. I cannot bear for that dream to be taken away again.

A man is waiting on the top step to greet me, a stooped fellow with stringy grey hair falling about his ears and a bald crown, like a monk's tonsure. Everything about him is grey as if he has sucked in the fat, dark clouds above. His skin has the papery look of the old and worn; a few straggly whiskers have escaped the razor's blade.

As the carriage draws up, he hurries down the steps, opens the door and sweeps a low bow.

'Lady Katherine, welcome to Ware Park. My name is Stone, at your service.'

He offers a wrinkled hand. I'm surprised by the strength in his grip.

He guides me carefully to the steps. 'Where is my husband?' I ask. 'And the other staff?'

'The master is in the library, m'lady, awaiting your arrival. I'll take you to him right away, if you wish.' He is eyeing Rachel as she climbs down from the carriage, hefting our travelling packs over one shoulder.

There is a hard pebble of nerves in my stomach as Stone takes me inside and leads me to the library.

In the hallway I learn that the house has not fared much better inside than out. The tiled floor is clean swept, but not scrubbed. There is no fire in the grate to welcome me. There are still a few portraits on the walls above the wide staircase we climb, but most have been slashed and ruined. It makes me think of my own image, stowed away on the roof of the carriage, soon to join this parade of dour, black-clad ancestors.

Sections of wood panelling have been pulled away from the wall in the upstairs corridor, exposing the brick beneath. Brackets for torches and candles hang loose. At one end of this long, narrow passage, a heavy curtain flaps in a breeze. I catch the scent of ash and charred wood.

The library was once a fine room, judging by the dark wooden cases that line the walls, though most of the books are gone, lending an empty, cavernous feel. But there is a good blaze in the hearth and comfortable high-backed chairs placed before it.

Thomas is waiting. He stands as I enter.

In all our years apart, I have seen him rarely, and then always in company. We have acted like the cousins we are, but nothing more, strangers to each other's beds and bodies. Now, receiving me as his wife, he seems much changed, the boy grown into a man.

We stand in silence for a few moments. The smattering of letters that has united us has done little to prepare me for this meeting. I know nothing of who my husband really is, or what is expected of me. There has been time enough for foolish dreaming, many idle hours spent rehearsing this moment, but I find the words of my practised speech seem like nonsense, so I say nothing. There is a tight, sinking feeling in my stomach, instead of the butterfly heart that I have imagined.

Master Stone makes a show of pouring wine and arranging my full cup next to Thomas's on a table by the fire. This duty dispensed, he tactfully withdraws. Rachel hovers by the door. I do not want to dismiss her yet – I'm not ready to be left alone with this man I do not know.

'Wife . . .' Thomas says, eventually. 'Come, warm yourself by the fire.'

I do as he says and stand, chafing my fingers in the heat of the flames, for want of something better to do. I eye him sideways. He seems thinner but broader across the shoulders. Where his cheeks were once full, they are now slack and pouchy. I notice threadbare patches and dangling buttons on his coat.

I can feel him appraising me, from the hem of my skirts to the curl of my hair. I hope he is pleased by what he sees. He is not alone in the changes that time has wrought. I am no longer the skinny doll-like child he married. I turn so that he might see the curve of my waist and the swell beneath my bodice – I can feel his eyes wandering that way.

Though, on first meeting, his looks may not please me, I know this is of little import. I am the one must do the pleasing. I know that any chance of happiness in this new life depends upon his goodwill. I have not forgotten why I am here, the duty that I must fulfil.

But Thomas's gaze quickly falls away. He makes no move to embrace me, or even touch me. We are strangers, hampered in our ease by the knowledge of such expectations.

Later, Thomas shows me the house, Rachel in tow. It is clear from the frown shadowing his brow that he is as shocked as I by the damage that has been done, but he speaks of employing builders and artists and gardeners to make it splendid once more. I do not understand how he means to pay for the works, but think it best not to ask.

When we reach the threshold of the stables, his awkward manner alters.

'Close your eyes,' he says, and holds out a hand for me to take. It is the first attempt he has made to touch me.

'Thomas, I . . .'

'Close your eyes, wife.' His grip catches my fingers, clinging damply. 'I have a surprise for you. It cannot be a true surprise if you guess at the thing.'

I have learned that I do not much care for surprises. Today has been full of them and, so far, none to my liking. I squint through half-closed lids as Thomas pulls me forward. He soon releases me, positioning me, a palm on each shoulder. 'Now . . . now you may look,' he says.

I open my eyes.

In the stall closest by is a dappled grey horse. It is as fine an animal as I ever saw, with a shining coat and a mane to match the rainclouds.

'Oh, Thomas! Is she for me?' I cannot keep the glee from my voice.

'Yes . . . to give you some means of entertainment while I'm away. I remember you liked to ride when you were young.' He looks pleased with himself. 'A fine beast, but gentle too. Suited to a lady, so I'm promised. She's bred down from the King's stables, as was.'

'She's beautiful.'

'Nothing better could be got.' He smiles for the first time since I arrived, but I cannot tell if it's my enthusiasm that pleases him, or his own good judgement. 'Cost a pretty penny too. Leventhorpe found her out from a dealer at Newmarket, good man. Now, where is the groom? You shall see how well she moves.'

He leans over the gate and reaches out to pat the creature's neck. He clicks his tongue to encourage her, but she ignores him, eyeing him suspiciously.

'But such an expense . . .' I say.

'Ah!' He flaps a hand. 'Not for you to worry about.'

'Surely, if we must furnish—'

'I do not mean to live like a pauper, wife, and I shall keep my business as I see fit.' His voice has a hard edge.

'I only mean to—'

'Do you not like her?'

'Of course . . .'

'Then don't complain. Damn it, where is that groom? Boy! Boy!' But no one comes. He lets out an exasperated sigh. 'Must I do everything myself?'

Thomas fetches a halter and slides open the bolt on the gate. As he steps inside the stall the horse presses herself against the far wall, kicking and spilling a water pail. Thomas advances slowly. I'm reminded of the pig breeders chasing piglets at weaning time – how the men creep, sly as cats, waiting for the perfect moment before their prey squeals and scatters. The mare chews, watching him warily.

When he is close enough, Thomas raises the halter, making ready to slip the thing over the animal's nose. I note the quivering muscles in her rump, the flick of an eye, the sudden switch of the long tail.

He moves closer still. At the first touch the mare tosses her head and whinnies. She backs away from him, eyes rolling.

'Come now, show your new mistress what a fine, good girl you are,' he says, but he cannot hide the irritation in his voice.

He makes the attempt again but this time it is too much for the creature. She paws at the ground, ears flattened. As Thomas tries to force the halter over her nose she rears, arching her neck, dancing on hind legs. Then she plunges forward and Thomas, stumbling away, is caught. He teeters, arms wheeling, straw binding his heels, and falls, landing with a grunt on his backside.

The mare retreats to her corner. I see the tightening and twitching of muscle in her hindquarters, the flex of sinew in her legs, as though she is ready to fly.

'Are you hurt, sir?' Rachel says, concerned. 'Shall I fetch help?'

'God damn the cursed thing,' Thomas mutters, already

climbing to his feet. 'Where is that groom?' As he dusts himself off, I suppress a smile.

'Are you sure you're not injured, sir?'

'Not a bit of it, girl.' His cheeks are flushed.

'Let me try,' I say.

'Kate, no.' Rachel puts a steadying hand on my sleeve but I shake her off.

'She's only frightened because she does not know us. Think how unsettling it must be, to be thrust from one place to another without a friend in all the world.' I throw Rachel a meaningful look. 'We must get to know one another. We must make friends.'

I open the gate and step up to Thomas's side.

'I cannot let you endanger yourself,' he says.

But now it's my turn to brush aside the concern. I shoot him a glance that says I am determined to try. He hesitates for a second and I see he is torn between his duty to protect me, his shame at being unmanned by the creature, and his fear of a repeat. He straightens his collar and retreats from the stall, the battle for his pride relinquished.

'Kate, we should wait for the groom.' Rachel is insistent.

'I will do well enough myself.' I think of the affinity I found with Glory. There was no finer or more troublesome a steed in Aunt Alice's stables. George said I shared his natural way with horses. Surely this pretty mare can be no different.

I stand a while, splaying my hands to show that I hold no halter, no whip or bit. She quietens, standing with one leg cocked, the tip of one hoof resting against the floor as if she might bend into a bow.

'Now then, my girl,' I keep my voice gentle, 'you and I must be friends. What do you say?' I take a step towards her, then another.

'Don't be afraid. I'll not hurt you.' Another step. She regards me with dark liquid eyes, ringed with long, silver-tipped lashes.

I put a hand up to her neck. 'There . . . see? I mean you no harm.'

I feel her tense and shiver but she does not shy away as she had done with Thomas. She tosses her head and shifts her weight from one leg to the other, letting out a snort of air, as though considering my words.

'Be careful, Kate,' Rachel whispers.

I put a palm gently to the horse's muzzle. She allows it, nostrils twitching, velvet softness nudging my hand. 'There now, we are friends, see?' I stay there a few moments, letting her get used to the scent of me, until it's clear she has had enough and butts me gently away. But not before I have run my hand along her smooth coat, and noted the strength in her flank, the glitter in her eye.

Returning to the gate, I take up Thomas's hand. 'Thank you.'

He pulls his fingers away, discomforted. I'm confused by his reaction. He seems to seek my approval but my heartfelt gratitude embarrasses him.

'A spirited animal,' he says gruffly. 'But we will break her, soon enough.'

'She's perfect as she is.'

'She'll soon learn who is master here,' he says.

'What will you call her?' Rachel asks.

Turning, I notice a pale feather caught upon the shoulder of her shawl, fallen from the beams above where the turtle doves roost. I pluck it and run it between my fingertips. It is so delicate, the little plume of down at the root softer than a dandelion clock. Dove grey, it darkens in ripples towards the tip, exactly like the dapples on the mare's flank.

'Feather,' I say. 'I shall call her Feather.' And for the first time in a long time, I cannot keep the smile from my lips.

Chapter 12

'Of course, Markyate Cell will have to go.' Thomas talks with his mouth full, scattering crumbs.

As the day goes on, we find little to say to one another. I assume that the cup of wine, so frequently refreshed, is a sign that Thomas is ill at ease. But now, over a meagre supper, it serves to make him more talkative.

'What do you mean?' I ask.

'The house, the land . . . it will all have to be sold. It's the only way to settle the debt.'

'But I thought . . .' I pick up my spoon and stir the bowl of broth. It smells of green meat. Memories bloom, of the busy kitchens at Markyate Cell, the extravagant feasts I knew as a child. 'Surely things would be better if we were to go there instead. My mother had a very good cook that we might employ again. We might live a fine life there.' A lump of gristle bobs in the thin brown liquor, white and fatty. It makes my stomach roil. 'Can nothing better than this be got?'

'At least there is meat.'

'It's turned. There must be something else, something better.'

'Eat it and be thankful.'

I put down my spoon and stare at him. I clear my throat, expecting a servant to hear and come running. No one appears.

Thomas sighs, leaning back and taking up his cup. 'Stone . . . Stone!'

Master Stone appears at the door. 'Sir?'

'My wife is done with her supper.'

The old man comes to my side and lifts my plate.

'Have you something better?' I ask.

'M'lady?'

Thomas is watching with scorn-filled eyes.

'A pie perhaps? Roasted birds, eggs?'

Stone looks bemused but nods and leaves the room.

'He'll come back empty-handed,' Thomas says, wiping his mouth on his sleeve. 'What did you expect? To find us as before? As if nothing has happened? What world have you been living in?'

'I thought things would be better here. I'm tired of living like this. I want a decent meal from my own kitchen, not food better suited to the servants' hall.'

'We must all eat like servants these days – servants to Cromwell, servants to Parliament and the Compounding Committee. They are the masters now.' His bitterness is written in the sour twist of his mouth.

I fold my hands in my lap and try to keep my voice level. His lack of understanding causes little sparks of anger to ignite in my chest. 'You promised me that all would be well, now that Ware Park is signed over to you. You said that your fortune would be restored. And I thought—'

He splutters into his cup. 'I said nothing of the sort. I've not a half of what should be mine. Not a third. Parliament has taken most of the land, the house is in ruins, and there's no money to settle with the Committee. If you are come here looking for feasts and gaieties, you will be sore disappointed.'

'I am come here because you ordered me to. You said—'

'You are my wife and I have a duty to perform. I could not

put it off any longer. Be thankful you have a house to run at all.'

'Yes, I have a house – Markyate Cell.'

'Ware Park is your home now.'

I have lost my appetite. I push my chair away from the table, making a loud, protesting scrape across the boards.

Thomas stares, and for a moment we are held there, silent, while my defiance begins to boil. He seems to think better of picking an argument. 'Come now, you must see that the land at Markyate is not so fine as here, and it's a good deal further from the road to London. Besides, they say the house has suffered far worse than Ware Park and it will take a deal of coin to make it good again. There are plenty of Parliament men, looking to take on the old family seats. I must make a bargain with one of them if Ware Park is to survive.'

'But you have no right. Markyate Cell is mine.'

'And you belong to me. You swore to it, remember?'

'It was the one thing my mother promised, upon her marriage to your uncle, that Markyate Cell would always be my home.'

'Your mother is long dead.' He has started on the sardines now, lips and fingers greasy with oil. 'You have a house here to make your own. Be grateful for it. And I have brought you the grey mare for sport – procuring that creature near emptied my purse, I can tell you. Most wives would be well satisfied with that.'

The sight of him suddenly sickens me. 'I will not sell my family's past for gifts and trinkets.'

'You have no say in the matter.'

'You cannot take my birthright away from me.'

'Yes, I can. I may do as I wish.'

I take up my wine and dash it across the table. The cold liquid courses across it like the tide across a causeway, until it reaches his platter and drips into his lap.

Only then does he turn his attention from the food. He pulls his chair back and glares at me, lips pursed tight. I see a flicker of that raging young boy in the gardens at Merton College, but the moment is brief and quickly quelled.

Master Stone returns, faltering as he sees the mess. He says nothing and ignores me, sitting there, trembling with fury. He goes to Thomas, lifts the platter away and finds a dry spot. Thomas stands calmly, as though nothing is amiss, while Stone adjusts his chair. He takes his seat again and resumes his meal. Only then does Stone come to me.

'M'lady, the cook says there's naught else but pottage, and no more manchet till Friday, but you can have a share of the maslin, if you would take it from the mouths of those who serve you.'

Thomas's eyes meet mine, triumphant.

How can my husband, the one man now charged with my care, sit so unmoved while our world falls about our ears?

Chapter 13

It has been a cold three days, the marital bed not yet warmed. Thomas and I have not begun our life together as I imagined it or, indeed, as anyone would wish it.

I am still smarting from the news that Markyate Cell is to be sold. I come to understand, after three days of failed negotiation, of tears and pleading and long silences, that my husband will not change his mind. In fact, he cannot. The matter is not his cruel ploy to distress me, as it might at first have seemed, but a necessity: the Fanshawe estate cannot be maintained without draining dry every last penny from the Ferrers fortune. I am the last of that line and, I now learn, the one that will see it fail.

It is a simple choice for Thomas: Ware Park or Markyate Cell. How can I blame him for choosing to save his own family seat above mine, when I would do the very same? But I do blame him, and what pains me more is that now I see the design in it all. One family fortune plundered to save another.

Who was it first saw the chance? Sir Simon, perhaps, or those other canny Fanshawe brothers, swooping down upon my grieving mother, with flattery and trickery, to steal and swallow the spoils? Such easy prey. She would never have agreed to the sale of Markyate Cell if she were still alive. I know we are in times like no other, and that sacrifices must be made, but somehow this knowledge does nothing to quell my anger.

I had once hoped for a husband who would stand beside me to fight the battles of this world, but instead our first skirmishes are against each other, in the stretches of silence between us, in tears shed on Rachel's shoulder, in his unspoken absence at night.

That is, until the evening he comes to my bed.

On the first night I was afraid he would come and find me weeping, rocking like a babe in Rachel's arms. On the second I was sure he would come, but I fell asleep with my candle burning and woke alone, in the dead hours, shivering in my flimsy nightgown. On the third he drank all day and fell to slumbering in his chair before supper. I did not have the inclination to wake him. But on the fourth night, as I take my leave, he catches my hand and presses his lips against it. I know then that the time has come.

An hour passes before he comes to my door. I can tell that he has spent the time with the liquor bottle. A waft of spirits reaches me, making a flutter of nerves about my heart.

He has already removed his doublet, his shirt hanging loose, and his cheeks have the flush of a drunkard.

'Well, then, wife,' he says, coming towards the bed, where I lie against the bolster, waiting. 'Let me see if you have fulfilled your promise.'

He pulls back the coverlet and surveys me, untying his breeches, kicking off his boots, rolling down his stockings, until he stands in nothing but his shirt. His legs are stark white, still almost hairless.

He climbs onto the mattress and tugs at my nightgown. 'Take it off.'

I slip it over my head. My skin shivers into goose bumps. It takes a deal of effort not to cover myself with my hands. He is my husband, I tell myself, and he has a right to see me. But I do not feel the stirrings I used to feel when George looked upon me. I feel none of the passions that torment me by night. Instead, I am fearful, wide-eyed, and awkward as a fawn taking first steps.

I expect him to lean in for a kiss, but he kneels next to me, looking over my body, in silence.

I wonder, for a moment, if he knows what to do. But, of course, he is no longer the fumbling boy of our wedding night. He is in his twenty-fourth year, with knowledge and experience far beyond my own. I'm not so naïve as to think that there have not been others to tutor him in all our years apart, but this is not the moment to think of my jealousy, my anger, or my disappointment: I must make myself the dutiful wife, willing to be taught.

Feeling bolder, I whisper, 'Won't you let me see you too?'

He starts as though I have slapped him. 'What?'

I try to make my voice soft, cajoling, as I imagine a man might like. 'Take off your shirt, husband, and let me see what God made of you.'

He pauses a moment and frowns. Then, without another word, he climbs on top of me and pushes my knees apart, lowering himself between my legs.

He struggles to enter, the length of him butting against me as though he cannot find his way. He grunts with impatience. And then it happens, and I am squashed beneath him, breath squeezed from me, confusion rising.

At first there is a sudden sore pain and I think something must be wrong.

I put my hands against his chest, trying to push him away. 'Stop . . . please stop . . .' But my whispers sound pathetic. 'Thomas, please . . .'

He ignores me, beginning to push, his face buried against my neck.

'Thomas . . . I . . .'

'Be silent . . .' He puts a hand over my mouth. He pants into my ear, liquor-laced sour-milk breath curling in my nostrils, mingling now with another scent, musky and unclean.

There are no kisses, no affectionate words, such as I have

imagined, just this unceasing pushing and panting. I struggle to catch my breath. The candle sends shadows spiralling on the canopy. I am too hot. I cannot breathe. A sudden panic overwhelms me – I must stop this, I cannot bear it.

Then, as abruptly as it had begun, it is over.

He shudders and lets out a low moan, crushing me as he collapses.

I lie still and silent, praying there is no more. The panic ebbs away, taking the pain with it.

After a few moments, he rolls aside.

I am ashamed and exposed, too afraid to reach for my nightgown.

'You will make fine sons,' he says eventually. 'Fine Fanshawe boys.' It is not an observation – it is an order.

Then he gathers his clothes and leaves.

Chapter 14

I could not tell you the way to Markyate Cell from Ware Park, but I find the house easily, turning Feather down the right lanes, making the left turn at the crossroads, passing familiar hamlets and farms, guided by an increasing tug in my chest, as if I am spellbound. When I left Ware Park, before dawn, sneaking from the stables before Thomas could insist on a chaperone, I knew it would anger him, but I was – am – determined to do this alone. His cruelty in the matter has cut me keenly and I am willing to risk his wrath, desperate to see the house one last time before it is sold.

Markyate Cell sits upon a rise in the land, parkland sweeping away on three sides, orchards and woodlands sloping gently to the north. It is late afternoon by the time I arrive and the midsummer sun is still high. From a distance, the house is just as I remember it. The light bounces and sparkles on diamond windowpanes. I can almost feel sun-hot red brick beneath my fingertips. I can imagine smoke rising from the bakehouse chimneys, can almost smell the oven-fresh loaves. My heart squeezes.

But as I draw closer, Feather's hoofs muffled by the bindweed on the path, it becomes clear that the house is long abandoned. The leads are blank eyes, blinkered here and there by climbing ivy. Broken panes wink back at me. One of the lower windows is boarded with planks of whitewashed wood, nailed in a lopsided crucifix, like a plague cross.

The trees in the orchards are grown wild, long branches hanging, piles of rotten fruit mulched at their feet. The walled summer garden, where my mother and I would sit in dappled sunlight, is given over to weeds, a mess of nettles and dandelions fit for an old crone's cook pot. A flurry of starlings rises from the roof where tiles are missing. Everything is silent and still, save the slow, consuming creep of nature.

The yard is empty but there is rainwater in the trough and I tie Feather there so she can drink. I want to call for a boy to see to the horse, for a maid to take my cloak, bring me ale and set a fire in the red chamber where I might spend the night. But it seems wrong to disturb the eerie quiet when the place is so clearly deserted. A bleak fear begins to take hold.

I always preferred the entrance from the yard and I go to the big wooden door and put my shoulder against it. Locked, no doubt bolted on the inside. I wander about, scuffing my boots in the dust, looking for a way in.

I notice a low window in the dairy, a little room I know is linked to the main house. A distant memory comes back to me of drunken servants, in the tavern too late and locked out, a broken window and docked wages. I find a large stone and use it to smash the panes closest to the door. The glass shatters easily. I reach inside, jagged edges catching on my sleeve. Stretching, I can just reach the bolt. It is stiff with rust and it takes a while but eventually it slides back into the holding. My fingers come back ochre red and smelling of iron. I turn the handle and the door swings open. I slip inside.

The room smells dank with a faint tang of old cheese. Mildew darkens the walls. Dirty churns are strewn about the floor and a three-legged stool lies on its side, one leg crooked aloft, like a pissing dog.

I leave quickly and follow the passage that leads to the kitchens. I ignore the stench of decay that hangs in the air here, the cold, bare space in the roasting pit, the spits lined up against the wall like pikes.

The staircase leading up to the main hall is slippery with dew, lichen creeping across the ancient stone, but I tiptoe up and reach the main hall.

I am racked by what I see. I remember this wide, high room filled with people, music and dancing, candles aglow, torches flickering in sconces, the old beams twined with ivy and red holly berries on Twelfth Night, logs blazing in the fine carved fireplace, tables laden with food.

The tables are still here, pushed up against one wall, but they are empty, save slivers of coloured glass that lie splintered: the Ferrers coat of arms, broken into pieces.

Only one tapestry remains, half of it burned and blackened, the rest dulled by smoke and tattered in rags. Two of the fine chairs from the high table lie on their backs, padded seats spewing stuffing as though someone has taken a knife to them. The rats have done the rest. Mouldering bales of straw sit stinking in a corner, with a clutch of broken wooden pales. There is a stench of dung and pondweed. Horses have been stabled here.

I cannot bear it but, then, I cannot bear to leave. It's like walking through my own nightmare. Thomas is right – Ware Park is in a poor state but Markyate Cell has suffered the ravages of Cromwell's soldiers far worse. You would think no one had lived here for decades.

I bend and pick up a ruby shard of glass. I look up at the big window, once the most splendid decoration in the whole house. We had had nothing like it elsewhere, not even in the little room used as a chapel, or in the village church. Made by craftsmen long before I was born, it was an object of great pride for my father. As a girl I could sit for hours on summer days like this one, watching the sun play upon the coloured panes, delighting in the way it made rainbows dance upon the stone flags. I would hold out my hand to catch the colours in my palm, but those little pockets of magic were always spinning and slipping away.

The painted glass is all smashed now. Beams of sunlight filter in, making the dust motes spark. Such delicate beauty makes a mockery of my memories.

I want to weep for what has happened here. But I'm too angry for tears.

I'm angry with Thomas for allowing my home to fall into such disrepair. I'm angry with the soldiers who broke the windows and dug up the kitchen beds and knocked the heads from the statues. I'm angry with my father for dying, with my mother for following him, with Sir Simon for abandoning me to a husband who has taken the one thing I cared about and cast it aside without a thought. But, most of all, I'm angry with myself for staying away so long.

A choking cry erupts from my throat, strangling me. I slump down onto a bench and bend double, trying to find clean air to breathe, but the air in here is tainted – poisoned by the realisation of my own failings. While I hid away in Hamerton, those long, dull years, I left my birthright to this destruction. I did not even try to return. I did not fight. I blindly accepted my husband's will, and the assurances of my elders, believing that nothing would really change and that one day I would come back and find my happiness here. I have been a fool. I alone have abandoned Markyate Cell to its crumbling, desolate fate. And now it will be taken away from me all over again. The aching, desperate loss that I've learned to live with, that has been lessened by the years, is suddenly fierce once more.

Just then I hear a noise from above. A door slams and something clatters onto the bare boards. I fall silent and listen. An animal, perhaps, got in through a broken window? Or a breeze, gasping through gaps in the tiles? Markyate is an old house; it always did have its own voice and it hid its mysteries well.

But then I hear footsteps.

My hairs at the nape of my neck bristle, my blood running chill. I follow the steady thump across the ceiling above.

I have the urge to run. But I calm myself. It may be the steward Thomas spoke of. I am still mistress here, and I have every right to know who is in my house. Perhaps it is even one of the old servants, someone who can tell me what happened. But despite my reasoning I feel as though I am the one trespassing.

I stand, shaking off my fear, gather my skirts and tiptoe to the staircase that leads to the upper floor, mindful to avoid the crunch of glass underfoot. I still remember which steps creak and sneak up them without a sound. I make my way along the gallery.

The damage is not so bad here but birds have come in through the cracked panes and nested in the cornice. The wooden panelling is spattered black and white with their lye. There are twigs and feathers on the floor. Some of the paintings remain, a few of the portraits slashed at the neck, the work of Cromwell's men, no doubt, taking the heads off enemies they could not slay on the battlefield. A blue and white vase I remember from my childhood lies in pieces. Anything else of value is gone.

My breath is shallow.

Sounds are coming from the chamber at the far end of the gallery. Of course, anyone would choose that room: it is the finest in the house, the most comfortable, the most beautiful, with windows looking out over what remains of the walled garden. It was my mother's bedchamber.

When I was a child I spent long afternoons lying upon the red velvet coverlet, fingers tracing the gold embroidered vines and the deep crimson roses on the hangings, while I listened to my mother's tales, and the hum of her song as she brushed out her hair or dabbed rosewater on her cheeks. I knew that one day I would take her place and that room would be mine. No one should be in there but me.

The thought makes my heart tilt and ache. But I'm frightened too. What will I do if I open the door and see her standing there? What if the noise in the gallery was the sound of her step? What will I do if she sits by the window, beckoning me to her for a sweetmeat and a story? My mouth is dry as I reach the door and pause for a moment, straining to hear any sign at all. I hear something, but it is not my mother's sweet tones. It is more like the panting of a dog, then the muffle of something soft thrown onto the floor, a low, gruff moan.

Before my terror can get the better of me, I ease the door open slowly.

There is a man standing at the foot of the bed. He has his back to me. He is of middling height, square-shouldered. Chestnut curls are tied back with black braid. He wears a plain linen shirt, dark breeches and leather riding boots covered with mud. A brown coat is tossed upon the bed. I see the red coverlet is gone, the mattress strewn with a rough woollen blanket.

As the door rests on its hinges, the man turns. His eyes, as they meet mine, flash with shock, then fear, then confusion, all in a moment. His face is drained pale, with dark hollows under his eyes. But I barely have time to decipher his expression before I see that the front of his shirt is stained, from waist to shoulder, with a lurid spray of scarlet.

I stagger backwards. In a flash he comes towards the door. I stumble away, back down the gallery, old leaves, straw and a discarded birds' nest tangling my skirts.

'Wait!' the man cries, his voice echoing loud in the empty space.

I reach the stairs and fling myself down, missing steps, almost tumbling. Then back across the damp chill of the hall, running now, into the kitchens the way I came. I can hear him coming after me, the uneven tread on the staircase, like the Devil on my heels.

I fly down the passageway to the dairy and out into the yard.

My fingers are clumsy and fumbling as I untie Feather from the post. She tosses her head as I tug on her reins to pull her around and clamber onto her back. I struggle into the saddle and dig my heels in sharp. As Feather wheels, I catch a glimpse of him, lurching from the dairy, one hand clutched to his chest, the other outstretched.

'Wait – please wait! I won't hurt you!' he calls, but I do not wait to find out.

1657

Chapter 15

Ware is not a large town, but it is renowned for its trade. These years of poverty and Parliament's taxes have only increased men's appetite for the gaining and spending of coin, or the barter of favours when coin cannot be got. The high street is lined with inns, always brimful of travellers making their way to and fro along the old North Road. The streets bustle with comings and goings. Fine coaches, carrying city gentlemen, jostle with gypsies' carts. Barrow boys, laden with sacks of grain, weave tracks between the malthouses. Bargemen loll outside the taverns, a tankard apiece, watching the world go by, waiting for a full enough load to make the trip to London worth their while. Young dandies on horseback doff feathered hats to any passing lady. Outside the alehouses, preening wenches with painted faces pout as the men go by. The air smells of warm barley, horse muck, night soil and the reedy marsh beds of the River Lea.

On market days the smiths ply for trade. The ring of iron on iron from the inn yards echoes the church bells in St Mary's. Hawkers call out their wares. There are beggars too, men with missing limbs who have been unable to work since the war, and ragged, haunt-eyed children in sackcloth, clamouring for a bruised apple, a crust of bread, a bacon rind. They gather around the stocks in the market square where a bald man is slick with the slime of putrid eggs, hoping to scavenge from the rotting vegetable scraps about his feet. An old friar in a long, grey robe preaches to the crowd, holding up his arms to the sky. A boy hurries a flock of raucous geese across the square as they scatter under stalls and beneath people's feet.

The street-sellers compete to catch the best business. Women balance baskets of warm loaves on their heads, shopkeepers' boys yell from trestles, everywhere is noise and commotion. After the quiet of Ware Park, the racket makes my head spin, but it is good to be out in the world again. In the two years since returning to Hertfordshire, I have rarely had the opportunity to venture beyond the boundaries of our land. With Markyate Cell lost to me, and Thomas so often away in London, my world has remained joyless and small, Rachel my only constant companion. She is with me now, close by my side, keen-eyed, on the look-out for cutpurses.

We find Hazel's butcher's shop, as instructed by the cook. Master Hazel, a thin, pinched man, who looks as though he rarely benefits from the meat he sells, greets me without a smile. Cleaver in hand, he continues chopping a joint of pork and makes no move to serve me. Hearing my name, the townswomen waiting in line fall silent and stare. They whisper behind their hands. The butcher's apprentice, tying a parcel of meat with straw and string, watches me sideways. My cheeks begin to burn as I am made to wait my turn.

Another woman enters and stands beside me. She is plainly dressed, and wears a neat coif in the fashion of the Puritans. Her black dress looks new, her white collar well laundered, and the burgundy shawl she wears has simple velvet trimmings. Her dark hair is parted and pulled back beneath her cap, lending a severity that does not serve her features. Compared to the goodwives, she looks a woman of quality, a little older than I but, I notice, there is no wedding ring on her finger. We exchange a nod of acknowledgement.

When it is my turn at the counter, I ask for a hock of venison, and hand over an order for the other meats that must be delivered to Ware Park over the next week. Thomas's letter included instruction to spare no expense. He wants only the best for his guests. This will be the first time he has brought his friends to Ware Park and I do not miss the implication in his words: I am being tested.

'I will take the venison now,' I tell Master Hazel. 'But the rest must be freshly slaughtered and delivered to Ware Park each day. Nothing but your best.'

Master Hazel nods as he takes the order and looks it over. Then he disappears into a back room and brings back a slab of dark red meat. I can smell the rank stench of rotting flesh before it reaches the trestle. He hands it to the boy, who pulls a face as he begins to tie it up. I know the cook will curse and mutter if I present her with such a challenge.

'Master Hazel, that will not do,' I say. 'That meat is not fresh.'

'It has been hung, madam,' he says. 'In my store.'

I go over to the trestle and prod at the hunk of flesh. It is poor, with signs that maggots have already feasted upon it. The women are turning away, holding up nosegays. One tuts and shakes her head. Why do they linger? Do I make such a show?

'You must have better. Let me see something else.'

'Madam, my apologies, but this is the best I can offer you.'

'I won't take it. Good venison, please, as I asked.'

He hesitates. 'I'm afraid, if this will not do, you will have to find trade somewhere else.'

'I was told you are the best butcher in Ware.'

He lowers his voice, making some attempt at discretion. 'Forgive me, m'lady, but your order is expensive.'

'Yes. The best, just as my husband requests.'

'That's the very nub of it, m'lady. I cannot take an order from the Fanshawe house without prior payment.'

'Why not?' I am aware that all eyes are on me. The goodwives have fallen silent, eyes sharp, talons primed.

Master Hazel clears his throat. 'By order of the aldermen, I can supply Ware Park only when Thomas Fanshawe's debt is settled.'

'I know nothing of any debt.'

'You'll forgive me, m'lady, but there is a large amount owing.'

I can feel a poker-hot flush creeping up my neck. Thomas complains about his lack of coin often enough, but I had assumed our bills were settled with the money from the sale of Markyate Cell. 'I see. How much is owed?' I say quietly.

Master Hazel shifts from foot to foot. 'Your husband has the details of the account, madam.'

'My husband is not here. How much is the debt?'

I know he means to save me shame but I am determined to know the truth.

'Near on five pounds and seven shillings to me. Much more to some others. The townsmen have determined that no one in Ware is to give credit until the debts are settled. Your husband has been told of this. I'm sorry, there's nothing I can do. In these straitened times, we must all have a head for business, and I cannot go against the guild.'

Five pounds and seven shillings. I have nothing like that much in coin. I have nothing like that anywhere.

I hear whispering behind me as the women begin their gossip. The story of Master Hazel's five pounds and seven shillings will surely follow me around the marketplace for weeks to come. If Thomas knows of this, how can he ignore it? How can he let me come here unawares, to be humiliated?

I open my pocket and pretend to count coin, but I know I have no hope of paying. Master Hazel looks away, cheeks flushing almost as red as my own.

'How much is the good venison?' Next to me, the dark-haired woman's voice is gentle but firm.

Master Hazel looks at her in surprise, then at me. She steps forwards, the only one not whispering with the others. 'How much?' she insists.

'For a side, five shillings.'

She fetches out her pocket, spills coin onto her hand, takes up a half-crown and places it on the trestle. 'Lady Katherine will take a quart of the good venison,' she says.

Master Hazel stares, waiting for a response. The woman looks at me. Her eyes are kind, but with no hint of pity. 'If you will allow me?' she says.

I give a curt nod. What choice have I? I cannot leave empty-handed and let this cabal of Ware housewives tittle-tattle about the fortunes of Thomas Fanshawe and his unfortunate degraded wife, who cannot pay the butcher's bill.

This time Master Hazel returns with a good-sized hock that is fresh, red and smells rich and gamey. I stand in silence until the meat is wrapped and the coin has been exchanged. I will not thank this woman in front of the others – I would not show myself so reduced.

I am desperate to know: who is the generous stranger who knows my name, and why would she come to my rescue? My curiosity does not burn for long.

'You will accept Lady Katherine's order,' she says. 'And you will write to me for settlement of the account. My name is Martha Coppin, and you will find me at Markyate Cell.'

Chapter 16

Martha Coppin's generosity serves me well. The next day we concoct a feast from our bare stores. The hock of venison turns dark mahogany on the spit, rich juices spitting in the dripping pan. The cook sets a boy to turn and baste the meat for the whole three hours of cooking, so it will be tender and full of flavour. There are young game birds too, from our own park, fresh caught by the falconer, plucked and gutted by a fat, bustling girl brought in from Ware. There are dishes of artichokes, skirrets and radish from the kitchen beds. There is a peach syllabub, made with early fruit from the glasshouse. The peaches are small and crunchy. When I pick them from the trellis I think they will not do, but stewed and whipped with cream and sugar, they taste of summer. Thomas has his claret, there are spirits for the men, a good brew of small beer and last year's cider. The air is thick with rich savours and humming with activity. My stomach gurgles and groans in anticipation. I catch the boy dipping his fingers in the dripping pan. Instead of scolding him, I do the same. The greasy, charred taste reminds me of days past. I push the scene in the butcher's shop to the back of my mind and imagine that better times have come at last.

Thomas arrives with his friend Leventhorpe, a baronet with a house some ten miles east at Sawbridgeworth. Thomas has spoken of him often and I'm curious to greet the man my husband considers his closest friend. I remember him from my wedding day – a tall, pale fellow, of about my own age, with dirty yellow curls and shifty blue eyes. Some might call him foppish, but 'sly' was the word that sprang to mind back then. Time has not much changed him. Like Thomas, he is too young to have fought at the King's side and lacks the haunted, sombre look that so many older men seem to wear.

The others come soon after: Anne, with her husband, Richard Fanshawe, trailing two mewling infants, and my little cousin Dickon, a boisterous lad who insists on carrying a stick at all times to beat off the Roundheads, though a messy beheading of spring daffodils has to suffice. Sir Simon arrives, the creases in his brow deeper than I remember.

Sir Richard Willis comes last, arriving late and alone, on horseback. I have no chance to wash the kitchen dirt from my hands and face. There is flour on my cheek in lieu of white lead, and my blush is from exertion rather than the apothecary's pot. So I let Thomas greet him while I peer from an upper window.

Willis is not much changed. He has not run to fat and ruin, like so many others of the old King's commanders. His hair is still coal black. His dress is simple and neat, seemingly untainted by the dust of the road. As he dismounts and joins the Fanshawe men, with much good-natured backslapping, he has the air of a man who knows that we have all been waiting for him. I wonder what he will make of the changes in me.

The meal is a success. When the food is laid out, Thomas nods his approval. I'm not sure he'll be so pleased when he finds out about our new debt to Martha Coppin, but for now he is satisfied.

Later, when enough wine has been supped, the talk turns to politics, as it always does when the Fanshawe men are gathered.

'Have you had word from the King?' Sir Simon asks of Willis.

'Is there progress with the Spanish plan?'

'I have no news that I can share. I'm sure you understand.'

'Our friend Willis is one of the privileged few to have His Majesty's confidence,' Uncle Richard explains, although there is no need – the whole world knows how Willis suffered in the Tower at the mercy of Thurloe, Cromwell's spymaster, the man they say would torture his own child if it gave him some advantage over the King's remaining supporters. It's no secret that Willis's loyalty has earned him a place as one of the six men chosen by the young Charles Stuart to lead the Sealed Knot, that fellowship of men still brave enough to work for the return of the Stuart bloodline to the English throne.

'The Spanish insist they'll not set sail until we are assured of an English port to receive them,' Willis says. 'And we cannot secure a landing place without their number . . . So, we are at a stalemate. You see how it is.'

I'm surprised that they talk so openly of plots and secrets while there are servants at table. I try to catch Anne's eye, but she is smiling demurely, delicately picking at the food on her plate, as though she is used to it.

'Of course,' Willis goes on, 'we're waiting to see if we're to have a different crowned head on these shores before the year is out.'

'Cromwell . . .' Spittle showers from Leventhorpe's lips. He has already drunk too much of Thomas's claret. 'I'll cut off his head before I see a crown upon it.'

'Is there news?' Sir Simon asks. 'Has Cromwell accepted Parliament's offer at last?'

Willis makes us all dangle for a few seconds before he shakes his head. 'I was at Whitehall yesterday and it seems there is still no confirmation. But all expect it soon. I don't know why the man tarries so – to create some false illusion of humility, perhaps. What a sham. We all know this has been his dearest wish these ten years.' He spears a piece of meat with his knife.

'King Oliver the First,' says Leventhorpe. 'What a joke.'

'It's no joke,' Uncle Richard says tersely. 'If he accepts Parliament's terms then a new royal family will be proclaimed. It'll be all the harder to re-establish the Stuart claim once Cromwell is the royal lineage in the statute books. Outright war would be the only way.'

'And we do not have the means for such a challenge,' Willis adds. 'Certainly not without the Spanish.'

'What about the French?' Sir Simon asks. 'Will Louis not be persuaded to help, with such a connection between the families?'

'The people won't take well to an English king at the head of a Catholic army, Spanish or French. History shows us that. Cromwell knows it too. That's why he's so assured of his position. That's why he dallies. He knows the whole of Europe is hanging on his word, like a lovelorn sweetheart.'

Thomas butts in, 'But surely any Stuart king is preferable to Cromwell?'

Uncle Richard raises his glass. 'Amen to that. If only more thought the same.'

'What hope have we if Cromwell takes the crown?' Thomas is angry now and I can see the wine has had its effect. His cheeks are red and his eyes watery. 'We'll be taxed all the more, our estates shall be ruined – what's left of them – and the moneylenders will tire of the endless credit.'

So, I think, he does know about the debts. A flicker of fury rises in me, fuelled by the wine, as I remember the shame of my visit to the butcher. If there is no money, why does he insist on spending more? I understand the desire for the riches that should be our birthright – I feel it keenly every day – but I curse his thoughtlessness and hypocrisy.

Willis puts his knife down and leans forward, elbows on the table. 'If Cromwell is so foolhardy as to put the crown upon his own head, we must hope that the common people will see clear the arrogance and pride of the man. They will see that he has cut off the head of one king to make himself the same, under another name. What is Lord Protector if not King in disguise? He promised them a *new* England, not this duplicity. There are already plenty among the army ranks, and the Commonwealth men in Parliament, who turn against their old general, who see these truths. They see that he's lied, that he has his own interests at heart. It will not be long before others see it too. They will see him for the tyrant he is.'

'Hear hear.' Thomas raises his glass again.

'Perhaps then we'll gain the support of the commoners,' Willis continues, 'for they'll soon see what's best for them. They'll see that if there must be a king upon the throne, better to have one who is born to it and understands the subtlety of kingship, not a greedy leech, sucking the country dry for want of his own power. Once the mob calls for the return of the Stuarts, we'll be assured of victory. I'm convinced we must bide our time, wait for this to play out, wait for the right moment.'

'So you will not give up, even if Cromwell takes the crown?' I ask. It is the first I have spoken and the men all look at me in surprise.

Willis considers. 'I prefer to find hope in every circumstance. I'll never give up this fight, but now is not the right time to challenge. I've been called reckless before, foolish even, and I've learned my lesson the hard way. My counsel would be for patience.' His eyes linger on mine.

'Tell us, Sir Richard,' Anne says, 'how was the Tower on your last visit?'

Willis pushes his plate away, takes up his cup and leans back in his chair. 'Tolerable, as always. It can be agreeable to revisit old haunts.'

Leventhorpe snorts into his cup.

'And did they treat you well? You are a little leaner, I think, since I saw you last. I hope you were not too . . . inconvenienced.'

Willis smiles. 'Madam, the food was not up to the standards I'm used to, but the company was, as always, diverting.' I see something in his expression then. Despite the jest there is darkness behind his bravado. It's clear he does not want to talk about this.

Anne sees it too and does not press. 'It seems our Lord Protector cannot dampen your spirits. I thank God there are still men like you, brave and loyal to His Majesty, willing to risk all to help him.'

Willis inclines his head.

'Tell us more of the King,' Leventhorpe says. 'And Prince Rupert. Is he with Charles now? When did you see them last?'

Although it is some years since Willis was abroad with the exiled Charles Stuart and his makeshift, penniless court, he has plenty to tell and holds the company spellbound. Thomas and Leventhorpe lap up his words, like eager pups at spilt milk. As I watch them, so impressed and fawning, I am slightly sickened by my husband. When compared to a man like Willis, he seems but a boy. By the time Willis has finished telling of the King's latest hopes to bring a Spanish army to England, Thomas and Leventhorpe are so awed and stupid, they look as if they would kneel down upon the flags and delight in licking his boots clean.

I admit there is something compelling in the way Willis talks. There is a passion in him, spilling into his words and making his eyes flash. His blood is up as he talks again of Cromwell and the impending proclamation of his kingship. He makes me believe that there is still hope for Charles Stuart's cause, even when all hope seems lost. Willis has the force and vigour of a man twenty years younger; mixed with the wisdom and experience of his years, it is an intoxicating brew.

'You must know,' Thomas says eventually, 'that in the Fanshawe family you've many allies. Of course, I cannot speak for my uncles and brothers, but I'd do anything to aid His Majesty's cause.'

'I too,' Leventhorpe adds.

The older Fanshawe men exchange knowing looks.

Willis acknowledges with a nod. 'There may come a time when I'm able to call upon you all. I'll remember your words. I know them to be heartfelt. God willing, there'll be a time when every faithful servant of His Majesty will be called upon, and we'll all be rewarded with the justice that is our due.'

The wine is almost finished. My head is beginning to spin. The fire is banked high and, for once, it is hot. The air seems cloyed with high-strung emotion.

Thomas, as host, raises his glass once more. 'To King Charles.' We all echo him and drain our cups. 'And to our sworn enemy, Oliver Cromwell.' He hurls his glass into the fireplace. There is a moment of stunned silence and all eyes turn to the hearthstone, now glittering with daggers of glass, splashed and dripping with claret wine.

Chapter 17

When I excuse myself, leaving the men to their politics and pipes, Anne follows me to my chamber. I'm exhausted from my long day in the kitchens and my mind is fogged with wine.

Anne perches on the edge of the bed as Rachel helps me undress. She rubs her temples and yawns, fixing me with her shrewd stare. 'My dear, how are things between you and Thomas?'

'All is well, thank you, Aunt.'

'How long has it been now, since you were reunited?'

'Almost two years.'

She contemplates this. 'And is he a good husband to you?'

'Of course.' I begin to unpin my hair, avoiding her eyes.

'Do not think me impertinent, Katherine. We're family now, and someone must counsel you – Sir Simon, dear man, has no idea what to do with a daughter – and I could not help but notice you are a little thin. I know times are hard, and we must all be frugal, but you're in sore need of fattening up. Keep back the best foodstuffs – shut them away from the servants. Men like a little plumpness in their women.'

I say nothing.

'My Richard tells me that Thomas spends much time in London, and you're often alone, here at Ware.'

'We are parted more often than not.'

'Ah – then that explains it.' She cradles her belly. 'I'm with child again myself, though it's early still.'

Rachel, now facing me, unlacing my stays, raises a brow slightly.

'My dear,' Anne goes on, 'you were very young when you married and there was plenty of time for such things. But now you are well ripened. Do not wait too much longer. I had two children by the time I was your age, though neither of them are with me any longer.' She casts her eyes down and I imagine her bending over a small grave, placing tiny coffins in the earth. 'But that makes it all the more important to begin.'

I know that Anne's marriage is built on mutual liking. I see it in the way that she and Uncle Richard look to each other, exchanging little smiles when they think no one is watching. There is an affinity between them that I cannot hope to match with Thomas. Anne cannot possibly imagine how it is on the infrequent occasions that Thomas visits my bed.

In the two years since that first night, I can count our liaisons on my fingertips. He comes to me drunk, or not at all. There is never romance, flattery or seduction. When he kisses me, eyes screwed shut, tasting of spirits and tobacco, our teeth clash and our bodies are at odds. He is quick and urgent, leaving as soon as our business is transacted.

Though I am getting used to the act, it is far from how I thought a marriage bed would be. It does not begin to match the fancies that come upon me sometimes at night, or the dreams I have that cause me to wake, breathless and sweating. I'm sure these imaginings come from the wickedness within me, and I pray every Sunday that I will be released from them, but at times I'm enslaved, finding no respite until I have answered the Devil's call.

Sometimes Thomas cannot complete the task. On those nights he is filled with contempt, as if he blames me for his failures. Just once, when it happened, he lay down next to me and sobbed like a child. I stroked his hair until he fell asleep – the closest we have ever come to affection – but in the morning he shunned my touch and would not meet my eye. Even in the heat of our regular quarrels, neither of us has mentioned it again.

I wonder if Anne has been put up to this task or if the concern is all her own. Whatever the case, I cannot tell her the truth.

'I understand,' I say.

'Good.' She rises and wanders to the fireside. 'You know, there are things that one can do, to aid the process. Of course, you do not have a mother to help you, so you must let me advise. I will send to my London apothecary for a remedy that I have found expeditious.'

'There is no need,' I say, but she waves away my protests.

'It is a woman's job to ensure the getting of children, though we are entirely dependent on a little help from our men.' She pauses and toys with the pearls at her neck. 'If you are without that help, then there are things that can be done. It's your duty to produce an heir, and you must do it soon. Tell me, is there a reason you have not yet been able to do so with your husband?'

I shake my head. I'm standing in my shift while Rachel folds my skirts. Rachel's expression is fixed in the studied vacancy required of a trusted maidservant. Ignoring her, Anne comes over to me and puts her hands on my shoulders. 'I say this as a friend. There are already questions raised about your union, about your . . . abilities. Perhaps it was unwise to marry you so young, but we cannot change that. Once there is a child, there can be no more questions. It is the only way to secure your place here. And there is only so long that a family can wait. If there is a problem, you must let me help.'

I'm certain now: the threat in her message comes clear. I will not let on that she chafes at the truth and it smarts. 'There is no problem, Aunt.'

'I say these things only out of concern for you.'

'There is no problem.'

She fixes me with an intent gaze. 'Then I shall expect to hear the happy news soon. You must find a way, Katherine. Do what you must.'

When she has gone Rachel is silent.

I think about Anne's insinuations. Of course the family is disappointed with me. I see that in Thomas's indifference, hear it in his spiteful comments. They have taken all they can from me, slowly sucking my inheritance dry, but I still have not given them the one thing that is needed most. I have not fulfilled my side of the bargain. Anne is right – a child would change this. A child would give some purpose to my life here and secure my position in the family. A child would be my protection. But what is this help that Anne spoke of? Could it be that she is suggesting something she could never outwardly condone?

When Rachel helps me into bed I pat the mattress. 'Come, sit a while.'

'I'm tired,' she says.

'What do you think she meant?'

Rachel shrugs and turns away to fetch a candle. Her mouth is fixed in a tight, thin line, like a thread of black cotton.

'Was she suggesting that I try outside my marriage? I can hardly believe that she would, but it seemed so.'

Rachel places the candle by the bedside. 'I cannot think what she meant.'

'But what was your impression?'

'You've had your chances in the past. What difference would it make now?' she says, bobbing a formal little curtsy. She turns and crosses to the door.

'Is something the matter?' I ask. But she just shakes her head and closes the door behind her.

I lie awake, staring into the darkness. I have heard enough gossip of men and their mistresses to understand that husbands will stray beyond the marriage bed. It is expected. But it's a different matter for a woman to look for such things beyond her vows. Have I misunderstood Anne's meaning, or have I wilfully imagined her sanction because the thought is not new to me? I wonder if her words were meant as a warning. Perhaps there are already plans, whispered in private rooms and scrawled in secret letters, to remove Thomas's troublesome wife.

Suddenly I'm angry. The lack of a child is not solely my fault, so why should I take all the blame? I've been married for nine long years and in all that time have had no pleasure from my husband. After two years at Ware Park, he is still a stranger to me. I have sometimes thought this must be a failing in me, but then I remember how George used to look at me. I remember those nights in the stables and the chances I did not take.

I think of the way that Richard Willis regards me with undisguised approval, the way his lips linger a little too long on my hand, the way he closes his eyes when he kisses my fingers. If these other men find something to admire in me, why do I fail my husband?

Is it so wrong to want the passion of a kiss, the touch of a man's hands on my skin, the heaviness of a child growing in my belly? I want these things, as a wife should, within the blessed bounds of my marriage. Yet if Thomas refuses to give them, I'm the one who suffers. I'm the one branded a failure. And I cannot say these things out loud, because the only thing worse than a barren wife is a wayward one.

I climb out of bed and go to the window. My mind races like the clouds scouring the round, fat moon. When I open the casement, a breeze rushes in, scented with the freshness of spring. I feel an urge to be outside, to breathe deep of the night air.

I notice another scent, sweet, charred and heady: pipe smoke. I watch a thin twine of it drift upwards past my window.

Peering over the sill I see Willis below. He is alone, slowly pacing the terrace, skirting the bay that juts out beneath my chamber. I hold my breath as he pauses and looks up at the moon, taking a long draw on the pipe. He exhales and watches smoke swirl. It can be no accident that he chooses to idle beneath my window. He would not turn away from me.

Before I can think better of it, I fetch out my thickest cloak and creep from the room.

Willis sees me the moment I reach the terrace. He does not seem surprised to find the lady of the house out alone, after midnight. Slowly, methodically, he taps out the spent tobacco against a stone trough where the gardener has planted night-scented stocks. He tucks the pipe inside his coat and stands with his hands clasped behind his back, waiting.

I turn away and skirt the wall of the house to a section of the garden that is well hidden. I know he will follow. I sit on a low stone bench, my heart drumming. It does not take him long to find me.

He sits so close that our sleeves touch. 'M'lady,' he says. 'What keeps you from your bed?'

My mouth is suddenly dry. 'I cannot sleep. I am . . . unsettled.'

He turns towards me and I notice him glance back towards the house, making sure we are unobserved. 'Perhaps it was the conversation this evening. Such fiery talk can be detrimental to a lady's nerves.'

'Not to me.'

He smiles at that. 'Hmm. It would take more than posturing and fighting talk to frighten you.'

He leans a little closer. I can smell the pipe smoke on his breath, ripe and woody.

I feel bolder than I have for a long time. I look him in the eye. He is striking, dark eyes and dark hair against moon-washed skin. Whether or not this is what Anne meant, I am suddenly determined.

'I'm looking for something,' I whisper.

'And what might that be?'

'I . . .'

He raises a hand and runs a single finger down my cheek and along my jawline, silencing me. He stops at the point of my chin and tilts my head, as though angling for a kiss. He has read my meaning and there can be no mistaking his intention.

'Something tells me you find little satisfaction in this quiet life. You were not made for it, I think.' He puts a palm on my leg, finding the shape of my thigh beneath my cloak.

I hesitate. Despite the resentment that has driven me here, a picture of Thomas comes into my mind's eye. I am bound to him in the sight of God and what I intend to do is undeniably sinful. Yet all the sermons in the world could not prevent the swell of desire I feel.

Willis takes my silence as acceptance. He brushes my hair aside and strokes the skin below my ear. His touch sends shivers to the tips of my limbs. 'We are alike, you and I,' he whispers. 'I have known it for a long time. We need more from this world than most. We cannot be happy within the confines of an ordinary life. We are different, not like the others.'

'What do you mean?'

He considers. 'Most people lead good lives. They do what is expected. They go to worship and settle their debts, they are faithful to their wives and make sure their children are fed. They live and die and are forgotten. They make no mark upon the world.' His thumb creeps to my mouth and traces the line of my lower lip. 'That has never been enough for me. And I think . . . it will not be enough for you.'

He is right. I want so much more. In this moment, my heart aches, though I cannot tell what for – the void that seems to open is too wide, too obscure. Images tumble: George stripped to the waist, reaching out his hand to me; the rush of the wind through

Feather's mane and the thrill of galloping across open fields; the glitter of the King's smile; a man with a slash of scarlet across his chest.

Willis parts my cloak at the collar and leans to kiss my throat. The hair of his moustache bristles my skin. I feel myself on the edge of a precipice. I have a sense that if I do this, it will be only the beginning. I'm not sure I will ever be able to stop.

'I knew this day would come.' His voice is muffled as he noses my neck, hand sliding beneath my cloak to take hold of my waist, pulling me closer. 'You're wasted on that fool Fanshawe. I can see it in you – such wickedness. You display it like a jewel. You cannot help it.'

I put my hands up to his chest, where his heart beats fast beneath the fine linen shirt. 'Such wickedness?'

He pulls back. 'Oh, Kate, don't deny it. You could never be satisfied with a boy like Thomas Fanshawe. You could never make do with a weak sapling like that.'

He tries for my mouth, but his words have triggered something inside me. He voices the very things I have feared are true. Am I so transparent to him? 'What do you mean by wickedness?' I ask.

'You know I'm right. I see it in you, as I see it in myself.'

'But what do you see?'

He runs his hand gently over my throat, strokes a fingertip along the neckline of my shift, then down to my breast. My breath catches. I feel dizzy and unreal.

'I see the torment in you. You feel it now, don't you? Let me tell you, that torment does not come from God.'

Still, his lips try to meet mine, but his words quell the stirrings in my body. Confused, I try half-heartedly to push him away. 'I don't know what you mean.'

'Don't play the maiden with me, Kate. He taunts you, does he not? He makes you dream of things the Bible tells us are sin.'

He moves his hand down to my leg and runs his fingers along

the inside of my thigh. My thin nightgown is the only thing between his skin and mine. I shiver, but this time not with desire.

'No.' I push his hand away.

'You cannot deny it. You came to me, did you not?'

'I . . . I do not like what you said.'

'It's the Devil brings you here as surely as he lights that hellfire in your eyes. You know as well as I that we are his creatures.'

My tumbling stomach turns to sickness. 'How dare you speak to me in this way? You know nothing of me.'

'But I think I do.'

Trembling now, I stand.

I try to walk away but he catches at my sleeve. 'You know I'm right.'

'Don't touch me. Don't speak to me again, so long as you are here.' I walk away.

He calls after me: 'The day will come, Kate, when you have to admit it. You'll see.'

As I climb the stairs I meet Leventhorpe. He grips the banister, cheeks turning a yellowish hue to match his hair. I knew he would not hold the wine. As he sees me he gropes to doff his hat, then, realising he is not wearing one, chuckles to himself and pats his head instead. He gives me a leery, knowing grin. I do not say a word. As I reach the turn of the staircase, I can feel his eyes on my back.

I am a fool to think I can dabble with a man like Willis. I am angry that he has shamed me. I am sickened by what he said, because, deep inside, I'm afraid that he is right.

Chapter 18

The men return from hunting in the late afternoon, clattering into the stableyard, hounds yelping and snapping at heels. Thomas sends a boy to fetch me to his study. I leave the kitchens, dishevelled and dirty, wearing plain brown worsted, hair tucked beneath a cap. I have been scouring pots, plucking grouse and milling flour all day. The work has been dreary, but a distraction from the thoughts that haunted me in the dark hours before dawn, and a convenient means of avoiding any more of Anne's interrogations.

When Thomas sees me, his lip curls in disdain. 'God's bones, you look like a drudge. Are you so determined to humiliate me?'

'There is much to be done for your guests,' I explain, wiping my hands on my apron. 'I must help in the kitchens.'

'Don't let anyone see you dressed like that. You may do as you like tomorrow, when we've gone.' He has been at the liquor already. I can hear it in his slurred speech, smell the sharp scent in the air.

'I thought our guests were to stay the week.'

'The visit is to be cut short. We leave for London in the morning.'

'But your letter said—'

'Plans have changed.'

I think of the work that has gone into preparing for this week of company, the foodstuffs that we cannot afford hanging in the cold store, purchased on Martha Coppin's account. Thomas has not recognised how hard I have worked to create the appearance of wealth where there is none.

He goes to the window and stands with his back to me, looking out across the park. 'It's time I took up my place at the Inns of Court. London is where I must be now. At the centre of things.'

'For how long?'

He shrugs. 'For as long as it pleases me.'

I swallow my gathering feelings. 'Perhaps, this time, I could come with you.'

'The Middle Temple is no place for a woman. Your place is here.'

'You've been away so long already. Am I to do without my husband altogether?'

'It seems you have little need of me.' He is terse. He does not turn to look at me. 'You are provided for, are you not?'

If he is to leave me alone again, then I must challenge him about the debt. 'There is a problem,' I begin, 'with the merchants in Ware.'

He says nothing.

'I'm told, by the butcher there, that none of the merchants will take orders from Ware Park until all debts are settled.'

'What does this butcher know of my business?'

'Is it true? Is there bad debt?'

'What of it?'

'It must be settled before you go, else I cannot see how I will manage.'

'Have you been gossiping in Ware? Good Lord, but you're an embarrassment of a wife. There are others, you know, ten times better, would have me in a trice, if I were free.'

He means to hurt me, but I will not be dissuaded. 'Then go to

London, if you must, but you will leave me coin to settle the debts.'

He spins to face me, raising his voice. 'There is no coin! Do you not understand?'

'What about the money from the sale of Markyate Cell?' I ask, trying to balance my own temper. 'That money is rightfully mine.'

He laughs bitterly. 'Gone to the Compounding Committee. They would have taken this house if I had not settled. You're a fool, Kate. You know nothing of business and fortune. Do not attempt to meddle in things you don't understand, and do not dare discuss my affairs with tradesmen and servants. Why do you insist on shaming me?'

A slow dread begins to beckon. 'The money cannot all be gone. Where is the rest?'

He is silent.

'Where is the rest?' I repeat. 'Have you spent it all?'

His eyes spark, fists curled. 'How dare you accuse me? I'm your husband and you should not question my actions.'

'Then be a true husband to me.' He shall hear my mind, while there is the chance. 'You are my husband in name only. When was the last time you visited my bed, the last time you offered any kind of comfort? When have I ever received a tender word from you, or any sign of affection?' I take a few steps towards him. 'We did not choose each other, Thomas, but we cannot change it. If you would but try to be a more considerate husband . . .'

'You blame me?' He is incredulous. 'You blame me for your failings?'

'Only that you are never here. How can we make a marriage, make a family, if we are strangers to one another, if there is no love between us?'

'I never asked for love,' he says, 'and you cannot expect it now. Our arrangement,' he hangs on the word, 'is one of convenience, nothing more.'

Even though I know this, it still smarts to hear it said so bluntly. 'But did you not hope for love?' I ask.

'Any foolish notion I might have had has been dead since our wedding day.'

My thoughts turn to our wedding night. Can it be that the shame of our failure then has poisoned him against me all this time?

'How can I be expected to love a wife who is so cold to me, who defies me and questions me at every turn? By God, but they sold me short with you.'

He turns away from me again, hiding his distress. Perhaps I'm imagining it, but I swear his eyes are growing wet. I am too fired up for sympathy, my own angry tears springing.

'It's you who has been cold to me,' I say. 'You treat me no better than a slave, or a prisoner. You keep me shut away here, while you fritter my inheritance in London, on drinking and gaming and whores, no doubt, while I can barely afford meat and butter. Perhaps you will never love me, but I do not understand why you hate me so much. I do not understand why you are so cruel. Is it any surprise that I . . . that I . . .'

'There!' He points a finger. 'What? Can you not say the words? You're nothing but a beggarly whore. How can I be expected to remain here, with a wife who so offends me?'

'If I am beggarly, then you have made me so. You have taken from me everything I ever had. But I am not a whore, sir. You are wrong about that.'

Thomas's voice is knife-edged. 'That is not what Leventhorpe says.'

I knew it. I knew that creeping, drunken fool would never hold his tongue. So this is the real reason for Thomas's sudden departure – he wants Willis away from me.

There is a pause. A log in the fire cracks and sparks, showering the hearthstone with embers. It seems to me there are sparks in the air between us; I am breathing them in and spitting them out. I cannot help myself.

'Whatever your friend has told you, I have done nothing wrong.'

'Leventhorpe has no reason to lie. He's the most loyal of friends. Only that I could say the same of my wife.'

'So you will punish me for something I have not done? You will condemn me before I can defend myself?'

'I need no further proof. I see it in the way you look at Willis. You pant after him, like a bitch in heat. And he . . . he indulges you. He laughs at you, you know, behind your back. You humiliate me, madam. You are as wicked as a Bankside whore.'

The echo of Willis's own words sting like a slap.

A sneer of disgust makes Thomas ugly. 'I will not have a wife who dishonours me, damn it. I turn a blind eye to your wilfulness and your tempers, the way you bicker and harangue, like a fishwife. But I will not be a cuckold. You will stay here and do your duty. If I hear another word against you, I will not hesitate to cast you out, do you understand? You will be cast out without a penny to your name. If you wish to play the role of beggar whore, then you need only continue along the path upon which you have set yourself.'

At that moment the door opens. Rachel appears at the threshold, but is drawn up short as she registers the scene before her. How we must look, Thomas with fists balled and trembling, while I am ready to spit hellfire.

'Oh . . . I'm sorry . . .' She lowers her eyes and turns to go.

'Stay, Rachel,' Thomas barks. 'You will see your mistress to her room and make her decent.' To me, under his breath, he adds, 'You will not make a show of yourself tonight.'

'Please, leave us, Rachel,' I say. 'We're not finished here.'

Thomas glares. 'I'm master of this house and Rachel will answer to me. Our conversation is at an end. I have nothing more to say.' He picks up the bottle of spirits and pours a draught. His hand is shaking as he lifts the cup to his mouth.

I see there is no point in trying to reason with him.

I turn to Rachel, who is staring at the floor, fingers twitching on the door handle. 'Come then, we have much work to do.' I can taste the sourness in my voice like bitter herbs. 'My husband and his guests will be leaving in the morning. We must make tonight's banquet a success, for it will be the last.'

Rachel, shocked, looks to Thomas for confirmation.

I cross the room, brushing away tears of frustration. Rachel puts a reassuring hand on my arm and throws a questioning glance over my shoulder at Thomas, but he turns his back and stares out of the window.

We close the door behind us, leaving Thomas to his drink. Would that I could turn the key, lock him away and never think of him again.

But no: here at Ware Park, I am the one who is trapped.

Chapter 19

I am in the scarlet chamber at Markyate Cell. It is night. A good fire blazes in the hearth. Shadows dance on the panels.

He is standing next to the bed, turned away from me. I can smell him, above the wood smoke and beeswax: a rich, earthy scent, like the woods after rain, mixed with spices and honey. His essence curls around me, makes rivers in my insides. I can almost taste it.

He turns slowly and reaches out a hand. 'Wait,' he whispers.

His hair is tied at the nape of his neck, a lone curl escaping, feathering his cheek, catching against stubble. His eyes are unusually large, but it is their colour that is most striking: a rich, golden brown like early horse chestnuts, with paler flecks of tomcat orange. They have a complexity I have never seen before. When he looks at me, I feel I am laid bare, as if he could reach in and tug out my most secret thoughts with a single glance.

He is deathly pale. Purple smudges ring those absorbing eyes. There is blood on his shirt. There is blood matted in the hair on his chest and on the pale slice of skin where his shirt is unlaced. There is blood on the fingers that stretch out towards me.

'Wait . . .' he whispers again. 'Wait . . .'

I put out my own hand, tentative at first, fingertips trembling. I want to touch him but find I cannot reach. I stretch further, yearning now to meet his skin, but he seems to retreat. He is still reaching for me, and I for him, but the harder I try, the further away he seems. And suddenly I am longing, my whole body hungry and craving. I must touch him. I must go to him. I reach . . . and I reach . . .

I wake, my heart plunging with a mixture of terror and something I do not understand.

I struggle towards wakefulness, sleep's clutches reluctant to release me. It's near dawn. In the half-light of my chamber, I cannot tell what is real and what is imagined.

The door swings open suddenly.

'Kate . . . are you ill?' Rachel stands on the threshold, ghostly in her nightgown, hair tumbling around her shoulders. For the briefest moment I see the man in my dream – something in the turn of her mouth, the searching eyes – but then my head clears.

'Rachel . . .'

'There were noises.' She crosses the room, clumsy with sleep. 'You woke me. I thought . . .'

The world is righting itself. 'A bad dream only. Go back to bed.'

She looks towards the window. 'It's almost morning. I cannot sleep now. Not today.' She smiles, finds my hand atop the coverlet and squeezes it. 'We must set off early if we're to reach Markyate Cell before dusk.'

It is almost two years since the day I visited Markyate Cell alone. I have never told anyone what I found then, not even Rachel, because I could not bear her questions. I did not want to talk about the ruined house. Markyate Cell's broken windowpanes too closely reflected my own broken hopes. The tangled weeds tethered me too tightly to the empty house, and those rooms, as hollow as my heart, were riddled with holes where my family should have been.

Neither did I want to speak of the man in the red chamber. I wanted to keep that secret as my own. Since then, I have almost convinced myself he was a conjuring of my own mind, standing for everything that is lacking in my life – so many parts of it are missing that I invented a mirage to fill the spaces.

I'm nervous as our carriage approaches, but I needn't have feared. The driveway is clear, the courtyard tidy, and the glass in the casements is whole and new. I glimpse men at work as we pass the orchards, making good use of the evening light. Dairymaids are churning butter, the dairy scrubbed clean and painted bright with new lime. Two grooms come running as we clatter into the yard. Chickens scatter. The scent of roasting meat drifts from the kitchens. A fug of hops hovers above the brewhouse.

Martha Coppin is waiting to greet me with a warm smile and a steady hand.

Inside the transformation continues. The hall is not as grand as in the old days but it has been cleared and painted. The long benches are back in place, there are smart new hangings to stop the draughts and fat, dry logs in the hearth. I notice that where the Ferrers crest once glittered red and gold, the windows now sparkle with bright, clear panes.

Martha is quiet, letting Rachel and me dawdle as we pass through the hall and take the stairs to the upper gallery. Here, too, the paintwork is fresh, the floorboards polished. The ruined portraits are all gone, all my Ferrers ancestors banished to a bonfire. There is no trace of the degradation I remember. And then I realise: we are headed to the scarlet chamber. The butterflies in my stomach begin to rise.

As we reach the door, Martha pauses. 'I must confess, I have taken a liberty,' she says. 'I have placed you in the finest room, Lady Katherine, but I will understand if you find it easier to rest elsewhere. You must tell me if I have done wrong, and we can make a change.'

I long for her to open the door but she waits, hand lingering on the catch.

'I hope I've not turned your father out of his bed,' I say.

'My father is not at home and, besides, he prefers simpler surroundings. This room is not occupied. It's yours if you would like it. I expect it has special meaning for you.'

I nod my acceptance.

As she opens the door I almost expect to see him there – my nightmare spectre, drenched in blood. My heart patters hard. But, of course, the room is empty. It is empty and it is perfect.

My mother's old four-poster bed remains, with new hangings of rich red silk, embroidered with golden vines and flowers. A red velvet coverlet is strewn across fresh white linen. The evening sun glows golden through diamond leads. Candles are already lit and a fire is set in the hearth. There is new furniture too: a heavy leather chest, with gold studwork, at the foot of the bed, a delicate table and stool beneath the window and a very fine Oriental screen, such as I have not seen since the Queen's chambers at Merton.

I wander over to the window and look out across the walled garden to the park beyond. I spy my favourite sycamore, standing proud and alone, luxuriant with summer foliage. On the tabletop there is a looking-glass and a set of combs, an inkwell, writing things and a little trinket box, made in intricate ebony and ivory. I run my fingertips over these luxuries, like so many relics from my past, from a life I have lost.

The sun is going down and the sky is turning orange, wisps of pink cloud at the horizon. The room is bathed in sunset. I look back towards the bed. It is as though at any moment my mother might drift through the door, sit down upon the stool and brush out her hair, humming lullabies for me as I lie upon the pillows. It feels so right and, at the same time, so sad to be in this room once more. Rachel comes over to me, her fingers creeping into mine.

'Have I done too much?' Martha asks gently.

I shake my head. 'No. This will suit very well.'

Later, when we have eaten a good supper, we rest in the parlour. A fresh-lit fire crackles and smokes in the grate. I have to admit that Martha Coppin has arranged things just as I would, were I still mistress of Markyate Cell. I feel a spike of jealousy as I watch her pour wine into thin-stemmed glasses. Her hands are smooth and pale, like my own not so long ago. Lately, the skin around my nails has been dry and cracked. Tough little calluses are rising at the root of each finger. But it's hard to be angry when my belly is full and my toes are warm for the first time in weeks. It's hard to feel spite towards a woman who has been so kind. Besides, I've come here with a purpose and I must set about it; indulging my grudges will not serve me well.

'Martha, there is something I must say to you,' I begin. 'But, first, I must be assured of your confidence.'

She looks at me with calm, clear eyes. 'Of course.' She places a glass of wine next to me, then sits, perfectly still, hands folded.

'I'm sorry to come here as your guest when, no doubt, you expect things between us to be settled. But, I'm afraid, I come empty-handed. Thomas is in London and I'm without the means to settle our debt to you . . .'

Her lack of reaction is unnerving. I expect judgement, perhaps anger or disappointment, not this peaceable silence. I sense Rachel's surprise at this honesty. A frown plays across her brow.

'I wonder, has he written to you, or your father perhaps?'

Martha gives a brief shake of her head.

'Then I must beg for your patience. I'm sure it's some misunderstanding, some oversight. Thomas is away so often that business at Ware can be easily neglected.'

I intended to try for her sympathy and I cannot understand

why she does not respond. Her refusal to speak causes words to spill out of me like tears.

'In truth, I have very little, and nothing of my own. We struggle to make ends meet. It may be some time before I am able to repay your kindness. I want you to know how grateful I am.'

When at last she does speak, her voice is low and gentle. 'If you think I do not know your circumstances, you are mistaken. I rarely pay heed to gossip, but sometimes gossip is founded in truth. When I met you, that day in Master Hazel's shop, I knew who you were. I could see the truth in what I had heard about the former mistress of Markyate Cell.'

I wonder what she has heard, what slander those prattling wives have spread.

'I know a little of your situation,' she goes on. 'But I did not help you out of pity, or charity. I helped you because I could not stand to see the pleasure that others took in your misfortune. They say we women suffer most at the hands of men, but I find that our own sex can be the cruellest of critics.'

'Your perception does you credit, especially when you do not know me, but may I ask, why continue to help me?'

She considers, sighing out a deep breath. 'It's no secret that my father was not always a rich man. His wealth has come from his own labour and God's good fortune. While so many others have suffered, first with the wars, and now with Parliament's demands, my father has prospered. There are many, like you, who were once privileged and are now learning what it means to go without. Despite my own good fortune, I know what it is like to have the things you care about most taken away. My father has grown wealthy but that does not mean I will ever forget it.' Her eyes are sad but she gives away nothing more. 'I'm conscious I'm now in the place that was once yours. I care nothing about your family's part in the wars, or their support of the King. We are the ones who now suffer, or profit, because of our fathers' arguments. Though you and I find our places exchanged, our stories are intertwined, in the history of this house. We should not be strangers. I hope we will be friends.' She gives the merest smile.

Rachel catches my eye and raises an eyebrow.

'What is it that you speak of? What is the great loss you suffered?' I say.

'A story for another time, perhaps.' She stands and takes up the fire iron to stoke the flames. Rachel is by her side in an instant, offering to help, but Martha will not hear of it.

When she has done, she returns to the seat next to me and fixes me with her frank gaze. 'I will agree to delay repayment. There will be a time for that. But there is something more I must say to you. If you are come here hoping to secure a further loan, then I will have to disappoint you.'

I curse inwardly. Can she see my purpose so clear?

'Sometimes God gives us challenges so that we might rise up to meet them,' she says. 'It is only when we face great uncertainty that our strength is called upon. I know you have that strength. One need only look to the story of your life – yes, I know a little of it – to see how much you have already overcome. You believe you are powerless to change things, but you are not.'

'I can do nothing without the permission of my husband.'

'Sir Thomas's absence may be inconvenient in some ways, but might it not allow you a little freedom to arrange matters more to your liking?'

'I think you cannot understand how marriage is. You do not know its constraints.'

She acknowledges with a nod. 'It's true I've never been married, and with my mother gone so long, my understanding of these things is based only on observation. But I've had many years to see how it is for others.'

'Then you see my hands are tied.'

'I believe you will find a way through your troubles. You must pray for God's guidance in this.'

'Prayer will not put food on the table.'

'But it will sustain you in other ways. Have faith. Ask, and God will send you a sign.'

We are silent a while, as I mull on what she has said.

Rachel, emboldened by the wine, speaks up. 'Mistress Coppin, why have you not yet married?'

Martha smiles, as though it is a question she has answered a thousand times. 'I will never marry. It is a choice I made some years ago.'

'But why?'

'My life suits me as it is. My father is often away, attending to business. I answer to no one but myself. There are not many women can say the same.'

'Do you not want little ones? A family of your own?'

'Once, perhaps, but that has not been God's path for me. I have learned to find my comfort in other ways.'

'But what about love?'

At this I shoot Rachel a warning look.

'Love comes to us in many guises.' Martha's hand goes up to a little silver crucifix strung about her neck. I sense some semblance of regret in her.

'Does your father not require you to provide him with an heir?' I ask.

'We have an understanding about these things. He has learned not to expect it.'

'So his estate, his fortune, will pass to you, as his only child.'

'Yes.'

'The suitors will come flocking then,' Rachel says.

'That may be, and I shall be an old maid by then, God willing. But come now, we are talking of money, not love. The two are not easy bedfellows.'

'If only that were not true,' I say.

Martha gives a wry smile. 'Let us talk of a happier future. I want you to know my home is open to you. I will keep the red chamber prepared, that you might always find a haven here, a place of refuge, in your old home. In return, I ask just one thing – a promise that we will be friends.'

Could it be that, despite her claim otherwise, she is lonely here at Markyate Cell? It seems an easy bargain: a foothold here for something as simple as a promise.

'Why would you do this,' I ask, 'when I am no one to you? When you hardly know me?'

'You have been so abused, Lady Katherine, that you cannot see an offer of trust when it is put before you. The Lord has guided me to you. I simply believe we are meant to be friends.'

Despite my envy, I cannot help but like her. I had thought she would be an easy mark, but I am wrong. There is much more to Martha Coppin than her demure appearance suggests. I put out my hand and she takes it with a firm grip. We shake on our agreement, like gentlemen.

Chapter 20

We leave Markyate Cell early with promises to return. Martha stands on the stone steps, watching as the carriage winds down the track. I crane my neck to see her shrink until she is nothing but a small dark dot against the light, like a smudge of ink on a printer's page.

Rachel is in good spirits: now we have visited my childhood home, we are to visit hers. Her brother's farm lies a few miles to the east.

'There now,' she says, settling in her seat. 'What a kind, generous soul Mistress Coppin is.'

'Not as generous as I'd hoped.'

'But so gracious . . . and I haven't seen a finer table these ten years.'

'You like her because she noticed you.'

'She doesn't put on airs she hasn't got. She might be mistress of Markyate Cell but she's not haughty. It's kind of her to welcome you in when she needn't.'

'I'm still Lady Ferrers. She's nothing but a merchant's daughter. It's kind of me to notice her.'

Rachel rolls her eyes. 'Be glad of her friendship, Kate. It may be of use yet.'

I find it impossible to dislike Martha Coppin, no matter how I might try. These last few days she has allowed me enough freedom to feel easy in my old home. I cannot fault her way with me. 'I just hope she keeps her word.'

'She will. A godly body like that wouldn't make a false promise.'

As the carriage rattles away from Markyate Cell I think about what Martha said. Though I come away just as poor, with no idea how we will weather the winter at Ware Park, should Thomas not find funds from somewhere, a chance has opened up to me. I am a little closer to finding my way back to Markyate Cell.

I draw out the heart-shaped charm from beneath my bodice and clasp it in my right hand. For the first time in many months, I close my eyes and pray wholeheartedly. A sign, Martha said. God will send me a sign.

We reach the hamlet by noon. The sound of our wheels brings the wives out from their cottages to gawp. It's a tumbledown place, with mean, squat dwellings, low doorways and thatched roofs. Thin smoke trickles from chimneys. A few scrawny hens cluck in the dirt, pecking at worms. Two toddling infants dip their fingers into puddles and paint each other's faces with mud, no sign of a mother to scold them.

Rachel jumps down from the carriage and goes up to one of the women, a broad-shouldered matron, as squat as her cottage. The scowl on the woman's face breaks into a wide smile as she recognises Rachel and folds her into her arms. There is laughing and excited chatter. Others gather round. I see Rachel indicate back towards the carriage and shrink away behind the blind, wanting to be left alone.

I have never given much thought to Rachel's life before she came to Markyate Cell so many years ago. When I picked her out it was for the prettiness of her looks, which so nearly matched my own. She was small and slight, like me, never meant for the land, as these women so clearly are. Seeing her here, amid the poverty and grime of this broken-down place, I wonder how she learned her manners.

Before long she comes back to the carriage and calls through the window, 'Rafe is in the field. I've sent a boy to fetch him. We'll wait in the house.'

The farmhouse is set back from the road on higher ground. To reach it we must follow a dusty path that the carriage cannot take. I pick my way through ruts and furrows, avoiding the dung of horses, bindweed snagging my skirts.

The house itself is larger than the dwellings in the hamlet. It has an upper storey, and behind it, an outhouse and a barn. Swallows dart above the mouldering thatch.

Rachel is apologetic. 'It was much better kept when I was a girl. Before the wars, when Mother and Father were still alive. But now Rafe is alone, it's much harder for him. He has no wife or sons to help.'

The remains of what was once a fine garden are now overgrown and tangled, a riot of May-time weeds. The shutters at the windows are peeling and flaking and the door is propped open with a barrel of small, bruised apples.

Inside things are not much improved. The hearth is large, and sturdy iron holdings support a black cauldron, a fire smoking lazily beneath. The only furniture is a large oak table and several three-legged stools. The floor is flagged but unswept, with reed mats that are worn to holes. In one corner sits a pile of grain sacks and a stack of pails. Across the way, in another room, I see hulking equipment of wood and iron, and leather horse tack – all the things needed to work the land. A low-beamed staircase leads to the upper rooms.

'Rafe will be so glad to meet you at last,' Rachel says, cheeks pink with anticipation. 'Your visit will be talked about for months. No one ever comes here.'

'We must be on our way in good time,' I remind her, drawing up a stool before the hearth and sitting, dusting off my skirts. 'We do not want to be on the roads much after dark, and it's still a good few hours to Ware.'

She paces the distance between the fire and the door. 'I just want to lay eyes on him,' she says. 'I just need to know he's safe.'

'Why should he not be?' I ask. But before she can answer there comes the sound of hurried footsteps and the boy Rachel had sent to fetch her brother comes panting through the door. He holds out a hand in expectation of reward. I have no pennies to give him. Rachel takes an apple from the barrel and presses it into his palm. He gives a disappointed sigh, shoulders slumping.

As the boy turns to leave, the doorway is blocked by another figure. For a moment he is just a dark shadow against the bright sun outside. Rachel makes a little bleat of joy and flings herself towards him.

I shift on my stool, feeling like an intruder. But then Rachel is leading him towards me.

'Come and meet Lady Kate.'

The man takes off his hat, exposing the same nut-brown curls as his sister, the same amber eyes.

I feel the blood drain from my face and rush to my chest as my heart takes a great leap. The breath is knocked from me, as though I have been punched in the gut.

I know him. I know this man. He has haunted me every day since I first saw him, covered with blood, at Markyate Cell.

Chapter 21

I am in the kitchen garden raising a crop of carrots from their summer beds. The season has turned. The October air has lost its kindness and become chill. The sun, breaking through the cloud now and then, sends pockets of warmth chasing across the soil, but it can do little to lessen autumn's grip. I'm warmed only by the work.

This morning, as I have done every morning as the seasons change, I dressed in the same scratchy, worsted skirts, and have bound up my hair under a plain white cap. I wear wooden pattens on my feet to save my ankles from the worst of the dirt but my petticoat is crusted with earth – a reminder of my long days in the gardens of Ware Park. When I look in the glass I do not recognise myself. I linger by my wedding portrait, wondering where that young girl has gone.

By donning this disguise I can make believe I am someone else. That way, my fate does not seem so real. I cannot find the satisfaction in honest toil that flint-eyed preachers speak about on market days in Ware. I see such sentiment in the eyes of Puritan wives, shining with a godliness I cannot hope to find in myself. All I see in my reflection is weariness and stubborn resentment. I will never get used to this life. I am not meant for it. I will never accept it as my own.

Thomas dismissed most of the servants the last time he was at home. Of course he did not tell me: it was all arranged with Master Stone, with instruction to turn the people out once Thomas was back in London, safe from threats and recriminations. Others have chosen to take themselves away, leaving land that their fathers worked, and their fathers before them, because I cannot pay a fair wage and they will have better chances elsewhere. We are left behind, the handful of us who have not given up, to fend for ourselves, while the fields lie fallow and our master enjoys the comforts of London lodgings. The place by his side that should be mine is denied to me.

I do battle every day with seething bitterness towards my husband. Sometimes Rachel or Master Stone bears the brunt of my frustration. So I go faithfully to chapel and pray for forgiveness, and for God's guidance. But as winter creeps towards us, and I receive nothing from Thomas, the only thing that thrives is my desperation. I'm still waiting for the answers that Martha Coppin promised would come.

I kneel, coaxing the long thin roots from the earth and laying them in a trug. My knees ache and my fingers are numb, tips turning blue beneath a coating of dirt. I rest back on my heels a moment, then climb to my feet to stretch my tired limbs. My back protests. My shoulders ache. The muscles in my arms are heavy and sore. I put my hands on my hips and arch my back to ease out the stiffness. I tilt my head, watching as the sun peeps from behind a cloud. The sky is the colour of a dress I once had – palest blue silk, garlanded with white trimmings.

I shiver suddenly, a chill winding itself about my naked neck and bringing my attention back down to earth. I catch a movement from the corner of my eye. Ware Park is so quiet, these days, that my senses pick out any unusual noise, any new scent, any unexpected presence. Even so, Rafe Chaplin has managed to enter the garden without warning.

He is standing in the corner, back against the wall, watching me. His arms are folded and one knee is bent, his foot finding purchase on the crumbling brickwork behind.

This time my heart does not leap into my throat as before, but there is a tightening in my chest, as though my stays are bound too snug beneath my bodice. I forget about my aching arms and stricken back. My knees no longer complain of damp and cold because suddenly I cannot feel them. My limbs rush with a tingling, whirling sensation as though I have stood too quickly.

I realise I have been waiting for this, expecting it.

Since that morning at the Chaplin farm, when I learned the true identity of my Markyate ghost, he has haunted me in both sleeping and waking. But in that moment, while my own mind reeled away from the farmhouse hearth, back to the scarlet room, Rafe Chaplin gave no sign of recognition. With Rachel beside him, the proud, doting sister, he was polite and respectful, the gentleman he should have been, and certainly nothing more. If he knew me at all, he did not show it.

How could he conceal the sudden shock that left me trembling and sick? How could he not betray the drumming heartbeat and tangled tongue that rendered me speechless? If he felt any of these things, he hid them well. Is it possible he did not know me?

I have since questioned my own memory. My thoughts of the man in the red chamber are so jumbled I have lost track of what is real and what is invention. But I dream of him still, and he has Rafe Chaplin's eyes and Rafe Chaplin's mouth and Rafe Chaplin's fingers. I have longed to see him again, to put these tumbling thoughts into order and find answers to my questions.

And now he has come, and I know that I am right. I am not mistaken. I would know this man anywhere.

He gives a quick nod, hiding his face beneath the brim of his hat, then slips away into the walled garden. I am rooted, like the carrots, my feet bound by the earth, but I hesitate only long enough to quiet the butterflies that rise, wild and unruly, in my chest.

He has found the same secluded spot where I once sat with Richard Willis. But Willis is a fleeting thought now.

Rafe sits on the bench, takes off his hat and leans back against the wall. I feel his eyes on me as I walk towards him and sit. The usual greetings and pleasantries seem to have no place here. He stares in silence. Every nerve of my body quivers. I cannot bear it. I stand up again and make as if to leave.

'Forgive me, Master Chaplin. Let me fetch Rachel.'

'No. Rachel mustn't know I'm here. Sit down.'

'She'll be delighted to see you.'

'I mean to speak to you alone. I've been waiting for a chance. Please . . .' He indicates the bench.

I sit slowly. In truth, I do not want to walk away and end this chance to be alone with him.

He keeps his voice low and leans in close. 'Would you promise to keep a secret?'

'Master Chaplin, I—'

'It'd be a favour, to me and to Rachel. I've something to give you and it's best she doesn't know.'

'I will not lie to her.'

He leans forward, elbows on knees, hat in hands. 'I'm asking for your confidence. I know you can be trusted.'

He looks at me and I'm sure this is as close as he will get to an acknowledgement of our shared secret. He's right. I have never told anyone about that day at Markyate Cell.

'You must believe me. Your silence will be better for Rachel,' he says.

'I cannot make such a promise before I know your intention.'

He accedes with a nod. 'I know you're a kind mistress to her. She puts you above any other.'

'Not above you, I think.'

'I would do all in my power to see her safe, but there's not much I can do for her. Not as much as I would like. No doubt she's told you the story of her disreputable brother.'

'I know that she cares for you, little more.'

He raises an eyebrow, surprised. 'Then she keeps her counsel well.'

We are silent for a few moments.

'Why are you here, Master Chaplin?'

He leans back again and stares directly into my eyes until I have to look away. I feel he is judging me, weighing me up. Then he reaches inside his coat and brings out a small leather pouch. As he drops it into my hand I hear the chink of coin, feel the weight of gold.

'What's this?'

'I want you to look after my sister,' he says. 'Because I cannot do so myself.'

'Rachel is well. You may see so for yourself, if you will let me fetch her.'

'She tells me you're in need here, and the truth is clear to see.' He glances at my muddied skirts, my dirt-crusted sleeves.

'We do not need your help,' I say, though the pouch stays in my palm and I do not want to relinquish the possibility it holds. My fingers twitch to open it.

His eyes run the length of my body, from the tip of my cap to the filthy hem of my petticoat. 'A mistress who works her own land is barely a mistress at all. Do not let pride stand in the way of sense.'

'We all have our part to play in these times.' I think of his broken-down home, the untilled farmland, the rotting apples in the barrel. I think of how much Rachel frets about her brother. 'But, surely, you need this more than I.'

'I have all I need.'

I tug open the drawstring and spill the contents into my palm. There are gold coins among the little pile. 'How did you come by this?'

'No matter. It's yours now. Say you will take it.'

'On what terms?'

'Terms? You think I wish to have a hold over you?'

'What are your terms, Master Chaplin?'

'I wish to see my sister warm and fed. If your feckless husband cannot even provide for his own wife, then why should he have a care for those in his employ? I would simply have your word that Rachel will not go without. There are no other terms.'

'I am not my husband. Do you think I would let your sister suffer?'

'I couldn't care less about the likes of you and your sort, but Rachel does. Lord knows why, but she would give up the world for you. She would stay with you to starvation, if you asked it. I will not let that happen.'

I study the coin in my palm as it glints in the sun. I have not held this much wealth in many months. It will keep us in grain and meat for weeks. Now I have it, I don't want to give it back. 'I will accept it if you tell me why this should be kept from Rachel. She would want to know. She would want to thank you.'

'I cannot give you a truthful answer. It's better this way. You must promise me that no one else shall know.'

'Then how shall I explain it?'

'You'll think of something.'

'I do not understand you, Master Chaplin. I do not understand what is at stake. Why the need for secrecy?'

He presses his fingers to the bridge of his nose, thinking. When he turns his eyes to mine, he has that look about him – the searching gaze that comes back to me in memory and dreams. Suddenly I cannot breathe.

'I'm asking that you trust me in this, as I have trusted you before.'

I consider. It is an easy promise to make for something that will benefit us all. I know I should not trust him but something compels me to take the chance. I swallow a sense of unease. 'I promise.'

He nods, satisfied, then stands, looking about to make sure we are still alone. The strangeness of our transaction is waning, the intensity of the moment passing.

'I must be gone,' he says, donning and straightening his hat, making ready to leave.

'Wait,' I say. I cannot let this opportunity slip by. 'What do you know about the secret passage at Markyate Cell?'

He hesitates only for the briefest second. 'I never visited the place, madam. Your family were not so kind as to extend an invitation.'

But as he turns to go, I'm sure I catch the faint flicker of a smile.

1658

Chapter 22

Martha's maid is sent to the red chamber to help me undress. She banks up the fire against the February chill and brings a fresh candle for the bedside. She barely speaks, going about her business with downcast eyes, dripping watery glances from under sparse lashes. I do not trust her.

I could not bear to have a maid like that. Not for the first time, I'm thankful for my good fortune with Rachel. My thoughts turn to her again. All this long evening they have not strayed far from the Chaplin family. I wonder what she is doing now, whether she has scraped together a decent meal for her brother, whether she is safe asleep under that rat-infested roof. I hope her bed is warm, her straw mattress soft, and that she will sleep soundly.

When the maid has stopped fussing I ask for wine, hoping that a little will still my nerves. She brings me a jug and a single goblet on a silver tray. When she has gone, I take a whole cup of the deep-red liquid and feel its warmth flood my body, quieting the churning in my chest. Then I comb out my hair until it rises in a cloud of curl and study my face in the hand glass. I see how my cheeks are wine-flushed, how my skin takes on the honeyed glow of firelight. It reminds me of the ladies I used to see at the court in Oxford – the ones with a certain laxity about their dress that made them seem smudgy and indistinct, as if seen through a haze of nectar and scent. My mother never talked to those ladies but I liked to look at them: they were sumptuous, inviting in some way, always smiling. I try a smile in the mirror now. Yes, I have that look about me, with my hair soft about my face and grape-stained lips.

But I am wakeful still, so I pace the room and stand by the window, watching the clouds chase across the moon. I trace the frosting on the glass with my fingertips until I begin to shiver and retreat back behind the shutters. And all the time I am waiting, a tightly squirming knot twisting in my insides.

When I paid the messenger double for his promise of secrecy, I knew I was taking a risk. I caught the puzzled look that Master Stone threw me as I insisted on instructing the youth myself and walked to the gates with him so that we were out of earshot. But Stone would not dare question me, and the boy swore on his sweetheart's life that he'd do as I asked.

I hear the clock in the hall strike ten, eleven, then midnight. The fire begins to die back and Winter's fingers caress my bare neck and ankles. I climb beneath the coverlet and lie back against the pillows, cradling the goblet in my hands, as if it were hot posset. I watch the flames curling around the blackening logs. The fire has a good few hours of heat left but the strength of the blaze is gone. The curdling in my stomach begins to transform into something else: anger at first, then disappointment.

He is not coming.

I do not want to admit it and think, over and over: there is time yet . . . there is time yet. But my eyelids are becoming heavy and there is a leaden feeling in my limbs.

I am disturbed by a faint scraping sound. Suddenly alert, I sit upright, ears straining. The goblet has slipped from my hand, spilling a red stain on the white linen. I slide from between the sheets and pull on the thick velvet robe that Martha has lent me. Drawing it close, I cross the room and press my ear against the wall. Yes, I hear it – the soft scuffle of careful footsteps, the unmistakable scrape of boots on stone.

I go to the hearth, the hairs on my arms bristling, and take up the iron poker that rests in the grate, still warmed by the embers.

Then a noise at once familiar yet so long unheard it brings a flood of memories – a soft click-clack coming from behind the panelling. Very slowly, one section shifts, only a fraction at first, barely perceptible. Then a little wider, until a dark crack appears, exhaling a gust of damp and mildew and cold starlit air.

He is breathing hard, as though he has ridden at speed. Swaddled in a winter cloak, wide-brimmed hat pulled low and a scrap of linen tied around his throat, he has a wild look about him. He slips inside the room, gently closes the panel and leans back against it. With a breath, recovering himself, he takes off his hat and tosses it aside. He eyes the poker in my hand.

'I trust you'll not be needing that,' he says.

Feeling foolish, I lower it to the hearthstone.

He sweeps his cloak aside and takes a few strides to the bed, draws out a handful of coins and scatters them on the coverlet. The red velvet glitters with silver and gold.

'It's not much, but it's all I could get,' he says.

'Master Chaplin, I —'

'Lord, can we not dispense with formalities? I think you and I are beyond that now.'

'I never asked for your money. I never asked for this secret between us. It's your doing.'

'But I'm right, am I not? This is what you wanted.'

'I—'

'You knew Rachel would tell me how things are set at Ware Park. You sent a messenger to summon me here in secrecy. What other reason could there be?' He leans against the tester, still catching his breath. 'This will have to be enough, for a time.'

He's right, and I'm pleased he has anticipated my reason for this meeting. The money he gave me has run out and, though I would never stoop to beg him, I can see no other means of getting more. Thomas continues to ignore my pleas – he is punishing me – so I have no choice but to try elsewhere. I go to the bed and cast my eye over the coin there. It is not half of what he gave before, but it is better than nothing.

'If you have what you want, I'll leave you,' he says. 'I must get back before Rachel wakes.'

I read the weariness in his stance, the shadows beneath his eyes. He is at the wainscoting, reaching up to find the secret catch before I say, 'Wait . . . Won't you rest awhile?'

I take up the goblet that lies discarded on the bed and go back to the hearth where the wine jug stands on a low table. I fill the glass and offer it.

'My horse is tethered outside. I cannot leave her for long.'

'Take a moment to recover yourself.' I hold out the glass. 'As thanks . . .'

'I must not be found here,' he says, but I sense he is wavering.

'No one will know. Everyone is gone to bed long since.' I draw up a second stool before the hearth and sit, taking a sip from the glass.

He considers a moment before removing his gloves and cloak, dropping both to the floor to meet his hat. He takes a stool and accepts the wine.

We sit, wordless, while he drinks. My nerves are on edge and the silence seems to stretch out. I have the urge to fill it. I pluck up my courage. 'Will you tell me where the money comes from? I've made many guesses, but I'd like to know the truth.'

'I told you before, do not ask me,' he says. 'For I would not lie to you and I cannot tell you the truth.'

'I'm imagining all kinds of misdeeds.'

He holds out the goblet for me to refill it. 'You seem happy enough to take the money without knowing where it came from.'

'I accept a gift from my maidservant's family, that's all.'

He lifts the cup in a mocking toast. 'For Rachel.' He glances around the room, taking in the fine furnishings, the rich carpets and the silver candlesticks.

'How things do change,' he muses. 'Was a time I could not hope to see inside a house such as this, let alone my lady's bed-chamber. Now I'm the one paying for your wine.'

'You know well enough this wine comes from Markyate's cellars. We have nothing so fine at Ware.'

'Cellars that were once yours. How that must grate.'

'I think I'm not the only one who misses the use of this house. You seem to know it well.'

'Better than some.'

'Better than most.'

'I remember this place in the days of your father. He was a good neighbour. My own father always said he was a fair man.'

'He was the very best of men.'

'You're lucky to have good memories of him.'

'Surely you have the same. Rachel speaks so fondly of your parents.'

'My father is passed, and my mother too, during the wars. God rest them both. But you know this, I'm sure.'

When Rachel first came to Markyate Cell, her orphaned state, so closely mirroring my own, was one of the reasons I took to her so well. But she has never told me much about that sad event, and I have never pressed. Whenever I try, her face takes on a strange closed look and she falls mute.

'Rachel prefers not to speak of it.'

'I expect she prefers not to think of it. She alone was left to nurse them in their last illness. Two whole weeks she tended them without help, watching them fail. When they passed, she prepared their bodies for the grave. No other soul dared go near, for fear of plague. It was a miracle she was not took herself.'

'Where were you?'

'I was away. She wrote to me, but the letter never reached me. We were never in one place for long that year.'

'We?'

'The army. I was a musketeer. She has not told you this?'

'Never.'

'Then she is ashamed still.'

'Why should she be? There is no shame in a brother who fought for the King. I know my own brothers would have done the same, had they lived, and I would have been proud of them.'

He gives a wry smile and shakes his head. 'Your sort will never change.'

'What do you mean?'

He fixes me with a hard look. 'Even now you see the world through blinkered eyes. You cannot imagine any other way. I did not fight for the King. I fought for Parliament.'

The blood turns in my veins.

He studies me, waiting for a reaction. I reach out for the goblet of wine, drain it and refill it once more from the jug, the last dregs, cloudy with sediment. Suddenly all I can see is the image of him, here in this room, a slash of scarlet bright across his chest.

'And now you are determined to hate me,' he says.

'Rachel always said your family was for the King. Your father raised men from among the farm workers. She swore he was loyal. She is proud of it.'

'He was. I chose another path.'

There is a shadow in his eye; something stirs darkly.

'Rachel never told me.'

'No. She would not. I am my family's shame. I'm not sure she'll ever forgive me. My father passed before we could reconcile. When I went home, at last, she told me that he died calling out for the son who broke his heart.'

The guilt is written in the creases in his brow. I know how it feels to fail your own kin, but any sympathy is crushed by this revelation.

'How could you go against your father?'

'It was a matter of conscience.'

'But to cause such a rift . . .'

He studies me. 'You are too young to understand. You must have been a child when it began.'

'I was, but I knew where my loyalties lay even then, and they lie with my family. They lie here . . .' I indicate the room in which we sit. 'Besides, you cannot have been so very grown yourself.'

'I was young,' he admits. 'Too young to realise what it meant . . . but the army took me anyway. They took anyone willing. If I'd known then how things would fall in the end . . .' He reaches for the cup. 'Every time I took to the field, it was as if I faced my own father. But I did it nonetheless. He could not forgive me, and I never cared, until it was too late.'

'It was a long time ago,' I say, swallowing my stirred feelings for the sake of our secrets and the coin on the bed. 'It is in the past.'

He raises his eyes to mine. 'You think it is past? Whether for Parliament or King, Cromwell or Charles, it matters little now because we all suffer for it still. You might not know it, tucked away from the world at Ware Park, but the argument is far from won. Mark my words, this story is not yet at an end.'

After he leaves, slipping out by the secret passageway, I lie in the bed and stare at the carvings in the canopy above my head, as I used to do when I was a girl. My heart will not be still. I take the charm from around my neck and dangle it, making it glint as it swings in the candlelight. I hope, beyond all reason, that Rafe Chaplin's words are true, and it is not too late to change the ending of my story.

Chapter 23

A few days pass quietly at Ware Park. I notice that Rachel seems distant and distracted, but I choose not to question her because I am so wrapped up in my own thoughts.

When I give Master Stone the handful of coin, I see the questions he dare not ask in his frown. 'From my husband,' I tell him.

'Is this all that can be spared?'

'I'm afraid so.'

He hesitates, chewing his lip, then, 'Forgive me, m'lady, but I must speak. Our larders are almost empty. We're struggling to feed the household as it is, and there's precious little for wages. May I ask when we can expect more?'

'I don't know, Master Stone. I don't know.'

'Then something must be done if we're to manage.'

I hear the ill-concealed accusation in his words. The welfare of the household is my responsibility – with an absent master, the burden falls to me, and I am failing. But Stone is waiting for a solution I do not have.

Rafe Chaplin haunts me. I think of him when I am in my chamber at nights, running over and over all my unanswered questions. I'm not surprised that Rachel never told me the truth about her brother

– she knows only too well the loathing I feel towards the men who killed the King. She probably feared for her own place by my side. What surprises me more is that, despite this, I find I cannot hate him. I'm convinced there is more to his story and spend sleepless hours filling the gaps, fitting together pieces of the puzzle. I could never share my suspicions with Rachel.

Then, one evening, I cannot find her.

I look for her in the kitchens, the bakehouse and the little room next to my own where her truckle bed lies untouched. I go from room to room, opening doors that have been shut up through the winter, disturbing the spiders and the creeping damp.

I find her in Thomas's study, looking out of the window into the dark night beyond. There is no fire in the hearth – this room is rarely used when my husband is not at home – and the air is chill. The only light comes from a single candle flame, burning high on Thomas's desk, casting long shadows. Next to it, writing things have been set out. A sheet of paper lies in waiting, ink has been poured and a new quill sharpened. Rachel is so lost in reverie that she does not notice as I slip into the room.

'What are you doing in here?' I ask.

She starts. As she turns, I see she has been crying, wet cheeks glistening. 'Oh . . . Kate. I shouldn't be in here. I'm sorry . . .'

She has a letter in her right hand, which she folds hastily, concealing it in her fist.

'What is the matter?'

'Nothing . . . nothing at all.' She wipes away tears on her sleeve. 'I'm being soft-hearted. That's all.' She turns back towards the casement, tucking the letter beneath her stays. 'It's such a beautiful night.'

I join her. The sky is clear and, beyond the reflected candle flame, stars blink in the blackness.

'Kate, do you ever think of your brothers?' she says.

'Of course. All the time.'

'Do you miss them?'

'Yes. Though it was so long ago, I still feel the lack of them somehow. My life would be very different if they were here. You're lucky to have a brother alive.'

She sniffs, and when she speaks, her voice is choked with feeling. 'I'm worried about Rafe.' She hesitates. 'He's foolhardy. He takes risks. We argued . . . We did not part on good terms.'

'Are you writing to him?' I ask, thinking of the ink and quill ready on the desk. 'To make it right?'

She nods. 'He means well but sometimes he can be cruel . . . and I can be cruel too.'

'We all say things we do not mean in the heat of argument, but you are never cruel. In all these years, I've never heard you say a bad word against anyone.'

She lifts her head, doubtful eyes searching mine.

A sense of trepidation rises but curiosity gets the better of me. 'What caused this argument?'

She sighs. 'We have an understanding and he broke his word. You see, sometimes when I visit he leaves me alone at nights. I don't like it. I don't like to be alone in that house. It reminds me of times I'd rather forget. He promised he would stay, but this time, on the very first night, he left me alone again.'

My mind's eye sees Rafe Chaplin seated before the hearth in the scarlet room in Markyate Cell. That now familiar sensation – a mixture of excitement and fear – squeezes the breath from my lungs.

'I waited for hours,' Rachel goes on. 'He returned just before dawn. He wouldn't tell me where he'd been.'

I'm afraid to speak, should I give something away.

'We fought bitterly,' she says. 'I'm not proud of my part in it. I said some things I should not have. But he refuses to see my side.'

'Did you fight about where he had been?'

'Yes. But he still would not be truthful with me.'

'Can you tell me what you suspect?'

She turns and looks at me. It takes a great deal of will to hold her gaze.

'It doesn't matter what I think. I can't change him. What frustrates me is that he's a good man at heart, but sometimes he makes it hard for me to love him as a sister should.'

I put my hand on her shoulder. 'I'm sure he knows how much you care for him and I'm sure he cares for you.'

'You are such a comfort to me, Kate.' Her fingers cover mine. 'I hope . . . I hope nothing ever happens to part us.'

'Why should it?'

She doesn't answer but bites her lip to stop it trembling.

I go to the desk and begin to tidy the writing things. 'Come now, there's nothing to be done tonight. Leave the letter-writing for the morning, when everything will seem clear once again. Your brother will surely forgive you for any harsh words. He's probably forgiven you already.'

'You are so good to me,' she says, but when I smile at her, I read the turmoil behind her eyes.

We go to the kitchen to make caudle. As Rachel bends over the fire, stirring the pot, she gives me furtive little glances. I pretend to turn my back and busy myself. From the corner of my eye I watch her take the letter from beneath her stays and cast it into the flames.

Later, when she is asleep, I creep back down to the kitchens and poke about in the hearth to see if I can find any remains, but there is nothing left. Whatever words she wished to keep from me, they are burned to cinders.

Chapter 24

I am running, as fast as I can, through the woods at twilight. Low branches catch at my hair, tugging and tearing as strands are torn away. Thorny brambles snag my skirts, rip at my petticoats and slice my bare feet. I'm fighting for breath, lungs aching, as though I have been running for a long time.

He is close behind me, the scent of him carried on the wind. The stench is one of decayed flesh, like a carcass left dead in a ditch. It has a half-human taint and another layer that catches in my throat, acrid and smoky: the sickly fug of a bone fire.

I stumble on a tree root and cry out as I fall. There is a sharp, tearing pain in my ankle.

He closes in.

I scrabble backwards but the brambles catch at my clothes. Their vicious, barbed lengths snake towards me, binding my legs, tethering my wrists. I am captured, unable to move, the stench filling my nostrils, making my stomach heave.

He comes forward, smiling, dark and toothless. This is no ordinary man: his body is humped and twisted, with the black, dead eyes of a snake. His face is a ruin. The flesh is rotting away to the bone above one ear and down along his jaw. His hands seem too large for his body, long fingers gnarled and malformed, like claws.

When he reaches me he waits and watches, as I lie on my back, struggling in vain, choking with fear. Then he drops and forces himself between my knees. I fight against my bonds, the terror almost blinding with fierce bright light, but still I cannot get free. He lifts my skirts, pushing them up, until he finds the place between my legs.

I try to scream, feel the pressure in my lungs, the rasp in my throat, but there is no sound. He looks up at me, from between my thighs. He grins. Then he unfurls his long, slick tongue.

As he meets me, my body quivers with violent white-hot fire. Though I know I should fight it, I cannot.

My hand knocks against something buried beneath the leaves on the forest floor. I grasp at it and find the cold edge of metal, the smooth curve of wood.

Suddenly my wrists are freed. There is a pistol in my hands, already cocked and ready to fire. In an instant, one wicked desire leaves me to be replaced by another. I do not stop to think. I aim the gun and pull the trigger.

The bullet finds a home in the centre of his forehead. It makes a small round mark amid the cloud of smoke and sparks. A trickle of blood oozes, dark and putrid between his eyes. He rears away from me. Somehow he stands. But the bullet wound is growing and a fissure begins to form, splitting his skull at first, then splicing his features, like a cracked nut.

I watch in horror as his body splinters, the bullet corrupting his flesh. His skin seems to fall inwards, a chasm opening in his chest, right down to the ribs. The flesh is slipping away from his cheeks. He crumples, in a hissing, spitting mess of blood and bone.

I struggle to my feet. The sky has turned flaming red, and the wind rages, branches thrashing above my head. A wild howl erupts from somewhere deep inside. I have not made a sound like that for years, not since the day my mother died. The pistol is still in my hand. My body still shivers with the echo of the creature's touch.

Low in the sky, to the east, I catch a glimpse of a single star, bright in the scarlet sunset. I pull the trigger, over and over, aiming an empty gun at that taunting, diamond light.

I wake to feel a pulling ache low in my belly. I am covered with sweat.

Then, as if borne by the nightmare, the thought comes to me. It is at once so simple and so clear that I laugh out loud. There is a way to get what I want.

Three days later I go to Ware. I travel alone. It's market day and the town is crammed with traders. Though I have business with some – the excuse for my journey – it will have to wait. Feather is not used to the hubbub. She shies and skitters as I urge her through the crowds, but when we reach the White Hart she goes with the ostler calmly enough.

The tavern is low-ceilinged, warmed by a fire in the hearth. A girl, dressed in neat green skirts, wipes a stack of pewter plates. A bucket by her feet collects drips from the tap. She watches, slant-eyed, as I choose a seat in the back room, furthest from the door.

Groups of men, cradling their tankards, take refuge from the clamour in the high street. I feel their eyes on me as the girl saunters over and I order small ale, simple pottage and meat pie for two. I turn my back, hoping they will not recognise the mistress of Ware Park dressed in servant's rags.

He arrives as the girl is setting the food upon the table. He says nothing, as if this meeting is the most natural thing in the world, and pulls up a stool to sit opposite. When the girl is gone, I pour ale for us both and slide a mug across the table towards him. He drinks greedily. He pulls one bowl of pottage closer, takes up a spoon and stirs. I have no appetite. His presence makes my blood rush too much.

When, at last, he turns his gaze upon me, I'm struck, yet again, by the flashes of gold in his eyes.

'So . . . my lady Ferrers,' he says, not without mocking. 'Here I am, at your beck and call once more. What's so important? Is something the matter with Rachel?'

'No. Rachel is well.'

He responds by slurping pottage from his spoon. 'If you're hoping for more coin, I'm afraid I have none to spare.'

I lift my own spoon and stir the contents of my bowl. The pottage is thin and reeks of old cabbage. I put the spoon down. 'I have a proposal to put to you.'

'I assume you need more money.'

'I always need more money,' I say, lowering my voice. 'But I'd thank you not to speak of it so publicly.'

He glances over my shoulder, checking for listening ears. 'I cannot help you. There's nothing to be had today. There's a limit to what can be got.'

'Master Chaplin . . . I would be frank with you.'

'Go ahead. We're not overheard.'

'I know the truth. I know how you came by the money you gave me.'

I see him falter then, though he tries to hide it. 'And what silly fancy have you dreamed?'

I lean forward so I can whisper. 'You are a highway thief. You are a man of the roads. Any wealth you have is taken from others.'

He stops eating and pushes the bowl away, though it is still half full. He takes a drink and leans back. Again, his gaze wanders past my shoulder, flitting from table to table.

'And why would you believe such a thing? Have you been listening to tall tales?'

'No, yet I am convinced of it.'

His frank stare makes my chest tighten. 'Is not all wealth procured in the same way – taken from one pocket and put into another?'

'But not taken by force. Not taken by robbery. Not against the law.'

He breathes a sigh out through his nose and takes another long draw on his cup. I expect him to defend himself against my accusation but instead he says, 'So . . . will you sell me to the thief-takers?'

'Then you do not deny it?'

'You have no proof, so you can do no real harm, but you're here to make a bargain all the same, are you not?'

I nod.

'And what is it that you want, in return for your silence? A slice of my earnings? You have that already.'

I take a deep breath. 'I offer a partnership.'

He regards me. His gaze makes my heart beat faster and the blood rise to my cheeks. But I will say my piece.

'I have a good horse, and can ride as well as any man. I can shoot a pistol. I was a fair marksman when I was young. With practice—'

'Am I to understand that you wish to join me in my work?'

'I propose a partnership,' I say again. 'With an equal split of profits.'

He laughs then, shaking his head in disbelief.

'I've thought hard about this,' I say. 'It's the best way to get what we both want. With a partner you would be able to take more coin, and I would earn my share.'

Perhaps he hears the determination in my voice because his laughter fades.

'By God, you're serious.'

'We both need money but I will take charity from you no longer. Not on pretence of helping Rachel, or any other reason.'

'If you have some misguided sense of honour, think again. There is no glory in thievery, despite what the pamphlets and the poets say. Be satisfied with whatever pittance your husband allows and I will do what I can for Rachel.'

'No. I need more. I want more. And I'm willing to take risks to get it. I can learn quickly, if you will teach me.'

Again he shakes his head. 'Best stay safe behind your parkland walls. The road is no place for a woman.'

'I have stayed safe too long. It has brought me nothing but poverty and misery. I must take a different path now.'

'What of your husband? Where is he in this?'

'He has all but abandoned me. I'm tired of living like a pauper, dependent on whatever scraps he throws me, waiting for a change that will never come. I will do whatever it takes to shift for myself now.'

'I'm not the man to help you.'

'But you must.'

He leans across the table. 'It's dangerous work,' he says. 'It's not for the likes of you.'

I fix him with a stony glare. 'You do not know me well enough to make such a judgement.'

'I will not put you in harm's way. You are asking me to risk your life. I will not be hampered by a woman.'

'Think a moment. I would not be the first woman to lure herself a victim. You could use me to advantage. It might benefit us both.'

He leans back then. 'You know the sentence for highway robbery is hanging. I will not be responsible for anyone else's life.'

'We shall not be caught.'

'You do not have the first idea of what you are suggesting . . .'

'Then teach me. You have not been caught yet, so why should that change?'

'The answer is no.'

'But think on it . . .'

'There is nothing to think about. It's impossible. I won't do it.'

'I never took you for a coward. Where is the man who defied his own father to get what he wanted?' I feel bolder as I see his eyes spark. His blunt refusal frustrates me, but I still have a final card to play. 'You will accept my proposal because, if you do not, I shall turn you in.'

He tries hard not to react but the muscles in his cheek twitch. 'You will not do that,' he says slowly. 'You will not do that because it would break Rachel's heart. And I do not believe you would wish that.'

'Again, you do not know me. And you do not know what I might do.'

'And where is the proof you would use against me?'

'It would be your word against mine, and I think the magistrate will listen favourably to me, especially when I tell how you stole my purse, and threatened my life, on the road to Ware.'

I feel braver than I have done for a long time. He knows I'm right. My word will carry weight over his. I have him where I want him. The air between us crackles with defiance. We hold each other's gaze, neither willing to back down.

'I would do it in a heartbeat,' I whisper. 'I care not if you live or die. You might be Rachel's kin, but you mean nothing to me.'

As I say this, I know it is a lie.

Chapter 25

Spring arrives late. Thomas returns to Ware Park in early April, bringing a sparse purse and a sour mood. He stays for almost a month, though he often rides over to see Leventhorpe at Sawbridgeworth, or is out shooting in the park. He locks himself into his study for hours at a time, with nothing but a bottle for company. I think it best to keep my distance.

When he visits me at nights, which he does three times during his stay, our liaisons are cold and cursory. He has not forgiven me for the argument over Richard Willis. But I cannot refuse him, no matter how much I want to. Our problem is not resolved. I have still not fulfilled the duty required of me. So I hold my tongue and make myself biddable, spending the days in dreaming, hungering for a time when things will be different, my new secrets cushioning me from the pain of my loveless marriage.

When he leaves for London, in early May, there is an almost palpable change at Ware Park, as if we all release a long-held breath. I think we are better off without him.

One afternoon, a few days after Thomas's departure, I find Rachel in my bedchamber. She is standing at a table by the window, rays of spring sunshine lighting the dust motes around her. There is a box on the table in which I keep my private correspondence. It is secured with a tiny key that I keep safe in a velvet pouch beneath my mattress.

But now the box is open, the key turned in the lock. A pile of papers is splayed on the table. Rachel holds one in her hand.

As I enter her eyes flood with shock, then horror. It is too late for her to hide. I have caught her red-handed.

'What are you doing?' I say.

Her mouth opens and closes but no sound comes out.

I rush the few steps towards her and snatch the letter. 'These things are private.'

I need only one glance at the paper in my hand to know it is from Rafe. There is no name or signature – he is too clever to make such a mistake – but it contains a set of instructions and a list of place names with which I am to make myself familiar.

Rachel's eyes go wide. 'What is that? Who is it from?'

'What right have you to look through my private things?'

I expect her to cower, to beg forgiveness as she should, but she does not.

'What does it mean, Kate?'

'It means nothing.'

'Tell me – who is it from?'

'You overstep yourself. Do not think that our friendship means I will tolerate this.'

She persists: 'I know there is something wrong. I know you too well. Something has changed these last months and I know it. You're hiding something from me.'

'I do not have to explain myself to you.' My cheeks burn and I turn away from her.

'Something has altered between us. I feel it.'

'You're imagining it.'

'No, I'm not. We used to be always together. Now you want to be left alone. You spend hours out riding. And Master Stone tells me you've asked for old Sir Thomas's pistols to be found out and cleaned. These are strange things, Kate. Admit it.'

'What nonsense. How dare you challenge me? How dare you sneak and gossip behind my back?'

'If you've nothing to hide, why won't you tell me?' She pushes the pile of papers across the table. 'That letter is not your hand. I know it. And there are others here too. So, who is it? Is it Richard Willis?'

I turn back to face her, part relieved she has not recognised Rafe's hand, but outraged all the same. I cannot believe she dares question me like this.

'What do you mean?'

'I know you have a liking for him.'

'Richard Willis is in the Tower at present, put there by Cromwell's men. Thomas told us that not a week since.'

'That does not mean he didn't write that letter. What does it mean, Kate? Is it some sort of message? Some sort of code?'

'I will hear no more of this. You will leave me. Now.'

'No. I won't let you silence me this time. You used to tell me everything. What has changed?'

'Get out. Get out of my room.'

'Why won't you tell me the truth?'

My whole body is tense with fury. 'By God, but you are taking a great risk, Rachel. Do not think I will stand for this. I could cast you out in a moment. If Thomas were here . . .'

Astonishingly, she smiles. She glances up at me from beneath her lashes. 'I think you'll find he takes my side in this.'

'What? What are you saying?'

'It would not be wise to discuss this with your husband,' she says quietly.

There is defiance in the set of her shoulders, a hard glint in her eye. For a moment I am stunned by the resemblance to her brother. I look across to the splay of papers on the desk, the little pile she has made of unsigned notes and I see it all. Of course – Thomas has set her to this task.

I back away from her, boiling with rage. 'What has he promised you to be his spy? Money? Well, there is none.'

'I'm doing this for you, Kate. I know something is amiss and I'm worried about you.'

Suddenly I feel sick. Sick with anger, sick with betrayal. How can the one person I thought I could trust act against me? How can she ally herself with Thomas?

I sit down on the edge of the bed, still clutching Rafe's note. The simple words seem suddenly incriminating. Why did I not burn it? How could I have been so careless? I needed something by me as proof that our agreement was real.

Rachel comes and stands before me, though she is wise enough to keep her distance. 'Is it Richard Willis?' she says again.

'How can you ask me such a thing?'

'You do not deny it.'

I can barely look at her. 'Why would you do this to me? Have I not been good to you? Have I not been a fair mistress?'

'I do it out of love for you, Kate. The world is not kind to women like us. We have to be careful. You have no children, and your husband is always away. People talk. They gossip. Any hint of adultery would be enough to ruin you. And, more than that, adultery is sin. I fear for your soul.'

'You know nothing of my soul. And it seems I know little of yours. How could you do this, when I've trusted you all these years?'

She stands in silence for a few moments, eyes downcast. Then, 'You were the first to break that trust, long ago.'

'What do you mean?'

She walks away, stares blankly out of the window. 'You broke it when you took George away from me.'

'George? What has he to do with this? I have not thought of him for years.'

'Exactly. You were always blind to other people.'

'What are you talking about?'

Her voice is measured, but I hear stifled feeling beneath the words. 'I loved him. And you stole him away.'

'You loved him?'

'Yes, and you knew it and could not stand it.'

'That is not true.'

'Yes, it is. You saw how I cared for him, so you flirted and flattered, like you do with all of them, until you made him yours. You play with people's feelings, Kate. You bend others to your will. You always have.'

I think back to those nights in the stable block at Hamerton, the sound of George's breath fast in my ears. I may have had a girlish fancy for him then, but it was never anything more. 'It was not like that,' I say. 'He never meant anything to me.'

'And he was everything to me. And you couldn't bear that I might choose him over you, that I might be happy when you were not, so you took him and you broke my heart.' She turns to face me and her eyes are blazing. 'My God, Kate, have you any idea how it is to live life in your shadow? Thomas knows what it's like, always to be belittled by you. You shame him. You make him less of a man. And now you betray him, just as you betrayed me.'

I'm stunned by the force in her tone. Never before has she dared speak to me like this. I do not recognise the Rachel I know in this fiery-tongued, passionate woman who stands before me.

'Tell me,' she says again. 'Is it Willis?'

My anger turns blinding white, icicle cold. I will never give her what she wants. All these years I have treated her as so much more than a maidservant, giving her a home, taking her into my confidence, sharing both my cares and my fleeting moments of happiness. Is this how she repays me, with suspicions and accusations and lies? What would she do if she knew that accursed note is in the hand of her own brother?

'Why would I trust you now?' I say. 'When you've gone behind my back like this. I can never trust you again.'

'You have to trust me, because there is no one who knows you like I do. Let me help you . . .'

'Why would you want to help me, if I have wronged you as you say?'

She falters then. 'Because . . . despite it all . . . I still love you best.'

She would not, if she knew the truth.

Once the door is shut behind her I collect up Rafe's notes and shove them inside my apron; I will burn them later. I go to the desk and gather the other letters, put them back into the box. There is one note, the most recent, buried beneath the others. I thank God that Rachel did not find it: it is the most important and most secret of them all. Reading it sends a thrill cascading like a waterfall from the crown of my head and the tips of my fingers straight to my flaming heart:

15 May, midday
The White Hart, Ware
Be ready to ride.

Chapter 26

I am alone on the old North Road.

I tie Feather by the roadside and wait. The trees, in full leaf, stretch skywards on all sides. This part of the ancient forest is dense with oak, ash and sycamore, the track cutting a well-worn path through a carpet of fern and low, thorny undergrowth. The sides of the road are banked, sloping gently upwards; beyond that, little but tree trunks and shadow, nothing but the whispering of the canopy above my head, the scent of earth and moss. Birds are busy in the treetops. The hollow knock-knock of a woodpecker echoes. Something scurries in the brambles.

Minutes stretch out.

The effect of the liquor that Rafe insisted I drink is fading, and I wish I had more. Without its false boldness my heart starts to clench again, but I cannot tell if its cause is fear or anticipation.

There is no sign of Rafe. The forest has swallowed him. It's possible that he's left me here alone, perhaps to teach me a lesson, to prove to me that I am not cut out for this work. The short dagger strapped to my hip offers no real protection against an armed man, or a gang of brigands, and I know these woods are famous for both. I search the shadows for movement, strain my ears for the sound of company, but there is nothing.

* * *

We met at the White Hart at midday. He had taken a room. Knowing eyes followed me as I took the stairs.

Once we were alone, he looked me over, making small adjustments to my green velvet riding habit, tilting the wide-brimmed hat to hide my face and tucking my curls beneath. When he helped me clip the black lace veil in place, his fingers brushed against my cheek, and the butterflies in my chest grew wild, dipping and plunging along with my heartbeat.

When he fastened the dagger around my hips, he said, 'Only to protect yourself, do you understand? There will be no blood today.' Then he asked me, just once, 'Are you sure?'

I looked into his eyes and knew: I had never been more certain of anything in my life.

I think of that long-ago day on the road to Hamerton. The lonely track through the woods was similar to this, but how my world has turned since then. I was still a child, thinking myself so grown and wise, on the verge of womanhood. I imagined a life ahead that mirrored my mother's – one of wealth and ease, of duty and respectability. I would have sworn on my soul that the King's army would claim victory in the end and the life we knew before the fighting would be restored. I never imagined anything different until they killed the King.

But on that day in the woods, I learned that life is delicate and fleeting. Was it by God's grace or the Devil's will that I escaped death? Was that when the Devil's bargain was struck? Was it that moment, as I stood against the rough bark of the tree trunk with that man's foul, stinking fingers inside me, which brought me to this place?

I am startled from my reverie by the sound of horses' hoofs. Someone is coming. I listen hard for the signal and am rewarded – a long, low whistle from the shadows.

I untie Feather, turning her about to face the travellers.

Two men appear from around a bend in the road ahead. Both on horseback, they look the godly sort, plainly dressed in tall black hats and plain white collars. Voices float to me, words indistinct. As they come closer I take the measure of them.

One notices me, standing there alone, holding Feather's reins. He says something to his friend. I wave my arm and call, 'Ho there!'

He eases his mount into a trot, reaches me and reins in his horse, smiling and doffing his hat. 'Good day, mistress.'

'Good day to you, sir.' My voice does not sound like my own. Surely he will detect the falseness that seems so obvious to me.

'What keeps you waiting alone in such a place? Have you some trouble?'

'My horse is lamed. She refuses to go on. Praise be that you came along, sir. Will you help me?' My throat is dry with nerves and the practised words sound sham to my ears.

His companion reaches us. 'What happened?' he asks.

'She stumbled,' I say. 'Almost threw me. Now she'll not take my weight.'

He runs his eyes over Feather. 'She stands well enough,' he says.

'Please, sir. I don't know what to do. Will you help me?'

The first man shoots his friend a questioning look. 'It's probably just a stone,' he says. 'No surprise on these roads. It's easily remedied.'

He dismounts and fetches a small blunt knife from his pack. 'My name is Beasley. At your service.' He bows, touching his hat. 'May I know your name, madam?'

'Mistress Silvester,' I say, bobbing a little curtsy.

'Well, mistress, let me see if I can solve this puzzle. Hold her steady.' He begins to run his hand down Feather's foreleg. She jitters and prances away.

'Hold her steady,' Beasley repeats.

'What are you doing out here without an escort?' the other man asks. 'This is not a safe road for a lady to travel alone.'

'I know, sir. Thank Heaven you came by, for I feared that I would be lost out here all night.'

Feather is shying away from Beasley and will not let him raise her hoof. For once her capriciousness is welcome – she is putting in a fine performance.

He tuts. 'Simeon, get down here and calm this beast.'

The second man sighs heavily but dismounts. He loops the reins of the two horses over a branch and comes forward to take Feather's head. Rafe's words echo: 'Never abandon your mount.'

'Oh, no, sir,' I say. ' She will not be handled by others. I will try to calm her. You help your friend.'

I soothe Feather by petting and whispering gentle words in the way she likes. She steadies at last and both men bend to the work. One hoof is checked and declared free of stones, then a second.

Minutes run by. A third hoof. The man called Simeon straightens up and looks about him.

'Your horse is not lamed, I think.' He comes towards me. I do not like the glint in his eye. 'And why wear a veil? Forgive me, Mistress Silvester,' he lingers on the name, 'but I would see your face.'

'I . . . I prefer not,' I say, but my wits are failing me and I falter over the words.

Just then, from the bracken behind me, there comes a great crashing, like the noise of frenzied deer escaping the hunt. Simeon wheels about, panicked. Rafe emerges from between the trees, urging his big bay mare down the bank, hoofs slithering to a standstill on the road. A pistol is drawn and cocked. He raises an elbow and balances the barrel on the crook of his arm.

'Thank you for your kind service, gentlemen,' he says. 'Now we will take our payment.'

Beasley, still crouched at Feather's rear is confused, stumbling as I grab her reins and pull her from him. His knife drops and bounces away.

Simeon curses. 'I knew it. Damn you, harlot!' He tries to make for his horse but I place myself between the men and their frightened mounts, my dagger drawn and glinting. Feather is nervous. I have to drag on her mouth to keep her steady.

But Rafe is quick at his work and the men do not put up a fight. How can they, defenceless and miles from help? They turn out their pockets. Two purses of coin and a gold ring are given into my hands. All the time Rafe keeps the gun levelled and ready.

I push the spoils into Feather's saddlebag and secure it with trembling fingers.

'On your knees,' Rafe says. The men obey. 'Now kiss the earth that God made, and thank Him that you met with an honourable man this day.'

Beasley clasps his hands in prayer, muttering under his breath, eyes squeezed shut. As the two men lie down, I struggle to mount. My skirts hinder me, wrapping around my legs, like tangled bedding. Feather wheels and paws but I manage at last.

Beasley is jabbering into the dirt, Simeon spitting curses that I know are meant for me. Rafe holsters the pistol and gives me a nod, and then we are away, galloping as though the whole of Cromwell's army is at our heels.

Chapter 27

We ride hard. The wind whips at my hat and snatches my breath. Feather sweats and snorts. I lean low to stay in the saddle, dry-mouthed with dust and exhilaration. We fly out of the woods and across a broad meadow, towards the lowering sun, long shadows stretching across our path.

Eventually Rafe reins his horse to a walk. We stay away from the roads, following old drovers' tracks across buttercup-strewn fields, then into a dark wood where the trees are close and the air is still. For a time we splash along the course of a shallow stream. I have no idea where I am.

'Where are you taking me?' I ask eventually.

'Somewhere we'll not be followed.'

'At Ware Park they'll be wondering where I am.'

'You'll not be back there tonight.'

'I must get home before I'm missed.'

'Make your excuses tomorrow.'

I should be angry and insist that he set me back on the road to Ware, but a clear thrill moves within me at the idea of a whole night of freedom, so I don't challenge him.

It's gloomy beneath the dense trunks but I soon see we are following a path through the trees, a narrow track that follows the line of the stream. Though overgrown, I spy stumps where trees have been felled to make way for travellers. The forest floor is thick with curling ferns and nettles and we make slow progress. After a long, silent stretch, we reach a clearing.

Here the stream carves a tiny valley, banks sloping gently on each side, the bracken and brambles giving way to a stretch of moss, dried leaves and low, scrubby bushes with yellow flowers. The last rays of sunlight reach us here, through a break in the canopy, lighting the mossy ground with bright emerald patches. To my surprise, there are five or six dwellings – or, at least, the abandoned walls that once served as such – small timber-built shacks, with patchy wattle walls and fallen roofs, crumbling into holes. They form a circle, gaping dark spaces where doors and shutters once kept out the forest. In the centre of the clearing stands a crude stone cross. A flurry of wings disturbs the silence as two woodpigeons flap to the branches. The whole clearing is no bigger than the walled garden at Markyate Cell.

'What place is this?' I ask. 'Who lived here?'

Rafe shrugs. 'Woodsmen, perhaps, or hunters. Whoever built it, it's long forgotten.' He urges his horse into the space and dismounts. 'We'll be safe here for tonight. No one comes this way now.'

One of the shacks is in better repair than the others. Nestling against the line of trees, rough-hewn lichened logs shore up the holes in the wattle, and the turf roof is patched in places with bundles of rushes. In front of the doorway a blackened spot surrounded by stones marks where a fire has been recently lit. Crude uprights support a makeshift spit. The stream burbles into the trees beyond.

Rafe takes Feather's bridle so that I can dismount.

It is strangely quiet. I have an otherworldly feeling, as though the ghosts of the men and women who once lived here watch me from those shadowed doorways. I do not like the creeping sensation it makes on my skin, so while Rafe attends to the horses

I explore the little house that still stands.

The slatted door is stiff and broken but gives easily enough with a shove. Inside I find a hard-packed earthen floor, a low truckle bed strewn with a dirty straw mattress and rough woollen blankets. There is a small table with a rusty candle lantern set upon it and a three-legged stool. As I open the shutters on the single window, cobwebs stretch their eerie fingers and spiders scuttle. The roof rustles with the crawl of hidden creatures. Leaning against the walls I see a few tools, a cooking pot, a barrel and a wooden chest covered with sackcloth. It smells of earth and damp, the faint taint of smoke and ash from the hearth outside.

I stand in the doorway, watching Rafe as he tethers both horses with a long rope, allowing them to roam, drink from the stream and snatch at the grass. Then he comes and dumps the saddlebag containing the day's spoils at my feet. He looks up at the sky.

'It'll be dry tonight. Warm enough to sleep outside, if I make a fire.'

He goes into the hut and returns with an earthenware bottle. He swallows a good measure, then passes it to me. The liquor is strong and sharp and hits the back of my throat like sparks. It makes me cough. He smiles, taking it back for another drink. The way his eyes linger on mine makes my chest tighten so much it hurts.

Later, when the fire is lit and darkness has fallen, I huddle close to the flames. I'm a little afraid to leave the circle of light. Rafe brings out bread, cheese and a dry heel of pie from his pack and we eat, listening to the horses stirring in the dark. I'm not used to the strong liquor. My whole body is warmed and loosened, a pleasant drifting feeling calming my spinning mind. Still, the silence between us lies heavy and I'm keen to break it.

'What do you call your horse?' I ask.

'She has no name.'

'Then how do you command her?'

He shrugs.

'A horse must have a name,' I say.

'Then you choose one.'

'What kind of horse is she?'

He frowns, as if I have asked a ridiculous question. 'Like any other.'

'I mean, is she lively? Is she troublesome?'

'What has that to do with it?'

'She must have a name that suits. Think . . . What do you like about her?'

'She's fast.'

'Fast as an arrow. Swift as a fox. Quick as a bawdyhouse whore.' The corner of his mouth tilts at my joke. 'What about Flight? As fast as a falcon. My grey is named Feather, see? Flight is a good name, don't you think?'

'If you say so.'

'Then Flight it is.' I lift the bottle in salute. Somewhere beyond the firelight, one of the horses snorts. Pleased with myself, I lean back and watch stars blinking through the gap in the canopy, thinking that the sky never looked quite so full and glittering before. My head swims a little.

When the praise I have hoped for comes, I'm surprised by it.

'You did well today,' he says. 'Stood your ground.'

'I was afraid they would see through me. I think one of them did.'

He draws out the two pouches of coin and spills the contents of each into his palm. 'Not bad for a first time.'

He counts it out, dividing it into two piles. There is the ring also, which he tilts to the light. It flares gold. 'You can take this,' he says.

'An equal split, remember? I will not take more than my due.'

'A prize, for your first success.' He holds the ring out to me. 'If you don't want to keep it, there's a man in Ware who will take it with no questions. Ask for Timbrell at the Saracen's Head.'

My fingers close around the simple band. It sits heavy in my palm. 'How soon can we do it again?' I ask.

He puffs out a sigh, thinking. 'Today was easy – they were not armed. It will not always be so. You did well, but you hesitated. I saw it. There can be no room for doubt. They sniff out fear like bloodhounds.'

'I'll do better next time.'

'You need a pistol, and a good blade.'

'I'll get them.'

'And you need to find reasons to be away from home. It's always safer to stay a night here, or at a backwater inn or hostel, to avoid being followed. You need to plan it. There can be no suspicion at Ware Park.'

'It's too late for that,' I say, under my breath.

'What do you mean?'

'Your sister suspects I'm keeping secrets from her.'

He snorts. 'She's a Chaplin. Of course she does. She's more canny than she seems, my sister.'

'She found one of the notes you sent. I thought she would know your hand but she didn't seem to recognise it.'

'My letters?' His jaw tightens. 'You should have burned them.'

'I know that now. But I had no reason to doubt their safety.'

He raises his eyes to mine. 'If you are so determined to go down this road, you must learn that you can trust no one except me. Your partner can be the only one who knows the truth.'

'I've never had reason to question Rachel's loyalty before, but I found her searching through my things.'

'What excuse did she give?'

'That she was worried for me. That she knows something has changed between us. But I'm sure my husband set her to it. She's convinced I'm hiding something.'

'Perhaps you're not cut out for this after all. Perhaps I've misjudged your capacity for concealment.'

'I will get better at hiding the truth. I will be more careful.'

'My sister is shrewd. If there's something to be sniffed out, she'll do it in the end.'

A thought comes to me. 'Perhaps I should tell her the truth. She would never do anything to hurt either of us. It might be easier to explain my absences if she would cover for me.'

'No.'

'But if she is part of it, then she may see it as I do – as a way to do what's right. Then neither of us would have to lie to her.'

He reaches for the bottle. 'Rachel already knows how I make my way.'

'She does?'

'Yes. And she hates it. We've argued over it many times. If she knew I'd agreed to this she'd never forgive me. This is our business and no one else may know.'

I think back to all the times I've seen deep concern in Rachel's eyes as she talks about her brother. I remember her fondness for Newgate pamphlets and the penny broadsheets that recount the hangings at Tyburn. I had thought it gruesome, but now I understand: she was waiting for the day she read her own brother's name in print. It seems I am not the only one who has been keeping secrets all these years.

I take up a stick and poke at the embers in the hearth. 'She suspects me of another kind of sin. She might tell my husband.'

He shakes his head. 'She won't do that.'

'How do you know?'

'I know my sister. She might threaten it, but she won't do it. Trust me.'

'There is a strong bond between you, I think.'

'Of course – we are the only family left.'

'She once told me that you're a good man at heart. She said you would do anything to keep your father's farm. Is that why you do it?

He bows his head, gathering the little pile of crowns and shillings that is now his and slotting it, coin by coin, into one of the purses. 'You've seen the farm. You've seen it's near ruin. The land has not been properly worked since the wars. It would take a lot more than a few gentlemen's purses to put it right.'

'But is that what you hope for?'

'It is a debt I owe.'

'To whom?'

'My family.'

'But Rachel is your only family.'

'I include those who are dead.'

I remember what he told me that night in Markyate Cell, of his father's untimely death and their sad estrangement. 'Do you blame yourself for the ruin of your family?'

He shifts, clearly uncomfortable with the question. 'There are many reasons I do what I do, why I've made the choices I've made.'

I see in him the same guilt I feel every day, knowing how all my family's hopes once lay with me and that I have failed them. We have more in common than he knows.

'When my husband took Markyate Cell away from me, the pain was so great I thought I would die, bleeding from the heartache.'

'He took it from you? How so?'

'It became his upon our marriage and he chose to sell. There was nothing I could do.'

'Did you fight for it?'

'I tried, but what could I do? What was once my property, my fortune, all now belongs to him. And the Compounding Committee took the rest.'

'He's your husband. Have you no love for him?'

'I hate him.'

He smiles, holding up a silver shilling so it glints in the firelight. 'Love and hate are often two sides of the same coin.'

'You're wrong. He cares nothing for me, nor I for him.' The drink is making my tongue run away. 'I hate my life at Ware Park. I'm like a prisoner there. Thomas is cruel and unreasonable. He refuses to give me money – he says there is none – and yet he demands a son. He blames me for his own failures. How can I have a child with a husband who is always absent? No doubt he is busy making bastards in other women's beds.'

I snatch the bottle from Rafe's hand and take another drink. I've never said these things so bluntly to anyone, not even Rachel.

He looks at me, searching. 'Then why do you stay?'

'What choice have I?'

'There is always choice.'

'Ha! How little you know about what it is to be a woman.'

'Perhaps the choice is too hard to make. It's often easier to stay in a bad situation than to find the strength to change it.'

'I have my reasons for staying. Besides, what is this but something to make a change?'

He nods. 'And what is it you hope to alter?'

I hold his gaze, fighting a swell of emotion as I think of my answer. 'I want what is rightfully mine. I want the life that should be my own. I want to go home.'

His eyes take on such strength of feeling that I think he understands, that similar desires drive us both. Then he says quietly, 'Why did you run, that day at Markyate Cell?'

My heart missteps. I had not thought ever to talk of the day I first saw him in the scarlet chamber. But there seems no point in hiding the truth. If we are to trust one another, we must have no secrets.

'I was frightened. I was frightened of you.'

'I would not have hurt you.'

'I didn't know that.'

'Are you frightened still?'

My breath is suddenly shallow. 'Perhaps a little.'

'What are you frightened of?'

Everything, I want to say. I'm scared that if you come any closer I will lose my heart to you. I will be fixed upon a path I cannot stop – that I do not want to stop – that can only lead to heartbreak and disappointment. I'm afraid it is already too late. But my courage fails and instead I say, 'I don't know.'

He stares into the flames as he speaks. 'I should have laughed at you when you came to me and asked to be a part of this. I should have sent you away. But you . . . are different. I saw it that first day, at Markyate Cell. You have no need to be afraid of me.'

Either the drink or his words send the heat of Hell's fire coursing through my veins, and I know that I could not stop this, even if I wanted to. The Devil has a hold on us both.

Chapter 28

S pring slides into summer. The bluebells die, foxgloves and dog
roses replacing the carpets of indigo. The air hums with insects.
Bumblebees, busy and nectar-swelled, dip hazy-headed from
bloom to bloom. I watch butterflies, white, yellow and the palest
green, flit among the honeysuckle. We have a few days of clear
blue skies and strong sun when it is too hot for heavy work in the
garden, pulling weeds or purging slugs from the cabbages. Despite
the brief relief that my share of stolen coin brought, there is still
endless work to be done, so I stay in the shady patches close to the
house, beneath the wall of the kitchen beds, half-heartedly
prodding at the earth.

Master Stone was pleased when I offered up the leather purse
and ordered him to make good use of it. Thomas had some luck at
cards was the story I told, and he accepted it without question.

I pause in my work to stretch my back and wipe away the sweat
that trickles at my temples. On the far side of the plot, beyond the
stable wall, I can hear Feather nickering at the boy who is trying to
groom her before she is let out into the meadow to graze. I imagine
her taking little nips at his hands, stamping her hoofs dangerously
close, flicking her tail into his eyes, and smile at his grumbled
curses.

Rachel comes around the corner of the house, frowning against the sun. Her mouth is fixed in a grim little line. She comes up to me and holds out a letter. 'This has arrived for you.'

The paper is folded and closed with dark red wax but there is no seal. I do not need to open it to know its sender. I can tell by the skip of my heart. I have been longing for this. The weeks that have passed since that night in Gustard Wood have been an agony of waiting. Each minute stretches in a succession of long hours and endless days. The late-setting sun cannot dim soon enough for me, yet barely has one long day ended than another begins. I snatch brief fevered sleep in the dark hours, dreaming of him. But now the dreams are different because they are based on promises.

Rachel's eyes are defiant.

'Thank you,' I say, taking the note from her, and, when she makes no move to leave, 'You may go.'

But she does not move. She stares at me in silence.

I turn away and tear open the letter. I know I should wait until I'm alone but I cannot.

The date is set two days from now, our meeting place the clearing in Gustard Wood.

For a moment I'm lost to all else. First comes relief, then excitement, then a wave of longing.

'Who is it from?' Rachel's stern tone brings me back to earth. I turn to face her, hastily folding the paper.

'Martha. She invites me to Markyate Cell. I will go the day after tomorrow.'

Rachel's frown does not falter. 'Take me with you.'

'I'm sorry, not this time. I'll go alone.'

'Then take me as far as the Chaplin farm. Give me leave while you're away. If you do not need me at Markyate Cell, then let me see my brother.'

'You are needed here.'

She takes a few steps closer to me and lowers her voice. 'You and I know that is not true.'

I ignore her. 'I need someone to watch over things while I'm gone. I'm not sure how long I shall be away. You will take my place here and help Master Stone.'

Her eyes spark. 'I know that note is not from Martha Coppin.'

We stare at each other and I see her lip quiver just a little before she looks away. She knows she cannot defy me without risk.

'I'm going to Markyate Cell,' I repeat. 'You will stay here and help Master Stone.'

She lowers her eyes to the path and bobs a mocking curtsy. Her lips are pursed. She turns and walks away.

As I watch her go a strange sadness wells in me and my heart pulls after her. I hate to keep my secrets from her but she has tainted our friendship and now my silence matters more than ever. If she learns the truth it will destroy any good feeling that is left between us. She will hate me for taking her brother away. She will blame me for making a distance between them. She will think I am trying to take her place in his affections, as she claims I did with George. In that moment I feel keenly the loss of my friend. But it is a fleeting thing, and once she is out of sight, I take out Rafe's letter and hug it to my chest. Nothing in the world can be wrong when he has kept his word.

Chapter 29

Nomansland Common is a broad stretch of heath that marks a low rise in the country some ten miles from Markyate Cell. An old road, running north, cuts it in half. Locals say a gallows stood here once, and that the restless spirits of those who met their end beneath its beams haunt the lonely road. The servants at Markyate Cell used to tell such stories to scare my brothers. They, in turn, would tell me, after bedtime, giggling and sleepless with horror.

Grazing rights bring some cottagers to build their rough dwellings here: they keep goats on the heath and their pigs rootle in the woods that skirt three sides of the common. But the hot summer has driven most of them away, and the dwellings are shut up. The ground here is dry and flinty, midsummer grass burned yellow, like barley stubble after harvest. It is not a kind place to make a home. It is wild, marked only by the long curve of the road and ancient marker stones, placed along the path long ago to show the way to London. At the northern edge sits a small, shabby inn, the kind of place where they serve rot-gut and ask no questions.

Rafe and I stay beneath the shadow of the old oaks, where we can easily see the stretch of track as it meets the common. From here the road stretches away, climbing the slope. If we ride straight across the heath we will meet any travellers the moment they are furthest from the shelter of trees. There will be nowhere for them to run. With the dry spell the roads are good and Rafe is sure that luck will be with us today.

We have been waiting an hour or more. Feather is jittery, champing at her bit and sidling up to Flight to nip at her hind-quarters. I am too hot in my green velvet skirts. My stays pinch at my ribs. I long to tear off my hat and loosen the neckerchief that lies looped about my throat. I have refused to wear the veil this time, for it dulls my sight too much.

We have already seen travellers on the road – one or two messengers, galloping hard to London, and a band of gypsies with a cartload of sacks and soot-haired children. Rafe shook his head and raised a steadying hand each time, as though he knows my impatience. He is waiting for something, silent and still, barely responding to my questions, until I give up and am left alone with my thoughts. My heart is busy and my mouth is dry with dust and heat. Insects buzz around Feather's eyes, alighting on her rump. I bat them away from my own face, patting my skirts to make sure the knife I stole from Thomas's store at Ware Park is still in place.

At last I hear the rumble of wheels in the distance. From the line of trees comes a black covered coach, pulled by two tired horses. Rafe steadies Flight, wheeling her about, squinting against the afternoon sun.

'One coachman,' he says. 'And one other next to him. But no livery. Reckon it's hired. They're not rich.' He considers. 'But I think there's promise enough. We cannot wait much longer. Are you ready?' His eyes have taken on a hard, determined glint.

I nod, raising the neckerchief to cover my face. I am more than ready. I've been waiting for this for weeks.

'Follow me,' he says. 'And keep to the plan. Whatever happens, do not hesitate and do not leave your mount. If you have to flee, then do it.'

We stay to the edge of the woods at first, keeping to the shadows while the coach climbs. We wait until they are near the brow of the hill, in the centre of the heath. I keep a check on the road behind and beyond, making sure there is no one else in sight.

At last, beckoning me to follow, Rafe spurs Flight out onto the common. I do the same, urging Feather to a gallop.

The coachman sees us coming. He calls out – a cry that contains both warning and panic. The other man clambers back along the roof to tighten the straps holding the baggage. The leather covers at the windows come down, flapping like bat wings. The coachman whips his horses and they break into a canter, but they are no match for Feather and Flight. We meet them just where the road begins its long descent.

Rafe pulls up his horse and draws the pistol from its holster, standing bold in the coach's path. 'Halt your horses!' He locks the flint into place and aims.

Flight does not flinch at the horses bearing down upon her. The coachman is forced to rein in. He cannot take the coach off the road here: the ground is pocked with tufted hillocks of grass and gorse that would surely turn it. The coach comes to a juddering stop, dust clouds billowing at the wheels. The two nags snort and stamp, almost nose to nose with Flight. Feather prances, made nervous by the commotion, but I manage to bring her round and up alongside Rafe. The coach windows are covered, whomever it carries cowering in darkness within.

Rafe points the pistol at the coachman. 'Throw your whip to the ground.'

The driver, a scrawny man in a shabby waistcoat, obeys.

'Are you armed?'

The man shakes his head.

'Show me.'

The man stands, lifts his arms and twists about in show.

'Climb down, man. Hold the horses steady.'

He does as he's told and comes shakily to their heads to grip the harness. I place myself next to him, draw out my knife and hold the long blade close so he cannot let the horses bolt. From my saddle it would be easy enough to swipe at his neck, or make a quick stab between his shoulder blades. His eyes are on me, taking in my skirts, my bodice, my gloved hands. I note a flicker of something other than fear.

Rafe shifts his attention to the passengers as he brings Flight up alongside the coach.

'You inside, open the door slowly and step out, one by one.'

A reedy cry starts up – the howl of an upset child. The door opens slowly. Rafe raises the pistol. From the dark interior comes a man, blinking and shielding his eyes against the light. The crying gets louder. The man is plain, with a tangle of ginger hair sticking out from under a brown hat. His beard straggles in thin ropes beneath his chin. He has the colouring of an earthworm, pale and pink, a rash of freckles across his nose.

'Please,' he says, 'have mercy. I am with my family . . .'

Rafe jerks the pistol to indicate the scrubby grass at the roadside. 'Stand there, all of you.'

The man holds up his hands and nods. He throws a quick, desperate glance at the coachman, who can do nothing to help with my knife at his throat.

The man turns back to help his family. The first child is passed into her father's arms. Barely more than a babe, she carries a wooden poppet and clings to her father, burying her face against his shoulder. The second girl is older. I recognise her scowl as the angry defiance of one with understanding beyond her years.

Last comes the mother, dressed for travelling but pretty beneath her white coif. She cannot be much older than I. She grips the hand of her eldest and I see her knuckles whiten. When she sees me, in my skirts, blade glinting, her eyes go round and her mouth gapes.

Rafe peers inside the coach, pistol first, to check there is none other. Then he turns to face the family, who stand huddled close by, on the rough grass of the common.

'You will hand over your coin, any jewels, anything of value that you carry,' he says calmly, as though he is asking for nothing more than a loaf of the baker's freshest bread.

The father takes a step forward, still carrying his sobbing child. 'Please, we have little to spare . . .'

Rafe repeats his request.

The man loosens the child's arms and places her on the ground next to her mother, poppet dangling forlornly. The mother gathers the little one up onto her hip and strokes her hair, sending pleading looks my way.

The husband comes towards Rafe with his arms outstretched. 'I beg you . . . I travel with all I have in the world. If you take it, we will be beggared. If you have any pity, think of my children, who will go hungry.'

Still Rafe is unmoved. 'I'm losing my patience.'

'You see I am unarmed. I am a peaceable man. I do not look for argument, but if you have any mercy, you will see I speak the truth. If you would but let us pass, God will bless you.'

'I did not come here to bargain with you or with God. You will do as I say.' There is a hard, vicious tone to Rafe's voice that I've never heard before.

'Think of the children, I beg of you. Think of the Lord's mercy . . .'

The man's earnestness is beginning to affect me. As I look at the little ones, guilt clenches my innards. But Rafe will not bend.

'You will do as I ask or the children will lose their father.' He raises the pistol level with the man's chest.

'Please, no!' the woman cries.

The man cowers and reaches into his jacket, bringing out a small leather pouch. 'This is all I have,' he says. In order to take hold of it, Rafe rests the gun against his thigh.

'And your ring, sir.'

The man twists a silver wedding band from his finger. There are tears in his eyes.

'And your wife. I must have her pocket, her jewels.'

'She has no jewels,' the man says, and I believe him, plain dressed as she is.

Beside me the coachman is shuffling from foot to foot, pale and sweating.

'What's in the trunks?' Rafe asks.

Too late I remember the second man with the driver. As if summoned, a figure leaps from atop the coach with a wild cry, catching Rafe around the neck and unseating him. Both men tumble in a flurry of sprawling limbs and dust. The pistol falls from Rafe's grasp, skidding and spinning on the path. Flight rears up, whinnying, her hoofs coming down dangerously close to the two men.

This other man is a burly fellow, clearly a seasoned brawler, and he has the better of Rafe quickly. He swings thick-veined fists, catching Rafe on the chin, on the chest, in the stomach before he can scramble to his feet. The ginger-haired man takes his chance and stumbles away from them. The child begins to scream.

There is a moment when I am shocked, stock-still, by the sight of them, rolling on the floor in a tangle of flying fists. Rafe's hat is knocked away, his neckerchief dragged aside, exposing his face. The man climbs on top of him, lands one hard punch, bloodying Rafe's nose. Rafe reels and slumps onto his back.

The coachman is muttering and twitching, glancing at me as though he is planning his own feat of courage.

'Do not dare,' I tell him. 'Or I shall end you.' I lean close and press the blade to his throat so he knows I mean what I say.

The man is on top of Rafe, one blood-spattered hand pushed into Rafe's face, fingertips searching for the soft wet give of an eyeball, his knee leaning heavily on Rafe's groin. Rafe's fists beat against the man's chest but he cannot see for the blood and he cannot land a powerful blow. The man's face is a grimace of anger and effort as he keeps Rafe down.

Never leave the saddle. That is what Rafe made me swear, but I cannot stand by uselessly.

I sheathe my dagger and slide quickly from Feather's back, praying that she does not bolt. I run to where the pistol lies in the dirt and snatch it up. The flint is already cocked, ready to fire. It is a miracle it did not spark when dropped. I need only pull the trigger to end this.

I spin round, afraid that the coachman will try for me, or the ginger-haired man, but they are cowards, quivering and blubbing like children. I have nothing to fear from them. A sudden sense of power overtakes me. With the pistol in my hands they dare not challenge me. There is a surging sensation in my chest, building like a laugh.

I hold the pistol with both hands. It's heavy, unwieldy, but my finger is on the trigger and I have both men in my sights.

'Stop! Stop now or I'll shoot!'

It's enough to make the man pause. He looks up at me, eyes crazed, teeth bared, like a wild animal.

'Stop, or I swear you'll meet the Devil this day.'

He takes his hand away from Rafe's face and leans back on his heels, panting. 'Thieving scum,' he spits. 'You're the ones who'll rot in Hell.'

Rafe lies between his knees, gasping for breath, eyes rolling. 'No,' he groans. 'Get away . . .' I know he means me. He wants me to flee.

I keep the gun as steady as I can. 'Stand up. Move away from him.'

The man curses and hawks spittle but is not brave enough to argue. He does as I say, swaggering and swaying, drunk with the power in his fists.

Rafe rises slowly, wiping blood from his eyes, spitting strings of scarlet. He winces, his hand going to his chest as he struggles, first to his knees and then to his feet. He grabs his hat and the bloodied neckerchief, stumbles to my side and snatches the pistol from my hands.

'Get back on your horse,' he says, strangled, urgent. 'Now.' He pushes me roughly towards Feather.

He snatches at Flight's bridle. She snaps and pulls before she'll let him mount, but he swings himself up into the saddle and trains the gun back on the little group. Their ashen faces are shocked and wordless.

I run back to Feather – thank God, she has not wandered far. Rafe waits till I'm on her back, then spurs Flight on, holstering the pistol as he passes.

We leave the little family standing on the heath.

Then there is nothing but the whip of the wind, the blood rushing, the thunder of hoofs and the thin wail of a child's cry ringing in my ears.

Chapter 30

Rafe says very little as we make our way to Gustard Wood. I can tell he suffers by the way he slumps to one side, touches his hand again and again to his lip, and carefully pushes hanks of dirt-matted hair away from his face. Whenever Flight takes an uneven step, jolting him in the saddle, he curses under his breath.

By the time we reach the clearing, fat yellow clouds are gathering and the midsummer air is thick and prickling. I am stifled and breathless. Now the thrill of the moment has passed, my body is tired and weak. I cannot imagine how Rafe must feel, having come so close to an entirely different end. As he dismounts, casting his hat and jacket aside, I see his face is crusted with blood, the flesh under one eye already beginning to swell and colour. I fight the urge to go to him.

When the horses are settled, Rafe shakes the coin from the stolen leather purse. He can hold all the day's spoils in the palm of one hand – a few coins, barely more than a pound. The silver band from the man's finger is thin and scuffed, no workings or jewels, a simple ring for a simple man. I am disappointed but Rafe is resigned.

'Not such a bad day's work,' he says.

'But at what cost?'

He raises an eyebrow, wincing as he does so. 'You should have run,' he says. 'What you did was foolish. I told you, never leave the saddle.'

'What would have happened had I not been there? If that man had had a knife or sword, anything more than his fists?'

The answer hangs unspoken between us. For a moment his eyes brim with a strange brew of emotion that I cannot read. He looks up at the sky and lets a long sigh escape his lips. 'This damned heat is going to break. Come, I have something to show you.'

We leave the horses tethered and he leads me along the bank of the stream, stepping over lichened tree roots that rise up in whorls from the earth. My petticoats catch and tear on brambles. Behind the clearing the land slopes gently downhill. The stream splashes over pebbles, eddying around rocks. The air is heavy with clouds of midges.

Before long I see where we are headed. Where the land levels off, the stream drops into a deep pool. We climb out from between the trees and stand on the bank as rain starts to patter in the canopy above.

The water is deep, swelling where the stream meets, calmer in the centre. The surface shivers with insects. Circles ripple as raindrops land, disturbing the glassy surface. The ground is soft and pliable beneath my feet. It smells of earth and damp summer foliage.

Rafe goes to the water's edge. Carefully he loosens the ties of his shirt, kicks off his boots. His forehead is tense with pain, movements slow and deliberate. He turns to me. 'Come . . .'

But I am afraid to join him, suddenly all too aware of myself, aware of him and the space between us.

I watch as he steps out of his breeches and pulls the shirt over his head. There are angry red marks across his chest and stomach that will be bruise-purple by morning. His neck is splattered with blood, ending in a weird crescent where his shirt covered his skin.

He does not hide himself but steps, naked and seemingly un-ashamed, into the pool.

When he is up to his waist he cups his hands and splashes water over his face and neck. Ribbons of scarlet trickle down over his chest.

I am rooted where I stand, unable to tear my eyes away, my body flooded with feeling as the rain comes down.

He turns to face me. 'Best not let your clothes get wet or you'll be cold later.' I understand his meaning, hear the challenge in his voice and devilment moves within. I know what comes next. I have dreamed of it all these long, lonely years.

I take off my bodice and untie my skirts, stepping from them, folding them and placing them beneath the ferns. I unlace my stays with shaking fingers, and stand at the water's edge in nothing but my shift. I feel his eyes on me. Slowly, I lift the shift over my head. The cool water laps at my toes. Summer raindrops splash my arms and chest, fresh on my heated skin.

The pool is cold and clean after the sweat and heat of the day. Water swells around my ankles, my knees and then at last over my hips. I let it take the whole of me, dipping my head to feel the chill on my scalp, floating on my back, hair softly billowing like riverweed. My heart is full and aching. Low in my belly, the Devil flexes his claws.

It is not long before I go to him. He puts his hands about my waist and pulls me close. With the blood washed away, the bruises and cuts are clear, but nothing can disguise the wanting in his eyes. When he kisses me, at last, I feel the split in his lip, taste salt and blood. My heart beats loud in my ears. He runs his hands over my skin until everything turns liquid, syrupy and sweet as the summer rain. Then he draws me back to the bank.

He lays me down, turns me, so that I'm on my back, among the leaves and twigs. He's heavy on top of me, hands journeying downwards. But I don't want it to be like this – to be forced beneath him, crushed by the weight of him: it reminds me too much of other times, other men, of things I don't want to remember.

I push him up and away. His brow creases, questioning, he comes back to try for my mouth once again. I put my hands firmly on his chest. He resists a moment longer, then senses what I want and rolls onto his back. I climb astride and pull him up to sitting, so I'm cradled in the valley between his body and his knees. I take his poor, ruined face in my hands and he puts his arms around my back, holding me tightly.

There is a look of wonder in his eyes, almost boyish, that I had not expected. Until now he has given so little of himself away, seeming so detached and cold-blooded. This changes him. For me, I think I have always been waiting for this. I knew – not in words but by some other sense – that it was somewhere waiting to be found, but with Thomas, I lacked the map to find it. I know, then, that I am right: this began all those years ago, in the scarlet chamber at Markyate Cell, and it is far too late to stop it now.

When it happens, there is rightness, inevitability, a synchronicity about our bodies. Here, a thigh raised, hooking over a hip so that we meet perfectly; there, a dip in his chest where the swelling of my own must rest; the turn of his neck, such that I might trace the soft flesh of his lobe, taste the rain-damp hollow at his shoulder.

I do not know how I know what to do. My husband has never taught me and there has been no other measure beyond dreams and fancies, but I find that my dreams are enough. I suspect the Devil gave me those dreams, and where he falls short, Rafe does the teaching. With a nudge of his knee or a firm hand, he moves me, places me, until we become two halves of the same. Where my imagination fails, he fills the gaps, with his fingers, his lips, a low whisper: kiss here, touch there, now with your tongue.

In the end, I cannot believe how easily I fall.

★ ★ ★

Afterwards we swim again. We splash and play like children. We float, fingertips entwined, feeling the glide of cooling skin in the push-pull of water until the rain stops. Then we lie on the bank and let the midsummer air dry our bodies. We are on our backs, shoulder to shoulder, gazing up through the boughs. After a time I turn to look at him, but he keeps his gaze fixed on the sky. There is a little furrow in his forehead.

'After what happened today, we cannot go on with our agreement,' he says.

'Surely there is all the more reason to continue. If I had not been there . . .'

'I may not have tried for the coach alone.'

'But it's safer with two.'

'I will not put you in danger again.'

I turn onto my side and prop myself on one elbow. 'We made a bargain. I intend to keep it.'

'And if I do not keep my side, will you turn me in?'

'Yes. I'll keep my word.'

He reaches over and runs a finger down my cheek. 'You won't do that. Not now.'

I suspect he is right, but he cannot be so sure. 'You have no idea what I will do.'

He is silent awhile, thinking. Then he says, 'There must be a trust between us, if we are to rely on each other, and protect one another. I cannot have a partner whom I cannot trust.'

I put my head on his chest and stroke the fine hairs there. 'You can trust me to keep my side of the bargain, if you will keep yours. Surely you know that by now.'

'I hardly know what to believe with you.'

I hesitate for a moment. There are so many things he does not yet know about me, and if I am more open with him, perhaps he will not like what he finds. In this moment I cannot bear the thought of being parted. 'Then let us make a new understanding,' I say. 'If you will agree to continue, I'll make no more threats. We will be partners because we want to be. I'll swear to be honest, if you will do the same.'

He takes my hand. 'You have a way of getting what you want from me. I cannot help but admire you for it.'

I place a gentle kiss on his wounded mouth. There are words building in me, important words, pressing in my chest as if they will burst out. But I dare not say them. Not yet.

Instead I say, 'If we are to have complete honesty, will you tell me the story of how you came to this life? I would better know the man to whom I make my promises.'

Again he pauses, holding my gaze as if searching for something. 'If you are expecting some tale of adventure and daring, you'll be disappointed. You'll find nonesuch here.'

'A gang tried to rob me once,' I say, 'some years ago on the North Road. Perhaps Rachel told you of it. Two of them died for their trouble. I've often wondered what might drive a man to such ends.'

'Desperation,' he says gruffly. 'Only desperation.'

'And was it so with you?'

'Yes, though the first time was by chance. I'd travelled to London, to try my luck with investors at the Exchange. I was hoping to find a buyer, a merchant, someone who might want the farm, and would keep me on as tenant. But I had no luck. On the way home I fell in with another man, a wealthy yeoman, travelling north to his lands in Yorkshire. We broke the journey at Ware. I dined with him, hoping to make my bargain. I spent the last of my coin on drink and a fine meal, thinking to coax him, to convince him I was worthy of his interest, but I failed even at that. He was a decent enough fellow but couldn't hold his drink. As he slept, his pocket fell from his coat, swollen with the gold he'd earned at the Exchange. I saw my chance and took it.

'He was a wealthy man. What meant little to him was life or death to me. When that source had run dry, it was natural for me to look elsewhere for more.'

'So, you stole from someone who had plenty because you did not.'

He shrugs. 'Is that not the way of the world? Those who are rich care nothing for the plight of the poor, and there's no harm in helping them to share their wealth.'

I think back to the days of plenty, before the wars, when my father would give Twelfth Night feasts for all of the Markyate workers, how he had helped the struggling families on his land with his charity. 'It's not quite so simple,' I say. 'Some people are rich but they spare what they can.'

'I've not found that to be true, not for many years. Rich men look to their own, and it is only worse since the wars. Oh, I had grand ideals once. I believed in the dreams of those levelling men in Parliament's army – I went to war for them. I hoped for a world where no man has too little or too much and the riches of the land are spread among its people. I believed in that dream, for a time, like so many of us did. We fought and died for it.'

'Many of the rich men you despise have lost everything too,' I say, the familiar flames of resentment kindling.

'No more than they deserve, after feeding off the poor folk for centuries.'

'Your Republic has taken everything from families like mine. All the things that were rightfully ours, cut away, along with the King's head. Now we are the ones who starve and struggle, because of other people's arguments. Where is the justice and equality in that?'

'There is none. It was only ever a concocted fancy, a pretty lie. There is no Commonwealth, not while fatted gentry are content to watch others starve. The men who promised us a new England soon changed their minds, once they found they were content to stuff their own bellies, and fill their own pockets with the fortunes they stole from the likes of you. Money will always turn a man blind to aught else. I've learned there is no "us", only "I". In the end we must all make our own way, and answer for our own sins, each man for himself, just like on the battlefield.'

There is a dark sorrow in his eye that makes my heart tilt. Perhaps we are not so divided by our pasts, after all. But as he talks a curl of guilt creeps back.

'That family today, they were not rich. What they had, we took from them. When the man begged, did you feel nothing of his despair?'

'It doesn't pay to have too much heart in this line of work.'

'But the children . . .'

'It's not the first time I've taken from a family. You cannot listen to the stories of those from whom you would take your living.'

'Do you not think he was in earnest?'

'You cannot always believe what appears to be true.'

'But the children will go hungry while we will not. If they starve, we will be to blame.'

He turns on to his side to face me. 'Kate, if you are determined to go on with this, you must harden your heart. You question too much.'

How can I harden my heart, I think, when you are cracking it wide open? I think of the little girl crying, the mother's pleading eyes.

'Do you feel no guilt?'

'Feelings do not come into it.'

'Never?'

'A little at first, perhaps, but it passed. It will be the same with you. You'll see.' He fixes me with those bewildering amber eyes. 'Listen to me.' He twirls one of my curls around his finger and hooks it behind my ear. 'We did well today. We made a profit and no blood was spilled. No blood save my own.'

'How can you joke about it? You might have died.'

'Remember, I've worked alone for many years. I've had to be my own saviour more than once. Today God was with me.'

Was it God or something darker that made me take up that gun?

He runs a finger over my lips. 'Tell me, then, if you will speak of sentiment, what did you feel today?'

I lie back, staring at the endless space beyond the treetops, trying to make sense of my tumbling thoughts. Up there, where the heavens are darkening and the clouds are clearing, I see a single brilliant star. I catch sight of it once, twice, and again, as the leaves shift in the canopy. I recognise it, from memories and dreams: a single point of light in a blood-red sky.

'At first I was excited, and a little frightened, guilty when I saw the children. Then I was afraid for you, afraid for myself, but when I took up the gun . . .' I recall the weight of the pistol in my hand, the calm that descended, the certainty that took hold '. . . then I felt powerful, as though no one could harm me. I felt as though nothing must stand in my way.'

'That's what you must cling to. Remember that feeling. Think of it every day.' He follows my eye to the glimmering star above. 'You see that?' He points. 'When I was a child my mother told me that the stars watch over us. She believed that our lives are written there. Each one of us has his own star, and we are bound to follow it. She said that one – the first star in the summer sky – that one is mine.'

I almost laugh. 'I've always noticed that star.'

'It's just a pretty story told at my mother's knee. I prefer to think I choose my own fate.'

'Surely we are all subject to the will of God.' As I say this, I realise I am no longer so sure of it. There is a battle in me that Our Lord is fast losing.

'We all make our own path, and whether it leads to God or the

Devil, it's ours to choose. I'm not made for piety and sacrifice. If I want something enough, I will do what it takes to get it.'

'Whatever the consequence?'

'If I pay for my wrongs, so be it. I think you understand me. I think you are the same. We are both trying to change our fate.'

As he reaches for me again, I think that, perhaps, I have already found mine.

Chapter 31

It begins, as always, with a child's smile.

I am watching her play in the walled garden at Markyate Cell – a girl with green-flecked eyes and the bloom of youth in her cheeks. It is high summer and the roses are drowsy. She collects dropped petals, placing them delicately, one by one, in the palm of her left hand, as though each is a living thing, a butterfly with scarlet wings. She hums to herself, snatches of an old ditty, making up the words she cannot remember.

She is perfect, as yet unmarked by the suffering of the world. I know there will never be another like her. I feel a hollow curl in my stomach, as though the place in me that made her still feels her absence. My heart aches with love.

She skips over to me, cupping the petals in her hand, hazelnut curls bouncing. She twirls and curtsies in the way I have shown her.

'A present for you,' she says, eyes dancing. She opens her palms.

Instead of the petals, her hands cup a pool of deep-red liquid. It begins to ooze between her fingers and drip languidly to the ground. I'm sickened, but she smiles, as a thin line of blood trickles from the corner of her mouth. I watch in horror as the trail runs down her chin and neck, to meet the white lace of her summer dress, staining it a horrid crimson, spreading downwards, blooming over her chest like a rose.

I put out my hand to touch her, unable to breathe for the rising panic, but she is just beyond my reach. Dread spirals. She smiles at me, red tears leaking down her cheeks. She stretches out her arms to me, expectant and eager for affection, as though she does not know that life is flooding from her.

I struggle to catch hold of her, to take her in my arms, to stop the flow of blood – her dress is drenched with it now – but no matter how hard I wrench myself towards her, how I cry and scream for her to come to me, she is always just beyond my fingertips. The poor thing does not understand the danger. She is all wide-eyed innocence, too young and too ignorant to see her own peril.

Then comes the dawning understanding. I am watching her from behind a wall of many years. She is unreachable because she is in the past. I am watching myself.

For the first moments after I wake, I think it must be the same blood that trickles between my thighs. My monthly bleed must have come, bringing the hot, fevered dreams that so often accompany it. I reach down between my legs and, sure enough, feel the familiar slick warmth on my thigh. I fight to pull myself back from that dark place of nightmare but the grip of terror still has hold.

It is a little before dawn and already the sky is brightening to grey, the morning stars blinking above. We had no need of a fire last night but we bedded down beside the hearth anyway, warmed by the sultry midsummer air. I'm tangled in my shift, the linen damp and sticky. Rafe is asleep beside me, lying naked on his back, one arm flung out. I can tell by the steady rise and fall of his chest, the soft parting of his lips, that he is undisturbed by my torment.

The horror stays with me, like the memory of last night's wine.

My stomach is still twisted in a knot. In the dim half-light the clearing seems smaller, the other cottages closing around us, black mouths yawning. There is a sudden burst of wings and a flutter of feathers as an owl takes flight, swooping from one of the doorways, low over the clearing and up into the trees, its white underbelly snowy as the moon.

I need air. I need water. I leave Rafe sleeping and make my way through the trees to the pool. It looks different at this hour, the waters still and black, the moon reflecting a perfect curve on the surface.

I slip out of my shift and take the silver charm from around my neck, placing them both carefully in a little pile on the bank, in the spot where earlier Rafe and I lay together. I step into the water. It's colder now than before, icy but welcome. My skin shivers and pimples but I push myself on, and it takes my breath. I want to be submerged, cleansed. I want to be rid of the feelings of guilt and helplessness and fear that linger. At last the threads of emotion unleash me. In this place I am safe, held in God's palm.

I swim a little to combat the chill, clean the blood from between my legs, and then float on my back, limbs drifting, water lapping over my body, my knees, belly and breasts making little islands. The dull ache that accompanies my bleeding has begun. I close my eyes and drift, enjoying the sensation of my hair flowing wild about my head.

I think about what Rafe said. Can I really make the choice to change my fate or is it already laid down? I have always believed that others would determine my life. From my earliest days I was bred to be a wife and mother, to obey God and my husband, to keep a fine family in a fine home. Death and war and misfortune have put an end to the life my mother had marked out for me, as a match for her own. I did not think there could be any other way. But duty and submission have not served me well. They have bought me a weak-willed husband, who will not provide for me or give me a child, a home that is not my own, while my own is lost, a life of hardship and struggle that I was never meant for. I was not born for these things. I'm meant for something more. I'm meant to live a different kind of life. I'm sure of it.

When I'm with Rafe I'm freed of all the confines, all the expectations, all the dull burdens of my life as Thomas's wife. He could be my escape. I want much, but this more than anything. Now I have him, I don't want to let him go.

I climb out of the water and take up the pendant, cup it in the palm of my hand and bring it to my chest. I close my eyes and whisper my wishes to the stars above.

When she gave me the charm, Queen Henrietta Maria had knelt in the mud and filth of Merton's courtyard so that she was eye to eye with me. I remember worrying about her fine blue satin and the intricate cream lace, though she did not seem to care. The bell was tolling at Christchurch. Everyone knew that the Roundheads were coming. Oxford was no longer safe. Merton was in a flurry with the Queen's household making ready to leave. No one else seemed to notice the lady herself, knee deep in horse muck, bending to kiss the forlorn, orphaned child she had taken under her wing.

She pressed the silvered heart into my hand. 'This is very precious to me, little one,' she said, her silky accent making the words sound full of mystery. 'It was given to me by my own dear *maman*, at a time when I was filled with the greatest sadness and fear. It protected me when I was carrying my little prince, and with its blessing, our Charles came safe into the world. I have kept it near me always, but you need it now, more than I. One day, it will protect you too.' Her hands were warm and soft, not much bigger than my own. 'If you are ever in great need, you must come to me and I promise I will do all in my power to help you. I will know you by this charm. There is none other like it in all England.'

She cupped my face in her hands, pressed a kiss to my forehead. 'Farewell, little one. May God keep you safe.'

I hold it up now. It gleams, twisting on its chain in the early light. The heart is no bigger than a shilling but it is beautifully patterned with intricate vines and flowers. On one side, the engraving has almost faded, where it has rubbed against my skin all these years. But on the other is a tiny crest: a shield filled with six perfect circles. I was once told that this mark of Henrietta Maria's family represents all the influence and wealth that she brought to her marriage with our king. It is ancient and powerful in its meaning.

It was a gift given to a child, but one containing such history, and promising such hope. I knew then what I would ask for if I ever gained the Queen's favour again, and it has stayed the same ever since. The image of my dream comes back to me: the girl in the garden. I would ask to go home. I would ask for Markyate Cell.

But what use is it now Cromwell's tyranny keeps us all cowed? Henrietta Maria walks under foreign skies and sleeps under foreign stars. The Stuarts are a fallen family, destitute as I in their exile. There is no way to claim such favour and she has no means of granting it.

I decide then, sitting on the bank as thin rays of morning sunlight reach through the trees: I have waited long enough for my hopes and dreams to come to me. One day, Markyate Cell will be the Ferrers house again. I will find a way to take it back.

Chapter 32

Rafe and I stay at the clearing in Gustard Wood for three days. I am living a waking dream. We spend each day in a cycle of swimming, eating and lovemaking, working together to make our own haven in this strange, deserted place. We do not see a single soul. The world exists for us alone.

I try to make the little cottage more inviting, discarding the mouldering straw mattress and drying rushes in the sun to replace it. I use a birch branch to sweep the cobwebs and animal mulch from the ceiling and floor. I strip my petticoats into rags and use them to stem my bleeding. I do not mind these workaday tasks that would, in my other life, oppress me so. Here, it feels like a game and I'm glad to do it.

Rafe traps two hares and we roast them over the fire, eating from the bone with greasy fingers, like gypsies. One day we take a slow ride through the woods, collecting wild garlic, wood sorrel and alexanders, eating berries until our lips are dark and sticky-smeared with juices.

I want my life to be like this always. I want to stay lost in this make-believe world. I put aside all thoughts of Ware Park, Thomas and Rachel. I do not even think about Markyate Cell again. Alone like this, as we are, Rafe is all that matters and his is the only company I need. Here, I can forget our arguments over king or

Parliament, poverty or privilege. That this man is one of those I am sworn to despise only fuels my passion for him.

But Rafe's wounds are healing. He looks as if he has taken a bruising in a tavern brawl, his brow purpled, turning yellow around the eye socket. His lip is healed enough for me to pepper his mouth with kisses. We both know that this magical time cannot last but it is Rafe who breaks the spell. Though my heart cracks when he says we must leave with tomorrow's dawn, I know he is right.

Master Stone is there to greet me as I bring Feather into the stables at Ware Park. There is a strange horse in one of the stalls.

'Whose is that?' I ask him.

'It's the horse the master hired, m'lady.' He eyes the length of me, noting the dust on my skirts, the tangled fall of my unpinned hair. He runs a hand over Feather's dirty rump. 'Have they no groom at Markyate Cell?'

A deep dread is pulling me back to earth. 'Where is Thomas now?' I ask.

'I cannot say, m'lady. He is somewhere about. He has not called for a horse today.'

If I were alone I would curse to the heavens. As I take the servants' stairs, and slip into my chamber unseen, my heart is heavy. I do not want my husband to drag me back from the blissful dream of the last few days.

I'm barely inside my room when Rachel comes rushing through the door. I see shock as she takes in my dishevelled state.

'Where have you been?' She is flustered and accusing.

I pretend indifference, take off my hat and place it on the table.

'Your husband is here,' she says.

'Master Stone told me. Where is he now?'

'Downstairs, in his study. Where have you been?' she asks again.

'I must wash and dress before I see him. Come, help me.' I lift the fall of my hair so that she might untie my laces.

She hesitates but comes to me and begins to tug at Rafe's knots.

'I know you were not at Markyate Cell,' she says. 'Thomas arrived two days ago. He sent for you. This morning a messenger came.'

My laces untied, she brings out a letter from beneath her stays and passes it to me. I recognise Martha's hand.

Sir,

I received your letter to Lady Katherine with surprise and not a little concern. Your wife is not my guest at Markyate Cell and has not been expected for some weeks. I pray for her safekeeping and hope that your message purports only some misunderstanding and nothing of greater portent. I trust you will accept my reply on her behalf and hope that you will forgive any transgression I may have made in reading your private correspondence. You will understand that I did so out of concern. I would ask only that I am kept informed of Lady Katherine's safe return to Ware Park.

In expectation, your humble servant,
Martha Coppin

My throat constricts. 'Has Thomas seen this?'

'No. I took it from the messenger's hand and have kept it from him. I didn't know what to do.'

I pace the room. 'You did right.'

I peel off my bodice and drop it to the floor, thoughts running ahead. If Rachel has such proof of my deceit, why has she not exposed me? Is she still loyal, despite our quarrel? She comes up to me, loosens my skirt and holds it while I step out of the stiff cloth.

'I was worried,' she says, gathering the dusty velvet in her arms. Her mouth opens and closes, as though she would add more.

'Will you fetch water so I might wash?'

She begins to walk away but stops, turns back. 'Kate, please tell me where you've been.'

'So that you may report it to my husband?'

'Kate, please . . .'

I tear Martha's letter into pieces and crush them in my fist. 'I was at Markyate Cell, with Martha Coppin.'

'Why won't you confide in me?'

'After all that has passed? How can I trust you?'

'By God, Kate, I've been imagining you injured on the road, kidnapped or worse. All day I've been fretting, thinking my silence might be to blame for some terrible tragedy.'

'I'm well, as you can see.'

'I cannot stand by and watch you endanger yourself. I don't know what you are doing but I can tell it's something bad. If you will give me no explanation then I shall have no choice but to go to the master.'

'And what will you say?'

'That you've been lying about where you go. That you receive strange, unsigned letters. That you're different from before.'

'Different? How so?'

'You used to care about me, about all of us here. Now it's as though you are wrapped up with something or someone else.'

'What do you mean?'

'There is a man, is there not?'

'So now I am guilty, without proof?'

'If you're innocent, then tell me. Deny it, I beg of you. Satisfy me that you're not in danger and I promise you'll have my silence. While I'm ignorant, I can only imagine the worst.'

Her reasoning infuriates me. 'And if you tell Thomas of these suspicions, what then? What do you think he will do?'

She is silent, cheeks flushing, eyes glittering. She knows she needs to watch her tongue.

'If you accuse me, he will turn me out,' I say. 'And remember, your place is by my side. Do you suppose he will think of you once you have served your purpose? No, he will cast you out, alone, friendless and disgraced. All this . . .' I indicate the room in which we stand '. . . all this will be gone for ever. What then?'

Her lip quivers. 'I only want to be sure you are safe.'

If it were merely another man then perhaps I would take her into my confidence, but I dare not admit even half the truth. Her anger would be too wild and her hurt too keen, if she knew that her closest friends had found a greater love in each other. It is better for her, I reason, if she does not know. And I will not break the promise I made to Rafe.

I swallow my frustration and try to make my voice gentle. 'Oh, Rachel . . . we have always been friends, have we not?'

She nods.

'Then you must do as I ask and be satisfied with that,' I say, resolute. 'I have been at Markyate Cell, with Martha Coppin. I returned the moment I received Thomas's request. Now, please fetch me some water and help me dress. I must see my husband.'

She shoots me one last look before she goes to fetch a jug of water. I hate to lie to her. I hate that my secrets now divide us, instead of uniting us as they once did. And yet I cannot help it. Though it is Thomas that I have made a cuckold, I feel little guilt. Rachel is the one I really betray and I cannot rest easy with that.

That night Thomas comes to my room. When I ask him what he wants, he says, 'An heir, wife. I want an heir.'

I had mistakenly thought that the coldness between us would prevent him visiting my bed, but it seems I am not to be spared that duty. I cannot refuse him without rousing either suspicion or anger. Besides, securing relations with Thomas will serve me well, should my time with Rafe prove to bear more than a few silver coins. So I say nothing and draw back the coverlet, inviting him in.

He climbs onto the bed and brings his face close to mine. I

breathe the sour scent of him, like curds left too long in the sun. He kisses my cheek and then my neck, but I do not turn my mouth to meet his. For a moment I wonder if he will be able to tell that I am changed, if somehow he will sense the difference in me. Will Rafe's touch have caused some alteration that my husband will detect? But as he tugs impatiently at my nightgown, he shows no sign of it.

I close my eyes and picture Rafe, trying to imagine that the clumsy pawing hands are his, but somehow it feels wrong to do so. Thomas takes my closed eyes as a sign of pleasure and puts his hands to work. I have a strong desire to pull away. I look down at the crown of Thomas's head and notice that the hair is thinning there – a small oval patch, no bigger than a chicken's egg, where the pale flaky skin of his scalp shows through.

I wonder if he is thinking of someone else. Is there a woman who makes his cold heart pound and swell, someone who makes his body sing and ache, as mine does with Rafe? Some fine lady from Cromwell's court, perhaps, sparkling with jewels and wit. Or a fat doxy who takes the remains of my fortune in exchange for the pretence of love. Despite myself, I do not like the thought. A tiny thread of jealousy rises. Still, I cannot find any desire for him. It is as though every part of my body knows that this act is wrong.

How can it be that this union, sanctified by God, feels so impure? I have endured Thomas's attentions before and have never found any pleasure in them, but now my feeling mounts to disgust – at him and at myself. I shut my eyes and picture Rafe. That is the only way.

When he is done, we lie side by side. I expect him to get up and leave without a word, as he has before, but he does not. He lies back against the bolster, one hand on his chest, displaying himself without shame, the length of him shrinking away on his thigh, like a sliver of greasy, uncooked meat.

'Word is that he will not last the summer,' he says eventually, as if we are conversing over dinner.

'Who will not last?'

'Cromwell, of course. Has word of his illness not reached you here?'

'I have little leisure for news books, these days.'

'I first heard it on the streets, but then I had a letter from Richard Fanshawe that confirms it. Our precious Lord Protector is taken very low again. They say he cannot rise from his bed, and his doctors do nothing but pray. We are all in God's hands now.'

I drag my mind from Rafe, suddenly interested in my husband. 'But what does this mean? What will happen if he dies?'

'Nothing is certain, but this illness of his has been a long one. We must all pray for a favourable outcome. And in the meantime, we must prepare ourselves.'

'For what?'

'If Cromwell dies, his son will rule as Lord Protector in his place. They say Richard Cromwell is weak, a shadow of his father, unfit for government. He will not last long. This country needs a strong leader, and he shows little promise of being such a man.'

'So what can be done?'

'I must keep my lips sealed on certain matters. But I can tell you that if the time does come for those who are loyal to His Majesty, I shall answer that call.'

'Will there be war again?' I ask, horrified by a sudden image of Rafe upon the battlefield. Thomas shrugs. 'Who knows what it will come to in the end?'

'I do not wish you to go to war.'

'Nor I, wife, nor I. I had word from Richard Willis. He expects to be released from the Tower any day now. I will meet him when that time comes. I have written today to invite him to Ware Park. I will find out what is planned by those closest to the King.'

Thomas eyes me sideways, no doubt waiting for my reaction. I have not thought of Richard Willis in these last months. I remember the night I made such a fool of myself with him and feel the coil of shame move inside me. I do not like the idea of him in my life again. I am surprised, after Thomas's suspicions, that he would suggest this.

'Would a London meeting not be more convenient?'

'It's not safe in London. Thurloe's spies are everywhere and one never knows who to trust. There are constant rumours about who is in his pay, or in his debt. It will be prudent to keep such talk away from that rat's nest. I will offer up this house. If the King were to return, it would sit well for my future to have played a part in bringing it about. I hope you will support me in this, wife. And I hope that there will be no questions about your conduct this time.'

My heart is suddenly leaping. 'You think it possible that the King will return?'

'All loyal men cannot help but hope for it.'

I smile then, for the first time that evening. My hand goes up to the silver charm at my neck.

'And can I count on your loyalty, and your silence, on these matters?' Thomas goes on. 'Does the King have a loyal servant in you?'

I am suddenly so hopeful that I clutch Thomas's hand and squeeze it. I see clearly now what it is that my husband can bring me. 'Of course. I wish for nothing more fervently.'

'Except an heir,' he says, seeming pleased by my change in mood.

'Thomas, you must do everything you can to help His Majesty. And whatever you decide, I shall be glad to help.'

He smiles at me and there is a moment of connection, the kindest thing that has passed between us for many months. But Thomas cannot know my real hopes. If the King is to return then surely his mother will return with him. And Henrietta Maria has a promise to keep.

Chapter 33

'Kiss the earth that God made and give thanks that you met with an honourable man this day.'

The two men follow Rafe's command. One has wet his breeches and lies down in the puddle, whimpering like a dog. Rafe holsters the pistol and then we are away, thundering across the dark stretch of Nomansland Common towards Markyate Cell.

Tonight it came so easy.

I retired at dusk, my kind hostess Martha handing me a candle to light the way to the scarlet chamber. A misunderstanding, I told her, quoting her own words, when she asked about Thomas's letter and my absence from Ware Park. There was some confusion among the servants, I said, inventing a journey to Hertford to visit a nameless friend. I saw the flicker of uncertainty in her eye and turned away so she didn't notice the heat creeping into my cheeks.

As soon as darkness fell and the halls of Markyate Cell were silent, I went by way of the secret passage out into the night air. It was easy to bridle Feather myself, muffle her hoofs with sackcloth, and ride out under a bright half-moon.

The two travellers asked for their fate. No man but a fool crosses the common with a bag of gold after twilight. But these men were not local and will not have heard the rumours that have begun to spread.

In the marketplace at Ware and the congregations at Hertford and St Albans, they talk of a devilish highwayman who haunts this barren place, a shameless harlot at his side. Some say he is a nobleman who lost a fortune in the wars, or a brigand on a black horse, seeking revenge for a wrong once wrought, others that he is the Devil himself.

Of his partner there are wide eyes, shaken heads and few prayers. A doxy, dressed in stolen skirts; a lady, disguised in boy's clothing; a witch, casting curses to lure her victims – they make me all these things and more.

The servants at Ware Park recount these wild tales, giggling in corners and whispering behind hands. Master Stone shakes his head, delivers stern rebukes, and does not doubt me when I tell him that my newly weighty purse comes from my husband.

But no one thought to warn these foreigners of the danger. They begged and stuttered in strange broken accents and handed over their riches without a fight. Our job was never simpler.

It has been three long weeks since I last held Rafe in my arms. Thomas stayed at Ware Park a fortnight and visited my bed several times, determined to get a son. I can only bear his touch because he brings me news from London. His pillow talk is all of plots and secret meetings and conspiracy. Now he has returned to the city, hoping to play his part in that drama, wanting to be closer to the beating heart of government, in the place where every man holds his breath, praying for either the death or the deliverance of Oliver Cromwell.

So I am free again. I sent word to the Chaplin farm on the day that Thomas left.

How I have yearned for Rafe these past weeks. Each night I lie awake and relive our days in Gustard Wood. I run our conversations over and over in my mind, imagining new ones, adding a word here, a look there, a touch, a kiss, to make each moment even more perfect, until I can no longer separate memory from fantasy. As I ride, the thrill of our success transforms me. To know that I will be close to him at last makes my heart quicken and my blood rush.

It is easy to tether Flight on the edge of Markyate woods, where Rafe will be able to collect her at dawn. It is easy to lead Feather quietly back to the stables. The place is in darkness, silent save the scurry of rats in the hayloft.

He is waiting for me at the entrance to the secret passageway – a low arched doorway at the back of the house, well concealed by briars and under shadow of tall elms.

His hands go to my face, stripping away the neckerchief. He pushes me back against the door, lifting my skirts, searching out the bare flesh of my thighs. He presses up against me, hips tilting so I feel his urgency.

'Wait.' I'm breathless, breaking away and tugging at the door. 'Come inside . . . the bed . . .'

We stumble up the spiral staircase, half blind in darkness. I brush cobwebs aside, feeling the cold, damp sweep of the wall. Rafe is close behind me, his hand on the curve at the top of my thigh. His breath is fast like mine. It's gratifying, intoxicating, to know he feels the same desperate need. The power of it makes my head spin.

There is a faint crack of light around the door to the red chamber, the candles I left burning still dripping wax, calling me home, calling us to the bed.

I push gently at the door and, as it opens, Rafe's hands come round my waist, his mouth meets my neck. I pull him into the room and put my arms about him, knocking his hat to the floor. And then I see them.

Rachel and Martha are standing by the bed.

At first I think it is an illusion, caused by the brilliance of light after the dark passageway, but then my heart leaps into my throat and I let out a little cry.

Rafe's hands fall away.

For a few moments – moments that seem to stretch endlessly – no one says a word. All my pleasure is crushed in a single heartbeat. All my passion, all my desire leaches out of me, instantly replaced by dread.

Rachel shakes her head. 'No . . .' Her eyes flit back and forth between us. 'No . . .'

Rafe steps forward. 'Rachel . . .' But there is nothing that he or I can say to explain this away. There are no lies or excuses that will save us. The truth is clear.

'How could you?' Rachel says, searching my face for answers that I cannot give. 'Why him, when you could choose anyone?'

Rafe tries to take hold of her arms but she shrugs him off. Her anger is all for me. 'I should have known. You cannot help yourself. I should have known you would do this.'

'Calm yourself, sister,' Rafe says. 'Do not blame Kate.'

'You fool,' Rachel says. 'You stupid, vain fool. You are no better than the rest of them. What has she promised you? What lies has she told to seduce you?'

'Stop this,' he says. 'You don't know what you're saying.'

Again she shirks his touch. 'Oh, I know what I see. I've been blind, but now I see.'

'Rachel . . .' I open my palms to her, but I cannot find any words to make it better.

All this time Martha is silent, watching us in tight-lipped composure. Now she steps forward, placing herself between the two siblings.

'Master Chaplin,' she says tersely. 'I think it best if you leave my home. You are, after all, not invited.'

He ignores her and appeals to Rachel. 'I'm to blame for this. Let me explain.'

'Master Chaplin.'

'It's not Kate's fault. I love her, do you understand?'

He has never yet said those words to me. Though I have repeated them a thousand times in my mind, they have never been uttered between us.

But Rachel laughs. 'You fool. You think she loves you? She cannot. She does not know what love is.'

'That is not true,' I say.

'I think it is. Well, the whole world will know of your deceit this time.'

'Rachel, calm yourself,' Rafe says. 'Don't say things in anger that you'll regret.'

'Master Chaplin!' I have never heard Martha raise her voice before and when she does it silences us all. She goes to the door of the passageway and holds it open. 'Your presence here is neither necessary nor desired. If you would be so good as to leave by the means that you came, you may be assured that no one else will know of your whereabouts this evening.'

There is a clear threat in her voice.

Rafe holds Rachel by her shoulders and tries to look her in the eye. 'Sister, you must calm yourself and think well before you act. Think of the consequences, for us all.' But she will not look at him.

As he bends to kiss her cheek, she stares at me over his shoulder and her gaze cuts like a dagger. I have never seen her look at anyone with such loathing, such fierce, burning hatred.

Then he steps away and turns momentarily towards me. I think he will come to me, hold me, whisper those sweet words in my ear, kiss me at least, but he does not. He hesitates, shooting me a pained look, and bends to fetch his hat from the floor. Then he is gone, disappearing into the darkness of the passageway without a word.

Martha closes the door. I cannot read her expression. Her

feelings are locked behind a mask of control and decency. Under her scrutiny I already feel judged and sentenced.

'I can explain,' I say.

'There is no need,' Martha says. 'Your intention is clear.'

'No, you don't understand.'

Rachel has turned away, her shoulders heaving. I must reason with her. I must find a way to mend this before the whole truth comes out.

'Please, Rachel, listen to me.'

'There's nothing you can say, Kate. He's my brother. He's the only one I have in the world. Why must you take away the one person I have left?'

'I knew you would think in that way. That is why I could not tell you. I did not mean to hurt you.'

She turns on me. 'Then why do you do so, again and again?'

'I love him.' As I say the words aloud for the first time, I know they are true.

'So again you must hurt me to get your own way. We must all bend to your whim, your fancy, your selfishness.'

'I cannot choose whom I love.'

'And no more can I. When Thomas hears of this—'

'You must not tell Thomas.'

'It's my duty.'

'Think on what Rafe said. Think on what is best for us all. What will Thomas do, if you tell him?'

'He will be rid of a cheating, lying wife.'

'Yes, and he will rid himself of you too.'

'He will not do that, not when I have proved myself loyal.'

'Don't be a fool. You are tied to me, Rachel. You think he cares about you at all? You will always remind him of me. Look in the glass if you don't believe me. Do you think he will want you about Ware Park, like a ghost of me, always reminding him of his shame?'

Martha holds up a warning hand. 'Enough of this.'

But I must say my piece. 'And what about Rafe? What will happen to him? Thomas will demand punishment. It will be the only way for him to save himself from scandal. Rafe will be arrested, he will be tried and he will be locked up. He will lose everything.' I catch hold of Rachel's arm. 'Is that what you want? Is that what you want for your family?'

I can almost see her mind working. She knows I'm right. She knows she is trapped.

'Stop this.' Martha steps between us. 'There is no sense and no profit in continuing here. We will talk more about what is to be done in the morning. God willing, the light of day will bring His clarity and guidance.'

She steers Rachel towards the door. 'Lady Katherine, if you will excuse me.' She has not addressed me so formally for months.

When they are gone I barely know what to do with myself. I want to go after Rafe, guessing that he will make for Gustard Wood, or the Chaplin farm, but I know that will only make matters worse. I must stay here and deal with Rachel.

It was foolhardy to bring him here, to think that we could get away with it. I was swept up in the idea, seduced by the thought of us in this place where we first laid eyes on one another. The more time we spend together, the more risks we seem to take, and the less I care about taking them. When I am with him, I am a bolder, wilder version of myself. And now, above all, and making everything else seem insignificant, there is his confession.

I knew it when I met him at the Chaplin farm, my Markyate phantom made flesh, and those unsaid words hung in the space between us. I knew it when he came to find me at Ware Park. I knew it that first night in Gustard Wood. Despite everything that has passed, despite the danger I am now in, nothing can stop the flight of my heart. It drowns all sense and reason. I will do anything to keep hold of this feeling.

★ ★ ★

Martha returns to my room less than an hour later and finds me still dressed and restless.

'She is calm now,' she says of Rachel. 'And trying to sleep.'

I nod. 'Thank you.'

We perch on the edge of the bed, the distance between us crackling with all the things that have not yet been said.

'You have betrayed my trust,' Martha begins. 'You have used my friendship, and my home, for your own sinful ends.'

I cannot deny any of this, so I say nothing.

'I cannot understand it.' Her hand goes up to her little silver crucifix. 'I see such goodness in you. I cannot understand why you would choose a path of sin and destruction. I fear for you.' Her eyes search mine. 'Whatever you have done, you must confess it. If you give up this folly, and if you are truly sorry, you will be forgiven.'

'I fear that that time is already past.' The words leave my mouth before I think better of them.

'It is never too late for God's forgiveness.'

'Rachel seems to believe there is no goodness left in me.'

'She is angry. She will see things differently in time.'

I do not know what to tell her. I cannot repent. I do not want this to end. Not yet. Not ever.

'I'm sorry for deceiving you,' I say.

'Save your contrition for those who need it. I do not know exactly what you have done, what sin you have committed, but if you persist on your current path, you may not be able to find your way safely back. Do you understand? You must cease now, Kate, before it is too late.'

'Will you tell anyone about this?'

She sighs. 'No. I do not see what good it would do. The law is not kind to adulterous wives. You are right about the consequences, and Rachel will see it too. She does not want to lose her brother. She does not want to lose her friend.'

'She seems set on it.'

'She will see sense. She loves you well, you know. You are lucky to have found her.'

'Why was she even here tonight when I forbade her to come?'

Martha bows her head. 'She came to bring the news – Oliver Cromwell is dead.'

She says it so calmly and so quietly that I think I have misheard. 'Truly? When?'

'Two days since, God rest his soul. Rachel arrived here late this evening to fetch you home. Your husband sent a messenger to Ware Park. He will return within the week and brings company. No doubt you must prepare for a celebration.'

Again my mind reels. So the tyrant is dead at last. A little bird of hope flutters in me. But I must be mindful of Martha's sentiments. Her father is a Commonwealth man, a Cromwell supporter. His fortune and position depend upon the twists and turns at Westminster. Martha must be feeling the pinch of uncertainty too. But her losses could mean my gain. It is a precarious path that I must now navigate.

'You have been a kind friend to me from the first,' I say. 'I am sorry it has come to this. I never meant to deceive you.' It is not hard to press a tear or two. 'I need a friend now. Will you help me? Will you forgive me?'

'You still have a friend in me, Kate, but I must see that you are in earnest. Will you promise to give up this folly?'

'Yes, of course,' I say. 'I promise.' But all the time the Devil coils his forked tail around my spine, and flicks his wicked red tongue over the places that most crave his attentions. His claws are embedded in my heart. Martha and her God have little hope with me.

Chapter 34

Thomas has brought a vat of good Canary from London and the men are already bleary-eyed and laughing by the time we sit down to eat. I sense a lightness that has been lacking for years.

Richard Fanshawe and Anne arrived early, my little cousins in tow. Anne showered me with kisses and compliments, but I saw the way she looked me up and down, taking in my shabby working clothes and failing to hide her shock.

Thomas's friend Leventhorpe is here too. Recently betrothed to one of Aunt Alice's girls, he has a new affected swagger about him, which I find ridiculous. He flatters and simpers, and when he kisses my hand, he leaves a damp slick, like a slug's trail.

Leventhorpe's greeting could not be more at odds with that of Richard Willis, who says nothing, but brings my fingers to his lips and locks eyes with me until I have to look away. I feel his gaze upon me all evening, any discretion melting away the more wine is drunk. The only time he turns his attention from me is when the talk is of politics – the real reason this merry party is gathered.

'We must look to the old king's supporters now,' Willis says. 'We'll see how Richard Cromwell rises to the challenge, but he'll be hard pressed without his father's guiding hand. The old guard is stirring once again.'

'They look to give the army command to Fleetwood,' Richard Fanshawe says. 'Where do his true loyalties lie?'

'He's a Cromwell man to the bone,' Willis replies. 'Married to one of the daughters, for his sins.' He laughs. 'But I've no doubt he'll try to bend Richard to his will. I expect he's just one of many swarming around our new Lord Protector, like flies to muck.'

'What sort of man is Richard Cromwell?' I ask.

'I've never had the pleasure,' Willis says. 'But Lady Dysart, who knew Old Nol better than most, says the son is too soft-hearted for government, most unlike his father. England needs a lion, not a lamb.'

'Plenty enough lions in the army,' Richard says. 'They'll all roar for power now, mark my words. And why should they not? Why should they take command from a man who has never proven himself on the battlefield? I know I would not.'

'And what of Charles Stuart?' Thomas asks. 'Is there word? Will he strike at once?'

'No,' Willis says. 'Though I'm sure a glass or two was raised in Antwerp when they had the news. Charles knows we must wait and see how the country responds. We still do not have the support of the Spanish. We must bide our time and wait for our moment.'

Leventhorpe bangs his fist on the table. 'We've been biding our time these ten years!'

'Then a while longer will not pain you,' Willis says. 'There's a chance now, the best we've had since Worcester, but we must be careful and clever. We do not want to go the same way as every other attempt. I, for one, cannot stomach another day on Tower rations.'

'I agree,' Richard says. He is under bail terms himself and cannot travel the country without the approval of the lawyers. He has taken a risk in coming to Ware. 'The days of hasty action are behind us. Stealth is what is needed now. We must begin a new rebellion in a more subtle way, building up support for His Majesty from within, raising troops secretly, so that we are assured of our strength before we strike. We must be certain of victory before we begin, for another failed attempt will not be forgiven. We would all be dead men.'

'And how shall we do that?' Thomas asks.

Willis and Richard exchange looks.

'It will come,' Willis says. 'And in the meantime, we must all ready ourselves for the fight. This time will be the last.'

Later I stand out on the terrace, escaping the fug of pipe smoke. Anne retired more than an hour ago, looking upset at Richard's newly invented scheme to travel abroad and seek direction from Charles Stuart. I'm tired of listening to the plots and plans of men but I know there is no point in turning in, for there is little chance of sleep.

It is a balmy autumn night and I idle, scuffing my last pair of old satin shoes in the gravel, gazing up at the stars. I wish I were in Gustard Wood, with the earth for my bed, boughs of oak and elm for my roof, and Rafe's shoulder for my pillow. I think I will never sleep soundly again, until then.

I have not seen or heard from Rafe since that night, one week ago at Markyate Cell. Every moment has been an agony of waiting. I sent a letter to the Chaplin farm, as soon as I returned to Ware, begging for some word or sign that things have not changed between us, but I dared not commit my true feelings to ink and paper, and I have had no reply.

So far, Rachel has not told Thomas of my infidelity. We have barely spoken ten words to each other. She goes about her duties in silence, helping me to dress this evening with downcast eyes and lips pressed shut as though she cannot trust herself to open them. It is an uneasy truce.

Others must have noticed the change, but Rachel and I have had our spats before, so no one comments, all assuming,

I expect, that we will make peace in the end, as we always do. But I know this is different. I'm not sure she will forgive me this time.

I catch the scent of Willis's pipe smoke before I am aware of his presence. He leans against the wall, watching me.

'I must apologise, Kate,' he says. 'Our talk of rebellion must bore you.'

'On the contrary. I hope as fervently as you for the safe return of our king.'

'Is it the wine, then, that brings you away? It is a little heady. I think your husband has more appetite than taste.'

'No, the wine is good.'

'Why, then, are you so distracted?'

'I'm not distracted, merely seeking fresh air.'

He comes towards me and lowers his voice. 'You cannot lie to me, Kate. Your mind is elsewhere and has been all evening. Tell me, what is it that you think of?'

'Nothing, other than that which a lady most usually dwells upon.'

He laughs. 'You've changed,' he says. 'I see it. Who's the lucky fellow?'

I stare at him in silence.

'Come now, it cannot be your husband has you so lovelorn.'

'I don't know what you mean.'

'It's clear to me. Something or someone has changed you.'

My hand goes up to my neck as I feel the blood rise at my throat. Still, I'm bolder with him, these days, and I won't let him know how close he is to the truth. 'You tease me.'

He gives me a perfect, seductive smile. 'You have truly bloomed, Kate, as I always knew you would. I can keep a secret. Tell me, who has had the pleasure?'

'My husband would be offended to hear you talk in such a way.'

He raises an eyebrow. 'I doubt that your husband has what it takes to satisfy a woman like you.'

'And you do, I suppose?'

He steps closer, puts one arm about my waist and pulls me towards him so that my body presses against his. For a moment I'm caught by the dark intensity of his eyes.

'Would that you would let me try.' He leans in, his mouth close to mine, but I push my palms against his chest and break away. A hoot of laughter rings out across the terrace. 'Stop. Thomas will see.'

'What does your husband matter? It's clear as day he's not the only one sharing your bed. Nor you his.'

'What do you mean?'

'Oh, come, Kate. Do you really think he spends his nights alone? He's a man and he will do what all men must.'

Jealousy beckons. 'If you have something to tell me . . .'

'I won't give up my secrets so easily. Besides, only a fool would not see it, when it is right before their eyes, and you are no fool.'

He looks towards the house and the sounds of raucous company within. I hear Thomas laugh at something Leventhorpe says.

'You cannot mean . . . ?'

'Do you not see the inclination between them?'

In a flash I understand why Leventhorpe is always at my husband's side, why Thomas mentions him constantly, why they share secret jokes and exchange knowing looks across the table, and why Leventhorpe tries so hard to ingratiate himself with me. Thomas's lack of any passion in our bed suddenly makes sense. Can I have been so naïve? Have I been so preoccupied that I did not see my own betrayal? The thought turns my stomach. My own misdemeanours pale in comparison to this.

Willis senses my shock. 'You did not suspect. I credited you with more cunning than that.'

'Is it true?'

'I only say what I see.'

'You would not make such accusations if you did not know something.'

'I'm accusing nobody. I'm merely suggesting that you consider your husband's behaviour before you decide your own.'

'I know there is more. Tell me.'

Again, the lazy smile. He knows he has me where he wants me. 'Oh, Kate, I'm a gaming man. I will not give up my hand for nothing.'

'I cannot give you what you want,' I say, turning my back.

'Then we are at a stalemate,' he says. 'And that is a shame.' He puts his hands on my shoulders, his face to my neck, and breathes in deeply, as though savouring the scent of my hair. 'A very great shame,' he whispers into my ear.

Despite my turmoil, my blood responds to his touch. The wine I have drunk makes me hazy. For a moment I close my eyes and teeter on the brink. Would it be such a bad thing, to get what I want? If Willis's suggestion of Thomas's foul infidelity is true, I would be well armed with such knowledge. It would give me some power over my husband, some advantage, should Rachel ever tell of my own sins. And I am angry – angry with Thomas. Willis would be a good revenge. But Rafe is ever present. To give myself to Richard Willis now, whatever my motive, would make me doubly the sinner.

I swallow hard, pressing down the temptation, and walk away from him, back to the house.

'I know, Kate,' he calls after me. 'I know there is someone else . . . but it should be me.'

I cannot sleep for fretting. I know I should not care about Thomas's betrayal, but I do. The thought of him with Leventhorpe sickens me. Without the facts I am left to fill the gaps. My mind whirls with possibilities as my anger grows. I get out of bed and pace the room. Of course I cannot trust Willis to tell the truth. He has a reputation as a man of honour, but I know better, and I'm not sure whether to believe his riddles. Still, I cannot bear the thought that I am made a fool. I imagine I am a laughing stock in London or, worse, that people pity me, the unwitting wife to this half-man. And, against all reason, I am jealous – jealous of a man I do not even want.

I must know the truth.

I make my way along the passage to Thomas's bedroom. But when I reach the door I hesitate. Perhaps it's foolish to accuse him of something of which I am guilty myself. I must not let anger govern me. The thought occurs – what if Willis is playing his own game and I am walking blindly into his trap?

I must do whatever I can to protect Rafe, and to save any hope I have of seeing him again. It is safer to say nothing. I must swallow these stirred-up feelings. What does it really matter if Thomas is unfaithful? A liaison in London will keep him away from Ware and that is exactly what I want.

I must harden my heart.

As I turn away I hear a low murmuring inside Thomas's room. I cannot stop myself – I press my ear to the door. I hear footsteps pad across the boards and the mattress rustle as someone climbs onto the bed. Then, again, the low hum of a man's voice. But I cannot tell if the voice belongs to my husband or another.

My own breath seems far too loud in the silence of the corridor. I hear a door open and close downstairs, the echo of boots upon the staircase, and I press myself further back into the recess of the doorframe so I will not be seen lurking in the shadows, like a footpad in my own house.

I listen hard. The voice has fallen silent. Though reason tells me to walk away, my curiosity is too strong. My whole body is alive with the need to know the truth. I put my hand to the latch and lift it very gently. The click as it releases seems so loud that I'm sure Thomas will hear. The door swings open a fraction, letting a tiny sliver of candlelight spill into the hallway. I pause for a moment, unsure whether I should stride in boldly with the pretence of speaking to my husband, but I can think of no good reason to call upon him so late. So instead I peer through the gap like a common sneak.

I cannot see the bed, just a pool of candlelight on the boards. Items of clothing are scattered, Thomas's muddy boots collapsed upon the turkey rug.

I hear the sound of quick, panting breath. This is not the steady, shallow rhythm of sleep. My ears strain. I hear a low moan and immediately recognise Thomas in his lust. Anger flashes lightning-white.

I fling the door open.

Thomas lies upon the bed. The coverlet is thrown aside and he is naked. The pale dome of his belly shines in the candlelight. His legs are splayed. He holds himself in one hand. With the other he presses a garment of faded linen to his face, his nose buried deep in its folds. But he is alone.

He jumps in shock. Our eyes lock. He gropes for the coverlet. Then, as quickly as I entered, I turn away and pull the door closed. Just before the latch clicks into place I hear him say my name.

Chapter 35

Rafe is waiting for me in the taproom, rolling a near-empty tankard back and forth between his palms. When he sees me he drains the dregs, stands and picks up his hat from the settle. He gives no greeting or smile to calm my frayed nerves. The knot in my stomach tightens, writhing like a nest of adders. He walks past me and up the stairs, taking them two at a time. I follow, barely able to breathe.

When I reach the landing there is no sign of him, but a door stands ajar at the far end of the hall. The golden glow of candlelight from within lights my path. I reach the door, my whole body tense, ready to take flight if need be. He is standing on the opposite side of the room with his back to me, next to the largest bed I have ever seen.

The chamber is the best in the house, decorated with a rainbow of tapestries. Crude, colourful scenes of revelry cover every wall. The window is draped with thick green and gold damask to keep out the December chill, but hangings are hardly needed, the heat from the hearth is so fierce. Under my heavy cloak, sweat springs at the nape of my neck and my palms grow sticky.

I've heard tell of this room before: the bed is big enough to hold a dozen men and is famous as far as London. The huge four-poster, intricately carved and painted with a riot of flowers and figures, is made for excess, made for lust. The hangings, heavily embroidered with looping vines and glorious blooms, fringed in gold, promise privacy for those who want it.

I put all this aside. All I can think of is him.

'Lock the door,' he says.

I turn the big iron key in its casing.

'Take off your cloak.'

I let it drop to the floor.

And then he turns and before I can say a word, before I can ask the thousand questions that have plagued me these last months, he is with me, arms around my waist, hand on my cheek, mouth pressed to mine. My heart near explodes with relief. From the pit of my stomach rises a desperate, clawing craving.

This time, when we come together, tears track from the corners of my eyes, and trickle down into my hair. He licks them away, hot desire dissolving to tenderness. When he moves inside me, a thousand stars glitter behind my closed eyelids. When I open them, I am blinded by a spectrum of tears. He stares hard into my eyes and puts a firm hand to my cheek, so I cannot turn my head to look away.

Afterwards he stays, propped up on his elbows, gazing at me. I have a lump in my throat where the words I long to utter are stuck. The need to confess my love for him builds in my chest, like a sickness. He strokes my hair away from my face and kisses each wet eyelid. All remaining coldness is gone from him, that hard wall crumbled, the distance between us closed in more ways than one.

For the rest of the evening we live as though we have no cares or duties to keep us from our pleasures. We don't mention Rachel or Thomas, or anything outside the room. I am caught up in the moment, unable to get my fill of him.

We eat late. Rafe, refusing to let me leave the bed, feeds me morsels from the cold plate that the innkeeper delivers. The bed becomes our dining table, our bedroom and everything in between. A bottle of sack melts away any remnants of anxiety, my whole body floating on a cloud of goose down and heady intoxication.

I do not press him for explanations or promises and try to put all questions from my mind. His intensity satisfies me that this will not be our goodbye. He is gentler with me than ever before, once his initial lust is sated, and looks at me with new affection. It surprises me when, some time towards midnight, he is the one to voice the things that have plagued my mind in these months of separation.

'I'm sorry I sent no word for so long. Things have been . . . complicated.'

'I couldn't bear not knowing if I would see you again.'

He nods slowly. 'I thought it best to stay away. I wasn't sure what Rachel would do. I feared I had ruined everything for you.'

'Everything I've done has been my choice. You're not to blame.'

He plants a kiss on my forehead. 'She was very angry with us both.'

'Have you had word from her since?'

'Yes. Did she not tell you?'

'No. She no longer speaks with me.'

He squeezes my hand. 'She wrote to me. She promised she would hold her tongue if I vowed to stay away from you.'

'I made the same promise to Martha Coppin.'

'And now we have both broken our word.'

I think of the poor excuse I made for my absence to Master Stone – an urgent trip to Ware to visit a dressmaker. Rachel knows I've had no new dresses for years.

'She will guess I'm with you tonight,' I say. 'But I had to take the chance. These months have been a kind of torture.'

'Then it will never happen again.' He kisses the palm of my hand, fierce conviction in his eyes.

Tears spring afresh, but I do not want to appear the weak, weeping woman, so I bite them back. I lean against the tester and run my hands over the carvings at the head of the bed to distract myself from the swell of emotion. Just above me, in the centre, is the figure of a bearded man with flushed red cheeks and a forthright stare. He is naked to the waist, one hand pressed to his heart. I run my fingertips absently over the little curve of his belly, the curls of his hair, smiling at his pretended modesty.

'This room must have cost a pretty penny,' I say.

'Do you like it?'

'It reminds me of the old days. Sumptuous enough for the King himself.'

He laughs. 'Then it's worth it.'

'How can you afford it?'

'Business has been good.' I detect a quaver in his voice.

'You told me that the winter months are hard. People do not use the roads so much.'

'I had a particular opportunity and I took it.' He pauses, sits up, releasing my hand, and suddenly my stomach is clenched.

'I wish I could have been a part of it. Will you tell me about it?'

'I cannot.'

I stroke his back. 'Why not? You know you can trust me.'

'And you should know not to ask too many questions.'

I am hurt. I don't understand this sudden refusal. I would share everything with him, tell him anything he asked, open up every last pore, spill every last secret, anything to fuel the affinity between us.

'I will never tell a soul,' I say.

'I will not lie to you, Kate, and I cannot tell you the truth, so it's best that we do not discuss it. I should never have said so much.'

'What have you done that is so bad you cannot tell me? I know what you are, Rafe Chaplin, and I won't judge you. Only God can do that.'

He hangs his head, hair falling to hide his expression. 'Be satisfied with my answer.'

'But we are partners. We agreed honesty, remember?'

'You must be satisfied.'

'Please tell me . . .' I reach out and run my fingertips down his back.

'Kate, stop.'

My own irritation rises to meet his. 'You make a mockery of our agreement if you do such work without telling me. Surely I should know all. Complete trust – that's what you said.'

'I'm trying to protect you,' he says, exasperated.

I pull the sheet up and cover myself. 'Good God, you are just like the rest. You think you can pick me up when you want and drop me again when you tire of me. You are no better than my husband.' I fold my arms across my chest. I know it's childish but I cannot help myself.

He leans against me and plays with a lock of hair that falls across my breasts. 'Stop toying with me, Kate. It won't work.' He places gentle kisses from my chest up to my neck and then to my mouth, until the argument is forgotten and all I want is to be bound with him again.

In the morning, candles still flickering, Rafe takes his knife and leaves his mark on the great bed. Unlike so many others before him, who have scratched their initials into a patch on the bedstead in a clustered jumble of letters and symbols, Rafe chooses his own place – the bearded man above my head. Into the figure's forehead, above those lusty, staring eyes, he carves a deep *RC*, the paint crumbling away around the letters.

How like Rafe, I think, to choose a spot that no one else has yet dared. How very like him to choose the place that a hundred lovers must have looked upon. I like the thought that he has marked out this night in a way that can never be erased. Those who come after us will wonder about *RC* and ask what kind of man he was. I am the only one who will ever know the answer.

We bid goodbye in the pale morning light as the December sun tries to find a way through the dawn mists. Standing in the inn yard I feel bold again, powerful, no longer afraid. I needed this night. I needed to know that Rafe had not abandoned me. Now I am reassured, I care little about discretion. I kiss him deeply, and we whisper promises of the spring, when we will ride out together and Gustard Wood will be our home.

As I make my way out of the yard, mounted on Feather, I twist in my saddle to see him one last time. Only then do I notice the man standing by the tavern door with his hat pulled low. He is well dressed, black clothes edged with lace, the gleam of a silver buckle in his hat. Even from a distance I know him at once. My world tilts.

Before I can turn away and hide my face he doffs his hat. It is too late. I can tell by the triumphant smile on his face that I have proved him right; that Richard Willis has seen it all.

1659

Chapter 36

'It seems our suspicions were correct. Richard Cromwell will be forced to resign.' Willis leans back in his chair, expansive, legs splayed. He cradles the bone-white bowl of his pipe, a coil of smoke snaking around his head. 'He has no support in the army – Fleetwood and Lambert clearly have the hearts of the men – and little more among the Commonwealth faction. He's played a good hand but he's losing friends fast.'

'His father must be turning in his grave,' Leventhorpe says, with a delighted grin.

'I'd like to turn him out of it,' Thomas adds. 'Drag his filthy corpse from Whitehall to Tyburn.'

Willis smiles in that slow, knowing way he has. 'A pretty picture for the ladies.'

Thomas flaps a hand. 'I doubt my wife is burdened with tender sensibilities. What we all want to know is what will happen next?'

'It's too soon to tell,' Willis says, 'but Parliament expects a rising. They know government is weak and the time for us to strike is drawing near. Why else issue more proclamations and send out agents to harry us all from the London streets?'

Thomas and Leventhorpe have been at Ware Park a fortnight, ever since Parliament declared that all known supporters of His Majesty were banished from the city. Their arrival puts all the more pressure on Ware Park's scant stores. Without the money I've stolen, I've no doubt he would be returning to a deserted estate and a destitute wife. I'm angry at his stubborn ignorance, his inability to acknowledge the burdens I shoulder on his behalf, but also terrified that he will start to ask questions. I find ways to ensure he and Master Stone are never alone together, because just a few words between them would untangle the web of lies I have spun.

I have endured Leventhorpe's presence as best I can, watching and waiting for a telltale sign of Thomas's betrayal. But when Thomas told me that Richard Willis was expected, I could barely speak, such was the panic that choked me.

For months now I have been waiting for Willis to make his move. He is too sly a man to let the knowledge he has go to waste. The constant threat is torturous. Whenever I meet his eye a wave of nausea washes over me. I feel like a condemned criminal, awaiting sentence, expecting the worst.

'My father tells me that the King has issued new orders,' Thomas says to Willis. 'I hope you're here to ask for our help.'

'As delightful as the company is,' Willis gives a nod in my direction but his eyes settle on Rachel who sits quietly in the corner, bent over her sewing, 'it is not the only reason for my visit.'

Rachel does not notice his attention. She is fixed upon her needlework. She does not seem to notice much, these days. She is more and more lost in her own world, separated from me by the secrets between us. I doubt our friendship will ever recover, though she has softened, and there is a grudging tolerance between us.

Willis sits forward. 'The Parliament men are right to prepare themselves. A number of us – those loyal to His Majesty – have been commissioned once again in his cause.'

Thomas and Leventhorpe are both eager, like stray dogs waiting for a butcher's scraps.

'A new group is established, named the Great Trust and Commission. Our sole purpose is the restoration of His Majesty. We've spent all these years gathering those about us whom we can trust. Now that loyalty is to be called upon.'

Leventhorpe's eyes are round and shiny. 'You can trust me, Sir Richard.' He's like a child, playing at soldiers, desperate for a chance to prove himself. My husband is little better.

'I hope you know the Fanshawe family remains steadfast to the King's cause. God knows we've suffered for it. I long for justice, for His Majesty and for my family.'

'I would not be here if I doubted you, Thomas, but may I count on you when the time for action comes? You were too young, I think, to see any fighting in the late wars.'

'That's true, but I was raised by soldiers and trained in their arts. I do not fear the battlefield.'

'And you, Leventhorpe?'

'I wish for nothing more.'

Willis turns his attention to me. 'And you, madam, does the King still have your heart?' I can't mistake the mischief in his eyes.

'Always,' I say.

'My wife takes a keen interest in matters of state,' Thomas says. 'Like all the Fanshawe women, she has a tolerable head for politics.'

'I'm glad to hear it,' Willis says. 'Perhaps we may find some part for her to play. What say you, Kate? Are you willing to take a risk? Would you stake your life, your honour, for the man who holds such a special place in your affections?' Willis gives me a look that only I will understand.

'I would do anything for him,' I say carefully.

'Such devotion does you credit, but it will be tested.' He lingers a moment.

My nerves spit and hiss. 'And your own wife, sir, will you ask the same of her?' I say.

Willis is recently married but has not yet mentioned his new wife. He smirks and sucks at his pipe. 'My dear Alice brings many things to our union but a passion for plotting is not among them. I prefer to keep her out of this business.'

'Very wise,' Leventhorpe says. 'Best to keep such things away from the ladies. No harm in a few secrets between husband and wife.'

Thomas shoots him a black look.

'To – to keep the peace, you understand.' Leventhorpe directs this at me. 'Most ladies do not have the nerves for such things. And, besides, did you not say, Sir Richard, that we should ever be mindful of secrecy?'

Willis looks amused. 'Calm yourself, Leventhorpe. We all know what you mean. There must be no risk of traitors or spies in our ranks.' His eyes wander again to Rachel.

Thomas sees it. 'Oh, don't worry about her. My wife's woman – she can be trusted.'

Rachel looks up. She has forgone her cap this evening and her curls fall about her shoulders. Those amber eyes, which remind me so much of Rafe, fix on Thomas.

Willis looks thoughtful. 'If you are sure, Fanshawe? If you will vouch for her loyalty and discretion?'

'I am. I will.'

Rachel's gaze catches mine. In that second I wish with all my heart that we could be friends again. How we would have laughed together at these men, puffed up in their bravado and self-importance. How we would have gossiped about Willis, made fun of Leventhorpe and mocked my husband. But now the gap between us is too wide and there is far too much at stake.

Willis stares at Rachel as she turns back to her work, the very picture of quiet obedience.

'What do you know of the King's plans?' Leventhorpe asks, desperate to steer the conversation.

'Viscount Mordaunt is commissioned to lead us. He's loyal,

one of the old commanders. He's with the King at present and will travel to England soon with instruction. In the meantime, we must make ourselves ready. We must recruit good leaders about the country that we can count on to muster when the time comes. You must arm yourselves and gather about you what men you can. You must wait for my word. Be stealthy and do nothing to arouse suspicion. For now we must hope that Richard Cromwell accepts his fate. He does not have his father's strength, or his will. It will not be long before he concedes. Then, the field will be open.'

Both Thomas and Leventhorpe are spilling over with enthusiasm.

Leventhorpe steeples his hands in mock prayer. 'God willing it will come soon. We have waited and suffered long enough, and so has our king.'

'What kind of man is he, Charles Stuart?' Thomas asks. 'We were both boys when I saw him last.'

Willis considers. 'He's a man whom other men will follow. He's young still, with all the fire and hope of youth. He'll make a fine king. He understands the need to play his enemies at their own games, to know every move before they do, to pre-empt their wishes. He grew up learning by his father's mistakes. He will not see them repeated, God willing, on these shores.'

'And the Dowager Queen?' I ask. 'Will she return with her son, or remain in France?'

'I imagine she'll want to witness her son's restoration to his throne, should that happy day come. You were with her at Oxford, were you not?'

'Yes, when I was a child. I have particular fond memories of her and have often longed to see her again.'

'Then you must keep her in your prayers, and hope that we will all receive due restitution for our pains.'

'Amen to that.' Leventhorpe drains his cup. 'Have you more wine, Fanshawe?'

Thomas lifts the bottle and swills the dregs in the bottom. 'I'll fetch more.'

'I will go.' Rachel stands. She puts her sewing down and goes to Thomas's side, reaching for the bottle.

For a second, Thomas refuses to release it. His fingers cover hers. He smiles up at her. 'Thank you, Rachel,' he says. 'I am right, am I not? I can trust you?'

'Of course, sir,' she says.

He releases the bottle, patting her arm before he lets go. 'Good girl.'

She bobs a curtsy and leaves the room. As she goes, all three men's eyes fix upon the sway of her skirts.

Chapter 37

I retire early, leaving the men to their wine and their plans. I undress alone, climb into bed and snuff out the candle. The moon is bright and I've left the shutters open, letting the blue light stream across the floorboards. Sleep eludes me.

The men are fired up with hope and it's infectious. Willis has been telling tales of his daring and bravery in the last war, and his time at Prince Rupert's side. Thomas and Leventhorpe hang upon his every word, no doubt conjuring dreams of such glory for themselves. My own hopes are modest by comparison: an audience with the Dowager Queen, a chance to ask her to keep the promise she once made. I will encourage Thomas in this new scheme, for if my husband plays a part in bringing her son back to his throne, Henrietta Maria will be compelled to meet my request. I want no glory or acclaim, just the one thing that is due: the return of Markyate Cell. But any hope of that is now dependent on Richard Willis. My future, my place as Thomas's wife, depends upon his silence.

I am drifting into dreams at last when the click of the door latch wakes me. I assume it is Thomas, come to do his duty, spurred by wine and talk of fighting to come. He will want to ensure the Fanshawe succession before he puts himself in harm's way. But it is not Thomas. It is Richard Willis.

Suddenly I'm awake, struggling upright, clutching the sheets about me.

'What are you doing?'

'Hush, Kate.' He closes the door, turns the key and slips it into his pocket. 'No one will disturb us. They are all . . . occupied.'

'Get out.'

He gives a slow smile.

'What do you mean by coming in here?'

'I would have thought that was clear enough.' He moves forward, shrugs off his doublet and drops it onto a chair.

'Stay back. Stay away from me.'

'Come now, there's no point in being coy. The time for that is long past, don't you think?'

In the moonlight his hair shines blue-black like raven's feathers, a streak of grey at each temple, his skin washed pale.

'I will not say it again. Get out, now . . .'

'Forgive me, Kate, but I think you have no cards left to play.' He sits on the edge of the bed. 'It would be a shame if I were forced to tell your husband about your friendship with a certain young man.'

I knew this would come and I have no answer. He has power over me and he knows it.

'I curse you,' I whisper. 'You are no gentleman.'

'And you think our young Master Chaplin is?' He reads my shock. 'Oh, yes, I know who he is. What a sorry, tangled affair.'

'You know nothing about it.'

'I know enough. It's surprising what can be bought for a few coins at the White Hart.'

He moves closer, kneeling next to me and leaning in. He smells of wine and pipe smoke, and the strong musk of a man who has spent his daylight hours in the saddle.

'I admit I'm impressed, Kate. I had no idea you were so bold. You're reckless . . . truly the Devil's daughter.'

'Don't say such things.' My courage is faltering. He could crush my hopes with a single word. He could ruin everything. I hold my breath as he brushes my hair away from my neck and says, close to my ear, 'Tell me, is it the coin you need or is it the thrill that makes you do it?'

My heart lurches, missing a beat. 'I don't know what you mean.' My voice wavers; the words sound unconvincing.

'Oh, I think you do.' He puts his palm over mine and uncurls my fingers from the coverlet. He pushes it down to my lap. Very gently, he runs a finger along my neckline, pausing when he reaches the ties at my chest, his fingertips stroking back and forth. 'But I won't tell, if you give me what I want.'

Despite my foreboding, despite myself, my body responds to his touch. But I'm no longer sure of his meaning. Can he really know the true nature of my dealings with Rafe? I dare not question him, for fear I will expose some vital clue.

'Your talk is nonsense to me,' I say, trying to push him away. 'Take your hands off me.'

Instead he moves to sit astride, his knees pressing the coverlet down on either side of my legs so I cannot move. I struggle but am held fast.

'Don't fight me, Kate. There's no point. We both know I have the better of you.' He runs his hands up over my shoulders and down to my breasts, all the time holding my gaze as if defying me to move or call out. His touch makes my breath falter. I feel myself starting to slip away, that fiery, consuming heat, now so familiar, kindling inside. What power is it that makes my body loosen and swim in this way, so that I cannot control it?

'You are a wicked man,' I say, my throat constricted.

'We are the same,' he whispers. 'We are the same, you and I.' He brings one hand up to my face and runs his thumb along my lower lip. I feel the calluses on his palm. His forefinger creeps into my mouth and I bite it, but not as hard as I should.

'Why him, Kate?' he says. 'Why such a common, pretending pup? Why choose him over me?'

The mention of Rafe brings me back to myself. I pull Willis's fingers from my mouth.

'Because I love him. And he loves me. Because he would never threaten me. And he would never force me.'

Willis hesitates. There is a sudden shadow in his eyes. He sits back, hands leaving me. 'Then you are a fool, for love never brought aught but heartache.'

'I think you must know nothing of love.'

He snorts a derisive laugh. 'And you know nothing of the world. You are blinded by infatuation, Kate. I thought you cleverer than that. You disappoint me, and that is not wise.' The crackle in the air between us shifts, desire melting, turning to defiance as quickly as it had come.

We stare at each other. 'What will you do?' I ask. 'Will you expose me? Will you tell Thomas?'

Willis is silent as he climbs off the bed and stands. He rearranges his clothes, one hand shifting himself about inside his breeches. 'We have yet to come to an agreement. Despite what you may think, I would not wish you harm. Our friend Master Chaplin, on the other hand, means nothing to me. What would you do to save him from the noose?'

'Anything.'

He shakes his head. 'Then there is little hope for your heart. But I have a task for you. If you complete it to my satisfaction, I'll keep my silence, for now.'

He brings out a small bundle of letters, tied with string. He tosses them onto the bed. 'You will take these to Ware, Tuesday next. You will wait at the White Hart – I know you are familiar with that establishment – and a man named Jove will meet you there at midday. You will know him by the black feathers in his hat. You will give him these letters. And you will tell no one – no one – where you are going or why. You will not open or read the letters. I will know if you have disobeyed any of my orders. If I find that you have done so, then your husband, and the magistrate, will know about your adventures with Rafe Chaplin.' He fixes me with a hard stare. 'Do we have an understanding?'

'This is bribery.'

'I prefer to think of it as a fair exchange.'

'Have I any choice?'

He comes to the side of the bed. 'There is always choice, Kate, and you must make the right one. I would have your word you'll do as I say, your word as a fellow soul on this path to Hell that we both seem so determined to follow.'

I pick up the letters. They are unmarked save one tiny black symbol on the corner of each. They are sealed with black wax but no crest or sigil gives away their author. If this is the price of his silence then I suppose I must pay it.

'You have my word.'

He bends and puts his face close to mine. 'Don't forget, Kate, that I will know if you betray me.'

'I will keep your dirty secrets.'

'If keeping secrets is our trade, then I would taste the tongue that keeps mine.'

When he kisses me, he tastes of claret and tobacco and lies.

Chapter 38

I set off early, before the household rises, to avoid questions. The morning is grey and drizzling, and I wear my hooded travelling cloak to hide my face, should I need to. I run the smooth fabric of my black silk kerchief through my fingers – it has become my favoured disguise – but today I must act as though nothing is amiss.

I take a winding route and enter Ware from the north. I'm well known in this town and the merchants and street-vendors are no longer surprised to see me without a chaperone, but today I feel more conspicuous than ever, as though I'm branded with some sign of my secret purpose.

I have thought long and hard about Willis's bargain. I've considered destroying the letters or sending them back with my refusal – but what then? I dare not risk angering him for fear of what he might do. I have no choice. I must do whatever it takes to secure Rafe's safety.

I've thought, too, about Willis's hands on my skin, the way my body rises to his touch. I'm sure it is the wickedness in me that is the cause. The devil in his eyes speaks to the one in mine, and I become helpless under his gaze. I despise myself for it.

And yet I glimpsed something that night, in the way his desire died the moment I spoke of love. Willis is a many-faceted man with experience far beyond my own. He has seen terrible things I cannot imagine. But at that one word, he faltered. Is there a broken heart beneath the steely, polished exterior? It intrigues me to think there may be some tiny speck of feeling behind those cunning black eyes.

I stable Feather at the White Hart and visit the butcher and the chandler, making idle conversation to pass the time. When it's almost noon I go back to the inn and find a secluded table in the corner of the taproom.

The inn is busy with travellers on their way to London, and post boys stopping to change horses, but the girl finds me and I order small beer. I'm supplied with the best brew the house can offer.

Four men, sitting in a group, doff their hats in my direction. I recognise two of them as traders from the market square. They begin whispering, throwing curious looks my way. I'm used to attracting unwanted attention and usually think little of it. But today I do not want their scrutiny. I see suspicion in the eyes of townsfolk where perhaps there is none.

I take out the bundle, hold it beneath the edge of the table where others cannot see and study it. There are six letters, parcelled with a crisscross of string. Each is identical apart from a small symbol, carefully marked, three with a tiny five-pointed star and three with a love heart. This must be to identify their intended recipient, but the symbols mean nothing to me. I fiddle with the string, loosening the knots until I can slip out a letter. I choose one marked with a tiny black heart. I turn it about, running my fingers along the edges and folds, but cannot see any ink or discern any hint of what might lie inside.

An overwhelming curiosity rises. If I must be a part of some dangerous plot then I would know the manner of my crimes before I am accused of them. I can only imagine that the letters are part of the same scheme that consumes Thomas and Leventhorpe, the new conspiracy that Willis spoke of at Ware Park, the night our bargain was struck. Perhaps these are meant for the other members of the Great Trust and Commission, Charles Stuart's new hope. What other reason can there be for such secrecy?

Making sure no one else can see, I slide my fingernail beneath the hard, black wax and prise open the letter.

At first I cannot make sense of it. The letter, addressed to a Master Tanner, seems to be about a shipment of goods. Several merchants are mentioned, along with a list of ships and a string of figures, presumably detailing the prices and amounts of goods to be transported. The name Tanner seems familiar, but I cannot fathom its significance here. What has this to do with the King? I feel like a child, studying a book that has no meaning without knowledge. It must be a cipher of sorts. Conspirators must have a way to conceal their correspondence and I've heard Thomas say as much. I pick out the odd repeated word here and there – place names, a date – but there is nothing I recognise and no clear sense to any of it.

I have no chance to investigate further. A man enters the room. He scans the place with sharp, hard eyes like a weasel's. I know before I see the black feathers in his hat that this is Jove. He asks the innkeeper a question, and the man nods in my direction.

Hurriedly I push the opened letter beneath my thigh, between the bench and my skirts. The others lie bunched in my lap. I cover them with my palms.

Jove comes towards me. 'Lady Katherine Ferrers.' He makes a cursory touch to the brim of his hat. 'I'm sent with a message from your husband.' He speaks louder than necessary. The townsmen turn their heads. I know they are listening.

I give Jove a look that begs discretion. 'Please, sit.'

He pulls up a stool and removes his hat, revealing lank,

mud-coloured hair. There is a rash of red spots across his forehead where the hatband has rubbed in the heat.

The serving girl is quick to pay attention. She lingers by the table. 'Ale for you, sir?' she says. 'And something to eat? The pie's fresh.'

'Nothing for me,' Jove says. 'I cannot stay. I'm only passing by to give Lady Katherine a message.'

The girl raises an eyebrow and gives me a disbelieving look. I know she has seen me here before, not least on the night I spent here with Rafe. She must recognise me and now Jove has made sure she knows my name. There was a time she would not have dared to look at her betters so, but those days are long gone.

'Very well, sir.' She dips a mocking curtsy and tosses me an insolent smile. 'M'lady . . .'

A girl like her must see more of the world than most, I think, wondering if she can be trusted to hold her tongue. No doubt I will be the subject of alehouse gossip today.

'Too clever for her own good,' Jove says, watching her, fingers twitching as though he would reach for the sword at his side. 'But let's not waste time on tavern wenches when we've business to do.' He leans forward across the tabletop. 'Have you the letters?'

'Who is your master?' I ask.

'That's no business of yours.'

'I would know before I give you the letters. Answer my question.'

'What is it to you?'

'I would know from whom you take your orders. By whose command are you sent here today?'

He smiles. 'I don't take commands. I take work, where I can get it.'

'You're not a soldier?'

He laughs. 'Do I look like one?'

It's true he looks like no soldier I ever saw. 'Then what kind of man are you and where do you find this work?'

'I've no time for chatter today.'

'At least tell me who pays you.'

'Whoever promises the best price.'

'Have you no loyalties?'

He leans forward. 'You'd do better not to ask so many questions, m'lady. Now, where are the letters?'

I hesitate a moment but then slide the bundle across the table towards him, all except the letter that sits out of sight beneath my leg.

He picks them up, counts them. 'And this is all?'

'All I was given.'

He squints at me and I hold his gaze, determined I will not give away any of the foreboding that tumbles inside.

'Very well,' he says. 'Then I'll leave you be.' He stands, tucking the letters inside his cape. He puts his hat on, straightening it with both hands. 'I bid you good day, m'lady.'

'Wait . . . Where are you taking them? Are they for London?'

He lowers his voice. 'You know I cannot tell you and it'll be better for you if you know nothing more. Take my advice – forget you ever met me. Forget this ever happened.'

He is gone as quickly as he arrived.

The servant girl watches him leave, then gives me a long, knowing look. I ignore her.

I fold the one remaining letter into a tiny square and tuck it safe beneath my stays. Now it comes to me: I remember where I've heard the name Tanner before. It was on the same night that Willis gave me the letters. He and Thomas were talking of John Thurloe – Cromwell's old spymaster – joking that they should choose an alias for him that matched the stink of the man's rancid soul. Tanner was the name Willis had chosen, for the stench that rises from the tanner's yard.

Master Tanner is John Thurloe, the man who has foiled many a royalist plot in these last years, the man who has a nest of spiders scuttling across his web with information and secrets, whose reach has been known to extend into the heart of even the King's most loyal families. If the letter in my stays is intended for him, then Richard Willis is a traitor.

I know Willis is capable of many things, but this makes my mind spin. There is only one reason he would be in communication with Thurloe. Is it possible that the man who fought at the old King's side, is famous for his loyalty and courage, now turns against the new King he is sworn to protect? I can hardly believe it. But if it's true, and this one letter is my proof, it may hold all the power I need. It may be the one card Willis will not expect me to play.

It is not until I am safely away from the White Hart that I realise it: by his blackmail Willis has turned me traitor too. If what I suspect is true, and those letters find their way to Thurloe, then it will be by my own hand. And Willis has made sure there were witnesses. I am traitor to the King, traitor to my husband, and traitor to my own wishes.

And there is only one end for a traitor who is found out.

Chapter 39

It is midsummer once more. Evening shadows stretch long across the common. Feather and Flight stand amid sunbaked scrub and yellow gorse.

Rafe and I watch the coach from afar as it climbs the hill, a single coachman commanding a pair of matching greys. Gilt finials glint in the honeyed light and I can make out the smudged colours of a crest on the door. It must belong to someone of significance, though I do not recognise it as any of the local families.

Rafe primes the pistol and puts it back in the saddle holster, his eyes rarely leaving the coach as it makes its way to the brow of the hill. He looks at me. 'Are you ready?'

I nod and smile, pulling up the black kerchief to hide my face. I gather Feather's reins, the butterflies awakening in my chest. How I have come to love this moment, when the tension of the stand, the power of a loaded pistol, the weight of gold in my palm are all yet to come, and anything is possible.

They're a dowdy bunch, lacking the finery we'd hoped for. A fat man with a veined drunkard's nose and the paunch of wealth is clearly the head of the party. His wife, a dumpling in a mob-cap, looks as though she's come straight from the bakehouse. There is a daughter, a younger version of the mother, drab in faded blue worsted with mousy, crinkling curls, and one other with more promise – a young man, swaggering in a scarlet coat. Fair-haired and handsome, in other circumstances I may have favoured him, but next to Rafe he seems little more than a preening boy.

I am in my usual place, securing the horses, blade drawn at the coachman's throat as he tries to keep them steady.

Rafe trains the pistol on the fat man. 'Hand over your coin, sir, and your ladies must give up any jewels.'

The man is self-assured. 'I will give you what I can spare and no more.' He rummages for his purse and draws out several half-crowns. They blink gold in the sun.

'You can spare more than that,' Rafe says. 'In fact, I insist upon it.' He twitches the barrel of the gun towards the two women. The daughter squeals and hides her face in her hands.

'I am Sir Mortimer Blanchard,' the fat man says. 'I trust you have heard my name. It will go better for you if you allow us safe passage on the King's highway.'

'The *King's* highway? The King's man, are you?'

The man puffs up his chest. 'I am for God, and the one true King.'

'Brave words, sir, in these dark days.'

'My conscience is no business of yours. It is my purse that interests you. I will give you a fair price, if you will let us be on our way unharmed. If you do not, then be warned, I will seek justice for this insult. I know the law men in these parts.'

'Is that a threat, Sir Mortimer? Or are you proposing a bargain?'

'I am a gentleman, sir, and I assume by your address that you were once the same. Surely we may reach some agreement that is amenable to us both.'

Rafe directs the pistol at the man's head. 'You are in no position to bargain, and I do not have time for this. You'll do as I say or pay a much dearer price.'

Sir Mortimer raises his palms in supplication while the women clutch at his sleeves. His courage is faltering. 'Very well. I can give you a good quantity of coin, and my young cousin may have a pound or two to spare.' He nods to the fair-haired youth, who scowls.

I see Rafe considering, his eyes settling on the two women. I know he will take this deal for the ease of it and to avoid bloodshed. He can be a cold man, but he is not cruel.

'My partner will relieve you of your purse,' he says.

I bring Feather round next to Flight and dismount. I feel bold as I go towards Sir Mortimer with my blade gripped firmly. I can sense the fear coming off the women, like a stench. The wife remains composed but the daughter has crumpled against her father, sniffling as a child might.

'I have heard tell of you, madam . . .' Sir Mortimer says, as I draw near. 'In the taverns at Puckeridge and Barnet. Tales of your wickedness spread as far as Huntingdon and Cambridge.'

'Hold your tongue,' Rafe says, and to me he mutters, 'Get back on your horse.' But I'm close enough to hear Sir Mortimer's whisper. 'They say the Devil has a hold on you, madam. Is that so? Or is it this man who keeps you captive?'

'I said, hold your tongue.'

'Confess it now, madam, and come away with us. Give up this sin.'

I snatch the purse from his hand and bring my dagger up to his throat. The women gasp, stumbling away, clutching at one another.

'You are no gentleman, and you know nothing of me.'

'Get back on your horse.' Louder this time, Rafe's command contains a warning, but I do not heed it. I twist the point of the blade to Sir Mortimer's throat. I feel it slice through the fabric of his collar and snag against the shirt beneath. One small slash and it would meet skin.

'You'd be wise to keep your filthy gossip to yourself,' I say.

'Don't taunt me, sir, for if the Devil drives me, then only he knows the lengths to which I might go.'

Suddenly there are strong hands pulling me roughly backwards. My right arm is twisted up and locked behind my back. I drop both the purse and the knife, crying out as a jagged pain shoots through my shoulder.

'Struggle and I'll cut your throat, you thieving whore.' The young man's face is close to mine, his mouth at my ear, beard bristling my neck. He is stronger than he looks and holds me fast, his own thin, sharp blade pressed against my neck.

Flight stamps in a scuffle of hoofs and dust. Rafe manages to rein her in and trains the pistol on Sir Mortimer.

'Release her, or I'll shoot.'

The fat man drops to his knees and holds up his palms. 'Peter, do as he says.'

'Not until you give back what you've taken,' the young man says.

I struggle against him but he is too strong. A sharp bolt of pain travels across my chest, making me cry out once more. He twists the knife against my neck and I feel the soft give of skin as it punctures, then the wet trickle of warm blood. Panic rises, a bitter iron taste in my mouth.

'Rafe . . .'

'Ah! So you do have a name,' the young man says. 'And it's one I've heard before . . .'

'Steady there, Peter,' Sir Mortimer calls out. 'We want no blood on our hands.'

'It's too late for that,' Rafe says. 'Release her or I'll shoot.'

'Fighting words, but you have only one shot, Rafe Chaplin,' Peter says, his voice loud in my ear. 'I'm right, am I not? That is your name. There are rumours about you. You've quite a reputation. Well, I'm not afraid of scum brigands like you, or their doxies.' For a moment the press of the blade leaves my throat and

Peter's hand comes up to tug the kerchief away from my face. 'You've got yourself a pretty whore. Perhaps I shall keep her when I'm done with you.'

'Peter, you must desist!' Sir Mortimer is earnest now.

Rafe brings Flight closer. I feel the edge of Peter's blade at my neck. I sense no pain, just the sticky warmth as blood creeps into the crevice between my breasts. My pulse is rushing. Tiny points of light begin to sparkle and blur my sight.

'Don't come any closer,' Peter says, 'I will kill her . . .'

Rafe ignores him. He aims the gun at Peter's forehead, so close he could not miss, but a shot might take me with him.

'You are unwise,' Rafe says. 'To assume what may, or may not, be important to a man like me. You do not know what I'm willing to sacrifice. Now, release her or you'll find yourself meeting your namesake this day.'

'Do as he says, Peter,' Sir Mortimer pleads. 'Let her go. She's not worth the stain on your soul.'

Peter is unsteady, panting hard in my ear. I feel him hesitate. I daren't move. I daren't even breathe. I fix my eyes on Rafe. He isn't looking at me: he's staring at Peter and his glare is as sharp and cold as the blade at my neck.

Then Peter makes a strangled cry of frustration and pushes me away. I stumble forward, almost falling. Sir Mortimer's purse and my dagger are on the ground nearby and I have the wit to snatch them up.

'A wise move,' Rafe says to the youth. 'You'd do well to pay attention to your uncle.' He keeps the pistol aimed at Peter as I stumble over to Feather and grab her bridle. The young man is spitting curses, fired up by bloodletting, angered by his failures.

I try to mount while Feather prances. When I'm in the saddle, Rafe wheels Flight about and spurs her on. He says nothing, does not look at me, gives me no signal to flee as usual. I dig my heels into Feather's flanks and follow.

As we thunder across Nomansland, towards the cover of trees, I know there is more at stake than a few coins. Those people knew Rafe by name and by reputation. They have seen my face. They know us both for what we are. How much longer will it be before others know it too?

Back in the clearing in Gustard Wood, Rafe draws water from the stream and uses a rag to clean the blood from my neck and chest. My shift is ruined, red rivulets tracking from shoulder to hip. I'm put in mind of my scarlet-stained spectre, that first day at Markyate Cell. What strange turns my life has taken since then, and now we are circled about, but this time the blood is mine.

The wound is not as bad as it first seems, the cut no bigger than an inch and not deep. Rafe fetches a clean rag and winds it around my throat. He is quiet, tending me, then bidding me rest while he fetches firewood and kindles a blaze. There is none of his usual exuberance after a successful stand, and he does not even count the coin in Sir Mortimer's purse. When at last he settles, dusk is creeping through the trees. He still will not meet my eye and there is a horrid lump in my gullet. I can tell he's angry with me and am compelled to ask why.

'I've told you many times – never leave your horse.' He makes no attempt to conceal the irritation in his voice. 'It's the first rule I taught you.'

'I thought it was safe. They seemed so tame. You were in command.'

'It's never safe.' Rafe's eyes glitter. 'You should know that by now. Besides, that's the least of it. You spoke my name.' I feel the accusation as a stab in the chest. He's right. I know I've failed him.

'It was a mistake. I thought that boy would slit my throat. I was . . . I was afraid.'

'And they have seen your face.'

'It matters not. They did not know me, or I them. There must be a hundred women would fit my description. It means nothing.'

'It'll mean everything when they are called to identify Lady Katherine Ferrers as a highway robber. You heard that man talk of seeking justice. He seems just the type to pursue it.'

I cannot bear the thought that, if this happens, it will be my fault. I'm longing to touch him, craving the comfort of his arms, but his displeasure makes me afraid to try. 'It will not come to that.'

He sighs. 'Sometimes, Kate, I believe I'm your curse. I've led you down this path and there's no returning. You do not heed the danger you're in. And now it's too late to change it.'

'I understand well enough, yet there is nowhere else I'd rather be. You know that.'

He sighs and looks up beyond the canopy. Early stars are blinking in the twilight. His eyes soften momentarily as they alight on the brightest. 'You could have died today and I would have been to blame.'

'You saved me, as I once saved you. Now we are equal. That man said I'm in thrall to you, but he knows nothing of my motives. I choose it. I would choose this life over any other. And, if I meet my end, then I will make a good, proud death by your side.'

'Kate.' He turns to face me. 'You talk like a child. This is not the stuff of folklore. This is not some romance or ballad. This is real.'

'You think I don't know that? You think I'm playing at this? I have everything at stake too. More than you know.'

Rafe does not even know the whole threat. It's time I told him about my dealings with Richard Willis. But I'm afraid that he will turn from me, when all I want is to be closer.

'They know my name,' he says. 'That is the beginning of the end. There will be talk. The thief-takers will come looking for me. I cannot go back to the farm.'

I take a deep breath. 'There is something more I must tell you. There is one other who suspects us both.'

He fixes on me, surprised. 'Who? Rachel? The Coppin woman?'

'A man named Sir Richard Willis, a friend of the Fanshawes. He saw us together that morning at the White Hart.'

I tell him everything. I admit that Willis came to me at Ware Park, though I do not mention when or where, and I detail the bargain that I have struck to keep him silent. I tell him about the letters I carried to Jove. As I talk, Rafe's expression is incredulous, then increasingly black.

'And you say these letters were in cipher, and marked with symbols?'

'I read only one, and I still have it.' I fetch out the letter, which I keep with me always, and hand it to him. He looks it over, tilting the paper towards the flames.

'How dare he draw you into this?' There is fury in his voice.

'Look, here.' I point to the name at the head of the page. 'I believe this is Thurloe. Why would Willis be passing messages to him? Do you think he's a traitor to the King?'

'We would do well to burn this,' he says, holding it out over the flames.

'No!' I snatch it back. 'It's our best chance against him. If he has any evidence against us he could turn us both in. He could tell Thomas. He could bring the law down upon you, take away your land, everything. Even without evidence people will surely believe him. He has that kind of power. But this gives us some power over him, don't you see?'

'Kate, if you are found with this letter they will take you for a spy.'

'I know, but it is my one safeguard. If he threatens me again, I will have a new card to play.'

'You should have told me about this sooner.'

'Well, it is done. I cannot change it now.'

'I might have been more careful. Willis is a dangerous man.'

'What do you know of him?' I'm surprised that Rafe knows the name, though, of course, Willis made his reputation on the battlefield.

'I know enough. It's not wise to cross him. He will find out that you took that letter.'

'He said the same.'

'Then why do it? You have put yourself in double the danger.'

'I'm willing to take that risk.'

He gives me one of his hard stares. 'Burn it, Kate. Mark my words, if you do not, it will come back to haunt you.'

I fold the letter and put it back inside my saddlebag. 'We shall see about that.'

Chapter 40

The night is hot, full of dry dust and honeysuckle. Though we have flung the casements wide, the air in the parlour at Ware Park is dense and crackling with a summer storm that will not break. It makes Thomas and Leventhorpe thirsty – they drink a bottle of Canary apiece, paid for by Sir Mortimer Blanchard's stolen purse.

I told Thomas that Master Stone got a good price for our early crop of cider apples. I told Master Stone that I sold my old trinkets to the moneylender in Ware. I told Rachel nothing, though I noticed her pursed lips and the questions in her eyes. She knows the orchards were plagued by sawfly this year and she knows I hawked all my pretty things a long time ago.

The cool linens on my bed are inviting but I know I will not sleep, so I sit up with the men, listening to their excited bragging about the preparations they have made. They claim dozens of others have promised to ride out with them when the order comes. There are pistols and shot and twenty carbines hidden in Leventhorpe's stables. They have both been fitted for new riding coats. Their talk is of silver buttons and lace trimmings and feathered hats, more fitting for the royal court than the battlefield. Anyone would think they speak of a hunting trip rather than a challenge to government.

Rachel feigns concentration on her sewing, but as the hours draw on, I notice that she darns the same section over and over. I catch her eye, raise an eyebrow and smile. The corner of her mouth twitches before she looks away.

Leventhorpe suggests a game of cards, and Thomas persuades Rachel to join us. To an outsider this may seem a comfortable party. I know better. But I'm keen to hear the latest from London, and Leventhorpe has just returned.

'We've heard all about your planning, husband,' I say, once we are seated and the cards are dealt. 'But when will you strike?'

Thomas studies his cards, places one on the table and indicates to Leventhorpe to take his turn.

'Can we trust you, Lady Katherine?' Leventhorpe asks.

'I'm keen to help, but cannot if I'm kept ignorant.'

'Then I'll tell you that the date is set. Two weeks from now, on the first day of August. We are well set up at Sawbridgeworth, but Thomas has promised to bring men from Ware Park.'

'And what will happen on that day?'

'We will muster and prepare to fight. Others will do the same all around the country. Our own men are ready. Fanshawe and I have visited every loyal man from Ware to Hertford and given instructions.'

'And who will be your enemy?'

'We expect to meet a detachment from one of the local garrisons. As soon as the rising is known, Parliament will move to crush it, I have no doubt.'

Leventhorpe plays his card and Thomas says, 'Rachel, my dear, you are the loser this time.'

Rachel gathers the cards and adds them to the little pile she is steadily gathering. She refuses to meet Thomas's eye, or mine.

I play my card. 'And do you have enough men at your command to be sure of a victory?'

'Provided our allies keep their promises,' Thomas says.

I have been aware of a change in feeling at Ware Park these last weeks. Thomas has recruited volunteers from the farms and villages on old estate land, and the few men in our employ are those still loyal to the Fanshawes, and to the King. They would not have stayed through these bleak, starving years otherwise. Our farm boys prepare to fight, just as their fathers did, for the old order that kept them in food and lodging for so long.

'Is there real hope that a rising will be victorious?' I ask. 'When others before you have failed?'

Leventhorpe grimaces as he loses the trick and gathers the cards. He takes a long draw on his cup, holding Thomas's gaze as he does so. 'Provided we have no turncoats in our ranks. We have been careful whom we approach, but at such a time, one can never be sure of the secrets in a man's heart.'

How close to the truth he is. 'Is there danger of treachery?'

Thomas and Leventhorpe exchange a look.

'Spymaster Thurloe is gone, along with Richard Cromwell, but his legacy remains,' Thomas says. 'His underhand way of dealing runs deep with those men. And the new man in his place – Scott is his name – will be keen to prove his worth. No doubt he'll do his best to persuade some that their better interests lie with him. But we'll see how many of those who were in Thurloe's pay stay loyal to a government with no clear leader. I know I would not risk my good name, even my life, for so aimless a cause. Where is the cause when there is no king? It is clear there is only one way forward now.'

We are silent as we play, Thomas taking the cards this time. Leventhorpe reaches across to pat Thomas's hand in pretend consolation. I notice how his fingertips linger. I see the meeting of their eyes before Thomas draws his hand away.

Thomas's gaze falls upon Rachel as she takes a sip from her cup. 'Come, Rachel, I know you can do better than that. What is the use of modesty in such company? Take a proper drink. I insist that you raise a full glass to our king.'

Rachel drinks, her cheeks flushing. 'Is it certain that you will fight?' she asks, eyes flitting between the two men.

'If God gives us the chance,' Leventhorpe says. 'If everything goes to plan and we are not betrayed.'

'Who would betray you?' I ask. 'Is there someone you suspect?'

'It is better that she knows,' Leventhorpe says, suddenly serious.

Thomas sighs. 'There are rumours about our friend Richard Willis. A placard was put up at the Exchange, accusing him of betraying the King. Of course Willis was not there to defend himself, and now London is awash with pamphlets saying the same. I cannot believe it myself. If there is a turncoat in our ranks, I cannot think it is Willis, when he has always worked so hard, and suffered so much, for the King's cause.'

Though perhaps I should not be shocked to hear this, I am. A public accusation would seem to have some substance, and serious consequence. I had thought I was alone in my suspicions. 'Who would dare accuse him?' I ask.

'I know Willis has been a long-time favourite of yours,' Thomas says, a prickle in his voice. 'I'm sure it will all come to nothing. He will prove his loyalty when our uprising is successful. No one will dare doubt him then.'

I feel Rachel's eyes on me. My mind is racing but I must play-act my feelings. I put a hand to my chest, and make my eyes round. 'I cannot believe it of him, when he has always been so steadfast. He has risked his life many times, suffered months of imprisonment for his loyalty. What would he have to profit by ruining the King's hopes now?'

'My thoughts exactly,' Leventhorpe says. 'There can be no truth in it.'

This strengthens my hand, I think: if the letter I hold is proof of this accusation, then I will have Willis in my palm. I find it hard to keep the smile from my lips.

'But there have been reports of preparations by the London

regiments, and rumours that ships are sent to guard against invasion from Flanders,' Thomas says. 'Parliament knows something is afoot and someone has told them.'

'A precaution,' Leventhorpe says, 'such as any sensible man might make at such a time. The situation is precarious. Those with any power left must do battle among themselves to take the lead – even those whose thoughts now turn to the King.'

'And do they turn to the King?' I ask.

'In any struggle for power there will always be those who try to claw their portion,' Thomas says, taking a drink. 'While the army and Parliament squabble among themselves, it can only aid the case for monarchy. The republican experiment has failed and the people are disillusioned. They long for the stability that only a true king can bring. And there can be no pretender this time. Charles Stuart is the one man who can unite us all.'

'Must you fight, if there is already such thinking?' Rachel asks. 'Is there not a more peaceful way?'

I imagine she is thinking about her brother, wondering which way his loyalties will fall should it come to it. He has already broken her heart once for the same arguments. If he were to fight against the King this time, he might break mine.

'God bless you,' Thomas says, 'but we are a long way from peace. Much depends upon a show of military strength. Such a victory would prove the support for His Majesty and quell all doubts. We are talking about men – men who saw a war – and they understand nothing better than swords and guns. It is the way of the world, the best way for a man to prove his worth. God will show us whose side He is on, in the end.'

The two of them talk as if they know something of war. They know nothing of the battlefield, save the stories they heard at their fathers' knees. I suspect I have witnessed more bloodshed than either. I have risked my life more times than they. The cut on my neck has healed well, leaving only a thin red scar that I cover with a neckerchief, but I have not forgotten how it felt to have that blade at my throat.

'We must clear a path for the King to return,' Leventhorpe continues. 'We must give him a sign that the country is ready. Only then will he come and take back the throne that was snatched from his father.'

Thomas raises his cup. 'Well said, Leventhorpe, well said.' He puts a hand on his friend's shoulder and their eyes lock. I see the understanding between them. They are become a pair, coupled by this endeavour.

I feel a pang of loss. This is how it used to be with Rachel and me, and now we sit here like strangers. I am jealous too, jealous that my own husband is able to live his life so openly, when I am forced to sneak and lie, divided from Rafe by the confines of duty. Why should Thomas have what I want most? He calls me 'wife' but he is no husband to me. Even his visits to my bed have ceased in these last weeks. The affinity I see between him and Leventhorpe convinces me that Richard Willis is right. I am not the only traitor to our marriage vows.

Chapter 41

Ware Park is quiet without the men. Thomas and Leventhorpe are gone, taking their horses, their weapons and most of the workers with them. Those of us left behind are listless, paddling in late-summer swelter. Petals drop from August roses and strew the paths in blood-red drifts. The borders are wild with weeds. Fat, lazy bees drone in the lavender. All is still and calm. We are waiting for the storm to break.

I wander the grounds, no energy or willingness for household tasks. I ride across the fields, fretting over how we are to bring in the rest of our meagre harvest. I stop in the village and watch the women pulling thin purple carrots from their kitchen plots, fetching water from the well, children and chickens fussing about their feet. They nod and bid me good day but I note the accusation in their looks. My husband has taken away their men, and we are all left behind with nothing to think about but what will happen if they do not come back.

I am alone when the letter arrives.

The youth who brings it is a stranger, with a head of unruly dark curls. I have no coin to give so I send him to the kitchens to find his payment in bread and cheese.

I know immediately that the letter is from Rafe. I recognise the slope of his hand. I run to my chamber and tear it open. The words are scrawled and the ink blotted, as though written in haste.

The rising is betrayed. Soldiers are sent to put down the rebellion and arrest the leaders. You are in danger. Come to me as soon as you can.

My body floods with panic. I read the note again.

How can Rafe know this? I'm sure the hand is his, but it makes no sense. He has no connection and no love for those men loyal to the King, so why should he have knowledge my husband does not? And who is the traitor? Richard Willis's image passes in my mind's eye, but there is no time to unravel the mystery. It is Thomas's fate that concerns me now. Despite everything, I would not wish a bad end for him: a dead husband will be of little use should the King eventually claim his throne. I would not have the watching eyes of the world turned upon Ware Park when I have my own reasons for discretion and privacy.

I snatch up my quill and quickly scratch a letter of my own. In the kitchens I find the messenger hunched over a bowl of pottage. Master Stone stands guard.

'Will you take this note to Thomas Fanshawe at Sawbridgeworth?' I ask the youth.

He looks up from the bowl, spoon midway to his lips.

'Now?'

'Yes, and with great haste. It is very important. You must deliver it into his hands alone, do you understand?'

The boy puts the spoon down and leans back. 'How much is it worth?'

Master Stone clips the back of his head. 'Mind your manners.'

The boy yelps. 'I'm not doin' it for nothin' but thin pottage and weak ale.' He pushes the bowl away.

'Master Stone, this is urgent,' I say. 'Do we have another boy to spare?'

Master Stone gives a brief shake of the head. The boy sees his chance slipping away. 'I'm your man, mistress. Just want what's fair.'

'Can we spare a penny or two?' I ask.

Master Stone frowns. 'If you wish it, m'lady, but should we trust—'

'Please fetch it.'

The boy grins. He wipes his mouth on his tunic and holds out a hand to take the letter. 'Thomas Fanshawe and no other, you say?'

'Yes. And you must be fast. Have you a good horse?'

'The best,' he says. 'Get me the silver and it'll be done.'

It is already darkening by the time I reach the clearing in Gustard Wood.

I had thought to find Rafe there, expected a fire to welcome me, have been imagining the safety of his arms on my long ride, but the place is abandoned. The shack stands empty, rabbit droppings and pigeon feathers strewn across the floor. The outside hearth is cold. No one has been here for days. But I'm sure he will come.

I lead Feather to the stream and tether her where she can drink and graze. In my haste I did not stop to collect food but my stomach is too cramped and churning to eat. I splash the cold, clear water on my face. It cannot wash away the misgiving that creeps in my gut, or the sickness that rises in my gullet.

Darkness creeps and still there is no sign of Rafe. I make a bed for myself beside the hearthstone. There is no need for a blaze, but once the heat of the day is gone, I shiver inside my cloak. I think about trying the truckle bed inside the hut but the doorway looks eerie and uninviting. Instead, I fetch candle stubs and the lantern, hoping to make a little light for myself, but I cannot find the tinderbox. The moon is thin and offers little brightness. Beneath the trees, all is black. I take comfort from the sound of Feather's movements; the snort of breath and muffled tread on mossy ground. My ears strain for the sound of Flight's hoofs – every rustle in the undergrowth has me staring into darkness, willing Rafe to appear. But he does not come.

By first light I'm wretched with sleeplessness and unease, worn out by a night of tormented waiting. As soon as the birds begin to sing, I draw out his note and study it, and these words in particular: *Come to me as soon as you can*. With no other rendezvous he must have meant me to come here, to the one place that is ours.

I wait until the sun rises, the treetops come alive with birdsong, and the shadowy place that terrified me by night has retreated once more.

When I fasten Feather's bridle she champs at her bit and skitters sideways. No doubt she thinks we are to ride out on Nomansland Common.

'Not today,' I say, letting her nuzzle my hand, wishing with all my heart that she were right. Though the fear of night has left me, I'm consumed by the conviction that something is terribly wrong.

I'm back at Ware Park by mid-morning, and just in time. I'm stabling Feather when there are shouts from the yard, the ring of hoofs on cobbles, someone calling for water. I leave Feather in her stall and hurry outside. The sight that greets me takes me back to another time. I am a child again, in Oxford, watching the King's troops return from battle.

A bedraggled gathering of men, dressed in a mismatched array of colours, beaten breastplates and iron pots, fills our little yard. The air rings with curses and the stench of saltpetre. Thomas is in their midst, Leventhorpe too, slumped in the saddle, head bobbing and rolling as though he might fall at any moment.

Rachel runs from the house, Master Stone close behind. She is drawn up short, her hands go to her face, eyes wide.

Thomas is caked with grime, cheeks streaked with mud. The strapping has come loose on his breastplate and it hangs lopsided and forlorn. There is no sign of the new feathered hat he was so proud of. He draws up his mount, surrounded by others, equally dishevelled. Master Stone moves to take the reins while Thomas eases himself from the saddle.

Thomas grasps his arm and leans heavily. He limps a few steps and I see a dark stain against the grey wool of his breeches.

I go to him. 'Husband, are you injured?'

He waves me away. 'A mere scratch. See to Leventhorpe.' He reaches the mounting block and sits, drawing deep, shuddering breaths.

I glance over my shoulder to see that others are helping Leventhorpe from his horse. His head lolls but he is awake and groaning in pain.

'Bring spirits!' I call. 'See to it that these men are looked after.' I realise there are few nearby to take my orders. Rachel hovers at my side.

I turn back to my husband. 'What happened?'

'They knew our plans to the letter.' Thomas winces as he speaks. His eyes are red and wet. 'They surprised us, attacked at first light. We were not ready . . .'

'I sent warning. Did you not receive my note?'

He looks puzzled. 'No . . . there was no note.'

'There is a traitor in the Great Trust. The rising was betrayed. I sent word as soon as I could.'

Thomas shakes his head. 'It did not reach me.'

'Then damn that boy. Damn him . . . and damn me for trusting him.'

Thomas looks from me to Rachel to Master Stone. His eyes cloud with bitterness. 'Then it was a sham from the start.' He puts his head in his hands. 'And I was the fool who was taken in. These men, they trusted me . . .'

'It's not your fault,' Rachel says quietly. 'Come now, you must rest. We must get you inside.'

I look about me. I see now that several of the men are injured. Leventhorpe is slumped on the floor next to his horse, one of the kitchen lads trying to make him drink something from a beaker. He pushes it away again and again, muttering to himself like a madman. 'Rachel, take my husband to his chamber and see to his care. Master Stone and I will look after the rest.'

Rachel nods. She puts her arm around Thomas's shoulders. 'Come, let me help you.'

He leans against her as he struggles to stand. There are tears, tracking their way through the dirt on his cheeks and he hides his face against Rachel's shoulder, so that his men cannot see.

Later that day a letter arrives from Viscount Mordaunt. He orders that the rising is to be cancelled immediately. The Great Trust and Commission has a traitor in its midst and Parliament has learned of their plans. Any action now is far too dangerous. His Majesty's loyal servants will have to wait a little longer for justice.

The letter is dated three days since. I wonder why such an urgent missive took so long to reach Ware Park.

Chapter 42

They come at night. They muffle the horses' hoofs to quiet the clatter on the cobbles. They brandish burning torches and their swords are drawn.

I'm sleepless yet again and at my window to witness the iron-barred coach draw up. It's a small party – about six men on foot, two on horseback and a driver to command the carthorse. All wear the russet coat of Parliament's army. I'm taken back to that long-ago day at Hamerton, when soldiers came to pillage our stores and left us desperate. The horror of it comes back to me, the filthy taste of Captain James's boot, quickly followed by the familiar flare of hatred that has still not died. There are some wounds that time will never heal.

The stable lad comes blinking and yawning from the hayloft. He moves sleepily to take hold of the horses' reins. The men confer, voices so low I cannot hear them. The boy gestures to the main door of the house.

My skin prickles into goose bumps, the hand of dread upon me. What can these men want, creeping like a band of brigands in the dead of night? My first thought is of Richard Willis. Has he sent them for me?

There has been no word from him in the two weeks since the failure of the uprising. Thomas received news that Willis is ordered to Brussels to face Charles Stuart and the charges of treachery laid against him. He and Leventhorpe, both now recovering from their injuries, disappointment and wounded pride, are reluctant to believe that Willis is the traitor. I feel sure of his guilt. If Willis knows I am in possession of a letter that proves it, might he not move to discredit me before I do the same to him?

How I wish Rafe were here. He would know what to do. But I've had no word from him either, since that brief scribbled note. My longing for him is a constant leaden weight. I have written cryptic letters to the Chaplin farm, and have returned to Gustard Wood twice more since that fearsome night, but each time the place was as deserted as the last. I have no idea where he is or when I shall see him again. I'm afraid that Willis has had a hand in this too.

My instinct is to run, but where would I go? I cannot reach the stables with soldiers watching the yard. I would get nowhere by foot and I cannot leave Feather behind. My mind races ahead, imagining myself trapped inside that closed cart, clutching at the barred windows as they take me away. No, I cannot run. There is only one real choice. I will have to face them.

By the time I've calmed myself enough to descend, I find Master Stone, dressed in nightshirt and cap, in conference with two of the soldiers. The poor man's face is haggard and drawn, bare feet turning blue on the cold flags.

They speak in hushed tones but in the silence of night, their voices resound.

'Do not raise any alarm, sir, there is no need to wake the household,' one of the men, likely the captain judging by his dress, says. 'Tell us where we can find him and we will do the rest.'

'Please, let me fetch him myself.'

'No, I insist. Show us the way to his chamber. You are delaying us.'

'I cannot let you disturb my master in this way. Can it not wait until the morning?'

'I'm afraid time is pressing.' The captain beckons two men who come forward, hands on the hilts of their swords. 'If you will direct them, my men will see it done with the least disturbance.'

'There must be no violence in this house,' Master Stone says. 'For pity's sake, there are women and children here.'

'This house is harbouring traitors. I cannot allow you to stand in our way or you become party to the same crime.'

Any relief that they are not here for me is quickly tempered by other fears. I take a deep breath and try to steady my trembling hands. 'Traitors, Captain? That is quite a claim.' I hitch my skirts and make my way down the staircase. The men's attention turns. The captain removes his hat and the others follow. 'This is my house and I do not harbour traitors. Please explain your presence here.'

Master Stone's eyes are panicked. 'M'lady . . .'

'Lady Katherine.' The captain gives a curt bow. 'Forgive the disturbance.'

'I take it you wish to see my husband,' I say, reaching him and standing as tall and proud as I dare, though the man towers over me. 'It's late and he is in his bed. Master Stone is right: he's not to be disturbed. May I be of assistance?'

'Madam, with regret, I have a warrant for your husband's arrest.'

Although I already know the answer, I ask, 'Under what charge?'

'Treason, m'lady. Conspiracy to overthrow the government.'

I pretend shock. 'Let me see this warrant.'

The captain beckons his second, who pulls a folded paper from inside his coat. He unfurls it and passes it to me. Master Stone tilts his candle so a pool of light falls upon the page. Thomas's name is there, alongside Leventhorpe's. They are to be taken to London and placed in the Tower.

I linger over it, trying to buy time. My heart is beating fast and I breathe deep to steady it. Whatever my feelings towards Thomas, this does not bode well for me. Whatever end they have in mind for my husband, if he is found guilty, they will strip away any remnants of his wealth, land, the house in which we stand, even his name. I do not want to be made a penniless nobody by a gallows death.

'Naturally, I would like to conduct this business with the least distress to yourself or your household,' the captain says. 'But I must carry out my orders.'

'I shall fetch my husband myself,' I say, working hard to stop the tremor in my voice. 'If you will grant me that one kindness, Captain?'

He hesitates a moment, studies my face.

'As you wish. Watkins, accompany Lady Katherine.'

The man at the captain's side steps forward.

Master Stone hands me a bunch of keys and shows me which one will open the door to Thomas's chamber, should it be locked. 'I'm sorry, m'lady,' he whispers, with desperate eyes. 'I'm so very sorry.'

Two others fall in behind Watkins as I lead them up the staircase. They are careful to tread lightly, and my hopes of creating some fair warning begin to ebb. Still, I go slowly, pausing at the head of the stairs and feigning a moment of distress. Watkins sighs and clears his throat, no sympathy for my poor play-acting.

We reach Thomas's door and I raise my fist to rap upon it. Watkins reaches out, catching my wrist.

'Just open it,' he says.

My heart is tumbling. I slip the key into the lock and turn. I open the door.

The light from Watkins's lantern spills across the boards, picking out the deep ochre of turkey carpet and a silver flask, slowly dripping a puddle of claret wine. Candles are burning low in the wall sconce, casting a warm, honeyed light. There is a pungent musk, sweet and heady; the scent of heated, spent bodies.

I see the landscape of two figures beneath the coverlet.

My heart leaps into my throat. 'Thomas?'

There is sudden movement and the coverlet shifts.

Then she sits up.

The candlelight catches the soft gleam of pale skin, the shine of auburn hair and amber eyes. She says his name, puts her hand out to nudge my husband awake.

For a few moments, I am turned to stone.

Watkins pushes me aside, strides into the room and draws his sword. 'Thomas Fanshawe, you are under arrest for conspiring to overturn the government of this country. I have orders to take you to the Tower, where you will await trial for treason.'

Thomas shifts, turns, wakes abruptly. He curses, says something, but I know not what, for my ears are made deaf by a pounding rush of blood. My vision blurs with a tunnel of white light, but still I cannot take my eyes from hers.

Rachel holds my gaze, brazen as a cheap tavern whore.

Thomas is not the real traitor in this house.

Chapter 43

Three days later and I'm alone in my chamber after dark, idling by the window, watching clouds scud across a yellow harvest moon. Since Thomas was taken I've been plagued by torturous dreams, snatching snippets of sleep that leave me wretched and exhausted. I cannot rid my mind of the images that taunt me. And I cannot stop the twin blades of jealousy and spite twisting deep in my chest. I have not cried – I am too angry for that – but every night I sit and wait for the grey light of dawn on the horizon, consumed by torment.

Rachel is gone. She left before I could cast her out, knowing, I suppose, that that was what I would do. By the time Thomas had been taken away in that iron-barred coach, shackled at ankle and wrist, like a common felon, she had slipped away, unseen, into the night.

Now both brother and sister are lost to me.

I have no right to be angry when the sin only mirrors my own. But fury and hurt do not abide by reason. There is no logic when a heart is betrayed. And jealousy is a cruel companion that dogs me night and day, snaps bitterly at my heels and allows me no peace at all.

Something glimmers faintly in the corner of the walled garden, drawing my eye. I strain to see through the bubbled glass of the casement. I make out the shadow of a figure, concealed in darkness beneath the wall. It moves, comes forwards into a patch of moonlight, takes form. My heart makes a great leap.

I am downstairs in a moment, unlocking the garden door. When he reaches me, I fling my arms around him, no longer caring whether we are seen. Beneath his air-cooled cloak Rafe's body is warm, heartbeat quick, matching my own. He smells of wood smoke and sharp sweat. His mouth finds mine and the taste of him is both familiar and freshly thrilling.

There is too much to say so I say nothing at all. I take his hand and lead him silently up the staircase and into my chamber. I turn the key and lock the world out.

Later, we lie side by side, bodies cooling. My head rests on his chest. He strokes my hair.

'I heard they arrested your Thomas. I feared they might take you too. I came as soon as I could.'

'They've put him in the Tower.'

'Thank God you're safe.'

'If they find him guilty, they could execute him,' I say. 'And make him a martyr for the King. I will lose this house, no doubt, and be outcast and destitute. I don't know what I'll do.' I tilt my head to see his reaction.

'They will not dare go so far.'

'He is a traitor to them, Leventhorpe too, and all the others caught along with them.'

'They say the Tower is so full of royalists that Charles Stuart might make himself a new court there, but there are others of more value than your husband. They will want to humble him, to be sure, but no one wants more killing. They will not execute these men for fear of reprisals, should the day come when a new king dictates who lives and who dies.'

'How do you know these things?' I prop myself on my elbows,

all my questions coming to the fore. 'And how did you know that the rising was betrayed?'

Rafe shrugs. 'Gossip.'

'I thought you'd given up on politics.'

He says nothing but strokes my hair absently. I know he is keeping something from me. 'Please be true with me, Rafe. That night, when I got your note, I went to Gustard Wood. You told me to come to you but you weren't there. I've waited almost three weeks with no word from you, fearing the worst.'

He catches my hand and squeezes it. 'Kate, I had to stay away. Your Thomas will be released in time, I'm sure of it.'

'Why do you call him that? He is not my Thomas any more.' I cannot hide the bitterness in my tone. 'I think he belongs to your sister now.'

Rafe is silent.

'Do you understand me?' I say it deliberately. 'Your sister and my husband – I found them together.'

As he gives a slow nod, I realise. 'You knew.' I pull away from him and sit up. 'You knew about this . . .'

'Yes.'

Suddenly I'm plunged back into a mire of secrets. 'How long? How long have you known?'

'Some months.'

'Months?' I drag myself away from him, standing, pulling the linen sheet and winding it around my shoulders. 'My God. Is it common knowledge? Am I the last to know?'

'Kate, come back to bed.'

I turn my back and pace the boards. 'How could you do this? How could you keep it from me?'

'I would save you further hurt. You distress yourself for no reason.'

'My husband and my oldest friend betray me, make a fool of me, and you say I have no reason. Are you so heartless?' I'm dimly aware that I'm walking a dangerous path but I cannot stop myself. 'You are the one who insisted on honesty between us, and now I find you have not kept your promise at all. Is there no one I can trust?'

'Kate, calm yourself.'

I'm trembling with anger, with Thomas, with Rachel and now with the man who lies naked in my bed. 'How do you know about this?'

Rafe rubs at his temples. 'Rachel told me herself. She told me she loves him.'

'When?'

'After she found us together at Markyate Cell.'

'But that was months and months ago. You have kept this from me all that time?'

'I had no choice. I struck a bargain with her – her silence for mine. Why do you think she's told no one about us? She's afraid of you, you know, afraid of your temper. She knew that you would cast her out if she spoke against you. The only way to stay near to Thomas, and you, was to be silent. She still loves you. More than anyone. So we agreed, on the condition that I told you nothing. And she has kept her word, for all our sakes. I thank her for it. She could have made things much harder for us.'

My mind reels, the facts of my life rearranging themselves. 'So all these months she has been with him when I thought . . .' I remember how I watched Leventhorpe, night after night, since Richard Willis first put the idea of Thomas's infidelity into my mind. Did I misunderstand his meaning from the start? I think of how Rachel sat with us in the evenings, quiet and watchful, a softer, kinder, more amenable version of myself. I have been blind all along, looking for betrayal in the wrong places.

'Why should you care so much,' Rafe says, 'when you do not love him?'

'He is my husband and she . . . I thought she was my friend . . .'

'You've chosen a different path. You gave them both up the moment you chose me. I'm glad of it. Now, come back to bed.'

But I'm furious with him. 'They've made a fool of me. And you have helped them.'

'No one makes you a fool except yourself. I'm sorry if I've added to your pain – I meant only to protect you – but I thought you would see it clear yourself, and when you did, it would not matter to you. Your pride may be injured but, I hope, not your heart.'

Perhaps he is right but my feelings are too tangled to decipher. Only one thing is constant: the way my heart pulls towards his, even in the midst of anger.

I climb back on to the bed and sit opposite him. 'You must never keep a secret from me again. Never. You must promise it.'

He leans back against the bolster. 'Kate . . .'

'You must promise me.' I'm afraid he is still holding back. 'Is there something more? Some other secret? Please, Rafe, I would know everything.'

'Kate, there are some things I cannot tell even you.'

A cold, hard bolt of steel slides in my innards. 'You demand my honesty but refuse to give it in return. That's not a fair bargain. I cannot go on with this if you keep things hidden from me.'

'For the sake of your own safety, there are some things I must keep back.' His wide eyes shine almost golden in the candlelight. He takes up both my hands, brings them to his lips. 'You must trust me, Kate.' He kisses each palm in turn. 'And I will tell you this: tomorrow I must leave Hertfordshire and will be gone some time. That is why I came. I had to see you one last time before I leave.'

Anger is instantly replaced by a low, curdling dread. 'Do not leave me alone again.'

He bows his head. 'I do not wish to, but I must. I must travel north. There is something I need to do – a commission I must complete. Our safety and our future depend upon it.'

'What commission?'

'If I tell you, I place you in greater danger. You have to trust me.'

'How can I trust you when you've kept secrets from me all these months?'

'I won't defend myself. I ask for your trust once more. It's up to you whether you choose to give it. I hope that you will.'

He holds my gaze intently. Though my guts are churning, I cannot refuse him.

'How long will you be gone?'

'A few months. Maybe more.'

I imagine the winter stretching out, alone at Ware Park through the hard, frozen months. The thought chills me. 'So long . . .'

'I will return. Do nothing hasty in the meantime. Do you have money?'

'A little, but not enough.'

'You must make it last. Do not think to act alone. Keep yourself safe.'

He pulls me close and strokes my cheek. 'Where is the letter you took from Willis?'

I think of it, hidden beneath the floorboards. 'Somewhere safe.'

'Good . . . keep it so. Show no one else.'

He wraps his arms around me. I cannot help but sink against him, feeling the tug of my body towards his.

'Will you be in danger?' I ask.

'Perhaps, but I'm used to that.'

'How I wish we could ride out together again.'

'We will, when I return.'

'It will be winter. It will be cold.'

'Then we will wear furs.'

I bury my face against his chest and breathe in the scent of his skin. 'I wish I were free to come with you.'

He shifts down the bed, pulling me with him and rolls on top of me so that his hair falls forward and tickles my cheek. He cradles my face in his hands. 'I will come back for you, I promise. Be patient. It will be worth it, in the end.'

I watch him leave in dawning light, early autumn mist rolling in the hollows. It swaddles him in its pale shroud, stealing away my last glimpse, leaving my battered heart doubly bruised.

When he is gone, I stand alone on the terrace for a long time, unwilling to turn back towards my cold, empty bed. I have never felt so alone. The mist swirls, creeping up my thighs, caressing my belly, dampening my eyelashes in place of the tears that will not come.

1660

Chapter 44

The air is bitter, numbing, scratching at throats. In the woods, on the edge of Nomansland Common, the trees are stark and bare, offering little protection and few places to hide. Fallen twigs snap and crunch under the horses' hoofs. Feather's mane glitters with frost. Holly berries droop, waxy leaves laden with the last of the Twelfth Night snowfall. The common is a white sheet, a giant's coverlet spread across the sleeping land. But here and there, where the snow is melting, gorse bushes rise in patches of green. And along the road, the thaw is evident.

Rafe is convinced that the weather will not stop them. He is sure they will come today.

I shiver, despite the thick winter clothes I wear, taken from Thomas's chamber: a doublet, breeches, a heavy cloak and leather boots that I have packed with yarn to make fit. Though these garments are not made for my frame, they offer more warmth and freedom than my skirts and, I hope, serve as a better disguise. My fingertips are turning blue inside my riding gloves, but I do not mind the cold. I would stand any discomfort. I have waited four long months for this day.

Rafe has heard that a rich transport will be passing this way – a coach containing some northern lord's profits from a Spanish ship taken at sea. If the spoils are already stolen, he reasons, why should we not take our share? I watch him as we make our way to the edge of the forest for a clear view of the road. His face is almost hidden by thick woollen wrappings, his hat pulled low, but I can still see the intense glitter in his eyes.

When his mind is on the task in hand, nothing will distract him. I know that this single-minded determination is the same quality that keeps him bound to me, and I would not change it.

The last few months have been a slow torture. Thomas still rots in the Tower and I am still too angry to care. Alone at Ware Park, I've had nothing to do but write begging letters to my Fanshawe relatives. Most of the servants have given up and left. Any money that the family can spare goes to keep Thomas comfortable in the Tower, and there's nothing left for wages. Without the extra coin from my work with Rafe, those of us left at Ware Park suffer winter's hardships more than ever. Scouring the pantry for half-rotten onions and mealy oats, scrounging the last dregs from the cider barrels, I have felt myself driven half mad with boredom and relentless hunger.

I have not seen or heard from Rachel, and even Martha Coppin seems to have abandoned me. There has been no invitation to Markyate Cell all winter long. I expect that the disgrace of Thomas's arrest is the cause, but it matters little. I do not think I could bear Martha to welcome me into that house, to compare her circumstances with mine. It would remind me too much of all the things I have lost, all the things she has that should belong to me. The injustice of it chafes like an open sore.

Rafe came to me at Ware Park, the night he returned from his journey north. He came with a heavy purse and a gift: a pistol, with fixings wrought in fine, shining silver. It is a thing of quality, the metalwork engraved with roses, the wood inlaid with ivory, the flint and workings all clean and precise. He tells me it belonged to a gentleman he met on the road, but will say no more than that. I am too pleased to care about its provenance. But he did not stay and would not tell me anything more about what kept him away so long.

We wait three long hours for any sign of travellers on the North Road, and at last they come.

A coach with no markings climbs slowly out across the common. The coachman sits huddled on the box, another man next to him, musket propped against one shoulder, barrel pointing skywards to the flat January clouds.

'It will be safer to take them in the woods,' Rafe says, frowning. 'We cannot make speed in the snow and we must give them no warning.'

We turn the horses and skirt the edge of the common. It is easy to get ahead of the coach, and place ourselves in its path, where the trees begin and the road narrows. Brambled banks slope steeply on either side of the road. Any coach stopped here will be trapped, unable to turn.

Hidden amid the tree trunks, I cannot see the coach make its progress, but I can hear it – the musical jangle of harness, the creak of a complaining axle, the squeak of wheels on the slippery ground. The snow drips from branches, making a rhythmic patter. The woods echo with the lonely caw of rooks.

I take my new pistol from the saddle holster, checking once again that the shot is packed tight and the flint gripped in place. On the opposite bank I catch glimpses of Flight's dark flanks moving between the trees. The butterflies dance in my chest. I smile to myself. I have missed this feeling.

I pull the black kerchief up over my nose and make sure the knot is tight. Feather's breath steams, drifts up to the branches, mingling with my own. I hold out the gun, finding a target in my sights, feeling the heft of it, weighing the balance. One shot is all I have, but it will be enough.

I hear the long, low whistle I know as my cue. I urge Feather forwards, positioning her at the top of the bank. I can see the coach now, the horses making slow progress through the woods, hoofs skittering on the ice, wheels juddering over the frozen ruts where the road has not felt the sun's reach.

When it is almost upon us, Rafe spurs Flight out from the trees and down the bank. She slides and stumbles. He has to pull on her reins to keep her head up, but they make it, slithering onto the road to block the coach's path.

He draws out a pistol. 'Stop your horses!'

The coachman reaches for his whip, flicks the horses' rumps, but there is nowhere for them to go. They cannot gain speed on the ice. The man with the musket fumbles with the powder kegs at his belt. If his gun is not loaded, we have time and advantage.

'Stop your horses!' Rafe repeats. 'Or I'll shoot.'

From my position above the road I train my gun on the musketeer. The coachman hauls the horses to a stand. They stamp and whinny at his rough treatment.

'We have nothing of value,' the coachman calls, 'and look for no trouble.'

The man with the musket is hurriedly tamping down the powder, but his fingers are numb with cold. He drops the rammer and watches, open-mouthed, as it bounces out of reach to the ground.

'Throw down the gun,' Rafe says. 'Now . . .'

The man hesitates, glancing around. He sees me. To my astonishment, his lips twitch into a smile.

'Do as he says,' the coachman orders, following his eye line.

The man tosses the musket to the ground.

Rafe keeps his gun trained on the coachman and brings Flight alongside. 'No doubt you have more protection than one pitiful musket.' He cranes to look down the side of the coach. He glances up at me. I make the signal – there is no sign of movement inside the coach.

'You inside,' Rafe calls out, 'ground your weapons and come out, one at a time.'

'There's no one inside,' the coachman says.

'Quiet. Come out, or your man will lose his life.'

There is something eerie about the silence. My ears strain but all I hear is the drip of melting snow and the creak of trees. I search the black and white landscape for anything amiss, but see nothing.

'I'm telling you, there is no one else here, and we have no cargo,' the coachman says. 'There is nothing for you to take, Rafe Chaplin.'

At the use of Rafe's name, my hackles rise. Something is not right. But Rafe ignores him.

'I will not give you another chance,' Rafe says. 'Step out now, or pay with blood.' There is uncertainty in his tone I do not like.

But still there is no reaction.

Rafe looks up at me and indicates that I should cover him. He cannot take Flight down the side of the coach for fear of becoming trapped there. There is no room for her to turn and flee should there be trouble. Instead he dismounts, disobeying his own first rule. My guts begin to churn. I keep my gun level, trained on the two men atop the coach, though the weight of it causes a dull ache in my arm.

Slowly, Rafe makes his way along the side of the coach. He has left his pistol in the saddle holster and, instead, draws out a sword. 'It's not wise to disobey me,' he calls. 'Open up and ground your weapons.'

Silence.

He puts one hand on the door handle and slowly turns it, slides the tip of the sword between the door and the wall of the coach.

The long, straight barrel of a musket meets it.

Rafe curses and tries to slam the door. He throws himself to the ground as there is a great, shattering crack. A plume of smoke and spark belches from the coach. Beneath me, Feather takes fright. She rears, loses her footing and begins to slide down the bank. I cry out, almost losing my balance, clinging to the pommel. She slithers on to the road, almost crashing into Flight. Both horses dance and kick, but I manage to keep my seat. I reach out and grab Flight's reins.

Rafe clambers to his feet, slipping on the ice. The door of the coach slams open and a man climbs out. He is squat and broad, with a mean ugly face. I recognise him: the constable from Ware. He tosses the smoking musket aside and draws a sword. Another man steps down behind him and another from the opposite door of the coach. They are armed with blades and cudgels.

I try desperately to steady Feather and struggle to level the pistol once again. I find my target in the constable, who now makes his way to Rafe. Rafe is on his feet, sword raised in challenge, tensed like an animal in a trap.

'Rafe Chaplin,' the man says. 'There is no point in fighting. You are outnumbered.' He widens his arms to indicate the woods around us and I see now, emerging through the trees on either side, several dark, shadowy figures.

Rafe gives a frustrated curse, but stands his ground, brandishing his sword.

The constable laughs. 'Save your fight for the lawyers.' He twitches a hand towards me, instructing his men, 'Take this one too, and the horses. Don't let her get away.'

My breath comes in short, hard pants but my mind is sharp, as though the sudden panic has cleared the confusion. From where I sit, there is a clear line to the constable's head. I raise the pistol. 'Tell your men to lower their guns or I will kill you.'

He laughs. 'Pull that trigger, you'll be dead in seconds. Give up. You've no choice.'

Rafe's words come back to me. *There is always choice.*

Rafe is steadily backing away from him and towards me. At last he catches hold of Flight's bridle.

The constable's expression changes as he sees his quarry slipping away.

'Shoot them!' he cries. I hear the splutter of matchlight, the burst of gunpowder, the hiss of a bullet as it rushes past, too close to my ear. The rooks flap and squawk in the treetops.

'Stop!' I cry. 'Call off your men. I swear I'll do it!'

'You do not have the stomach, girl, nor the will. You may dress as a man, act as a man, but you do not have the mettle of a man.'

His words spark something in me – something that has been buried for too long, some kindled rage that suddenly burns white-hot, so scorching it can only be Hell's flame.

For a moment I am crazed, intent on destroying this man. I am raw, desperate and powerful. I swear, if I had a knife I would gut him and laugh as his innards spilled. If I had a sword I would take pleasure in watching the arc of blood as I spliced his neck.

I raise the pistol, using both hands so my aim is sure and steady. I do not even give him another chance. I pull the trigger.

I'm shocked by the force of the blast, and Feather jumps and quivers beneath me, but the bullet finds its home. The man crumples to his knees. The one eye that remains is rolled back, white and wild. The other is a dark, charred hole, where blood begins to spurt. He falls to the ground.

'Go!' Rafe yells, swinging himself up into the saddle. Then the air is rent with the crack of musket shot, the acrid stench of powder and the shouts of men. I wheel Feather about, the pistol hot and smoking in my hand, and will her to fly faster than she ever has before.

Chapter 45

'It was a trap. I'll make it my business to find out who set it.'

Rafe is lying on his back on the truckle bed inside the hut in the clearing at Gustard Wood. The tiny space glows with the honeyed light of a single candle flame. I try to ignore the scratch of rushes, the rough woollen blankets and the itch of biting fleas. We are safe here, for now.

I want to lose myself in the closeness of Rafe's body, pressing against him and burying my face in the hollow of his collarbone, but every time I close my eyes, all I see is the bloody mess of the dead man's face.

'I've been a fool,' he says. 'I should have suspected that word of the transport came to me too easily.'

'Where did you hear of it?'

'I overheard some men at the White Hart. Perhaps their conversation was meant for me.'

'But who would go to such lengths?'

'Those who would profit by my end. There's a price on my head – on yours too.'

The thought surprises me, although it shouldn't. 'How much?'

'I don't know, but after today yours will be worth more than mine. The thief-takers won't like the loss of one of their own. They'll certainly seek revenge.'

'That man was the constable from Ware.'

'And a known thief-taker. We could not have picked a worse fight. The only protection you have now is that they did not see your face, and they don't know your name. But it's only a matter of time before they find us both.' He sighs. 'I should not have come back. It was foolish to think they would not come after me.'

'Do not say that.'

He is silent awhile. Outside the night resounds with the hoot of a single owl, and the muffled shifting of the horses from their makeshift shelter in one of the other dwellings. I shiver and wrap myself around him, drawing the blankets close.

'It's time to put an end to this,' he says. 'I would never forgive myself if something happened to you.'

I feel a thrill of nerves. Now is the moment to tell him. 'It is not your choice. No one makes choices for me any longer. I have a husband in the Tower and a friend who betrayed me and abandoned us both. There is not much left for me to lose. I have no one except you. You and one other.'

I take his hand and move it down to rest upon my belly.

I watch his expression alter as he understands. His frown melts. 'Truly?'

I smile and nod.

'When?'

'Before midsummer, I think.'

I have known since the weather turned and the leaves curled and dropped from the oaks in Ware Park. I suspected when I did not bleed, but I knew for certain when my breasts ached and my stomach turned at the savour of broth from the kitchens.

I had thought, after so many years, that I could not bear a child. I am barren, I told myself, and not a worthy wife. I thought that God had ignored my prayers, that the Devil had planted his own evil in my womb, and his seed kept me childless. But it seems it is not so; with Rafe, the curse has been banished.

'A child . . .' he whispers, his voice cracked and awed.

All these weeks I have hidden the truth, with no one to share my secret. I did not know whether Rafe would welcome the news as I do. But now he reaches for me, kissing my face again and again. He presses his lips to my eyelids, my cheek, my neck, moves down to my throat and chest, his hand gently stroking my stomach.

'We must go away from here,' he says, from between my breasts. 'You must come away with me.'

I take his face between my palms and he pauses, raises his eyes to mine.

'I cannot leave,' I say.

'We're not safe in Hertfordshire, and you have nothing left here.'

'Where would we go?'

He thinks for a while, propping himself on his elbows. 'When I travelled north, I stayed for a time in a place well hidden from prying eyes. It's far from any town or highway. We might be safe there.'

'What place?'

'It's on the northern coast. Some people have set up a home there, a gathering of like minds. They are good people. They might take us in.' There is a wistful look in his eye. 'They take shelter in an old, deserted castle, on the edge of the sea.'

I laugh. 'Then you would make our lives a fable indeed. Tell me, when did you dream this?'

'It's real enough.' He is not smiling with me. 'The castle is long abandoned, but there's food and warmth. The people there told me a widow by the name of Alice Craster made it a haven, in the days of old Queen Bess. She's long gone, but others carry on her work. They farm the land and take in those willing to help. They sheltered me for a while. They seek a peaceable life, and the land-lord turns a blind eye, provided there's no trouble. It's a forgotten place. No one would think to look for us there.'

'But who are these people?'

'I did not ask for their stories and they did not ask for mine, but they welcomed me like a brother all the same. I think, if I were to return, they would give us refuge.'

'What took you to such a place?'

'That does not matter now. What matters is that I keep you safe.'

'But how would we get money? How would we live?'

'We would join with them and work the land. The people there share all.'

'They are Diggers? By God, are there still those who would live in that way?'

'Think on it – if we had a home and food and a fire, what need have we for aught else? I would be a farmer once again. We would be free of this constant danger. I could return to a life I once loved. We would not have to worry about the law or the thief-takers or where to snatch the next purse.' His eyes are earnest. 'And you . . . you would be my wife.'

There is a tightening in my throat. This picture does not tally with the hopes I have for myself. 'I already have a husband,' I say.

'I am more husband to you than he has ever been.' He fixes me with such a passionate look that my heart squeezes.

'But, still, the law says I am his.'

'Since when did you have a care for the law?'

'I have a home here.'

'At Ware Park? You hate it there. Why are you making reasons to stay when there are none?'

'I don't mean Ware Park but Markyate Cell.'

'Markyate Cell has not been your home for years.'

'Markyate Cell will always be my home.'

He shakes his head. 'It belongs to the Coppins now.'

'It is the Ferrers house. It is rightfully mine.'

He takes my hands in his. 'Kate, if we are to have any chance of a future, you must give up this childish obsession.'

'I will never give it up. I cannot.'

'What is there to gain from a dream that will never come true?'

I pull my hands from his and take hold of the heart-shaped charm around my neck. 'You think it pointless but I know that one day Markyate Cell will be returned to me. That is why I cannot leave.'

He sits up. A draught of freezing air rushes beneath the blankets. The shine is gone from his eyes and instead a hard glint settles there. 'You accuse me of creating fables yet you are the one living in a fantasy. I believe in hope, Kate, but there comes a time when we must leave the past behind and move ahead. We have a chance now, a real chance, to choose a different path. You tell me you hate the life you were born to, so why not leave it behind?'

'I do not hate it. It was a good life, once.'

'Kate, those days are gone. They will never return. You are waiting for something that will never happen.'

'But if Charles Stuart returns—'

'What then? Everything will be restored to the way it was before the wars? Don't be a fool, Kate. You cannot believe that your story will end so neatly. You are not suited to that life – you never were. I've watched you. I've seen how desperate you are to be free. Why else would you do the things you've done?'

'I do them for need of money. I do them for you.'

'You do it because you like it. Because it makes you feel alive. Because it makes you feel free. I know, because I'm the same.'

His words silence me. I do not want to admit that he is right. I may have taken this sinful path out of desperation, but it has become so much more.

'You have a real choice now,' he goes on. 'You can leave all that behind, take on a new name and make a new family – one made from love, not riches and duty and subjugation. Make a new life with me – with me and our child.'

'You mean for us to live as beggars, gypsies, wandering the lanes, begging our bread from outcasts in a broken-down ruin. I cannot live like that. I was born to better things. My child will be born to better than that.'

'Have these last years not taught you that your birth no longer grants the privilege it once did? What happiness has it brought you?'

I pull myself away, tugging the blankets around my shoulders so that he is exposed to the cold air. 'I will be happy when Markyate Cell is returned to me.'

'So you will choose this foolish dream over a life with me?'

'And what is your castle by the sea but a foolish dream?'

'I tell you, it's real. And if not there, then some other place where we might live free. I'm tired of always watching over my shoulder. If today proved anything, it's that it won't be much longer before I'm caught, or killed. People know me, and what I've become, and there are those with a hold over me. If I'm ever to be free, I must get away, and soon.'

I stare at him. 'What do you mean? What people?'

He makes a dismissive gesture. 'I'm decided. I must leave Hertfordshire. I want you to come with me.'

Suddenly my heart is writhing in my chest, and a sharp pain strikes between my eyes. 'You cannot leave.'

'I must. We were lucky to escape today, but now they have all the more reason to find us, and next time they'll be better prepared. If I want to live my own life, be my own master once more, then I have no choice.'

'You said there is always a choice. Why can we not go on as before? If we are more careful . . .'

He shakes his head. 'We cannot risk it. Not now, not with the child. If I'd known, I would never have let you ride out today. We must leave and begin anew. It's the only way.'

'And if I cannot, will you leave me here alone?'

'You are carrying my child. You must do as I say.'

'I will do as I please.'

'But the child is mine.'

'The world does not know that. The world will know it as a Fanshawe. If it's a boy it will be Thomas's heir.'

Rafe's face crumples. 'You cannot wish that for our child.'

'I must think of what's best. If Thomas is released and the King returns, the Fanshawes will be rewarded handsomely for their loyalty. My son will have Ware Park one day, and a house in London, and Markyate Cell too, God willing. When he's grown he'll be rich and have a place at court. In the meantime he'll be warm and well fed. He will be safe. What mother would not wish that?'

Rafe stares at me. Then he tosses back the blanket and climbs out of the bed. Despite the pinch of cold, he stands naked in the glow of candle flame. 'Rachel is right. You can be cruel.' He picks up his breeches and undershirt and pulls them on. 'Why even tell me, if you mean to keep the child from me?'

'I only want what is best.'

'Best for whom? It seems you care more for wealth and position than you do for truth and love.'

I open my mouth to protest but he cuts me off. 'Well, if it's riches you want then you shall have them. There's to be one last robbery before I've finished with it. I'm promised gold and plenty of it – enough to buy the freedom I want.'

'What robbery? What are you talking about?'

'I do not have the details yet, but they will come. If I attempt it, it's certain I can never return here, where I'm known. I will leave for good.'

'Is this more tavern talk?' I ask. 'The same as nearly cost your life this night?'

He pulls his coat on, breath steaming, and steps into his boots.

'This time, I know it's true. I have it direct from Richard Willis.'

Now it's my turn to be shocked. 'Willis? What has he to do with this? Has he spoken with you? You cannot trust him.'

'I'll take my chances.' He picks up his hat in silence and collects his saddlebags, slinging them over one shoulder.

'Wait, where are you going? How do you know Richard Willis?'

He shoulders Flight's bridle and drapes his riding cape over one arm. He leaves the hut, a rush of icy dawn air taking my breath and making me shiver. I swaddle myself in my cloak and follow him outside. The birds have started to sing. Pale light creeps through the canopy.

'Rafe, don't leave me here alone. Come back inside and tell me about Willis. You mustn't listen to him. He can't be trusted.'

He strides over to the horses and untethers Flight. He flings the saddle over her quarters. She gives a disgruntled grumble as he tightens the girth, then fixes her bridle.

'Please . . .' The ground is freezing and my feet are turning numb. 'Come back to bed. Don't leave me here.'

But my pleading does not sway him. He mounts, brings Flight about. The two horses whicker to one another.

'I'm done with your double-dealing, Kate. You must make up your mind. You must decide whose side you are really on, and if you are for anyone other than yourself.'

He clicks his tongue and urges Flight to a steady trot down the pathway between the trees. He does not even look back.

Chapter 46

The chimneys of Markyate Cell are swathed in low grey cloud. The casements are blank, shuttered against the chill. But smoke is billowing from the bakehouse and a fresh-faced stable lad comes running to take Feather's reins when I ride into the yard. Though he tries to hide it, I see the enquiry in his eyes as he registers the pistol holster still attached to my saddle. I know how I must look to him, my face streaked with dirt and tight with salt.

When I left the clearing in Gustard Wood, I could not go back to Ware Park. I could not face another day alone in that prison. When I reached the road, I turned Feather west instead of east without a thought, as though Markyate Cell called me home.

Rafe's words have cut deep but I'm angry with him, too – for leaving, for trying to impose his will upon me, for trying to make me choose between him and the one thing that means more to me than all else. If he thinks I would throw away my long-held hopes for some momentary fancy of his, he does not know me. He is not alone in his iron-cast determination to get what he wants.

Though I have lived long in the poverty of these stricken years, I was not born to it. I turned to the road, and to Rafe, out of desperation. He is right about some things – I have come to like this wild life – but I would give it all up in return for the riches that are my birthright. The child in my belly might be born with the name Fanshawe, but he will have Ferrers blood in his veins. If there is the faintest chance that he might be master of Markyate Cell one day, I must hold fast to it. To turn away from that would be to betray myself, my parents, and everything the Ferrers family once stood for.

If the rumours are true and the King is close to returning, then surely Thomas's estates will be restored and we will profit. That is the life I was born to, the life I should have. I intend the same for my child. I cannot give up everything to live as a beggar in some forgotten corner of England. If Rafe truly cared for me, as I'd thought, he would not ask it of me. Our affinity, which I believed perfect, is tarnished in my eyes.

The stable lad holds Feather steady as I climb down by the block. I take the pistol from the holster and hide it inside my saddlebag. Martha comes out of the house. The boy darts sly little glances from the corner of his eye and I press a finger to my lips to beg silence.

'Lady Katherine . . . what a surprise. I received no word to expect you.' Martha wipes her hands on her stained apron, quickly removes it and tosses it onto a stool by the kitchen door. She comes towards me, noting my reddened eyes and the dirty, tattered state of my dress.

I take her hands in mine. 'Martha, may I stay here with you awhile?'

She searches my face, a little cleft appearing between her brows. Others have gathered in the yard. They stare and whisper.

'Of course,' Martha says. 'You are always welcome here.'

She would not say that, I think, if she knew what I had done.

'Is it possible,' I say, 'that God will forgive even the most grievous of sins?'

Martha says nothing. We are settled in the parlour, the remains of a barely touched meal beside me. She leans back in her chair and leaves a long silence, a space into which my voice starts to spill.

'I have done something. Something terrible. But I did it to help someone I love. Surely God will understand that.'

Still she does not respond.

I remember the feeling that came upon me as I aimed the gun and knew I was not afraid to fire. In that moment, I wanted the man dead. There was no doubt, no hesitation, and, if I'm honest, I do not feel the remorse I ought. I would do the same again. This frightens me. The Devil has a tight grasp on my heart. He is slowly turning it to stone, while he sets other parts of me alight.

'I think I am damned.' I look up at Martha. 'I will never be good, like you.'

Martha folds her hands in her lap. There is no judgement in her expression; neither does she move to comfort me.

'You know, my mother loved this room,' I say. 'I remember playing here when I was young. Markyate Cell always seemed to be filled with sunshine then. I know it cannot be true, but I do not remember a single winter. It seemed always summer, before my brothers fell ill.'

Martha breaks her silence. 'We do not always remember the hard times. Sometimes our memories are kind to us and lock such things away. Especially when we are too young to understand them. But if we are not careful, they stay inside us, like slow poison, sickening us from within.'

'You think I have such a sickness?'

'It is not for me to judge. What do you think?'

'There is something . . . something I have never told anyone.' I long to unburden myself but I'm afraid that if I tell, Martha will cast me out, and I cannot bear to leave this house again.

Martha sits forward. 'If you choose to, you can trust me.' She has such a plain way of speaking, such calmness about her, that I believe it.

'I fear . . . the Devil came to me, a long time ago.' I am shaking as I speak, the horror of last night finally coming to rest. 'And ever since . . . he makes me do things, puts thoughts into my head.'

The little crease reappears in Martha's brow. She watches me intently. 'Did he come to you in worldly form?'

'I . . . I don't know. There was a man, once, when I was young . . .'

'Did you enter into a pact with him?'

'Not in words, but . . . perhaps in deeds, though it was not of my choosing.'

Martha lets out a little sigh. When she speaks her voice is without blame. 'I once asked if you were ready to renounce your sins. You promised me that you would. You have not kept that promise. I would help you, if I can, but I cannot if you continue to lie to me.'

'There is so much . . . so much I cannot tell you.'

'I am not as unacquainted with the truth as you might believe.'

'You do not know what I have done.'

She pauses, watching the flames lick the burning logs. 'There are tales of highway robbers, at large in these parts. I hear the servants' gossip. They say there is a woman who robs innocent travellers, as boldly as any man. They say she is some man's doxy, a wild and wicked thing.'

The blood turns in my veins.

'Some say this woman has the strength of ten men, and bested some big brute in a tavern brawl, that she will slice the neck of any man who dares challenge her, that she takes man after man into her bed, giving herself to strangers, but can find none to satisfy her. I've heard all this and more. Now, I'm not one to believe in tall stories, but I can pick out the fact from the fiction.' She fixes me with a frank stare. 'You are that woman, are you not?'

For a moment I hesitate. To confess is tempting but I cannot begin to imagine the consequences. She leans forward and reaches out a hand to bridge the gap between us, her voice gentle and coaxing. 'I know, Kate. I know it is you. Please own it, so that I may help you.'

In that one moment of tenderness I am done with the hiding and the lying. I feel a powerful compulsion to tell her everything. How sweet would be the relief of all my wicked secrets shared.

'There is no truth in those stories. It is not like that . . .'

She understands my confession and squeezes my hand. Then she releases me and sits back, the ghost of a smile upon her lips.

Now it is done there is no turning back.

'Will you turn me in?' I ask, my voice small, like a child's.

'No,' she says. 'I have suspected the truth for some time and I have considered it. I will not be the reason for your disgrace. Both you and Master Chaplin would hang and I would not have that on my conscience. There are better ways . . .'

'Then will you help me?'

'If you will allow it.'

A sudden rush of relief overpowers me. I had thought myself utterly abandoned and now Martha offers herself as a new ally. I knew there was a reason I had felt the need to come to Markyate Cell. I kneel on the floor next to her chair and put my hand gently upon the cloth of her skirts.

'You are so good to me. How can I thank you?'

She shakes her head. 'I offer you time, that is all. I offer you a safe place to stay while you decide your path. I offer you the opportunity to repent, to prove your intention in God's eyes. The outcome is not within my control, or even yours.'

'What must I do?'

'You have already begun. I felt sure that you would come to me one day, when you were ready. Then, and only then, might I help you find your way back to Him. This is only the beginning for you.'

'It feels like the end.'

'Every end is also a beginning. You must put all your trust in God.'

'There is something more . . . Yesterday I . . .' But I cannot say the words aloud: I killed a man. I am a murderer.

'Do not tell me your sins,' Martha says. 'I cannot offer the redemption you seek.'

'But you can forgive me.'

'I can offer you a warm bed, and sustenance, as is my Christian duty, but I do not pretend any more than that. Only God can forgive you. It is between you and Him. Confess all and there is hope for you.'

At this moment, all I want is to sleep in my mother's bed in the scarlet chamber – the thought of a soft mattress, a warm fire, a safe retreat into memory and dreams . . . I want to hide away there for ever. I would do almost anything for it.

Martha stands, dusting off her skirts. 'Will you do it?'

'If you ask it.'

'You must do it for yourself, not for me. And you must mean it. Can you do that, truly?'

'Yes.'

'Then come with me.' She rises and offers a hand.

I stand. My legs are weak and I feel small and insubstantial next to Martha's solid surety. She takes my hand and leads me from the room, towards the family chapel that we used so often on Sundays.

We pass through rooms that are filled with memories: here the corridor where the servants would gather to gossip, the turn of the staircase where the cook would leave titbits for us children to find; there my favourite window seat, with a view across the park, where I would sit on chilly mornings, making patterns with my breath upon the panes.

I crave sanctuary. Markyate Cell is the only place I feel safe, the only place I belong. What I said to Rafe was true, and in this moment, the prospect of respite from the world is worth everything.

I do not know if God will be as forgiving as Martha, I doubt that He will even hear my pleas, but Martha's request is a small price to pay for what I might gain.

We reach the chapel. Martha stops outside the door.

'I will give you some time alone. Remember, Kate, God is all seeing. He already knows what is in your heart. Confess it all, unreservedly, and ask for forgiveness. He will see that you are in earnest.' She kisses me on the cheek. 'I will wait here for you. Take your time.'

I open the door to the little room and slip inside. This chamber was not built as a chapel but was made into one many years ago and I have always known it as such. It has no grand decoration, no church paintings or patterned walls. It is a simple room with a makeshift altar and several benches, just enough space to seat a family and their guests. Thin January light filters in from the single high window.

There is a figure kneeling at the altar.

I know it is Rachel before she turns her head. I can tell by the familiar slope of her shoulders, the strands of auburn hair come loose from her cap, winding down her back.

My heart tightens.

She turns at the sound of my footstep on the flags. She blanches, eyes wide and full of shock. She struggles to her feet. And as she does so, her hands go to her belly, cradling it where it begins to swell, just like my own.

Chapter 47

It is past four o'clock and the light is already fading when Thomas's carriage draws up outside Ware Park.

All day I have been fretting about what I will say to him, running the words over and over in my mind. I must be careful and clever. I must not let my temper get the better of me. Survival is what matters now. I have nowhere else to go and no one to turn to, so I must turn to the man who is bound to me by law.

When I received word that Thomas was to be released from the Tower, any relief was soon tempered by churning apprehension. It bodes well for the King's cause if his supporters are set free, but my concern now is my own fate.

Though my belly is not yet large, Thomas will see the changes in me. He will note the thickening at my waist, the swell of my breasts, and he will guess what it means. I have counted the months since he last visited my bed and, if he does the same, he will know the child cannot be his own. He will see my betrayal clear. Will he be kind to me, knowing that his own conscience is not clear? This is the only thread of hope I have left.

After I found out the truth about Rachel, I could not stay at Markyate Cell. The darkness that consumed me was like a black fog. I became crazed by fury. I rushed forward and pummelled her with my fists.

I tore at her hair and scratched her face, like a wildcat. Her screams brought Martha running and she pulled me away. A man held me down as I cried out against all the pain and betrayal, my last hope shattering into a thousand pieces. I swore curses against God. Why has He given Rachel the things that should be mine?

Martha tried to calm me. She tried to explain how Rachel had come to her after finding the Chaplin farm deserted and no sign of her brother, how she had taken her in, hoping she might play some part in our reconciliation. She told me that Rachel is penitent, praying for hours every day in the chapel, as if she were a convent novice. But I care nothing for Rachel or her new-found piety – I have no more faith in God.

So I ran.

In the end, I returned to Ware Park, carrying a raw emptiness, as if I had swallowed a hundred ravening crows. They pick and tear at the meat of me, consuming from the inside out.

Master Stone takes Thomas's arm as he steps down from the coach. I barely recognise my husband: he looks exhausted, hollowed out. He leans on a cane. He's been gone for five months, but it has aged him as many years.

He does not greet me as a husband should but gives me a hard, disappointed look as he climbs the steps and goes into the house. He says he's tired from the journey and wishes to go straight to his bedchamber. But now we are together, I have a burning urge to confront him. After so long, it is torture to wait a moment longer. So I follow him to his bedchamber, the room where I last saw him with Rachel.

I see that Master Stone has prepared well. A fire is lit and candles glow in the sconces. A jug of wine sits upon a table. The bed has been made ready to receive him. At the sight of all this, sparks of anger ignite. Despite my own sins, I have not forgiven him.

'Husband, why do you not greet me?' I notice his eyes are ringed with new creases.

'Why have you neither visited nor written these five months?'

'You know why.'

He sighs. 'Katherine, I'm very tired. I must rest, and you must wait until tomorrow. We shall talk then.'

'I have waited this whole winter.'

'Then one more day will not matter.' He goes to the table and pours the wine. There is only a single cup and he offers none to me. He stands, one hand rubbing the small of his back.

Despite all my best intentions, I flush with fury. 'I am your wife and you will not dismiss me as if I'm some serving wench. You will speak with me now.'

I step quickly to his side and knock the cup from his hand. The red liquid splashes onto the white linen of his undershirt and drips onto the floorboards. The cup bounces on the rug and rolls away towards the fire.

'What, in God's name—'

I cannot help myself. 'How could you betray me in my own house – and with her?'

'Five months in the Tower and this is my welcome?'

'Answer me.'

I raise my hand to strike his chest but he catches my wrist. 'For God's sake, calm yourself.'

'I will not be calm! Five long months I've been trapped here, not knowing what might become of me, deserted by my husband—'

'You think I deserted you? I've been captive in the Tower, in fear for my life.' His own anger is stirred. 'And this is how my wife greets me? By God, I know you never loved me, but do you even have a heart?'

'She was my friend.'

'From what Rachel told me, your friendship was ruined long ago.'

'And you have ended it for ever. It was you took her away from me. You took my only friend. You do not want me to be happy.'

He snorts. 'You are being ridiculous.'

'You are no husband to me. You are selfish and weak, and I knew it the day we wed. I am not surprised your uprising was a failure. You are incapable of such things. You are barely a man at all.'

His eyes flare then. 'You will not speak to me in this way.'

'You will hear what I have to say.'

'You will go to your room and calm yourself. I'll speak to you in the morning when you're recovered and ready to obey me. And you will send her to me.'

'What?'

'Send Rachel to me.'

For a moment I cannot speak, I am so astonished by his cruelty. But now I have the upper hand. 'She's not here.'

'What do you mean?'

'She does not live here any more.'

'Where is she?'

'I have no idea. In some bawdyhouse, no doubt, along with the other whores.'

He comes close and takes me by the shoulders, fingertips digging into my flesh. 'What did you do? Where did you send her?'

'Did you imagine us both pining away for you? I was glad to see you gone. And it was a pleasure to be rid of her, for she reminded me of you.'

'If I find that any harm has come to her . . .' His voice is strangled. He slumps on the bed, drained by his outburst. 'You were never a good wife, not even for one day. You were always cold to me. You laughed at me, despised me, made a fool of me. It's true this was never a love match, but we might have been comfortable together. You made that impossible.'

'How dare you blame me?'

For a moment there is hurt in his eyes, but it quickly dissolves. 'A man must have a wife and a marriage bed. It is his right. A man must have heirs. You are no use to me. You cannot even do the one thing you're made for. You are nothing but a spiteful, barren harlot.'

I cannot help but say what comes next. 'You're wrong about that. I am not barren.'

He looks at me, shaking his head. 'God has not blessed this union. Not even once.'

'I am not barren.'

He must read the triumph in my expression, must see something, because he stops short then. I put my hand to my skirts and cradle my belly. He stares. I feel his eyes move over my body. Now it's his turn to be astonished.

'How long?'

There is no point in lying, for time will surely expose me. 'I believe there will be a child born in June.'

There is a long silence. Then Thomas stands. His fists are trembling. He comes towards me and takes my wrists, pinching the skin so it burns. 'You accuse me of sin when you are no better. Whose is it?'

I say nothing.

'Is it Willis? I've seen the way you look at him, the way he pants after you, like a dog.'

'Not him.'

'Who, then?'

'I will never tell you.'

'You are my wife and you will do as I say.' There is a strange level to his voice that I've not witnessed before. There is a threat in it that frightens me.

'I will not. I will never do as you say. You cannot control me.'

'We'll see about that.'

He drags me to the door and slams it open, calling for Master Stone.

'Let go of me.' I twist against him but his grasp is surprisingly strong, his sword arm still well muscled. He drags me along the hallway. I trip and bump into an old oak chest, bruising my shins. I cry out, 'Stop – stop this!'

'You will do as I say,' he repeats, through gritted teeth.

Master Stone comes running up the stairs as we reach the door to my chamber, followed by one of the kitchen lads. Thomas opens the door and drags me inside.

'Stone, Lady Katherine is unwell,' Thomas says, panting and red-faced. 'She must rest, undisturbed.'

I run at him and begin to beat my fists against his chest. 'Liar!'

Thomas grabs hold of me again and forces me back towards the bed. 'She's extremely disturbed, as you can see. She's not herself. For God's sake, help me, man.'

Master Stone and the boy stand agog, but at Thomas's order they come towards me. They take hold of my arms and legs. I do not have a chance against them. The three of them manhandle me onto the bed, while I kick and struggle, cursing like a Bedlamite.

'There now, Lady Katherine,' Master Stone says, putting his hand over my mouth. 'You must be quiet.' I snap at his fingers.

Thomas turns to the kitchen boy. 'What have we to calm her nerves? Can you fetch brandy? Master Stone, what have we in the way of herbal?'

'Help me, Master Stone,' I say. 'It's a lie, I'm not ill.' But they are holding me down, talking above my head as if I'm insensible.

'An agitation of the mind, I think,' Thomas is saying. 'Brought on by her condition.'

I see a glimmer of understanding dawn on Master Stone's face. 'So, there is good news, sir?'

'Yes, Stone. We must do everything we can to make sure Lady Katherine is kept calm and undisturbed until her confinement.'

'Oh, glad tidings indeed,' Master Stone says, smiling, his hands loosening a little. 'I'll attend to her myself. What a happy day for us all.'

'Master Stone, don't listen. He's lying . . .'

The kitchen boy soon returns, carrying a tray, upon which sit a mug and a small, stoppered bottle.

'Ah! Tincture of poppy . . . clever boy,' Master Stone says. 'Take her legs.'

Thomas leans over me heavily, his knee pinning my chest to the bed. Beneath him, I cannot move.

'Please, Master Stone, there's nothing wrong with me,' I gasp, as he comes towards me, stirring the mug. 'I'll be calm now, I promise. Just let me go.'

Master Stone looks to Thomas, who shakes his head. 'I'm sorry, Katherine, but this is for the best.' He nods to Stone. 'Continue.'

Master Stone positions himself by my head. I turn my face away.

Thomas buries his fingers in the flesh of my arm. 'Drink.'

'Please, Lady Katherine,' Stone says. 'It will help. Just a little, enough to calm you.'

I try to resist them, using all my strength to force myself up, but they are too strong for me. I twist and turn, screaming for all the demons in Hell to rise up and burn them to cinders. Foul words fall from my lips but that only makes Thomas more determined.

In the end they pour the stuff into my mouth. The boy holds my head so I cannot spit it out onto the pillow.

Once it is done, Thomas orders a rope fetched from the stables. He lashes my wrists to the bedpost.

Soon, a strange sensation begins in my belly – waves of gentle, pleasant sweetness, as my mind begins to drift. I no longer have the desire to struggle, or even lift my limbs from the bed. I want to sleep. I am bone-weary. Nothing would be more pleasing than to close my eyes and fall into a deep and dreamless slumber, where I can forget everything.

'Now, where is the key to this chamber?' Thomas's voice seems far away.

'In the lock, sir.'

'Good. We'll leave her now. Let her sleep. Keep watch over her, Master Stone, and put a boy outside the door through the night. She must not leave this room, under any circumstances. For her own good, you understand.'

That is the last I remember before my lids slide shut and I am lost in swirling, velvety darkness.

Chapter 48

'Where is she?'

Thomas is standing by the window, back to the room. Rain patters against the panes, wind screams down the chimney. I do not know how long he has been standing there. I am swaddled in a waking dream.

'Where did you send her?'

I'm dimly aware of a movement in my belly. I move my hand down and rub at the underside of the deep curve. It grows heavy and taut with the child inside. The baby is shifting. Beneath my palm I feel the sudden kick of a limb. I smile to myself.

'If you tell me, and she is brought back safely, I will allow you a little more freedom.'

It is hard to focus on Thomas's words, or discern his meaning. I would like to be left alone, alone with my dreams, alone with the child in my belly. My world has become small, the only fragments of joy to be found in the child's occasional stirrings.

'I have told you, I don't know where she is,' I say quietly.

'I don't believe you.'

I turn onto my side and close my eyes, willing him to leave me so I can sleep.

'If you ever had a care for her, you must tell me what you know. Anything.' Thomas's voice is like an echo. In these last weeks, sometimes he is here and oftentimes not. I do not know which times are real and which are of my own imagining.

'You must not let your jealousy be the cause of future regret. I only wish to find her and make sure she is safe. Surely you would not wish her harm. Please, Katherine, tell me where she is.'

'I have nothing to say.'

I open my eyes and see him turn towards the bed. With the light behind him, his face is in shadow.

'Very well, then. I have given much thought to our . . . situation. I have decided that you will stay here, at Ware Park. When the child is born, I will accept it as my own. If it is a boy, he will become my heir. You are my wife, after all, and no one else need know that the child is not of Fanshawe blood.'

Rafe will know, I think, remembering the shine in his eyes when I told him. I picture him smiling as he stroked my belly, kissing me again and again. Through the dreamlike fog, my heart gives a little twist. Where is he now? I wish he would come for me. But I fear he will not forgive me. I fear I have made a terrible mistake.

'The child will be mine by law and mine by name. Do you understand?'

The child will never be yours, I think. The child is mine. You will not have him.

'The child will be given to a wet nurse. You will stay here and be a dutiful wife and mother. You will not leave Ware Park without my permission. You will make no visits and receive no guests without my approval. You will not ride out beyond the bounds of the park, without a chaperone chosen by me. Is that clear?'

I realise that my cheeks are wet. I am too tired to argue.

'Katherine, do you understand?'

'Yes. Please leave me alone.'

'Tell me where Rachel is.'

But already I feel the heaviness of sleep. His features blur and his voice becomes an echo.

I wake in a sweat. Flames are blazing high in the hearth and the room is airless. It is daytime, though the light is peculiarly dim. Mist shrouds the window. I rise, thick-headed and uneasy on my feet. My mouth is parched, drool crusts my chin. I am fully clothed, though I do not remember dressing. I go to the door and try the handle. Locked, as always. I tap against the wood.

'Please . . . let me out.'

There is a shuffling outside. I don't know who Thomas has stationed there as watchman, but there is always someone, day and night.

'I need air. Please . . . open the door.'

'I cannot.'

'I beg of you . . .'

'Are you ill, m'lady? Do you need a physician?'

'I just need to step outside for a moment.'

There is a pause. 'That's against my orders, m'lady. Let me call for Master Stone.'

'Please don't. Never mind.'

I go to the window. The gardens are mostly hidden by a grey veil of mist. I fumble with the handle to the casement. It is jammed shut. Looking closer I see that a nail has been driven into the wooden frame to fix it in place. I do not remember this happening either.

I feel faint. Has Thomas really gone so far as to make my chamber into my prison cell? I do not know how long it has been since I left this room but it must be weeks. Days bleed into one another.

I slump down on the seat by the window and put my fingertips to the pane.

I cannot live like this. I cannot be captive for the rest of my days. If I stay here, if I agree to Thomas's conditions, I will run mad before the year is out.

If I accept, my child will be brought up a Fanshawe. My child will be kept safe and given riches, while Rachel's child, Thomas's true blood heir, will have none of these things. My child will be assured of position and status. It is what I thought I wanted. But now I see the true cost. And I find I am not willing to give up my own life to make sure that my child bears a certain name. I am too selfish to make that sacrifice. My own title has never brought me happiness. It has only constrained me, making me trapped and bitter, bringing me, step by step, to this miserable, wretched state.

By keeping me here Thomas means to break me, to make me the submissive wife he always wanted me to be. He has achieved the opposite. I see now that I cannot stay with him, not for all the titles and riches in the world. I have been blind to the things that are most important.

I think of the stars, blinking in the blackness over Gustard Wood and my heart lurches. Rafe was right: I want to live free. I want my child to be brought up in love, not in bondage and lies. I want a life where I can make my own choices. If I stay at Ware Park, life will be nothing but a slow, torturous crawl towards death. I will not be a martyr for any cause, not for all the coin in the country.

I must find Rafe. I must tell him that he knew me before I knew myself, and that I'm ready to give up everything for a life with him.

Just then I see a figure in the garden below. Someone is walking swiftly away from the house – a woman, dressed in a long dark cape. I recognise Martha Coppin.

I'm on my feet in an instant, rapping upon the glass. 'Martha! Martha!'

The woman stops, turns back a moment and scans the gardens.

It's hard to see through the mist, but I'm sure it's her. I call louder and knock my fist against the pane until it rattles in the casement.

She raises her face to look up at the house. For a moment I'm sure she sees me and I wave frantically, but her expression does not alter. She lingers a moment, then turns and walks away.

'Martha Coppin was here,' I say to Master Stone, when he brings my supper. 'Why did no one fetch me?'

'I know nothing of it, m'lady.' He will not meet my eye.

'Come now, Master Stone. I saw her in the gardens. What did she want?'

'Here is your physick.' Stone puts the cup next to me. I have not taken my draught these three days. I have disposed of it in the chamber pot when Stone turns his back.

'Did she speak with my husband?'

'There was a lady visitor. And she did speak with the master.'

I try to still the panic that rises. Has Martha told Thomas about Rachel? Is she done with harbouring a sinner in her home? Is Rachel coming back?

'What did she say?' I ask.

'They spoke in private, m'lady.'

'Master Stone, you are my friend, are you not?'

'Your willing servant, as always.'

'No.' I clutch at his sleeve. 'Not my servant, but my friend. I need a friend now. Remember all those winters when Thomas was away in London? Remember how we struggled? How we worked together in the gardens to bring in enough food to get us through? How I worked alongside you, and you taught me to sow the cabbages, how to know when the carrots are full-grown. We were friends then, were we not?'

He nods, a little sheepish.

'Will you help me now, as I helped you then?'

'The master has given strict instructions . . . I cannot disobey him.'

'All I require is a tool, something I might use to loosen a nail. Can you bring me such an implement?'

'For what purpose?'

'Will you do this one thing for me, as my friend? No one else must know.'

He makes a mumbling sound that might be consent and will not be drawn on the subject again.

The next day, when he brings my supper, in place of a spoon, there is a knife and a small, pronged fork beside my plate.

Chapter 49

Three days later he comes for me. I knew he would. I could feel it in every breath, every heartbeat. I knew it when I watched the sky, the night after Martha's visit, and the mists cleared to reveal a full moon and a single brilliant star glimmering on the horizon. But I was sure of it this afternoon, when I found the note beneath my bowl of pottage:

Tonight. Be ready to ride.

The hand is Rafe's.

Master Stone has proved his loyalty.

I have loosened the nails in the casement so I can slide them out with ease. I have packed a small bag with a few clothes, though I find the breeches and the black kerchief are missing from my closet. I pick my simplest garments, leaving the threadbare velvets and silks for someone who still cares about such things.

I wile away the hours, staring at my wedding portrait. That young girl is dead and gone. I feel sorry for her, sorry that she suffered under the yoke of her birth for so long, sorry that I held her captive. Now she looks so small and innocent in her borrowed dress and her mother's jewels – playing a part for which she was never meant. I must forgive her follies and mistakes. I must leave her behind, in the past.

I snuff the candles in my room so that no one can tell I'm awake so late and wait silently by the window. A glow filters from beneath the door and every now and then I hear the gentle sounds of sighing and shifting as my guard settles for the night. It must be almost one, the house fallen still and silent, when at last I see him, a dark shadow skirting the lawn.

My heart starts to skip as I slide the nails from the casement, turn the handle and open the frame. I must be as silent as I can. Climbing up onto the window seat, I lean out. Beneath there is a small drop onto a flat roof, where the downstairs chamber extends in a rounded bay. From there, I must climb over the crenellations, and lower myself to the terrace below.

I wait for him to reach me. When he tips his face upwards, the moonlight catches the slope of his cheek and the glint of his amber eyes. I almost cry out in relief.

'Are you ready?' he whispers.

'Yes.'

'Then come. Feather is waiting for you.'

I toss my bundle down onto the roof, wincing as it makes a dull thud. I draw myself up onto the sill, step through the opening and sit on the edge with my legs dangling. I will have to duck and squeeze through but, despite my belly, I'm still small enough to fit. I protect my stomach with one hand as I push through the gap, the edges of the casement scraping my skin.

A few moments and I'm through. I drop to the roof below. It is not far, but still I crumple to my knees, my legs weak with lack of use.

Quickly I toss the bundle down to Rafe and take a moment to prepare, peering over the ledge.

'I'll catch you.'

I climb over the barricade of stone and find a footing on the outside rim, a thin ledge above the window. The height can be no more than two men, I tell myself, but it seems much more, and my body, once so bold, quivers. I'm frightened for the child. But then I look down and see Rafe there, arms outstretched, ready to receive me. I make my choice. I let go.

The inn is shabby, a small wayside establishment set back from the North Road, where Rafe has paid more than he should for a room, stabling and the keeper's silence. The taverner is long gone to his bed by the time we arrive in the dead hours of night and the place is in darkness. We put Feather and Flight in the stables and Rafe finds a lantern to light us to our bed. The room is small and meanly furnished with whitewashed walls, a lumpy mattress, a low table and stools before a cold hearth. But I don't care. I am free.

Rafe shuts the door and fixes the latch without letting go of my hand. He pulls me to him and our mouths meet, teeth clashing in urgency. His hands are under my cloak, pulling at the fastenings, flinging it away so that he can wrap himself around me. The swell of my belly is crushed for a moment until he draws back to look at me.

He puts one hand to my stomach, one to my face. 'I'm sorry I left you. I'll never do so again.'

'Nor I you.'

'I must know that you are with me, for good this time.'

'I'm sorry for all the things I said before. I was wrong.'

'Will you come away with me? You and the child?'

'Yes.'

'What about Markyate Cell?'

A lump rises in my throat. I swallow it, put my palm to his cheek and say, 'I will give it up.'

'Then, I promise you, all will be well.'

He kisses my neck, unties the lacings at my throat. I know I have done the right thing, and I want so much to believe him, but I am afraid. I cannot go back this time. I can never go back.

'All will be well,' he whispers, slipping his fingertips beneath my shift. A wave of wanting sweeps from the pit of my belly. I close my eyes as his tongue plays lower. Yes, I must believe it – all will be well. I can believe it, when I am lost in him.

Just then the door slams open with a splintering crack as the latch is torn from its fixings.

Rafe moves suddenly, reaching for a pistol that is missing from his side. Men spill into the room. In the dim light I cannot tell how many.

Then the world becomes a blur: the thunder of boots on bare boards, the grate of steel on steel, the stench of latrines, pig fat and stale liquor, the guttering candle, a blade at my throat.

A man with a lantern comes into the room. He wears a black hat with a glinting silver buckle.

'Well, well, two fish caught in one net. My luck has turned at last.'

'Willis—'

The man with a dagger at Rafe's throat lifts it, silencing him. Rafe swallows hard and raises his hands as Richard Willis smiles.

Chapter 50

'My terms are simple.' Richard Willis takes a sip of wine. 'You will each play for the other. If Kate is the winner, then you, Master Chaplin, will be allowed to go free, for now, but she will be placed in my care.' He takes another sip and turns to Rafe. 'If you beat us both, sir, then Kate will be free, but you shall come with me to face the magistrate and, no doubt, the gallows. And if I am the victor, I will decide on the justice that is due and you will both accept it without argument.'

He puts his cup on the table and draws out a small ebony box. Inside is a pack of playing cards and a handful of small bone counters. He fetches the cards out and shuffles them idly, one hand to the other. 'Do we have an understanding?'

'I would not stake Kate's life in such a way,' Rafe says. 'She is not some possession to be wagered.'

'I took you for a gaming man, Master Chaplin. You disappoint me.'

Rafe lowers his voice. 'You promised protection. We had an agreement.'

'That suited me, for a time, but no longer. You played your part well enough, but now the tide is turning. I no longer have any use for you.'

'Then you're a liar as well as a traitor.'

Willis smiles. 'I've been called much worse than that in recent months. You'll have to do better if you mean to insult me.'

Rafe's jaw is flexing, eyes fiery. I rest my fingers on his forearm. We must keep our wits about us now. Argument will not help our cause, so we must humour Willis. We are outmanned and cannot fight. They have taken our weapons. Two rough men, armed with swords and cudgels, bar the door, and there are more waiting outside in the yard.

'Let us play,' I say. 'What choice have we?'

'There now, she has the truth of it. You always did like a little sport, did you not, Kate?'

Willis divides the counters into three piles and slides one towards me, another to Rafe. Then he leans forward and deals the cards face down into three hands, twelve apiece. The pack is brightly painted, colours flashing between his fingertips. 'A game of tricks seems most apt. Best of three seems fair.' He places the remaining cards in the centre of the table, turning over the trump to reveal a seven of spades. I know the game. I've played often enough. It might seem simple, requiring luck, chance and a steady will, but I've watched enough gamesters at work to know that cunning will always determine the victor.

'Come, drink,' Willis says, nudging two cups towards us. Rafe does not touch his but I drink and am grateful for it. The wine is bitter-edged, stinging my throat, tasting of sour blackberries, but it warms me. Willis has had a fire lit in the hearth but I'm still cold, shivering with shock.

I saw Willis's own surprise when he first noted my swelling belly, though he has not mentioned it. This gives me some advantage. He will not dare harm me while I have a Fanshawe child growing inside me. I expect he is calculating how best he might profit from my condition, how he might balance his own precarious position against that of a Fanshawe heir. Or perhaps he read the truth in the way that Rafe tried to protect me against his men.

'Are we clear on the terms?' he says.

Rafe nods. Our lives are held in each other's hands.

'Then, Kate, start the play.'

I turn my cards. I have a poor hand, but I make my bid, pushing counters to the centre of the table. 'If I win, and Rafe goes free, what plans have you for me?'

Willis smiles. 'You are very sure of your luck. I imagine we can come to some arrangement.'

'I will never be your whore.'

He laughs, adding counters to mine. 'I remember a time when the prospect was not so unpalatable to you.'

I cannot deny it and flush deeply, thinking how my body had risen to his touch in the past. 'You are a despicable man,' I say. 'You have no honour. I will die before I lie with you.'

Rafe scowls, eyes focused on the cards in his hand. He makes the highest bid, collects the stock and slides counters back across the tabletop. Willis turns to me. 'Do not wish for death, Kate. The gallows have ruined pretty necks before. Do not think your beauty protects you from justice. I know it was you shot the constable on the Ware Road. I have witnesses who will testify to it.'

'I don't know what you mean,' I say, fixing him with an icy stare. How does Willis know about the dead man? Is it possible that he set those thief-takers on our path? If so, then he is even more cruel and determined than I'd thought. I cannot unravel the game he is playing.

We vie for the ruff, Willis winning with a set of spades, and begin to play tricks. We turn cards in silence for a time, my heart tripping every time a new one is played. Willis wins the first game easily and smiles to himself as he collects counters, gathers the cards and gives them to me to deal. My fingers shake as I divide the pack and we begin again.

I bid high for the stock this time, desperate to prevent Willis, but it does not help my hand. And I cannot concentrate with my temper so fired up.

'You think yourself above justice?' I say to Willis, as we begin to place cards. 'You are a traitor to the King's cause. If he returns, there will be swift retribution for any man who hindered him. Your former fame will count for nothing when Charles Stuart hears how you betrayed his hopes. My husband suffered in the Tower for five months because of you. Loyal men died because of you. The King is sure to find out the truth and you will pay the price, in the end.'

'I would look a little closer to find the real traitor, if I were you.'

'What do you mean by that?'

'Be quiet, Willis,' Rafe says, frowning.

Willis's smirk is revealing. 'Ah, it seems our friend's conscience is not so clear. And neither should yours be, on this matter. Those letters you gave to my associate, Jove? Those letters betrayed your husband and his cabal of glory-seekers to Thurloe and his nest of spies. They contained details of the uprising – plans I knew to be true because I communicated them directly from Mordaunt myself. But the betrayal was all done by your own hand, Kate.'

Though I had suspected this, to hear confirmation makes my hatred writhe. I think of the sixth letter, the one I kept back, still lying hidden at Ware Park. In my haste to escape, my mind so muddled, I did not even think of it. It can be of no use to me now that I can never return there.

'Why include Rafe in this? He knew nothing of the letters. The agreement was between us alone. He has nothing to do with it.'

Willis laughs again. 'Oh, such innocence! Kate, you do not know the man who shares your bed as well as you think.'

'Willis, hold your tongue.' Rafe's eyes are stormy. As he places a card, he stares at Willis steadily. But Willis does not heed the warning.

'I hardly think you are in a position to give orders,' he says.

'Rafe, what does he mean?' I ask.

Willis leans back in his seat, clearly enjoying himself now. 'Our friend here is one of Thurloe's spies, and has been for years,' he says. 'You have allied yourself to one of Cromwell's dogs. What do you think of him now?'

I search Rafe's eyes and find the truth there. This is the secret he has kept from me all this time. 'You never told me.'

'I could not.'

'You said no secrets . . .'

Rafe stares at his cards.

I feel a cold, dead hand slide its fingers around my heart. He has lied to me.

Willis cannot hide his glee. 'Oh, but it doesn't end there. We came to a mutual agreement some months ago. Our Master Chaplin has been working for me for some time now. He's an excellent courier, at ease with the King's men as he is with Parliament's. I betray the King's cause and Master Chaplin betrays his Parliament masters, for our mutual benefit.'

'Is this true?' I whisper.

Rafe's face is grim. 'He promised to keep his silence about us if I worked for him and held my tongue. He guessed everything, Kate. I did it to protect you.'

'By lying to me?' I feel as if I barely know the man at my side.

'I had no choice.' He still will not look at me and I understand that he will not show his true feelings in front of Willis and his men. He does right. We must not give Willis any more fuel for his fire.

'So many secrets.' Willis gloats at my shock. 'And what a shame that you will never know each other better.' He places a card, winning a trick, then drains his cup and pours more wine. He refills my cup too and indicates that I should drink. I do so, longing for respite.

'And what a waste of time the whole endeavour was from the

beginning,' Willis goes on. 'All these years spent intriguing and double-dealing, when the King will return anyway, despite the best efforts of those army fools. They should see the people have had enough of generals and tyrants. The country wants its king.'

I gather myself. The horror at what I've learned, and the questions crowding my mind, will have to wait. This is no time for anger, doubts and recriminations. Rafe's life is what matters now. I play another card, but they are not falling well for me.

'You seem very sure of that,' I say. 'How will the King return?'

'You have not heard?'

I look blankly at the two men. 'I have received no news lately, at Ware Park.'

'Parliament is restored and any hope of army opposition is crushed,' Willis says. 'I have it on good authority that secret talks with the King's representatives are taking place. I predict Parliament will declare for the King before May Day.'

'My God! Is this true?'

Rafe, scowling, slams a card down. 'Yes, and then all these years of suffering will have been for nothing.'

'There speaks a true Commonwealth man,' says Willis. 'Your time is over, my friend. The experiment is failed. The Good Old Cause is a thing of the past. It's time to return to king and prosperity.'

'You speak as though you are loyal to His Majesty still,' I say. 'Though everyone knows you're accused of treason, and you've just admitted as much.'

'All lies,' Willis says, eyes glittering. 'All you've heard is easy words, spoken in jest. The evidence against me is fake – forgeries all. No one can prove anything.'

Again, I think of the letter, safe beneath the boards at Ware Park, and curse my stupidity.

Rafe wins the hand. His eyes flick to mine with a glimmer of relief. Willis curses. They are even, one game apiece. Unless I can win the next, one of them will be the victor.

My mind is reeling with this news of the King and my discovery about Rafe's duplicity. I hardly know my own feelings. But one thing is clear above all: whatever Rafe has done, and whatever his reasons, I do not want to lose him again.

'Swear that you'll keep your word,' Rafe says, gathering the cards to deal them for what may be the final time. 'Swear that if I win this hand, you'll let her go free.'

Willis's expression is changed, his smile gone. He gives me a long, penetrating stare. I force myself to hold his gaze. I will not let him see how my heart thumps, how my skin crawls. He blinks, once, twice, eyes dark and intense.

'I swear it,' he says.

The trump card is a heart.

Again, Rafe takes the stock. I see his disappointment as he gathers the cards. Willis reads it too and smiles to himself. My hand is weak but I will not give up hope. I pretend confidence. I will not let Willis read my distress. I will not show Rafe that I'm afraid I'm failing him.

We play tricks, silent as the cards come down, wine discarded, the other men ignored. And each pretty painted picture takes Rafe further away from me. My whole life comes down to the cards on this table in this shabby little inn in the middle of nowhere. I could almost laugh at the futility of it.

At last the cards are falling well for Rafe. He wins more tricks than Willis and, each time, Willis curses, losing a little more of his composure. Rafe's eyes are hard and determined, as they are when we ride out, just before a stand.

The last trick is played. Rafe is the victor.

He sits back on the stool breathing heavily, holding out both hands to take mine. But I cannot respond. He has saved me, but I could not save him.

Willis is angry. Things have not gone his way. He slams his remaining cards down upon the table. 'Bind him and take him down,' he says to the men by the door. 'We will ride immediately.'

Rafe does not struggle against them. He does not fight. He lets them tie his wrists and march him from the room with a blade at his back. I sit there, stunned, wrung out, unable to take in what is happening. I cannot even raise myself from the stool to kiss him goodbye.

Willis stands, towering over me. He drains his cup, pulls on his gloves and picks up his hat.

I look up at him. 'Where are you taking him? Please . . . do not do this. I will do anything you want.'

He comes close and cradles my chin in his hand, his leather glove cool on my skin. 'We had an agreement,' he says. 'You accuse me of having no honour. Well, now you'll see that I can be true to my word. Be thankful for this outcome, Kate. It could have gone very differently for you.'

Within minutes they are gone. I do not watch as they set off in the pale dawn light. I cannot bear to see Rafe ride away from me again. But I hear them. I hear the clatter of hoofs in the yard, the raised voices of Willis's men, the slamming of doors and boots on the staircase as the inn's inhabitants are disturbed. I hear the sounds of the party as they move off and the terrible silence that follows.

After a time, I pour the last of the wine and swallow the whole cup, ignoring the protest of my stomach. Willis's remaining cards still lie face down on the table. I flip them over. Faces stare up at me. A smiling king and queen, proud and gaudy in rich silks and golden crowns, tabards emblazoned with scarlet, a jack and ace in the same design. A straight flush of hearts: the winning hand.

By rights, Willis is the victor. He should have taken us both.

Chapter 51

For two days, I hide in the shack in Gustard Wood. I lie on the little truckle bed, shivering inside moth-eaten blankets, trying to find the truth in the things that Richard Willis had said. I cannot untangle the maze in which I now find myself. There are too many questions left unanswered. Only one thing remains clear: there is a child, beating out its hunger in my belly, and I will do anything to protect it. In the end, this drives me back to Ware Park, to face Thomas's wrath.

By the time I reach the house I am worn out, too weak and weary to care. Let Thomas lock me up, let him curse and shout – my heart is already so bruised and aching, it is not possible for him to hurt me any further.

He meets me in the entrance hall, storming from the parlour with blood-shot eyes and balled fists. He is drawn up short as he takes in the state of me – this filthy, desperate version of his wife. His anger turns to shock.

I feel myself sway, as though my legs no longer have the strength to hold me up. My vision seems to blur with gauzy white mist. A man comes out of the parlour behind my husband. He says something, though his voice sounds far away and I cannot decipher the words. He puts a steadying hand on Thomas's shoulder. It takes me a few seconds to realise it is Richard Willis.

★ ★ ★

The letter is where I left it, slipped beneath the floorboards in my bedchamber.

I wait until late, when Thomas has gone to bed, drunk and muttering. Willis's presence has tempered his rage – he cannot be seen to treat his pregnant wife cruelly, so instead of the locked doors and threats I was expecting, a physician is ordered and Master Stone is given over to my care. After a few hours of sleep and a good meal, fed to me by Stone himself, as if I am a sickly infant, I am much restored. And at last, when night falls, I am left alone.

Willis is awake. He is sitting by the fire in his chamber, studying a pamphlet by the light of a single candle. He starts up as I enter without knocking, grabbing for the blade that hangs in a sheath on the bedpost. Upon seeing me his hands drop to his sides. For a moment we stare at each other, wordless. Then he sits again. He picks up the pamphlet and pretends to scrutinise it.

'I'll confess I'm surprised to see you, Kate,' he says. 'I thought you had more sense than to cross my path again so soon.'

'What are you doing here? What have you told Thomas?'

'I'm here to see my friend Fanshawe. We've been celebrating a small victory of mine – the capture of a wanted man, some local highway thief, currently residing in Hertford gaol.' He lowers the pamphlet. 'Thomas knows nothing more. Not yet.'

'Do you know why I'm here?'

'I would flatter myself that you've seen sense at last, but that look in your eye suggests otherwise.'

'You must rescind the charges against Rafe and let him go free.'

'Now, why would I do that?'

'If you do this one thing for me, I promise you'll never see or hear of him again. No one need ever know the truth.'

'Begging does not suit you and, besides, it's too late.'

I go towards him. 'I think not.'

'The constable at Hertford is very pleased to have the infamous Rafe Chaplin in his cells. There are far more charges laid at his door than those I might make. Our friend has made quite the nuisance of himself, over the years. Many men have claims against him. Robbery, arson, treason – need I go on? It will serve me well to be the one to bring such a dog to heel.'

'You do not need to add his death to your list of petty glories. I do not think you are so cruel.'

He puts the paper down on the table. I see his name on the page in bold black letters, married with the word *traitor*. It is one of the slanderous pamphlets that Thomas and Leventhorpe spoke of all those months before.

I point to it. 'You wish to clear your name. I can help you do that, or I can condemn you.'

He sighs, the flames casting dark shadows beneath his eyes. 'You and I both know that I'm unlikely to find the King's favour again. The best I can hope now is to escape the gallows myself. It is only because Charles Stuart has more important concerns that my fate is undecided. But that man does not forget for long. I assume you've come to offer me a promise of your silence in exchange for Chaplin's life.'

As always, he guesses my wishes before I have the chance to speak them.

'I've come to offer new terms.'

'You think you have some influence over me, Kate, because you know what I am. You think you've heard my full confession. But all you have are a few words uttered in drink over a card table. The only witness is Chaplin himself, a criminal and traitorous wretch, soon to meet his fate at the assizes. Why would anyone believe your word over mine?'

'Because I have proof.'

'What proof?'

I draw the letter out from beneath my shawl, unfold it and hold it up so that he might comprehend the power in my hands.

He licks his lips and takes a drink of sack. The corner of his mouth twitches. 'You think you have outwitted me. Think again.'

'With this letter I could condemn you in the eyes of everyone we know: Thomas, Leventhorpe, Mordaunt and the rest. Word would soon reach the King . . .'

'Come, you are cleverer than this.'

'If you help Rafe, I will give you this letter.'

'My dear girl, that letter is worthless.'

'It's one of the letters you had me take to Jove. One of the letters betraying the Great Trust, telling of the uprising.'

'I know what you think it is. But you're wrong.'

'No – see? It's written in cipher.' I brandish the paper. 'I know this Master Tanner is John Thurloe, and others know it too.'

'It is marked with a heart, is it not?'

'What of it?' My breath is starting to constrict.

He stands and comes over to me. I hide the letter behind my back, away from his grasp. But he does not reach for it. He runs a fingertip down the side of my face and pinches my chin between his forefinger and thumb. 'I knew you would choose so. I know you so well.'

'What do you mean?'

He drops his hand and turns away. 'Keep your letter. Give it to whom you like. You will find it contains nothing of import.'

'But—'

'It's concocted nonsense. A distraction. A dummy.'

'I don't understand.' The tightness in my chest chokes me, strangles my breath. 'You mean the whole thing was a trick?'

He walks back to the table where he picks a second glass from the tray and fills it with sack. 'Will you take a drink with me?'

'You – you lied to me from the beginning . . .'

'Not entirely. Three letters of the six found their way to

Thurloe. The others, the ones marked with a heart, were decoys. I knew you were likely to keep back at least one, and I was right. But three were real enough. You are not blameless, Kate. You have still betrayed the King. It changes nothing, other than the strength of your proposal.'

'I don't believe you. I cannot believe anything you say.'

'So what will you do? If you turn me in, with or without your false letter, you'll have to admit your own part in the plot. It will soon be found that I'm blameless and that you and your husband are the real traitors. Jove will be willing to confirm that. And I've made sure there are others who saw you with him and are keen to come forward. Thomas Fanshawe will return to the Tower, and this time he won't be alone. Are you willing to take that chance?'

Again he has the upper hand. I feel stupid and dim-witted, dizzied by his revelations. How many more layers of my life will be peeled away before the truth is laid bare?

'Have a drink, Kate. This may be the last time we are alone together.'

My legs are weak and I sit down opposite him. I take the glass and drink down the rich, sweet sack.

'Why do you persist in this?' I ask. 'Why do you hate Rafe so much? What do you care if he robs rich men of their wealth? A hundred others have done the same. Why involve him in your schemes at all?'

He holds my gaze for a long time. The fire dances, shadows spin.

'A condemned man cannot give evidence against me. And I despise any man who does not know his place. He should never have reached above his station.'

'His station means nothing. He is more of a man than you will ever be.'

'There we disagree.'

He stares at me, such intensity in his eyes. The fire pops and crackles. The sack runs warm in my belly.

I have one last bid to make. I stand up and cross the room. 'I will do anything to save him.' Slowly, I lower the shawl from my shoulders and let it drop to the floor. 'I will do anything you want, if you promise me that he will go free. Tell them you are mistaken. Take me instead of him.'

He swallows slowly. 'You really would do anything for him.'

Then he moves closer, the space between us barely more than a hand's breadth. I smell the scent of him: sweat, tobacco, leather and sweet sack. He will have me now, I think, and Rafe will be lost to me for ever. It will have to be enough to know that, by my surrender, Rafe will live. I ask the devil inside me for strength, close my eyes and tilt my mouth, ready for his lips.

But Willis places his hands gently on my shoulders. 'The child is his, is it not?' he says.

I nod.

Then, abruptly, he takes a few steps towards the hearth and stands, gazing into the flames, one hand on the mantel.

'Sometimes we find ourselves doing things we never thought to do,' he says quietly, the arrogance gone from his voice. 'Sometimes our hands are forced by circumstance, or by causes greater than our own. Sometimes we have to make difficult choices. You cannot always judge a man's conscience by his actions.'

I swear I hear regret in his voice, perhaps disappointment. I'm no longer sure what he's talking about, but the alteration in him is clear. He is refusing me.

'So many years, and for what?' he says, shaking his head. 'I'm tired, Kate. Tired of it all.'

I don't know what he wants of me. I don't know what more I can do, so I do nothing.

'I make no promises,' he says, still staring into the fire. 'But I will do what I can for you.'

'You will?'

'Do not hope for too much, Kate. My influence is not what it once was.'

'Why change your mind, after all you have said?'

He will not look at me. 'You have what you want. Do not question me more.'

I do not understand his change of heart, this shift in the air between us, but I will certainly not challenge it. I fetch the letter from the seat and go to the fireplace. I smooth out the paper and cast it into the flames. We both watch it curl and flare, until there is nothing left but ashes.

Chapter 52

The gaol at Hertford is a meagre, cramped place, just two cells in the old castle gatehouse where the constable keeps the drunkards and thieves while they await their fate with the magistrate. A stinking fug thickens the air – the stench of unwashed men and fetid, open drains.

Willis pays the gaoler a handful of coin to bring Rafe to a damp, sparsely furnished room. The child is unsettled today, making great kicks of protest. My back aches. I sit on a hard bench next to a cold hearth, longing for the comfort of Rafe's arms.

When he comes at last, I'm shocked by the change in him. The clothes he wore on the night that Willis brought him here are now torn and soiled. His hair is loose, its chestnut shine muted by prison-cell muck. One eye is circled with a dark bruise, blood crusted on his temple. His wrists are manacled and there are bleeding sores where he has clearly tried to free himself. When he sees me his eyes flood with disbelief, and he shakes his head as if trying to wake. He has been here only ten days and already he looks a man beaten.

He sees Willis, brooding in the corner. 'What's he doing here?' His voice comes out parched and gruff.

'Release his hands,' Willis orders the gaoler, who shakes his head and clicks his tongue.

'I take full responsibility for this man. I'll guard the door myself. There's no other way out.'

Willis is right – I have already considered the tiny leaded window high up on one wall, and the narrow chimney: there is no way to escape.

The gaoler is persuaded by yet more coin. He unlocks the manacles, mumbling half-hearted threats. Rafe rubs at his wrists. Then the others leave the room, closing the door. The key scrapes in the lock. At last, we are alone.

I could sob as he puts his arms around me and I bury my face against his filthy chest, but I must be strong now. I must show him that I have not given up. He kisses my face, strokes my hair and runs his hands over my belly, marvelling at the gentle pummelling of the child's kicking.

'I thought I would never see you again,' he says. 'I'm so sorry . . .'

His eyes well and, for a moment, he looks as though he may crumble. I cannot bear to see it. I wrap my hands around his and grip hard.

'No tears,' I say. 'When there is no need.'

He glances to the door where Willis waits outside. 'Why are you with him?'

I tell him about my return to Ware Park and all that has passed between Willis and me. He listens, eyes growing rounder.

'He will help us,' I say. 'You'll be released soon. And you and I will go far away from here, as we planned.'

'How can you put your faith in him?'

'What choice have we?'

'Kate, I cannot believe you would trust him.'

'I don't, but what better hope is there?'

'Willis is a man who cares for nothing but himself. He has nothing to gain by helping me.'

'I thought so too. But now I'm not sure . . .' I remember how

Willis looked at me when I offered myself to him, the torment in his eyes. 'It was his idea to bring me here. He told Thomas that he was taking me on a long drive, for the air. I heard them arguing.' I almost smile as I recall the echo of raised voices in the hall at Ware Park. My husband is less inclined to indulge Willis, these days, but he still grants hospitality to the man whom so many others have branded a traitor. 'Thomas wants me to enter my confinement, but it is just another way to keep me prisoner. Willis argued against it, and he has a talent for getting his way. It's as if he's protecting me.'

'That's what I'm worried about.' Rafe gives me a hard look. 'Kate, if you have made some arrangement with him, I cannot stomach it.'

I clutch at his hands. 'No! It's not what you think. Truly.'

'Then what motive can he have, when he's tried so very hard to be rid of me?'

'I asked the same but he will not say. I think he's growing tired of his old games. He's no longer a young man.'

'Men like him don't change. They live for nothing but their own power.'

'But he has lost all his. I think, perhaps, the loss of favour has affected him deeply. He has forfeited much for the King's cause in his time and now it's all for nothing. Perhaps he regrets what he has done. Perhaps there is some sense of honour left in him yet.'

Rafe raises an eyebrow. 'Forgive me, Kate, but you're a fool if you think he speaks anything but lies.'

'He's our last hope, and I will not give up on that . . .'

He is exasperated. 'Let's speak no more of Richard Willis. We have little time and there are things I must tell you.'

'We will have all the time in the world soon enough.'

He takes up my hand. 'I want you to be prepared.'

'Do not talk in that way.'

'Kate, you must listen to me.'

'Let us talk of our future together. Once you're released you must come to me at Ware Park. I'll be waiting and Thomas cannot stop me. Willis has stabled Flight at Ware. Thomas thinks she is Willis's horse and makes sure she is well cared for—'

'Please, Kate, hush.' He puts a blackened fingertip to my lips. 'Let me speak.'

There is desperation in his manner but I do not want to talk about what will happen if Willis's efforts fail. We both know that if Rafe faces the magistrate, there is only one possible end for him.

Rafe lowers his voice to a whisper. 'Do you recall the robbery I mentioned to you?'

I nod.

'I want you to know all. If it's a success, there would be enough gold to set you up in a new life.' He pauses a moment and glances to the door. He pulls me closer so our heads are almost touching. 'All depends upon the King. If the King returns, a carriage will be commissioned by Sir William Cobden to transport his gold from the city to his house in Lincolnshire. Sir William is a Commonwealth man who profited greatly after the war, with land and money taken from Royalist hands. He fears for his wealth should the King return. He's afraid of the taxes that the King and his advisers will no doubt demand of the men who grew wealthy after the war. He wants to keep his gold close.'

'How do you know this?'

'I first heard of it from Willis, who charged me to find out more. Now I have it directly from Sir William's man. I know him a little, from my work for Thurloe, and I trust him, as much as anyone can trust a spy.' At this a little flare of distaste rises in me. I have tried hard not to think of the secrets I learned that night at the inn but they seem of little worth or importance now. Still, though, I do not like to hear the man I love admit his duplicity so freely. I do not care what lies he has told to others – the Devil knows I have told my fair share – but I do not like to think of the secret life he kept from me, when he swore his honesty so convincingly. I still feel taken in.

'The carriage will travel through Hatfield and take the road across Nomansland,' Rafe goes on. 'They wanted protection on the highway and I promised them safe passage, for a price. They know who I am but they think I'm still loyal to Parliament. We agreed a good sum, but it's not enough for our wants.'

'So instead of protecting the carriage, you will rob it.'

'The only missing piece is the date of transportation. Sir William is awaiting news of the King's return before he takes any action. He's a cautious man and will avoid drawing unnecessary attention.'

'So all depends upon the King.'

He looks me steadily in the eye. 'Of course, when Sir William hears of my arrest they'll make other plans for protection, but I'm sure they'll still go ahead. If some other thief was to target the carriage on Nomansland Common, someone who knows the lie of the land . . .'

'Rafe, I—'

'I would not have you put yourself in danger. There is a man in Ware who will help you. Go to the Saracen's Head and ask for Timbrell. He has men who follow him, enough to mount an ambush. You need do nothing but tell him when and where, and agree a price with him. It's no small undertaking – there will be plenty of coin for you both.'

'I could not . . . Never without you.'

'The only thing you need is the date. Tell Timbrell to set up lookouts at the inns and turnpikes out of London. It will be a black, unmarked coach with a heavy guard. They'll give themselves away. If they're spotted before Barnet, there'll be time enough to send word. But they'll know they've been betrayed. As soon as you have the money, you'll have to leave. Sir William is a harsh man and will certainly seek justice. He will never forgive the loss of his fortune.'

'Please don't talk like this.'

'It's a way out for you,' he says. 'A way for you to start a new life. And there is one more thing I must ask . . .' He pauses, takes up both my hands again and gazes into my eyes. 'You must look after Rachel.'

'Rafe, she despises me.'

'That's not true. Please listen, Kate. You must reconcile with her. This is my greatest wish. Tell her, if I'm gone, that she must sell the farm and find a way to join you. The money should go to support you both, and my child . . .' He reaches for my belly.

'We will go together, the three of us. You and I will ride out again, like before.'

'Remember the place I told you about? The place in the north?'

'The castle by the sea?'

'Yes. You'll find safe harbour there. Tell them I sent you.'

Now it's my turn to hush him. 'I'll hear no more of this.'

But he is determined. 'Kate, promise me that you will do this. You will free yourself of the life you hate so much and bring up our child in freedom, as I would wish.'

I do not want to acknowledge that there is any chance of these things coming to pass, but I see the anguish in him.

'Please, Kate, promise me.'

What is a promise if I'm sure I will never need to honour it? I would do anything to comfort him now. There is no harm in saying the words to quiet his mind.

'I promise, my love. I promise.'

He breathes out a great sigh of relief and wraps his arms around me. 'That is all I ask. Thank you. God protect you. God protect our child. God protect you both.'

I'm glad he does not know that God has abandoned me. It's the Devil who owns me now, making me tell lies, and make promises I will never keep.

Chapter 53

We set out early to reach Hertford by noon. The sky is overcast, promising rain, but I have persuaded Master Stone to take me in the cart. He will not hear of me riding Feather so close to my time and we bicker over my safety. He is trying only to protect me and I'm glad to have him by my side. He is disobeying his master's orders by taking me outside Ware Park, but Thomas and Willis are gone away to London, where the whole world waits for news of the King.

Since Charles Stuart issued his declaration a week ago, promising clemency to all those who fought against his father in the late wars, word is that even the old Cromwell supporters are turning in his favour. Now they are assured of their estates, and their heads, suddenly they are all the King's men.

'Keep her close, Master Stone,' I heard Thomas say, as he left. 'And lock her door by night. Do you understand? I hold you alone responsible for the welfare of my wife.'

Thomas is mistaken in thinking that Master Stone's loyalty is to him. He does not know that he has trusted his captive to the wrong man.

It starts to drizzle as we near Hertford but the rain does not dissuade the swell of people on the roads. Ragged children run alongside, splashing in puddles, darting between groups of women in mud-spattered skirts. We pass a train of tarts, painted and curled, petticoats hitched. Men, stipple-cheeked and smiling, slap backs and exchange good-natured greetings. Their glad anticipation sickens me. I wish I could run them all under our wheels.

They are heading to the castle gates. Word has spread fast. There will be a hanging today.

I could not attend the assizes. When I tried to ride out, Thomas locked me in my room and put a man outside the door, another beneath my window, and threatened to lash me to the bed. It is only the child that keeps him civil now.

I spent the day fretting and crying, feeling as though my whole body were turned inside out. I heard the galloping hoofs of a messenger's horse in the early evening, and a man's voice in the entrance hall below, but it was not until Master Stone brought my supper that I found a note beneath my plate. Willis admitted, in his own bold, sloping hand, that his attempts with the justice have failed. Rafe is convicted as a highway robber. The sentence is death.

But I have not given up hope. Willis may still find a way. The man has connections I cannot begin to grasp and a tongue that could persuade a convent novice to sin. Of what importance is the life of a single man when the fate of the country is at stake? Who will notice if one petty thief slips through the hangman's noose? In London these three weeks, Willis left me with no knowledge of his progress, with nothing, in fact, except words offered in place of a promise. But I must believe that he will try, for any other truth is too terrible to bear.

The throng overflows the castle green. We barely find space to hitch the horse. Master Stone takes firm hold of my arm and pushes his way through the crowds, clearing a path. The ground is already slippery, turning to mud.

Traders make the most of the day, hawking their wares from makeshift stalls, barrels and trestles, the air clamorous with patter. Townsmen and the richer merchants are turned out in their good clothes, seated with their gossiping wives on a raised scaffold. Gangs of labourers and apprentices sup outside the taverns, eyeing each other warily. A gaggle of milkmaids preen and pout. It seems the whole of Hertfordshire has turned out for the spectacle.

I curse every one of them, from the lowest to the highest, from the squalling newborn in its mother's arms to the half-blind crone selling nosegays to dour-dressed goodwives. I hate them all with fierce fire.

I was like them once. As a child I watched, fascinated, as a man swung beneath the tree at Tyburn. I laughed at the spiked, rotting heads on London Bridge. I stared at the gory innards of a traitor, one day in Oxford, when the cobbles were slick with slithering guts, bloody as slaughtering day in the shambles. I did all this without a thought for the men or those they left behind. Widows, weeping at the gallows, were to be mocked and scorned. With their deathly faces, their ragged weeds and their bone-thin children, they were so far from the life I knew as to be barely human. I did not understand how it feels to be one of them. I did not understand, then, that there are things we all share. I could not imagine that riches and position can be taken away and mean so little, that there is nothing can protect any of us from the agonies of love.

The gallows have been put up outside the castle gates; a cross hatch of wood and nails that does not look strong enough to hold a man. Next to it, a maypole stands in mockery – the first I have seen since the early days of war. Master Stone tells me that there were May Day celebrations this year, a sure sign that the world is turning once again.

We find Martha and Rachel, squatting on a low bench at the foot of the scaffold. Rachel looks drawn, with fevered spots of colour in her cheeks, and when she sees me, she clutches at

Martha's sleeve, panicked. Martha puts a reassuring hand on her shoulder, then stands and comes towards me. My heartbeat is racketing but making things right with Rachel is one part of my promise to Rafe that I intend to keep.

Martha greets me politely enough, but before she can say more, I interrupt.

'Please, Martha. I must speak with Rachel. I've seen Rafe. I have a message from him.'

'She is very distressed. I would not have her suffer more.'

'Please, she will want to hear what I have to say.'

Martha considers, looking to Master Stone, who gives an encouraging nod. She accedes and leads us to the scaffold, where Rachel sits, hugging the round of her belly. I sit down next to her, feeling her flinch. But then our eyes meet and I see that the sorrow in hers reflects my own. Her heart is breaking too.

Suddenly we are those two young girls again, bound together by our struggles, finding our strength in each other. All the anger and resentment that has fired me for so long seems petty and pointless in the face of what we once had, and what we both now stand to lose. Our battles seem senseless. The speech I had planned seems trite and stale. I cannot find the right words to voice these things. Instead I put out a hand and find hers. She is shaking and there is a sour, sickroom smell about her.

'He loves us both, you know,' I say. 'We should not be enemies. I promised him . . .'

'Oh, Kate,' she says, as tears begin to spill. 'I cannot bear it. He's all I have left.'

I shake my head. 'Not true. You still have me.'

Her fingers grip mine and hold on tight.

She looks at me with watery eyes. 'I'm so sorry.'

I shake my head and dredge up a smile. 'There will be time for all that. We will all be together again soon, you'll see. These people will be disappointed today.'

I notice Master Stone, hat in hand, exchange a doubtful glance with Martha.

'There will be a reprieve. I'm sure of it,' I say.

Their expressions expose their misgiving.

'You don't believe me? Well, I shall prove you wrong.'

I will not let go of Rachel's hand. As we wait, I tell her everything – about my visit to Hertford gaol, about Willis and about the promises I made to Rafe. She looks at me through tear-glazed eyes.

'Kate, can you really believe . . .' But then she trails off and says no more, as if she cannot trust herself to speak. Her fingers tremble in my palm, like a terrified child's.

I look about me. Several of the townsmen, sitting above on the scaffold, recognise me and doff their hats. A group of young men are decked out in rich, bright cloth, lace cascading at their cuffs. It has been some time since I saw such finery on display. I have dressed in one of my old brocade gowns today, wanting to distance myself from the plain, serviceable clothes that I've used for thievery, and needing Rafe to see that my spirit is not dampened, but this glittering cabal, with their air of youth, confidence and wealth, brings to mind the days of the old King's court. Has the game of favour-seeking begun so soon, before Charles Stuart is even on these shores? No doubt, there will be a mad scrambling for position in every town in England. Once, I might have led the way, but now, I find I have no care for it, or for the pretty young men who might once have turned my head. Now I want a different kind of life.

I notice one of the peacocks whispering to his friend and watch from the corner of my eye as he makes his way along the scaffold and down the rickety steps towards us.

He stops a little too close, jostled by the crowd so that he steps upon my skirts. He ignores the blunder and bows deeply, sweeping his hat. 'Lady Katherine. How delightful to see you again.'

I recognise him vaguely from the parade of local gentry that Thomas entertains from time to time at Ware Park. I'm sure I have supped with the man in years past, but I do not recall his name. I acknowledge him with a nod.

'The aldermen of Hertford are honoured that you would attend to see justice done this day. It is encouraging to see people of quality take an interest, especially in such circumstances.' He unfurls a pale, thin-fingered hand in the direction of my swollen belly, shooting a slant-eyed glance at Rachel.

'And Mistress Coppin.' He makes his obsequious bow towards Martha. 'My friend and I would be greatly satisfied if you were to take our seats. There will be a perfect view of proceedings from higher up.' He turns and points. The men above are all staring expectantly. Anger blooms. I want nothing to do with these provincial fools and their perverse bloodlust.

'Thank you, sir,' Martha says. 'But it would not be safe for Lady Katherine to sit so high, in her present condition. We prefer to stay with our feet on the ground.'

The man makes a face of false concern. 'I understand perfectly. Then perhaps we can prevail upon you to take a little refreshment after the entertainment, at the house of Master Flood. He is laying on a little celebration for us all, in prospect of the restoration of His Majesty. Only the best people, of course, none of this . . . rabble. We would be honoured if you would consent to join us.'

Desperate to be rid of him, I accept.

'Good . . . good.' He smiles. 'Until later, then.' He bows a third time and makes his way back onto the scaffold, looking pleased with himself. He sits next to a handsome youth with flaxen hair and a scarlet coat with gold buttons who stares at me intently. He looks familiar but I cannot place him. Another local, I expect, another of Thomas's eager gaming companions. Still, his concentrated frown unnerves me and I make sure to turn my back.

We wait for at least an hour. With every moment of delay I'm sure that word will come from Willis. Perhaps the constable is waiting for the pardon. I slip the silver heart from beneath my stays, clasp it between my steepled palms and pray that this is so.

The crowd becomes impatient. The rain starts to come down and we take shelter for a time in the space beneath the scaffold. The taverns make good business. The apprentices are drunk and rowdy, singing maying songs and catching the arm of any girl who will join them. The women chatter and slap the legs of their unruly children. Flagons of wine and flasks of liquor are passed among the men on the scaffold. Their wives fuss and complain, holding up their shawls as protection against the rain. But, at last, the doors of the gatehouse swing open and the constable steps out. Behind him is an open cart, drawn by a single, pitiful nag. And there, blinking against the daylight, is Rafe, tethered and manacled at wrist and foot.

In the weeks since our meeting, he has grown thinner. His cheeks are hollow and yellowing bruises circle both eyes. He wears the same filthy shirt and soiled breeches, but his boots are gone. A seeping scab crusts one cheek and the shadow of a dark, ruddy stain spreads from shoulder to waist. For a moment I am taken back to the red chamber in Markyate Cell and my ghostly spectre with the flashing, amber eyes and a slash of scarlet across his chest.

My heart strains against the cage of my ribs. The child starts to kick.

A great hubbub goes up as he is drawn into the centre of the green next to the gallows. People cheer and taunt. They prefer their highwaymen with swagger and show and find nothing to their liking here.

'Now,' I whisper to Rachel, as she struggles to stand. 'Willis will come, you'll see.' I wrap my fingers around hers and feel her quaking. We are flanked by friends, with Martha on one side and Master Stone on the other, but I dare not let her go.

Rafe scans the crowd and when he finds our little group his face is all confusion. I raise a hand but Martha catches my wrist and pulls it down, shaking her head.

Some of the milkmaids I noticed earlier, bold after their ale, push their way to a spot near the cart. They blow coquettish kisses. One lifts her skirts and shouts, 'Any last wishes, my darling?' There are howls of laughter. How I despise them all.

My guts are churning. For the first time, I begin to doubt. 'Where is he?' I say. 'Where is Willis?' Rachel splutters and covers her mouth with her hand.

The cart is drawn up beneath the gallows. The hangman climbs up next to Rafe and checks the rope, measures the length of it, tugging on it with all his weight. It stays secure.

The constable climbs up too. He pulls out a scroll of paper, tries to shelter it with one arm to stop the ink running. Now, surely, here comes the pardon.

The crowd quietens.

The constable begins to read out a list. He names each of Rafe's crimes in turn, detailing dates and places both familiar and unknown to me. At each, a groan of mock horror goes up.

Fierce panic closes its talons around my heart and surges in my veins. I search about me frantically, expecting to find the tall black hat, the glint of a silver buckle, but there is no sign of Willis.

When the constable is done with his list, he turns to Rafe. 'Rafe Chaplin, before you meet with a higher justice, will you speak?'

Rafe gathers himself. I sense his fear. The rain has drenched him. Wet strands of hair cling to his jawline. He shuffles forward, hindered by the ties at his ankles. They will not allow him dignity even in this moment. The noose dangles behind, twisting slowly.

He searches the crowd until he finds me. He holds my gaze. Even from this distance, I can see the message in his eyes: there is apology, there is regret and longing, but most of all, there is love.

The pain in my heart is savage and true, like a dagger twisting deep.

I cannot bear this.

I cannot.

Just then a shout goes up from one corner of the green. A man is waving his arms. 'Stop!' he cries. 'Stop! A messenger comes! A messenger!'

Please, God, I beg, let this be Willis.

Sure enough, a cloaked man comes riding at speed up Castle Street, reining in roughly as he meets the crowd.

Rachel grasps at my hands.

'I told you,' I say. 'I told you.'

There is confusion and grumbling as the man dismounts and pushes his way towards the townsmen on the scaffold. The people part for him, shoving each other to get a better view. As he comes closer, I see he is tall and broad enough to be Willis, but his cloak is too shabby, his bearing too coarse.

Has Willis sent this messenger in his place?

'Who's in charge here?' the man shouts, bringing out a letter from beneath his cloak. Eager fingers point to a fat man in a green hat who sits close by.

Rafe's gaze is flitting, uncomprehending, between me and the messenger.

The fat man takes the letter, snaps open the seal and reads. His friends crane their necks. When he is done, he looks up and his expression is altered. He cannot suppress a wide smile. He beckons the constable over, says something low in his ear and gives him the letter. The constable reads. His mouth falls open. The fat man nods and flaps his hands, smug and grinning, as though giving some sort of dispensation. The constable climbs back up onto the cart.

The crowd caws for action, cries of 'Hang him!' and 'Justice!' still echoing.

The constable holds out his arms and gestures for silence. Rain drips from the brim of his hat.

'Ladies and gentlemen, townsfolk of Hertford, I bring you great news.'

This is it, I think. This must be it. Willis has done it. They will free him.

The constable makes a show of clearing his throat. 'On this day, the eighth of May 1660, Parliament has declared Charles Stuart to be the one true King of England.'

There is a suck of breath like a gust of wind in a storm.

'On this day, Parliament decrees that all Englishmen are restored as loyal subjects to His Majesty King Charles the Second. God save the King!'

Where is the reprieve from Willis? Where is Rafe's pardon?

The green suddenly rings with a great cheering. The townsmen behind me on the scaffold are all shaking hands and clapping each other on the back, as if they themselves have brought about this momentous thing. Hats are tossed. Men twirl their sweethearts about, raise their tankards and hug their friends. My sight of Rafe is lost in a sea of waving arms and cacophony.

'This cannot be,' I say. 'Where is Willis?' Master Stone is close behind me. He puts an arm around my waist as my legs threaten to give out. I look up at him. 'Where is he?' I demand. But, of course, he has no answer.

Minutes fly by and I am lost in clamour and racket. My mind is wild and I can barely hold onto a thought. All I know is that Rachel's hand is still in mine – I will not let it go – and Rafe is still somewhere beneath the gallows.

I try to pull Rachel forward, to push through the rabble, but Master Stone holds me back.

'Mistress, that's not wise.'

'I must go to him,' I say, fixing on the thought. Rachel releases me and slumps down onto the bench, her head in her hands. She begins to bleat, high and tremulous, like a newborn lamb.

Master Stone puts his hands on my shoulders and grips me firmly. 'No sense in two bodies on the gibbet,' he says. He gives me a purposeful look and I realise he knows everything. He touches his fingertips very softly to my stomach. 'Even less sense to make it three.'

The constable is trying to make himself heard above the din.

'There is much cause for celebration, but let us return to the business in hand.'

There are shouts of assent all around. A man on the scaffold above raises his silver flask and yells, 'Hang the wretch, in the name of His Majesty!'

I shake off Master Stone and climb up onto the bench. At first I cannot see Rafe and for a moment I think he is gone. But then I realise he has crumpled to his knees. His hair hangs wet and lank, hiding his face.

'Stand up,' I whisper, beneath my breath, willing him to show something of the man I know. 'Look at me.'

The constable gestures to the hangman to go about his work. They take Rafe, an arm each, and drag him to his feet.

The crowd jeers. They like a show of courage and are disappointed here. Is there no end to their cruelty? Will they ever tire of other people's suffering?

Rachel is slumped on the bench, sobbing in Martha's arms. She cannot watch. But I cannot tear my eyes away. I cannot believe that what I see is real. It's like watching a nightmare unfold, vivid and terrifying, unable to wake, compelled to the end.

The hangman puts the noose around Rafe's neck. His wrists are still tied and he intertwines his fingers. He closes his eyes, lips moving, muttering in prayer. Then he looks down again, searching the crowd.

I burn inside with dawning horror: this is going to happen and it is my fault.

'No!' I shout, the word erupting from somewhere deep inside. 'No! Stop!'

Then I am pushing my way towards the gibbet. But Master Stone grabs my arm, tugging me back. 'Please, m'lady, hold your tongue.' He casts worried looks back towards the townsmen. 'You must not make a show of yourself. Think of the child.'

I follow his eye and see the young man in the red coat is standing now, pointing down at me. He is animated, talking loudly to those about him. Some are frowning and shaking their heads, others gaping in disbelief.

It comes clear then. I know where I have seen him before. He is Peter Blanchard, the man who held a knife to my neck and sliced into my veins on Nomansland Common, the man who would have taken my life, if Rafe had not saved it.

For a moment I am stunned. Master Stone's arms come round me, holding me fast. The hangman climbs down from the cart, leaving Rafe alone, the noose tight around his neck.

A weird sob bubbles up from my throat. And then, 'Let me go!' In this moment I care nothing for Peter Blanchard. I do not care if the whole world knows who and what I am.

'Let me go!' I cry. 'Stop! You must stop this!' Master Stone clamps his hand firmly over my mouth. He is strong and determined and I cannot escape. As I struggle, the hangman gives the horse a great thwack with his whip and the cart jerks forward.

Then the world becomes nothing but screaming noise and bright, white light. A sharp pain stabs in my chest and brow. When I open my eyes, all I see are twisted faces, jeering and grotesque, crowding in about me. My knees give out and I begin to sink downwards. I am drowning in demons. If there is such a thing as Hell on this earth, then I have found it.

The Devil has his sacrifice at last.

And as the rope twists and turns beneath the gallows, taut as a bowstring, bells of celebration ring out.

Chapter 54

The bonfires burn every day. Three weeks later, when the royal party makes harbour at Dover, the land is aflame with passion for our new king.

Thomas orders me to London, where he waits to receive me at a house in the Strand. Richard Fanshawe and Anne are expected there too, having travelled with the King on his journey from The Hague. Thomas's letter brims with uncharacteristic tenderness. He addresses me as 'Dear Wife' and speaks of the prospect of a comfortable life together, and the birth of his heir. I know he hopes for honours from the King, for the part he played in the uprising and his suffering in the Tower. His joy at this possibility spills into his words, as if he has forgotten everything that went before. But I have not forgotten and I do not forgive so easily.

Despite my low state, and the size of my belly, I am compelled to go. Besides, I long to get away from Ware Park. I would rather be anywhere but here, in this place where every tree, every stone and every face reminds me of all I have lost.

Each evening I sit, wakeful, at my chamber window and watch the moon track across the night sky. Thomas no longer keeps a boy outside the door, but there is no need. Where would I go when there is nowhere I want to be? My heart aches. Would that I could cut it out and never feel this pain again. I long for relief and beg

Master Stone for tincture of poppy to help me sleep away my grief, but he will not supply it. I think he fears I will take too much and never wake again. Perhaps he is right.

But I have another reason to make the journey. If the King returns to London, then surely his mother will too. Thomas writes that an audience with the royal family is a certainty: Richard Fanshawe is close to the King and travels by his side. So I pack the best gowns I own, poor as they are, and make sure that the silver pendant is secure about my neck. I cherish it now, more than ever.

London is a city turned upside down once more.

On the day of the King's return, the pealing bells of a hundred churches wake me at dawn. In the Strand, crowds begin to gather with the sunrise, each citizen claiming his place along the procession route, all hoping to catch a glimpse of Charles Stuart on his way to Whitehall. There has never been a day like this and no one wants to miss it. Farmers and labourers come from miles around, streaming through the city gates in droves, all in search of the tale they will tell their grandchildren. The apprentices are drunk by midday, carousing down the Strand in eager gangs, flirting and making lewd gestures at any pretty maid who comes by. Hawkers sell bread, pies and sweetmeats from baskets atop their heads, fighting to be heard above the hubbub of the crowd. Billingsgate fishwives quit their stalls and put ribbons in their hair, sweetened by the wine that runs free from barrels outside the richer houses. By midday, the cobbles run crimson with claret, in triumphant mockery of the day they ran with a king's blood.

Thomas is like an excited, restless child, bobbing down into the street to catch the gossip, bringing back reports: the King is at Blackheath where the army has pledged its allegiance; the King is feasting at Southwark and has knighted the lord mayor; the King has crossed the bridge, scattering silver pennies as he goes. My husband arranges a makeshift viewing platform on the steps of the house, and hires a boy with a stick to keep the crowds at bay, but the attempt is futile and we are soon overrun.

The Strand is decorated like a tableau from the playhouse. The old maypole is winched up, fresh painted and newly crowned in glimmering gold. At its foot, children link hands to make a circle and spin about until they fall, laughing and dizzy. The usual street muck is covered with boards and strewn with flowers and herbs, making a verdant carpet for horses' hoofs. But even the abundance of lavender and rosemary cannot conceal the London stench. Night soil and coal smoke mingle with the marshy scent of the Thames and the unwashed multitudes to make a rich, stinking brew.

A riot of colourful banners and flags streams in the breeze. The old families, those who've managed to regain their riverside homes, are proud, once again, to display their crests and pennants. And the houses are decked with branches of oak, new spring leaves and blossoming hawthorn. Rich turkey carpets drape from upper sills. After so many years of hardship, I never thought to see such a thing in this lifetime.

When Anne first sees me, she rushes to my side and puts her hands on my belly. 'Oh, my dear! But you must be so very near your confinement. How wonderful you look.' She must not recognise the sadness in my eyes. 'Tell me, is everything as well as can be?' I know by her expression that there is no point in telling the truth. Like everyone else, she has no mind for aught but the King today.

'Yes, all is well.'

'But of course! How can it be otherwise on this most glorious day?'

She is accompanied by a bevy of chattering acquaintances, all desperate to hear of her recent journey across the Channel in the King's retinue. They crowd about us, smiling and kissing my hand as Anne makes introductions, and soon set to making good use of

Thomas's liberal supply of wine. Anne brings forward one man, a Master Evelyn, whose pretty cousin, Sarah, brings a flush to Thomas's cheeks.

Anne insists that Evelyn sits by me. 'He's a bore, but very attentive,' she whispers, loud enough for him to hear. 'He will look after you.'

I do not take to Evelyn. He seems the pious sort, with a pinched, serious face and a soft voice that requires me to lean too close. But he's polite, making idle observations about the fortuitous sunshine, as time passes and the day grows hot, requiring little response from me.

We hear the approach of the King long before we see him. The tumult of the cheering crowd rises in a great racket that makes me want to stop my ears and run back to the silence of Ware Park.

Ranks of soldiers come first, buff coats adorned with swags of purple, green and silver lace, swords all polished and glittering in the sun. A group of trumpeters heralds the King's coming, drummers beat a rousing rhythm, competing with the constant church bells. Ladies lean from upper windows and scatter apple blossom in flurries that catch and swirl in the breeze.

And then, he is here, our king, on horseback, dressed in a sparkling silver doublet, a plume of bright red feathers in his hat. He is a tall man but slighter than I'd imagined. Black curls fall about a thin, dour face. I saw him once, in Oxford, when I was just a girl and he was barely a man. He was England's shining prince then, swelled with pride and promise. That boy is long gone. Instead, I see a man like any other.

The years that have passed since he left England's shores show in the lines upon his face, the dark, flinty eyes and the fixed expression. How strange it must be, I think, to be cast into this mêlée after so many years of exile. How unreal it must seem to live the very thing you have dreamed of but never thought to have. How conflicting to be welcomed by the very people who were once the cause of such cruel betrayal. He looks a little mystified by the ceremony, searching about him with a half-smile that does not quite reach his eyes. Despite all the pomp and all the glamour, there is nothing of the Stuart magic I remember.

Is it he who is so very changed, I wonder, or is it me?

'Forgive me, Lady Katherine, but are you unwell?' Evelyn says, close to my ear, concern written in his frown. 'You look a little faint.'

'I'm well enough, thank you.'

'Does the spectacle not make you glad?'

I look up into the enquiring depths of his eyes.

'Does it not strike you as odd, Master Evelyn, that this crowd is made up of the very people who once called the old King tyrant, and cheered when they cut off his head?'

He looks taken aback for a fleeting moment, but then pleased. 'I have pondered upon that very question. It is a marvel indeed, Lady Katherine, that His Majesty is restored by the same hand – indeed, the same army – that rebelled against him. Sure proof of God's providence at work, I should think.'

'So you think it by God's work that the people's hearts and minds are so utterly altered?'

'Perhaps helped by the suffering we saw under Cromwell's rule. I've heard it said many times that the people are tired of tyrants. We cut down one, only to find another in his place.' He stops to take a delicate sip of wine, sneering disdainfully as some of Anne's fellows raise their cups and make whooping noises to attract the King and his brothers as they pass.

'But if it's God's will that a king should have the throne, for what purpose these last years? Why should God allow such bloodshed, such suffering, only to put things back as they were before?'

'You ask the question that many have struggled with of late. There are always lessons to be learned in suffering, even if that lesson is simply that His ways will ever be beyond our under-standing. Besides, it's not quite so simple as that. I understand Charles Stuart has undertaken to work alongside Parliament. He knows he owes his new-found power to his people. There are great hopes for a more tolerant future. I, for one, bless Our Lord for this deliverance, and trust in His wisdom. All of us, whether once for the King or Cromwell, all of us now hope for peace.'

'I find it unlikely that those who believed in the Commonwealth with such passion, who would fight and die for that belief, can be swayed by a pretty show. Surely the King will still have his enemies. Surely there are still those who hold true to the rebel cause.'

Just then, as if to prove my point, an old man at the front of the crowd takes a few steps out into the street. Drunken and swaying, arms waving, he hawks and spits onto the trail of petals.

'A pox on all kings!' he cries. 'A pox on all kings!' He unties his breeches, fumbles and begins to piss at the feet of the Duke of Gloucester's guard.

He is soon shouted down. People jeer and laugh as two soldiers take him in hand and bundle him away through the crowd, disappearing into a side street. I doubt he will stand to piss again today.

Evelyn is laughing with the rest. 'It seems you are right. Let us hope that all the King's enemies will be dealt with so swiftly.'

Anne interrupts us: 'Your cousin is charming, Master Evelyn. You must allow me to champion her at court.'

We turn to look at Sarah. She sits, demure and simpering, while Thomas fills her cup. He is pink-cheeked, blurry-eyed, regaling her with some tale. I expect to feel a spike of jealousy, but there is none. If I thank God for anything today, it is for the discovery that I no longer feel anything for my husband, except perhaps a little regret that I could never see the goodness in him that others seem to. He may do as he pleases now: I am safe in the knowledge he cannot hurt me.

'Katherine, your cup is almost empty,' Anne goes on. 'Shame on you, Master Evelyn. Where is your civility? You cannot keep her all to yourself, you know.' She waggles an admonishing finger. 'I have no doubt our beautiful Lady Katherine will soon be the darling of Whitehall, especially once she has a little Fanshawe in tow. The King is so fond of pretty children.'

Evelyn inclines his head. 'Forgive my oversight. Lady Katherine and I have been engaged in such interesting conversation, I quite forgot myself. Allow me . . .'

'Well, well,' Anne says, as Evelyn takes my cup and goes to fill it from the cask. 'You've made an impression there, my dear. He's a bit of a stiff-back, but a thinking man and headed for a good position, or so my Richard says. You'd do well to make an ally of him.'

I listen as she prattles on, speaking of the King's attention to her young daughters and the sad passing of her only son, Dickon, October last. 'Have you had a midwife look at you?' she asks, turning the conversation back to me. 'The good ones can tell if it's a boy or a girl. Of course you hope for a son, but daughters can be such a comfort.' She pats the back of my hand, her other palm settling on her own belly. 'Though with four girls already, I'm praying for a boy this time.' There is no sign of a curve beneath her beaded lace bodice. 'Oh, hush now,' she says, seeing my surprise. She smiles, conspiratorial. 'I've not yet told Richard. Look! Here comes the Marquess of Hertford with his troop. The King appointed him to the Order of the Garter at Canterbury just four days ago. You should have seen how he stuttered and blushed. But how splendid he looks in his robes.'

She smiles and raises a hand to wave at the marquess. I wonder how she keeps the grief she must feel at the loss of her only son locked so deep inside. I remember Dickon as full of life, with all the confidence of a firstborn son. His is yet another death to add to the depth of my grief. Anne has aged since I saw her last, deep wrinkles around her eyes an outward sign of all she has suffered.

I decide to take my chance and ask the question that has been burning inside all day. 'When will the Dowager Queen come by?'

Anne looks at me. 'Oh, my dear, Henrietta Maria stays in Paris.'

'She's not here, with her sons?'

'No, for shame. How she would love this spectacle.'

'When will she return to England?'

Anne shrugs. 'I expect she will wait for reports of Charles's reception, though if she could see this, she would not doubt the love that England has for her sons.'

My hand goes to the charm at my throat. It feels weightier than ever before.

I cannot say that the day is not glorious. I cannot argue that London has never seen the like, or that the people are not jubilant at the return of their king. But I cannot share in their joy. It is tainted in my eyes.

Soon after, I use the excuse of my belly to leave Anne, Evelyn and the others. A coach waits at the side of the house, ready to take us to Whitehall for an audience with the King. I seek refuge inside, pull down the blinds and sit alone in the dark space, letting the tears come.

The door opens and the carriage tilts as a man climbs in. I assume it is Thomas and don't look up to greet him, for fear he will see my wet cheeks and be angry that I dare display my sadness on such a day.

'Kate.'

The unexpected voice sends a shock through me.

He is wearing a suit of coal black velvet, intricate lace at his collar and a splay of raven's feathers tucked beneath the gleaming silver buckle on his hat.

'I'm glad to see you safe.' His tone is without a hint of shame or remorse. Why should I expect otherwise from Richard Willis?

I have imagined this moment. I have run this meeting over and over in my mind a hundred times in the last few weeks. I have invented my cool revenge, dreamed of a glinting blade at his throat, revelled in imagining his pleading as I slice it deep and blood begins to spill. But now he is before me, I'm lost to all reason. Fury blazes like a white-hot furnace. I'm blinded by it. I fly at him, making a strangled cry, scratching at his face. 'You dog! You devil! You vile, merciless liar!'

He is quick to catch my hands. 'By Christ, Kate, calm yourself!'

I rage like a madwoman. 'How dare you speak to me? How dare you come near me? I swear I will kill you!'

'Be still, woman, you are in no fit state to fight with me.' He grabs my arms and tries to pin them to my sides. As he struggles, trying to avoid crushing my belly, I manage to swipe at his face, my nail drawing a thin red line across his cheek. 'Be still, you wildcat. God's bones . . .'

He is too strong for me.

I slump back against the seat, panting heavily. 'If you touch me again I shall scream murder. They'll take you away and hang you as the traitor you are.'

He wipes the thin trail of blood on the back of his hand. 'Calm yourself, Kate. I mean you no harm.'

'No, for you have done enough already.'

He fixes me with those dark, turbulent eyes. 'I knew you would blame me, and I cannot reproach you for that. But let me have this one chance to speak—'

'He is dead because of you,' I say, pushing the swell of my own guilt aside.

'Kate, that's not true.'

'If it were not for you, he would still be free. We would both be free.'

He holds up his hands. 'Perhaps, but Rafe Chaplin chose his own fate on the day he took to the road, the day he allied himself with Thurloe, the day he climbed into your bed.'

'You promised me. You promised me you would save him.'

He takes off his hat and rubs at his cheek. 'I promised nothing. I was quite clear on that.'

'Tell me, did you even try? Or was it all just a lie to silence me?'

He sighs. 'I did my best for you, Kate. But I could not save him.'

'It's your fault he's dead.' As I say the words, the tears come once again. My God, will they ever stop? I bite them back. I will not let him see my weakness. 'He told me I was a fool to believe in you . . .'

My heart is raw as fresh-killed beef. The pain surges in my veins in accord with its beat, as if the pulsing of it will split me in two.

He shifts, moves to the seat next to me, one hand reaching out for mine in a gesture of comfort.

'Don't touch me. Come no closer.'

He sits back and waits, tiny beads of scarlet forming along the line of his cheekbone. Eventually the wave of feeling is quelled, and I sit, my face turned away from him.

'I don't blame you for thinking so ill of me,' he says. 'But I want you to know that I did try. I tried to bribe the gaoler, that day I took you to Hertford. I spoke to the magistrate and offered gold I do not even have. When that failed, I came to London, hoping to get a pardon from the chief justice, but you must understand how little influence I have now. You will have heard, I'm sure, that I'm condemned as a traitor to the King.'

I shake my head. 'All I know is that you betrayed me.'

'Old enemies have made certain I'll not find favour with Charles Stuart again. I thought, for a few days, I'd be joining our friend Chaplin, but in the end, the King has been kinder to me.'

'He has pardoned you?'

'He has granted mercy.'

'Why should you live, when others more worthy do not?'

'You are not the first to ask that question,' he says. 'But I remain grateful it is so.'

A sudden shaft of sunlight falls across his face. I see the creases beneath his eyes, where the skin begins to sag. The light illuminates the hairs in his beard, more white now than black.

'Truly, Kate, I tried, as I said I would. But I failed, as I have failed at so many things of late. I wanted you to know . . . I did all I could, but no one listens to the wishes of a condemned man.'

I will not give him what he wants. I will not let him manipulate me again. This new skein of self-pity wound about him angers me. 'I will never forgive you,' I say.

He indicates the curve beneath my gown. 'You have the child. Surely there is some comfort in that.'

'It means nothing without Rafe. You say you are a condemned man, but I am condemned to a life no better than a slave's. Once my child is born, Thomas will lock me away at Ware Park. The child will be taken from me and made into a Fanshawe, with a head full of money and position, living by the favour of the King. He will never know his true father. And I will never be happy again. My only chance of happiness died with Rafe Chaplin. I may as well have died by his side.'

Willis rubs his chin, sits forward with his elbows on his knees, looking up at me. 'The girl I know would not give up so easily.'

'What do you mean?'

'I will retire to a quiet life at my house at Thames Ditton. There, I will live out my years unremarkably. I'm done with matters of king and Parliament. I'll never pick up a pistol again. But you, I always thought you were meant for something different.' He regards me. Even after all these years, I still cannot read him. 'You are still young and in time this pain will lessen,' he says. 'It may never leave you completely. Instead, it will become part of who you are, and you will learn to treasure it, because it will have given you something more valuable than you can imagine.'

'And what is that?'

'You will have to find your own treasure, Kate. But if anyone can do it, you can.'

We sit in silence for a few moments. Outside the crowd jostles the carriage, rocking it gently. Church bells peal in a great crashing swell. A chime of laughter sounds from a woman, just outside, high and excited.

'You must be brave now,' he says, voice low.

I feel so tired all of a sudden. 'I am not brave, not without Rafe by my side.'

'You have courage of a different kind. I have always seen it in you. I have always admired it. You will make your own fate . . . if you are brave enough.'

My heart twists at his words – words that remind me so much of another time, another place, another man.

He holds my gaze for a few seconds. 'But now I must bid you farewell, Kate, for I think I will not see you again.' He picks up his hat and puts it on. He fixes me with those deep, stormy eyes that have fooled me so many times. 'I see you are determined to hate me, but know this: whatever your chosen path, I will always think of you.'

He stands, opening the carriage door to a great hubbub. Stepping out, he stands tall, pushes his shoulders back and takes a lungful of London stink. Turning to close the door, he pauses. There is a glint in his eye, something of the old Richard Willis – the handsome, swaggering man to whom once, as a girl, I would have given myself so gladly.

'I've heard tell that Sir William Cobden's coach will travel from London on the sixth of June,' he says. 'It will overnight at Hatfield before taking the North Road across Nomansland Common. They say that the route is made safe, these days, so the guards expect no trouble. I'm sure we both wish Sir William's gold a very safe passage.'

Before I can respond he puts his hand upon his heart and makes a low bow. Then, as he closes the coach door, he shoots me one last wicked grin.

Chapter 55

I lay the pistols on the table in my bedchamber: my own, with its smooth turned wood and intricate silver filigree, and Rafe's, simpler, heavier, more suited to the task.

I take a keg from Rafe's old bandolier – at least half are still full of powder – and put it next to the wadding, the scouring stick and my leather pouch of lead shot. I have a rag ready to clean the mechanism. I must be sure there is no chance it will fail.

When I am prepared, I sit and stare at the two guns. I play my fingers along the barrel of each in turn. They are cold, hard and unyielding, yet so beautiful, powerful and deadly.

I choose my own, pick it up and open the pan cover. The metal is charred and blackened. I wipe away the remnants of old powder, noting the little cross hatch of scratches where the flint has struck the steel. I check the flint itself, making sure it is secure and still sharp. Then I tap a measure of powder into the priming pan and close it. Carefully, I tip the rest of the charge down the barrel. I choose a bullet, taking my time to find one that is most perfectly round and smooth. I slip it into the barrel of the gun, then push the wadding home with the rammer.

The gun is ready. But I am not. Not yet.

I have slept little since I saw Richard Willis in London. My belly is huge now and I can find no respite from the tugging weight, the draw in my innards, the aching back. But that is not the reason sleep eludes me. Each morning since I returned to Ware Park, I am up with first light. I stand at my window, watching the world come alive, resentful at the June sunshine, the riot of blooms, the cacophony of birdcall. I hate the things that remind me of a world that keeps turning, unceasing and insensible, when my world is ruined. Each morning I think I lack the strength for another day. And yet, somehow, I go on. And each stretch of time between dawn and dusk brings unfathomable grief.

What rest I find in the dark hours is broken and tormented by dreams of Rafe. Sometimes they come as wicked nightmares, conjuring twisted images of those last moments beneath the gallows. I stir, trembling and terrified. Other times we are together again, beneath the bright, blinking stars in Gustard Wood. Those times, my mind answers the craving of my flesh and I wake, always just at the very moment of my pleasure, reaching out to touch his skin, desperate for the scent and warmth of him, as the sensation of his body inside mine fades and tears wet my cheeks. When it is like this, I wish I could close my eyes and dream of him for ever.

Willis's words haunt me. I have counted out the days, and as each passes, the tight clenching in my chest grows steadily stronger. And now the day is almost here. Sir William Cobden's coach leaves London today. If his coachman follows the usual route, they will cross Nomansland Common by noon tomorrow. Willis has given me the key to decide my own fate. But I've taken no action. I have not visited the man in Ware, as Rafe suggested. I have no gang of thieves awaiting my instruction. There will be no robbery because I cannot see the point. What future can there possibly be without Rafe?

I stand and go to the window, pistol in hand. My heart is halting and interrupted, but the heft of the gun by my side is somehow calming.

Outside, day is dawning, ghostly mist swirling in the ditches. I watch a single blackbird bob along the terrace below, beak bright as a beacon. The roses are budding on the trellis and late blossom drifts in lazy flights. Two white butterflies dance above the lavender, up and up, into the pale blue. But the pleasure I once found in such things is dead and gone. I cannot find the joy in God's creation when I am so cruelly abandoned by Him.

Slowly, I lift the gun, pull back the cock, and put the barrel into my mouth.

My finger tightens on the trigger.

Seconds run by.

The child kicks.

Richard Willis thinks I am brave, but he is wrong. If I were brave I would pull the trigger. If I were brave I would face the Devil and all his demons, in a bid to find Rafe amid Hell's flames.

But I cannot when there is new life inside me and that life belongs to Rafe.

I let the gun drop.

I turn away from the window and, instead, aim the barrel at the portrait hanging beside the bed. The girl in the picture stares back at me with defiant, wicked eyes.

The child kicks again. Once, twice. Sure and strong.

I know then that the Devil has plans for me yet.

A noise interrupts my reverie – the unmistakable thunder of galloping hoofs. I turn back to the window, just in time to see dust settling on the path.

I put the gun down, quickly wrap a shawl around my shoulders and leave the room. One of the dairymaids comes panting up the stairs, meeting me halfway. She pushes a note into my hand.

Lady Katherine,
Rachel struggles in childbed and asks for you. I pray you come to her
as soon as you can. It may be your last chance.
    God speed.
    Martha Coppin

Chapter 56

Rachel is lying on the bed in the red chamber, propped against the bolster. Her skin is sheened and grey as rainclouds. She rolls her head to look at me and reaches out a hand.

Quickly, I cross the room and kiss her. 'I'm here now. I'm here.'

The midwife, a meaty woman of middle years in plain cap and gown, is banking up the fire, despite the summer heat. 'Don't tire her with talk,' she says.

I shoot her a mean glare.

'Hannah is the best midwife in these parts,' Martha says. 'We must do as she says.'

Hannah gives a curt nod of acknowledgement. 'You're near your time too,' she says, eyeing my belly. 'Very near indeed. You should be at home.'

'This is my home,' I say, turning back to Rachel. I don't miss the sharp look that Martha gives me.

Rachel begins to grimace as the pain takes her. She lets out a tearing cry and beats her fist against the mattress. I squeeze her hand. 'I'm here, Rachel. All will be well.' She digs her fingernails into my palm.

When the pain has subsided, Rachel falls back, exhausted. Her head lolls from side to side and she murmurs nonsense under her breath. Martha takes me outside the room.

'She's very weak,' she says. 'Hannah says the baby lies the wrong way round and does not want to come. She's been like this for hours with no progress.'

I'm unprepared for this. I have no idea how best to help my friend and no idea how best to help myself. I have been alone in a world of men for many months, with no one to advise me. My hands slide over my own stomach.

'Are you well?' Martha is concerned. 'Hannah is right – I think you must be very near your time. I should not have sent for you.'

'No, no.' I put a hand on her shoulder to reassure her. 'You did right. I'm well enough. I have a little while yet.' But even as I say it, I feel the press and shift of the child low in my womb, the ache in my spine, and a trembling weakness in my legs that makes me unsteady. I must stay strong, for Rachel's sake.

Rachel's pain goes on into the night.

Hannah stays calm, dosing her patient with mugwort and calamint to make the baby come quicker. She says very little, but she has no need – the deep crease in her brow tells me all I need to know.

I stay close by Rachel's side. By nightfall, she starts to bleed. Racked with pain every time her body convulses, she bucks and kicks as though in a fit. She cries out, cursing and weeping for God to take her.

I am helpless and horrified. It is not that I have never witnessed a woman in childbed before, but never one so precious to me. I wish I could take the pain for her. With every new agony, my own body aches, my limbs grow heavy, my eyes are sore and there is a dull throbbing in the pit of my stomach. Martha and I work together, swabbing the red trickle that flows from between Rachel's legs.

In the darkest hours the pains come so quickly that there is no respite. Rachel sets up a great caterwauling howl. I'm reminded of a deer I once heard, badly injured but not killed by the arrows of the hunt, bellowing its last misery in a cry so full of anguish that I had to turn away when the dogs went in to finish it.

Hannah is by Rachel's side, reaching between her legs to feel the child inside.

'It's time,' she says. 'Rachel, you must try to stand, to help your baby on its way.'

At first it seems that Rachel cannot hear us. Her head tosses, eyes rolling and flecks of foamy spittle flying.

I put my arm around her shoulders. 'Rachel, you must do as Hannah says. I'll help you.'

With Martha and I taking an arm each, we manage to lever Rachel off the side of the bed. She crumples to her knees, a gush of bright red spattering the linen we have spread across the boards.

'Keep her upright,' Hannah says. 'Now, Rachel, you must start to push.' Her hands are between Rachel's legs. 'Your baby is coming into God's world feet first, like a pilgrim, ready to walk on God's earth. You must help and push as hard as you can.'

Rachel's face twists as a wave of pain takes her and she crumples forward onto all fours. 'I cannot . . . I cannot . . .'

'Yes, you can, Rachel,' Martha says. 'It is what you are made for.'

We keep her that way for what seems like an age and yet still the baby does not come. She is so weak, clutching my hand with grappling desperate fingers, imploring me to help her. She cries out for Rafe, like a child calling for a lost mother. I can hardly bear to hear it, for it echoes the yearning in my own heart.

I feel lightheaded and sick, spattered with Rachel's blood. Time seems to stretch and shrink around us. I can tell that the hours are passing only because the candles burn down and new logs are needed for the hearth.

In time, Hannah orders Rachel placed back on the bed. 'I must turn the baby around,' she says, grim-faced. 'You must hold her down. If we leave it, they will both die.'

Suddenly I am back in the courtyard at Merton College, listening to the echo of my mother's screams.

'I cannot bear it,' I say, backing away. My hands go up to my face, leaving smears of blood.

'Then help us. It's the only chance now.'

'Dear Lord,' Martha starts to pray, taking hold of Rachel's shoulders. 'We ask for your mercy. Help us now, your children, help us to bring this new soul into your world . . .'

Swallowing the horror that threatens to choke me, I take hold of Rachel. 'Look at me,' I say. She rolls her eyes to mine. Her expression is wild, as if she does not know me. 'I will not leave you. And you will not leave me. I promise we will never be parted again. Just stay here with me.'

'Kate . . .' she croaks, but then her eyes squeeze shut and her face contorts in a great howl of suffering as Hannah begins her work.

It takes only moments for Hannah to reach inside, but the pain is too much for Rachel. She has no strength to hold herself up once again and Martha and I must keep her upright so that the baby can come. A bloody mess drips from between Rachel's legs, thick purple clots that look like something tossed aside by the butcher, as if she is bleeding out her insides. She is insensible, whimpering, eyes showing white, body shuddering when the pains come. I cannot tell if she is pushing, but at last, Hannah finds the baby's head and pulls.

With one last torturous roar, the thing slides free in a rush of liquid and gore. Rachel slumps to the floor.

Hannah parts mother and child with the flick of a blade. She takes the tiny body in her arms. I wait for the rent of a child's cry, but it does not come.

'Get her onto the bed,' Hannah says, and Martha and I obey, struggling to lift Rachel.

'Does it live?' I ask, but Hannah turns away. I cannot see what she is doing with the small, red creature in her arms.

Rachel moans as we push and pull her onto the mattress. Her lips move as though she is trying to form words.

'Rest now,' I whisper, stroking away sweat-drenched hair from her face and neck.

There is a sudden cry, a splutter and a high wail. My heart flies.

Hannah turns about and the child in her arms is squirming, like a newborn piglet. 'It's a girl,' she says, unable to hide her relief.

'Oh, thank God.' Martha falls to her knees, one hand holding Rachel's, the other to her heart.

I press my face against Rachel's shoulder. 'You have a daughter.'

Rachel's breathing is ragged, her chest juddering, but she seems to understand. She lifts her head and reaches out her free hand towards Hannah.

Hannah quickly wipes away the worst of the blood. She lays the baby gently upon Rachel's chest. Tears leak from the corners of Rachel's eyes and trickle downwards. I wipe them away, ignoring my own. I cannot take my eyes from the tiny puckered face in Rachel's arms.

But Hannah does not give us long before she puts the child into Martha's arms and tends her patient. As she begins to wipe away the blood and gore, ready for the delivery of the afterbirth, she frowns, saying nothing. Rachel falls almost immediately into disturbed half-sleep. When I feel her cheek, she is flame hot. I meet Hannah's eye.

'She is not out of danger,' she says.

A hard lump rises in my chest. 'What can we do?'

'I will give her a dose for the fever. Beyond that, there is nothing to help her but prayer.'

★ ★ ★

It is dawn, a streak of hazy summer light creeping through a crack in the red velvet drapes, when Rachel stirs. Both Martha and Hannah have fallen to dozing by the fire. The baby rests fitfully, making little snuffling noises, with its head on Rachel's breast. I'm watching over them both, when Rachel opens her eyes. The wildness is gone. She seems almost herself again.

I stroke her cheek.

She holds her daughter close, plants a tender kiss on her head. 'Rafe would have been a proud uncle,' she says.

'The proudest. He would have taught her to ride, and to steal apples from the orchards here at Markyate Cell. He would have taught her to master a pistol before she could walk.'

Rachel smiles. She puts her head back against the pillow. 'I'm so tired, Kate. So very tired.'

'The worst is over. Now you need do nothing but rest.' I put my hand to her forehead. It is still burning. 'Rest, so you're strong for your little one.'

Her eyes are sad. 'Will you promise me something?'

'Of course.'

'A child should be with its rightful parents. My child . . . my child is Thomas's.'

'But you're her mother.'

'Thomas does not even know. He's a father. It's wrong that he doesn't know.'

'All Thomas cares about is an heir.'

'And now he has one, if he so chooses. Your child is Rafe's. You must not let Thomas bring up Rafe's child as his own. He did not want it . . . and nor do you.' She pauses a moment and takes a deep breath. 'I know you think him cruel, but Thomas is not a bad man. He was kind to me when I was lonely, a comfort when I thought myself abandoned. I know you and he have struggled but, Kate, he can be tender and loving, and he truly does long for a child. I know he will love his daughter.'

This picture of Thomas is at odds with the man I know, but now is not the time for argument.

'If I am gone,' she says, 'then she should be with her father . . . He will take care of her. He will give her a good life . . .'

'Do not say such things.'

'I'm sorry, Kate. I never meant to hurt you. Forgive me . . .'

I hush her. 'Don't distress yourself. There's plenty of time to decide the best course.'

'No, there is no more time.' She sighs. 'The promise you made to my brother, will you keep it?' She searches my face.

I am taken aback. 'Rachel, I—'

'Promise me, Kate . . . promise you'll do as he wished. Promise me you will be free.'

I have already broken the promise I made to Rafe. I do not want to break a promise to his sister.

'Go far away from here,' she goes on. 'Take your baby and go far away . . .' Her head sinks back to her pillow. 'Promise me . . .'

The words come out of my mouth. I will say anything to soothe her. 'I promise. We will go away together, just as Rafe wanted. I promise I will find a way.'

She looks pleased, and cradles her baby's head in her palm.

I climb on to the bed and lie next to her, my own belly aching, sharp pains travelling down my legs. The tiredness overwhelms me and my head sinks onto the pillow beside hers. I put my arm around her and the baby, as if I could protect them from the world, and all the pain and suffering and sadness that they will have to endure in the years to come, wishing with all my heart that I could see a way to keep the promises I have made.

I am woken by a child's cry.

The sun is high, slivers of bright sunshine slicing the dust motes. The baby is squirming, flush-faced and wailing, little arms punching the air. By the hearth, Hannah stirs, stands and stretches, peering over to the bed. I find Rachel's hand and squeeze it. Her fingers are cold.

Her skin is pale, the fever spots gone. Her lips are grey. Her daughter's cry does not wake her.

'Rachel?' My mouth is dry and my whisper does not sound like my own. I put a hand to her shoulder. 'Wake up, my love. Your baby needs you.'

Hannah comes slowly to the bedside. Martha is stirring.

I give Rachel a gentle shake. 'Wake up now. Wake up, Rachel . . .'

Hannah puts her hand gently on top of mine to still it. Silently, she touches Rachel's cheek, then to her neck. She shakes her head.

'Her suffering is over,' she says. 'God rest her soul.' Then she picks up the child and holds it close, rocking from side to side.

The child's cry is so loud, so piercing, that I think my mind will crack into a thousand pieces.

I lie there, unable to move or speak. I put my head on Rachel's chest, where the child lay a moment ago. The baby has left a small patch of warmth, just beneath Rachel's breast. I put my palm there as the heat fades. I try to cup it, to keep the smallest sign of life alive. But there is no beat beneath the cold, smooth skin.

Until this moment I did not know that a heart, already shattered, could be broken all over again.

Chapter 57

It is gone noon by the time I reach Nomansland Common. I pray I'm not too late.

A strange thick yellow fog has settled, choking the fields with sticky, damp heat. I lose my way more than once, even though I know the roads through this country like my own veins. Feather is tired, her tread heavy and stumbling. She tosses her head and champs her bit, protesting at my insistence that we go on.

My own body resists, every step sending a jolt through my aching limbs. Sharp pains arrest my breath every so often. I fight to stay upright in the saddle as my head swims, dense and stifling as the mist.

But I will not give up.

My mind hangs on images of Rachel's pale face, the parchment touch of her skin and the desperation with which she bade me make my final promise.

I see now I have been selfish, blinded by my own anger and petty resentments. I did not understand that she was the one who always loved me best. She loved me in spite of my failings, even when I hurt her, when I put my own wishes before hers, when I tossed aside her cares as though they were worth nothing.

I drove her away. I drove her into Thomas's arms. She was no more at fault than I. We turned away from each other to seek comfort in the arms of men. And because of that my friend is gone.

I blame myself. Will there ever be an end to the blood on my hands?

But I made a promise to her, and this time, I intend to keep it.

I'm half blinded by the fog, so I must go by other senses. I take the road across the heath, listening for the sound of travellers. There is no wind to carry the trundle of carriage wheels or the whicker of a carthorse. The fog brings an eerie silence. Even the birds are quiet. It provides protection of sorts, for I have little else to help. I'm wearing my riding cloak, but I'm still dressed in blood-stained skirts, no kerchief to cover my face. My best guard is the two pistols, now loaded and holstered on my saddle.

I check the guns, stroking the smooth wood where Rafe's hand rested so many times before. He is with me now, a part of him deep inside, in the blood and bones of my unborn child.

I think back to that day in Hertford gaol, when Rafe first told me of Cobden's gold. The memory makes tears sting, but I cannot let melancholy overwhelm me. It is far too late to seek the help that Rafe intended so I must do this alone. In my hampered state, my chances of success are slim, but I'm determined to try.

Rachel's death has changed everything. My eyes are no longer shrouded by the untruths I have told myself. I cannot go back to Ware Park to live as Thomas's prisoner. I cannot lie about my child's father. I will not condemn myself to a half-lived life of unhappiness and regret, for that would be a slow kind of torture.

If my end must come, I had rather it was swift and honest. Grief brings utter despair, but with it, a conviction that I must seize the only chance of freedom left open to me, no matter how mad and reckless it seems. And if I fail, then the Devil will take me, and the child will be lost, but rather that than the living death that lies ahead.

In the woods, where the track leaves the common, I find a well-hidden spot, up on the bank overlooking the road. Once a coach is stopped between these steep banks, it cannot turn or go back.

From here I have a view through the trunks to the common and, if the fog clears, a view ahead. The murk does not sit so heavy beneath the trees but wreathes around the trunks, ever shifting, like the flow of a brook over stones.

I dismount and tie Feather's reins to a low branch. Flashes of pain torment me, cramping me double. I have a sudden image of myself, all alone here in the woods, bleeding and helpless, crying out in agony with no one to hear. I fear a fate like Rachel's. My own body is so like hers – small and unmatronly, not well made for these things. I'm terrified that I will be rent in two by the child within.

Just then I hear a noise coming from the direction of the common, the jangle of harness, the steady trot of horses' hoofs. With a great effort of will, I push these thoughts aside.

Quickly, I unleash Feather and struggle into the saddle. I go to the top of the bank and strain to see through the mist. The noise draws near. Whoever it is, they are certainly taking this path. I hear the rattle of carriage wheels, the creak of ungreased axles. Then, through the gloom, a dark shape emerges.

An unmarked black coach, drawn by two horses, heaves into view. The windows are shut. A driver sits atop the closed carriage, a second man to his left. A further two are perched facing the road behind, the barrels of two muskets pointing skywards.

This must be Sir William Cobden's coach. Richard Willis was true at the last.

They move slowly, the horses hesitant and the driver mindful.

My heartbeat patters like battlefield drums. As they come closer a swelling agony rears, making me swoon and almost cry out. I have to bite on my sleeve while it passes. But then my hands rest against the heavy swoop of the pistol butts. I think of Rafe. I think of Rachel. I think of my unborn child. I remember the look in Richard Willis's eyes as he bade me goodbye. 'You will make your own fate,' he said. 'If you are brave enough.'

And then Feather is moving, taking sure steps down the bank

to meet the road. I have no idea if I have urged her on, but it is all the sign I need.

My hand goes to the pistol on my left – Rafe's pistol – and I draw it out, fixing the cock into place. With the gun ready, a powerful sense of calm descends.

Swaddled in mist, I reach the road. The coach is almost upon me.

'Halt your horses!' My voice rings out loud and strong in the eerie silence.

There is commotion as the driver tugs on the reins. The man next to him leaps from his seat and disappears into the trees. The horses whinny and stamp as they draw to a halt, stones scattering. One of the coach doors swings open but I cannot tell if anyone leaves before it slams shut once more. One of the armed men is hurriedly loading his musket, but I've lost sight of the other.

I aim my gun at the driver. 'You will deliver the gold to me,' I say.

Then comes a voice: 'We are armed and will not hesitate. Step aside or lose your life.'

I cannot see the owner of this voice. It seems to come from beyond the coach. The man with the musket has completed his task and fixes the eye of the gun upon me.

I stand my ground. 'You will give the gold to me, or your man will meet his maker.'

'So . . . the doxy returns without her keeper. Move aside and let us pass unharmed, or you shall join your sweetheart in his sinner's grave.'

'I will not ask again. Ground your weapons and hand over the gold.'

I hear movement in the woods to my left, catch a whiff of matchlight.

'You are outmanned and outgunned. Step aside and we will not harm you.'

I urge Feather forward, until we are almost level with the horses and I have a clear shot at the driver. He sits hunched, clutching the reins. I see him swallow as he takes in the gun, my blood-spattered dress and the swollen mound of my belly. His eyes slide momentarily to mine and they contain a warning. He gives the tiniest shake of his head.

The coach is a black hulking box, refusing to give up its secrets.

What would Rafe do?

'I will strike a bargain with you,' I say. 'Half the gold for your safe passage.'

'I don't think my master would like that.' There is more than a touch of arrogance in the man's tone and it makes me angry. 'You're surrounded. Lay down your pistol and dismount.'

I don't know if he tells the truth. I scan the woods but see no one amid the trees.

'Do as I say or this man will die,' I say, and the driver cowers.

I see now there is just enough room to take Feather down the side of the coach. If there are men in the woods, they will not dare to fire on me so close to their own horses.

Keeping my pistol trained on the driver, I draw level with the carriage door.

'You inside, open the door slowly and ground your weapons,' I say.

'You are making a mistake,' comes the voice. 'Leave now and we will not harm you. We do not look for trouble.' Whoever it is seems to be behind me, somewhere in the woods, but I'm right, and they do not fire while I'm so close to the prize.

There is no reaction from inside, so I reach down and try the handle. It turns. I open the door slowly, the barrel of my pistol first, my finger on the trigger.

My gun is met with its match, the dull iron of a flintlock, black barrel, like an eye, trained on my breast. The man behind it is young and scared. He uses both arms to balance the weight of the gun. He fixes me with a nervous stare, the muscles in his cheek and brow twitching.

'Hold your fire, Atkins!' the man's voice calls from the trees. 'We want no bloodshed.'

I raise my pistol to the youth's forehead. 'It seems we are at a stalemate, Atkins,' I say, making my voice quiet so that only he can hear. 'Your head for my heart.' He says nothing. I pull my cloak aside so that he can see the swell of my belly. I see his shock. His arms waver a little.

'You would not take an innocent life, I think, and nor would I. Now, put the gun on the floor and hand me the gold.'

'I – I cannot.'

'Do as I say, Atkins.'

'They'll have me flogged.'

'Better that than Hell's eternal fire.'

I see hesitation pass across his face. A strange calm overcomes me. This boy will not dare hurt me. My belly is my protection. 'Do as I say and I promise I won't hurt you.'

I'm aware of movement in the trees behind me, of cracking twigs and whispered commands. I am running out of time. Atkins looks down at my stomach and back up to meet my eyes. He is shaking. He lowers the pistol and places it on the floor of the coach.

'Well done, Atkins,' I say. 'You've done the right thing.'

Until now I had not dared take my eyes from his, but glancing inside, I see that there are several strongboxes and sacks on the seat opposite.

'Give me whichever sacks have the most coin.'

His hands tremble over one, then choose another. 'I'm not sure . . .' he says, holding it out to me.

It is heavy with the chink of coin. 'Now, reach out and put it in my saddlebag,' I say.

He does so, glancing over my shoulder into the woods with frightened eyes.

'Now another.'

Atkins does the same with a second sack, and a third. I can feel the weight of the gold, dragging down one side of the saddle.

Behind me I hear the crash of men making their way through the undergrowth. I must not be too greedy.

'Thank you, Atkins.'

He shies back behind the wall of the coach and gives a nod. Poor soul, I know he will pay dearly for this.

I urge Feather on, passing the coach, back towards Nomansland. If I can reach the stretch of common and give Feather her head, the fog will cover me.

Then comes the pain, this time so sudden and so terrible that I cry out. It begins low in my guts, sending sharp, evil tentacles all through my body. For a moment I'm lost to anything else. I clutch at my belly, dropping the pistol. As it hits the ground, it fires, a great crack of smoke and sparks at our feet. Feather lurches forwards, crashing against the back wheel of the carriage. I almost lose my seat. Clutching at the pommel, grappling for the reins, I just manage to keep hold. And then we are off, a volley of shot and shouting behind me.

'Home, Feather, take me home . . .' I gasp, swooning with the agony. I have no strength to press her on, but she knows the game by now, and it takes only moments before we are hidden in the swirling mists.

It is only miles later, when the pain has lessened and I draw Feather to a walk that I notice the flush of bright red, seeping along my cuff, dribbling into my palm. There is a tear in my riding cloak. I push it aside and see that the sleeve of my dress is stained dark and wet.

Suddenly a great smarting soreness rises to match that in my womb. I clutch at the wound and a surge of blood spills down my arm. Bile rises in my throat. And then the fog comes down.

Chapter 58

My journey is little more than a series of hazy images and muffled sounds. I'm made almost insensible by the pain that racks my body, and half blinded by the fog. The agony consumes me until I can think of nothing else. I try to concentrate on the steady tread of Feather's hoofs, the musk of her sweat-foamed flanks, but every time a new wave comes, it is all I can do to stay in the saddle. I slump forward, the mound of my belly wedged against Feather's mane, to stop myself falling. And with each vicious cramp I become more aware of a pressure, drawing ever downwards, as though my insides would come spilling out, slithering and splashing on the dusty road.

I reach Markyate Cell by twilight, as the fog clears to reveal a star-studded sky. There are shouts and running footsteps as Feather takes me into the yard. Eager hands steady me as we are guided to the mounting block, but I cannot make my limbs do as I wish. I slip sideways, falling from the saddle, into waiting arms.

I do not want to be separated from Feather, or the gold in her saddlebags, but when I open my mouth to give instruction, all that comes out is a strange animal moan, a faraway echo of myself. Another crushing pain makes me crumple to my knees. There is a splitting sensation low inside, an opening up, and a rush of warm wetness soaks my skirts.

* * *

I am in the scarlet chamber. Fire flares in the hearth. There is a sore tugging at my arm: someone is tending the wound there, wrapping it in wide linen bandages. I turn my head to see Martha.

'Hush now,' she says, as I struggle to speak. 'Save your strength. You are safe, but the baby is coming. I have sent for Hannah.'

Another pain begins. This time it is poker-hot and scorching, taking me deep inside myself. I pulse with each contraction of my body, the flow of blood, a blinding light behind my eyelids. I am naught but muscle and flesh and bone. I am a base and feral thing, panting like a birthing bitch. There is nothing but the smarting and a powerful urge to expel the thing inside. I am moving with it and fighting against it all at once.

I claw my way back to sense. 'Rachel . . .' I gasp. 'I want to see Rachel . . .'

Martha hushes me, stroking my forehead. 'Rachel is at rest in the chapel. You can see her later. You must stay calm, Kate. You have lost too much blood and must save your strength. You must help your baby to come.'

I try to push myself up. 'I don't want to die in this bed.'

'God will not let that happen,' Martha says. I see the worry in her eyes. 'Please, Kate, be strong for Him. Bear this suffering and you and your child will be delivered.'

I do not know how long it takes.

There is no sign of Hannah, so Martha is the one who helps me from the bed and onto my knees before the hearth, where they have covered the boards in straw and an old blanket. She gives calm orders to a young woman, with a frizz of orange curls and big, frightened eyes, whom I've never seen before. But I don't care who she is. I care about nothing but the fiery stinging between my thighs. I'm lost to this ceaseless agony. I'm become low – a heaving, breathing thing, bellowing out all my hatred, all my fury, all my heartbreak.

I am angry – angry with God. First, He took my brothers and then my father. When I had borne my share of that grief, He took my mother. I replaced her with Rachel and then, in time, with Rafe. Now, He has taken them too. All the people I have cared about are gone. There is no one left to love.

As the pain crashes over me once again, and I bear down hard, I feel the child move within. I squeeze my eyes tight shut. Behind the lids, all is blood-red; a blood-red sky, a single star, the Devil's talons hooked deep inside.

For a time, I want it all to end. I ask God to take me. I scream at Martha and she holds my hands and bids me push my child out into the world.

I cannot bear it. But at the same time I cannot bear to have this thing inside me any longer. I swear I will be cloven in two. I feel the beginning of the tearing, knife-like pain as it begins to happen. Images of my own lifeless body swim before me. I see myself laid out atop a marble tomb, with painted, dead eyes and crossed hands, like those ancient stone women in St Mary's. I see the child laid upon my chest, a red and grizzled thing, ugly and sightless as a baby rat, squirming and squealing in its own bloody gore.

I am on my hands and knees, Martha behind me. She tells me to push but my body is doing it anyway and I feel the raw, flaming rend of my insides as the child travels.

The silver heart-shaped charm, always around my neck, glints in the firelight. I clutch it in one hand, feel the sweat-slicked metal in my palm. Henrietta Maria's sweet face drifts in my mind's eye. If this trinket has the power to deliver a king safe into this world, surely it can help me now.

And then Martha is saying, 'One last time . . . one last time . . .'

The pain is boundless, but then, in a sudden slippery rush, the child comes tumbling out. I feel it. I feel it leave me, and know it is over.

And then I am crying and the ginger-haired girl is babbling something I cannot hear above the sound of my own sobs. I slump forward onto the floor, tangled in the wet linen, as Martha cuts the child free.

I am pulsing and shuddering, the pain dulled now, like a memory of what came before. A severing in my heart tells me that the child is dead. God has taken the one thing I had left. I beat my palms against the floorboards and beg Him to take me too.

Then I hear it – a thin, high mewling, reedy and pitiful at first, mustering to a loud squall, like the call of a kittiwake.

Martha is there. In her arms lies a tiny wrinkled thing, flopping like a fresh-killed leveret.

Martha smiles, and as she does so, the baby starts to move, tiny arms bending and kicking as though protesting this rude awakening from deepest sleep.

My tears are suddenly stopped. I am transfixed.

Martha gently wipes the blood from the child's face. 'Another girl,' she says. 'God be blessed, you have a daughter.'

She brings the child and places her in my arms. All my anger is gone. I look at her tiny face and see Rafe there. She has a few wet curls of fine hair and long lashes. When she opens her eyes, I see that, amid the newborn-blue, they are dappled with amber, just like his.

Chapter 59

All is silent in the scarlet chamber. A single flame stretches from a candle stub on a table next to the bed. Embers glow in the hearth. The shutters are closed, barring the moonlight and the cool, dark night.

Martha sits next to the fireplace, cradling a mug of something hot and steaming, contemplating the dwindling flames. I don't know how much time has passed but the floor is swept and the room put back in order. As I struggle to sit, wincing at the smarting between my legs, she stands and moves quickly to my side.

'Where is she?' I ask.

'With the wet nurse. She is well.'

'Bring her to me.'

'Soon, Kate. You need to rest for a time.'

'I have strength enough.'

Martha shakes her head, sitting next to me on the bed. 'Give yourself a moment to recover. You have suffered much these last weeks, but now God has been merciful. He has seen fit to save you, and through your suffering, you have proved yourself to Him.'

'How can you speak to me of God's mercy when He has been so cruel?'

'No,' she says gently. 'The world has been cruel. But God has brought you through it all. He has further purpose for you.'

I feel the thin veil of pretence between us falling away. 'Oh, Martha, the terrible things I have done . . . God is punishing me.'

She turns to face me and puts her hand on mine. 'I will not ask how you came by the gunshot wound. I will ask nothing about where you went yesterday, or why your saddlebags are laden with coin . . .' She presses a firm hand against my shoulder as I start up. 'Yes, the stable lad told me. Do not fear – I will make sure no one in my employ ever speaks of these things. I do not want to know anything more about what you have done, but I do know this: God has saved you. He has given you the chance to right your wrongs.' She fixes me with those calm, certain eyes. 'I heard the promise that you made to Rachel before she passed. If you intend to keep it, I would help you do so.'

I had thought that my whispered promise was for Rachel's ears alone, but now I remember that Martha was there too. With her gentle breath and closed eyes, I had thought her sleeping.

'Why would you help me when to do so goes against everything the world says is right?'

'Because the world is not always right.' She sighs. 'Kate . . . there is something I want to tell you. Something I have never spoken of . . . but if I am to hold your secrets then I would have you know mine. Perhaps, then, you will understand a little better. Have I your confidence, as you have mine?'

I nod.

She takes a deep breath and releases it slowly, as if preparing herself. 'I knew a man, once. He was the youngest son in a family of Catholic recusants and, as such, our friendship was forbidden. Both families made sure to prevent it. When war came, he was sent away, to fight for the King. But by then it was too late. There was a child inside me.' Her hands go unconsciously to her belly and rest there, her downcast eyes reflecting a sadness I have never seen in her before. 'After Marston Moor, I lost them both.'

She swallows hard. 'For years I thought this was God's judgement on my sins but, with time, I have come to see it differently. Even now, I cannot find it in me to regret what I did – I only regret what I did not do. I could have fought for the things I loved, but I was not brave enough. God puts challenges in our path that we might prove ourselves, but I was too weak.'

This revelation should surprise me – such a dark secret for such a godly woman – but somehow it does not. 'What was his name?'

'Edward.' Her breath catches.

'And the child?'

'She never had a name. She came too early for that. They took her away and I never saw her.' She takes a few steadying breaths, collecting herself. 'I have watched you, Kate, and I have always held to the belief that you have a good heart. I have seen how you strive for the things you want with the fearlessness that I lacked. I will not let you give up now, to live a life tainted by regret, as I have done.'

'It is already too late . . .'

'It is not. Let God help you. You must stop fighting Him. You cannot change the past and you will never find peace until you accept it.'

My heart tightens. 'How can I accept it when I am damned, and destined to lose everything I love?'

'Not everything.' Her eyes are clear and open, shining once more with faith.

'We all must find reasons to live. I found mine eventually, and you . . . you have plenty. God will help you find them.'

'I think your God must be different from my God. He abandoned me long ago.'

'He never abandons any of His children. It is we who turn away from Him.' She stands slowly. 'You must rest now. I have not yet sent word to Ware Park, and will not do so until tomorrow. There is still time.'

'Time for what?'

'For you to decide your path. I will keep your secrets, Kate, if you ask it. Just tell me what I must do.' Her fingers squeeze mine. 'No matter what you think, there are still those who love you, and those who will forgive you. I have told you many times, God will always forgive, but first, you must forgive yourself.'

When I wake again, I think, at first, that I am alone, but then I hear the quiet snuffling of my child. There is a wooden cradle next to the bed, the gentle undulating shape of a wakeful baby inside. I push myself up and look at her.

Her eyes are still small and tight closed, her skin raw and blotched. She has a tiny nose and a delicate pink mouth. She reaches up one little fist and splays her fingers.

I push back the coverlet. My head swims and I take a moment to steady myself. My breasts are tingling and heavy. There is an ache, deep in my belly, a stinging heat between my thighs, but I'm driven by something more powerful than pain. I take the few steps to the cradle and lift my daughter into my arms. As I bring her close, she makes a spluttering sound and rests her head upon my chest. I can feel the patter of her heartbeat, quick like a puppy's, and the gentle hiccup of her breath. My heart strains to meld with hers. I know then that we must never be parted. She will never know her father but, I swear as I stand in the scarlet chamber at Markyate Cell, she will not have a false one.

I dress slowly. A clean set of clothes has been laid out and I put them on, ignoring the ache in my limbs, the shiver on my skin. I wrap my baby in swaddling linen and blankets from the cradle and make a sling from my shawl, as I have seen the peasant women do when they carry their children in the fields.

I go to the hidden door beside the hearth and find the catch concealed in the wainscoting. Cold dawn air rushes in, carrying the scent of mildew and ancient stone. Pausing for a moment, I take one final look about me. Memories crowd in: my mother at her dressing-table, pinning pearls into her hair; sitting at the leaded panes, watching my brothers scamper in the walled garden below; Rachel, clutching my hand with sad, desperate eyes; Rafe, pale and ghostly, with a slash of scarlet across his white linen shirt.

All these memories make me what I am. It's hard to leave them behind. But as they comfort me, they also keep me trapped. If I am to have a future, I must let go of the past.

I hold my daughter close and step into the darkness, feeling my way, through cobwebs and dust, down the cold, damp sweep of the secret staircase.

Outside the moon is low and almost full. It is the hour before sunrise, when stars blink out, one by one, as black night turns to grey dawn. Any trace of yesterday's fog is gone. The air smells of honeysuckle and the sweet, pungent rot of the slurry pit.

My daughter wriggles and kicks inside the sling. I plant soothing kisses on her forehead and hush her until she settles, burrowing against my chest. I make my way to the well, and then to the old sycamore tree. Lowering myself to the ground, I lean back against the trunk, feeling the hard scratch of bark against my head. I loosen my bodice and pull my shift aside, cradling my daughter to my breast. I encourage her to drink. At first she splutters and grizzles, wailing a little with hunger, but after a time we both learn how, and when she is done, she falls asleep. Her gentle breathing becomes one with the first sounds of morning – the scurry of small animals, an owl's hoot, the caress of breeze in the sycamore leaves.

I watch the sky. On the horizon, a single star still shines bright. It seems close enough that I could reach out and touch it. I want to roll it in my palm, like a brilliant gem. I remember that night in Gustard Wood when Rafe told me how our story might be written in the stars. I do not doubt that he knew and accepted his own end when it came – though God knows I still cannot – but perhaps our story is not ended after all. It begins again, with the tiny, peaceful creature bundled in my arms.

I find a place where the roots of the tree make a deep triangle with the earth, twisted and gnarled, rising up from the ground to make a hollow beneath. When I was a child I used to think this was a place where the fey people made a home – hidden and yet not hidden, a secret pocket away from prying eyes. The memory raises a smile that feels unfamiliar on my lips.

I dig with my fingers. Then I take Henrietta Maria's charm from around my neck. It has worked its magic for me and I will not need it again. I press my lips to the silvered heart one last time, whispering my own secret wish, and then I place it inside the hollow and bury it, packing the earth tightly.

I will never see Henrietta Maria again and I will never ask her to keep her promise. By doing what I mean to do, I forfeit all such claims. All my dreams, all my longings, I leave here in the earth, along with my memories, along with my birthright, along with the past.

In the stables I find that Feather has been well cared for. Her saddle and bridle are cleaned and laid on a bench. The sacks of coin are still in the saddlebags, as are the remaining bandoliers and shot. My pistol rests in its holster. When I take it out and weigh it in my hand, the silver edging gleams as brightly as that first summer star.

The air in the chapel is cold and damp, as though summer cannot reach inside. My skirts, sweeping the stone flags, whisper like spirits. My heart leaps as a bat flutters in the beams.

She is here, a still white shape beneath a silver threaded cloth, laid out on a trestle at the side of the room.

I pull back the sheet.

They have not yet cleaned her, or sewn her into a winding sheet. She still wears the blood-crusted nightgown in which she died, the stains now turning black and hard. Dark purple bruises bloom around her eyes and her lips are strangely shadowed, revealing a slice of white teeth. Her body shows evidence enough of her sufferings in childbed, but beneath the blood, she still has the smooth, ivory skin we shared and her hair still shines the same rich chestnut.

She is like a doll, a manikin, an effigy. I place a single kiss on her marbled forehead, as if touching her might make it all real.

'I promise,' I whisper, the sound eerie in the shadows. 'I promise I'll do as you asked. Your daughter will want for nothing. I will do right by her. I will do right by you, in death, as I did not in life. You can trust me.' I put a hand to her cheek, expecting warmth, and am momentarily shocked by the cool slackness of flesh. I wish she could hear me. There are a hundred things I never had the chance to say.

'Forgive me, Rachel,' I begin, but I know, in my heart, she already has.

Chapter 60

I'm woken early by my daughter's cry. She is lying next to me, tucked close beneath the woollen blanket, safe in the crook of my arm. Her pink face is creased in frustration, little fists punching the air, fighting against the tent of fabric that keeps us warm. She is hungry.

I sit up, take her into my arms and put her to my breast. She latches on easily and begins to suck, making undignified snorts. I stroke and kiss the dome of her head. Her hair is fine and fair, soft as goose down.

The fire, which I've kept burning these five nights past, is almost out. Thin coils of smoke twine up into the canopy from blackened logs. Even at this early hour, it's warm enough to do without the heat, but I must protect my child from wild animals, and any wandering woodland sprites, that might roam too close in the darkness beneath the trees. I'm not worried about being found. No one will be looking for me. They think I am dead.

I've been here, in the clearing at Gustard Wood, since the morning I left Markyate Cell. I've marked the passing of five nights by carving a nick in the bark of a tree: I do not want to lose track of time. My daughter has no care for day or night. She follows her own rhythms, her own hunger and her own desires. She has no care for aught but the next feed, the next sleep, and the comfort of my arms. It is selfish and silly in a grown woman, perhaps, but I envy her simplicity. I wish I could be so carefree.

I wash her in the pool. I clean the soiled linen and bind it about her dimpled body to keep her warm, promising I will soon buy better. I bathe myself too, remembering happier times. Day by day, the wound in my arm begins to heal. The cutting pains between my legs lessen to a dull throb. When the sun is high, I strip away my clothes and step naked into the water. I float on my back, cradling my daughter between my breasts, feet tangling with the pondweed, tongues of cool water lapping softly at my skin. It soothes us both.

At night, when the dark walls of the forest close in, I tell her stories. I tell her everything. I tell her about Markyate Cell and the time before death came, when I played in the orchards with my brothers and watched butterflies disappear into the sun. I tell her about my mother, her fine dresses and sparkling jewels, about the King's court in Oxford and Henrietta Maria's promise. I tell her about Rachel, my dearest friend, who had the kindest, most forgiving soul I ever knew. I tell her about George, about Aunt Alice and Anne Fanshawe, about Thomas, and Richard Willis.

And then I tell her about her father.

I tell her that the world is mistaken in him. He will be remembered, if he is remembered at all, as a highway robber and a treacherous spy – a bad man. But the world did not know the man he really was. That is not the true picture. My heart aches when I think that my daughter will never know him, so I weave tales for her – tales of his courage, his daring and his sacrifice. I tell her that her father was a good man, and one day, a long time from now, God willing, she will find out for herself, when she meets him at the gates of Heaven. She will know him by the shining love in his amber eyes.

As I talk, I watch the stars. I think of the nights that Rafe and I spent here, bound so tightly to one another, talking of a future that will never come to pass. He spoke of a life made by choices, and the chance to live free. It is a thing I never thought to have. I believed for so long that my life was chosen for me, a path set out by other people upon which I would always tread. Was it Rafe who shook me from my long sleep and set me upon a different course? Was it the man in the woods with his foul fingers and Devil's curse? Perhaps Richard Willis, the night he spoke of my wickedness, and I believed him because I already thought it was so?

No. I do not think it was any of those men. I do not think it was God or the Devil. By each small choice, each decision, I have made my own way here. I have chosen this life. There is no one to blame but myself. And I cannot change it now. I'm grateful to find I do not want to.

Martha said I must accept the past if I am to find what I seek. I must embrace the whole – every mistake, every failing, every petty thought and jealous passion. I must own all my sins. There can be no freedom while I am bound by guilt and shame and regret, no matter what the church men say.

I promise myself this: my daughter will not have a mother bridled by suffering and remorse, or thwarted by the ties of money, property and wifely duty. She will have a mother who answers to no one – no preacher, no husband, no man. She will have a mother who lives free, as wild and as wicked as she pleases.

If there is one gift I can give my daughter, it is this.

This morning I let the fire burn out. After my daughter has fed, I take a little bread and cheese myself, then prepare Feather for travel. Her saddlebags are heavy with coin. I have counted out the spoils that almost cost my life. Sir William Cobden's wealth will keep us fed and clothed for some time, if I am careful.

I pack the rest of the foodstuffs, and collect the clean swaddling, washed out in the pool and dried on the low boughs of the forest, flapping like white flags of surrender. From the hut I take as much powder and shot as I can carry. I strap my pistol into the saddle holster. Then I make a sling and tie the child tight to my chest. She rests there, content and cocooned.

The sun is strong by the time I reach Ware. I dismount and go on by foot, leading Feather through quiet back lanes, avoiding the high street to reach St Mary's.

The church bell tolls a single mournful note. I find a place in the trees at the edge of the churchyard and tie Feather there. I creep to the tree line, keeping low in the shadows until I have a clear view of the church door. A man leans against the wall, chewing tobacco. I watch him hawk and spit onto a nearby grave. He coughs, clears his throat, mutters something under his breath, shifting his weight and rubbing the small of his back.

It's not long before a coach draws up. My heart flutters as I recognise the Fanshawe horses, and the Ware Park groom dressed in ill-fitting, faded livery that has not been worn since before the wars. Thomas descends, closely followed by Leventhorpe and his wife. Thomas is soberly dressed, pale and thin, playing the part of the grieving husband well. Leventhorpe wears a fine green coat with gold buttons, hat adorned with a rich plume of feathers. Diamonds sparkle at his wife's throat.

A cart travels close behind, a trail of dark clad bodies in its wake. Master Stone climbs down from the driver's seat and directs the boys who will carry the coffin. He takes the fourth corner of the plain wooden box, head bowed. I feel a twinge of guilt at his evident grief, a price that must be paid for my freedom.

Others are gathering in the churchyard – several townsmen and their wives, onlookers, come to stare. Martha is there, arm through the crook of her father's. She wears a look of calm composure. I wonder how she does it – never giving away the things that she must feel inside. On the surface she is my opposite, choosing the path of duty, obligation and gentle, uncomplaining submission. But I know that there is so much more to her than that – a secret inner life of which she never speaks. When she confided in me, I knew I could trust her to complete my plan. And now she is the keeper of my secrets. My future lies in her hands.

I swear I will find a way, one day, to pay her back.

I watch them gather, this little group of mismatched souls. I watch as the coffin is taken into the church to be put into the Fanshawe vault, and they all file in behind. I creep a little closer and find a sheltered spot against the church wall, below a small window. From my hiding place, I can hear the faint echo of the vicar as the service is read; the words I have heard so many times before, for so many other people.

I wonder how many of the mourners have seen the body inside the box. What has it cost to silence the stable lads, the nursemaid and the midwife, Hannah? For how long will they stay silent about the things they have seen? I imagine Martha tending Rachel, alone in the cool, dead air of the chapel – cleaning her, binding her and sewing her into a winding sheet, so that no one else would see the body that takes my place in the family vault.

Just then another figure steps down from the Fanshawe coach. I recognise the ginger-haired nursemaid from Markyate Cell. She wears a neat apron and cap and cradles a bundle in her arms. She paces, jiggling and cooing. A high, thin wail wheedles above the steady incantation of the vicar. Martha swore there was nothing to fear from this girl, that she could be trusted, and I wonder what she has been promised to hold her tongue. I wonder how much of the truth she knows.

In time, when the service is over, I make my way back to the shadows beneath the trees and watch the gathering leave the church. Thomas's face is grim. Leventhorpe puts a hand on his friend's shoulder, leaning close to whisper in Thomas's ear. The nursemaid goes up to them and carefully hands the child to

Thomas. One tiny arm emerges, fingers splaying, reaching up towards his face. He looks down and his expression alters. His frown dissolves and his eyes grow tender. He makes a gentle rocking motion to quiet his new daughter.

There is a thick feeling in my throat, choking me so I can barely breathe. Rachel was right: though Thomas will never know that the child he holds is truly his own, he will care for her all the same.

I stay there a few moments longer, watching, holding my own baby to me as she pushes her face against my chest.

Feather is waiting, sweating and stamping, as the day grows hot. I climb slowly into the saddle, checking that the pistol is safe inside the holster. I take off my hat and fasten it to my pack. I unpin my hair and let it fall about my shoulders, feeling the breeze lift it away from my neck. When I reach the crossroads, I take the road north.

I close my eyes and imagine I can catch the scent of sand dunes, marram grass and fresh-tilled earth, feel the heat of sunbaked stone and the salt-scoured whip of a northern wind around the battlements of a castle by the sea.

My daughter squirms inside the sling. I take Feather's reins in one hand and, with the other, stroke my baby's cheek. Her skin is softer than a butterfly's wing. She smells of milk and pine cones and wood smoke. Her heart beats against mine. She reaches up and curls her tiny fingers around my own. She looks up at me, searching my face with amber-flecked eyes.

She is my past and my future.

She is my new life.

I shall name her Rachel.

Epilogue
1674

I do not believe in ghosts.

When the stories first began, I dismissed them as the gossip and prattle of idle minds. I assumed that the fancy would soon pass, as these things do, and be forgotten by midsummer. But the rumours persist.

She is seen in the village at Markyate. Widow Falmouth says she caught a glimpse of a swift, fleet figure, with wild auburn hair, on the very day that a new-baked pie went missing from her kitchen. I do not think that ghosts eat pies.

She is spied by one of the altar boys at St Mary's, kneeling on the carved stone seal above the Fanshawe vault. The youth said his blood turned to ice when she looked upon him and her eyes were the colour of Hell's fire. His story, growing ever more elaborate with each telling, attracts a crowd of gossips in the marketplace, and the boy has to be comforted by the goodwives of Ware.

The tales grow wilder.

The drunken innkeeper from Nomansland says she rides a pale grey mare across the common in the dead of night, galloping as though the Devil were at her heels. The gaoler at Hertford says he saw her by the castle gates, in the black hours before dawn, idling in the very spot where the gibbet is put up on execution days. He said she was singing softly to herself – old ballads about outlaws and hanged men.

One of my own kitchen lads catches her in the walled garden, here at Markyate Cell, stretching on tiptoe, peering into the parlour through the leads. When I ask him what he was doing, wandering in the gardens past midnight, he pales and says no more.

I have long understood that simple folk will create their own truths as a way of making sense of the world. Instead of turning to God, they turn to their folk tales and superstitions, explaining God's mysteries so that they can go on living each day without question. The need for such understanding is common, and when I was young, I quested after it myself. But now I am older, I find I am of a more accepting mind. I no longer need to understand the workings of God's world. I no longer need to rage against its injustices and its sorrows. I have given up trying to understand the secret longings of every heart, even my own. Each one of us is so complex and unique, such a task would never be complete.

The peace I once strove for lies in the simple things. That is the lesson I failed to teach Katherine Ferrers all those years ago. Or perhaps I did not fail, in the end.

I have kept my secrets close these fourteen years. I have never told another soul my own wild tales. The morning I found the red chamber deserted, I knew that Kate had done as I'd hoped. She had chosen to make her own future, and I understood exactly what she asked of me.

As I sent the sad news to Ware Park and handed the child into Thomas Fanshawe's care, I knew it was what she intended. As I sewed Rachel Chaplin into her winding sheet and laid her to rest in the Fanshawe vault, I swore that my part in the tale would be laid to rest too. But these rumours have woken the sleeping doubts. I ask God, Are these long years of loneliness my punishment for the lies I told then? Is she come back now to stir my conscience before the end?

It is early evening and I am in the library. This room was my father's favourite and, since he passed, it has become mine. I write my correspondence here and attend to the business of the estate from the old oak desk next to the window with a broad view across the gardens to the park, and beyond, to the line of trees at the edge of the woods.

The midsummer light is golden, playing upon the riotous blooms in the flowerbeds. The air is laden with insects, wings catching the sun, glowing like fireflies. A cool breeze comes through the casement, bringing the scent of warm earth, roses and something sharper – an unfamiliar tang of salt and sea marsh.

I pause in my letter-writing and go to the window. The workers are all finished for the day, safe in their homes, or supping in the village alehouse, and there is no one in sight. I look out over this land of which I have become custodian: the pretty walled garden, full-planted with the first burst of summer roses, alive with the flutter of cabbage whites; the skeps, busy with the hum of bees; the stretch of scrubby parkland, stretching down towards the farm and beyond that the village. And the old trees, dotted here and there, as though they have stepped out of the woodland to unfurl their leaves and bask in the last warmth of the day. Everything is peaceful and still.

And then I see her.

She is standing beneath the boughs of an old sycamore, staring towards the house. She is dressed in patched skirts of dirty brown that may once have been scarlet. She is small and slight, just as I remember. Her hair is loose and shines russet in the evening light.

My heart seems to stop for a few moments. My chest pinches. A sudden chill makes the hairs on my forearms prickle.

She seems to be looking straight at me and, like a fool, I duck away from the window. It cannot be, I tell myself. It is a fancy of the mind brought on by servants' gossip and my own daydreaming. I must be overtired. I have worked too long today.

I peep around the edge of the stone sill. She is still there. But now she is bending beneath the tree, on her knees, face hidden by a fall of hair. I watch, heart pounding. It cannot be. It is not possible.

★ ★ ★

Outside, the air still holds the heat of the day. I walk quickly, stopping by the old well to steady my breath, and then on towards the tree. She is sitting now, leaning back against the trunk, gazing intently at something in her palm.

I stop a good distance away and wait.

She becomes aware of me.

At first she starts up, like a frightened animal, springing to her feet. She snatches up a pistol, snaps the flint into place and aims it steadily at my chest. The barrel glints silver, reflecting the sun's low rays.

'Wait!' I call out. 'Please . . . I will not hurt you.'

She hesitates, unsure, ready to fly. Something dangles from her wrist, catching the light.

Now I am close, I see how young she is. But, by God, she has the same looks – the same rich curls, though this girl's are tangled and matted with leaves and dried grass, as if she has been sleeping in the hedgerows. She has the same slight frame, budding with the promise of womanhood, the same skin, the colour of almond milk, the same pointed oval face and small pink lips. She has the same wide eyes, burning with that unmistakable fire.

'I promise, I will not hurt you,' I repeat. 'I just wish to speak with you.'

She measures me, makes her judgement.

Sudden recognition lights her expression. 'You are Martha,' she says, matter of fact.

'Yes . . . yes, I am.' I take a few steps towards her and spread my palms, but the pistol stays in place.

'Come no closer.' There is a spark in her tone. I see it all – the tinder of her anger, the ready temper, the flash in her eyes. She is surely her mother's daughter.

For a few moments we are silent. A rook caws in the trees at the edge of the woods and is answered by its fellows.

'You are welcome here,' I say. 'Please do not run away.' I indicate the ground beneath the tree. 'May I sit with you awhile?'

Her gaze never leaves me, but she gives a curt nod and lowers the gun. She takes a few steps back to the trunk where she sits, folding her legs neatly beneath her. I see that she has dug out a hollow beneath one of the tree roots. Her hands are dirty, fingernails black with soil. She eyes me warily, keeping the gun cocked and within reach.

'You are not what I thought you would be,' she says eventually, and I note the strange lilt of her accent.

'People seldom are.'

'She said your hair was black.'

I smile, touching my temples. 'Time is not kind to we women.'

She sighs deeply. 'Her hair was the shade of a gull's wing, by the end.'

'You are speaking of your mother.'

'She said that she owed you a great debt.'

'Where is your mother now?'

She studies the thing in her hand. She wipes the earth from it. It is a tarnished silver pendant, made in the shape of a heart. I recognise it. The feeling it stirs in me is akin to recalling a sad memory, long forgotten.

'She is dead.'

I knew this, I think, but my heart tilts to hear it said aloud, to know it is certain.

The girl goes on: 'I'm come back to settle her debt.' She fixes me with a clear-eyed look. There is a pride about her that is so familiar it makes a knot rise in my throat.

'And how will you do that?' I ask.

'That is up to you. She bade me come here and find this.' She holds up the necklace. 'She said you would know. She said you would do right by me.'

It takes me a moment, but as I look deep into the young woman's fearless eyes, it all comes clear. Oh, Kate. Clever, constant Kate. I see now that you never gave up on your long-held hope. I have kept your secrets these lonely years, never expecting aught in return for the lies I told, except the stain upon my conscience. But now you have sent me the one thing you could – your most precious legacy. It is the thing I have most desired, the thing that my whole life has lacked. It seems that, at the end, you have bequeathed to me the greatest of gifts.

'Do you have a place to sleep?' I ask, though I can already guess her answer. She shakes her head. 'Then you shall stay here.'

The girl's eyes widen. She has no expectation. 'Here, at Markyate Cell?'

'For as long as you want. You belong here.'

I see that she suddenly understands – that this is why Kate sent her, though she says, 'You would do this, though you do not know me?'

'I know you,' I say. 'I was the first to hold you when you came into this world.' I stand, dusting down my skirts.

She smiles then and the brightness in her eyes is glorious.

'Come,' I say. 'I have the perfect chamber for you. It was your mother's favourite and the room in which you were born. Let me show you . . .'

She loops the pendant around her neck, the silvered heart resting upon her breast. Then she stands. I hold out my hand. 'Tell me, what is your name?'

'Rachel,' she says. 'My name is Rachel.'

My heart is glad.

She comes close and slips her hand into mine. I feel her fragile bones, the scratch of dirt between our fingers.

'Come then, Rachel,' I say. 'Let us go home.'

Together we turn and walk slowly across the park, back to Markyate Cell.

Acknowledgements

I am very grateful to Leeanne Westwood for granting access to the Fanshawe portrait collection at Valence House Museum, and to Jonathan Ferguson for a memorable day at the Royal Armouries and advice on seventeenth century firearms.

Huge thanks to the whole team at Headline; to my editors Claire Baldwin and Leah Woodburn; to Caitlin Raynor, Vicky Palmer, Yeti Lambregts, Darcy Nicholson, Amy Perkins and Hazel Orme; and to my agent Annette Green.

Heartfelt thanks to all those friends, family, fellow writers and cheerleaders who continue to give invaluable support and encouragement. Special thanks are due to Jan Clements, for her red pen, and to Ian and Paula Madej, to whom this book is dedicated, for so generously giving me a room of my own.

The Silvered Heart

Bonus Material

The Real Wicked Lady: Fact or Fiction?

Reading Group Questions

The Real Wicked Lady: Fact or Fiction?

This book is a work of fiction based on the legend of seventeenth century highwaywoman, the Wicked Lady, and historical research into the life of Katherine Ferrers, the real woman with whom the legend has traditionally been associated.

Stories of women disguised as robbers, soldiers or sailors are common in folklore, but the particular tale in question goes something like this: Lady Katherine Ferrers, a young orphaned heiress, is forced into a marriage of convenience. Years of devastating civil war and pressure on the fortunes of royalist families see Katherine's inheritance quickly devoured. Trapped in a loveless marriage, bored and frustrated by a neglectful husband and her reduced circumstances, Katherine finds escape when she meets local farmer and highway robber, Ralph (or Rafe) Chaplin. The two embark on a wild crime spree, targeting travellers on Watling Street and Nomansland Common – a seventeenth century Bonnie and Clyde.

Before long, Ralph is captured and hanged. Driven mad by grief, Katherine's behaviour becomes increasingly ruthless, her violent crimes including arson, the slaughter of cattle, and the murder of a local constable. One night, she is fatally wounded during a hold-up on Nomansland Common. Her body is discovered the next morning, at the foot of a concealed staircase at her ancestral home, Markyate Cell. She is buried in secret, by night, at St Mary's church in Ware.

But the story doesn't end there. Sightings of Katherine's ghost have been reported ever since. She's been seen and heard wandering the staircases at Markyate Cell and swinging beneath the branches of an old sycamore tree in the grounds. When the house burnt down in the 1840s, those fighting the flames are said to have sensed her malevolent presence. Ramblers on Nomansland Common report the sight and sound of a ghostly rider. At nearby stables, owners have been puzzled to find their horses exhausted and sweating, as if they've been galloping across the heath.

It's a swashbuckling adventure that has inspired novels and films, including a classic 1945 version starring James Mason and Margaret Lockwood, but the life of the real woman tells a different tale. Katherine Ferrers certainly suffered grief, hardship, and the devastation of a family fortune, as did many women during the English Civil War and its aftermath, but did she really turn to crime? And what does her story tell us about the position and fate of women during this tumultuous time in British history?

From historical records we can glean the following information. Katherine Ferrers was born at Markyate Cell in May 1634 into troubled times; by the age of six, her father and two brothers had died. Her mother soon remarried to Simon Fanshawe, a member of the prominent Fanshawe family – wealthy landowners with strong links to the King. The marriage was most likely a practical arrangement. But these were the years of civil war and the life that Katherine would have recognised as a young child was to be turned upside down.

The family moved to Oxford for a time, to enable Simon Fanshawe to be close to the King, who established his Court in the city in 1642. Katherine's mother died there in 1643, leaving

Katherine as sole heir to the Ferrers' title and fortune. She became a ward of the Fanshawes and was married in 1648, just before her fourteenth birthday, to her cousin Thomas; an amalgamation of property and assets that should have been mutually beneficial. The wedding is mentioned in the memoirs of Anne Fanshawe who described Katherine as 'of very great fortune and a most excellent woman'.

The ceremony took place at Hamerton Manor in Cambridgeshire. Katherine probably stayed there for some time afterwards, under the protection of Alice Bedell, another Fanshawe relative. It was not uncommon for young couples to live apart until they reached a more appropriate age to start a family.

Although Katherine retained her hereditary title as Lady Ferrers, her money and possessions became the property of her husband. Financial pressures resulting from the war, the sequestration of Fanshawe estates and subsequent fines and taxes quickly swallowed up Katherine's fortune.

Some years later, Ware Park was restored to the Fanshawes and Katherine presumably returned to take up her life as Thomas's wife, but she is hard to track down. We do know that Katherine's family home, Markyate Cell, was sold in 1655, and passed to the Coppin family in 1657.

We can piece together a picture of what life might have been like for Katherine during those years. It's likely that her husband was often absent. Thomas took up a place at the Inns of Court in 1657 and probably spent much of his time in London. Although Anne Fanshawe thought Thomas 'of excellent understanding, and of great honour and honesty', Earl Clarendon was not so convinced, claiming him to be a 'rash, foolish, and hotheaded man'. We can only guess which of them was right, or how Thomas might have viewed his marital obligations, but the union produced no recorded offspring – something that would have been a significant problem.

The Fanshawes remained loyal to the Monarchy throughout

the Interregnum and were involved in the various royalist conspiracy rings that sprang up in the 1650s. Thomas was arrested for his involvement in the Booth uprising of 1659 and was imprisoned in the Tower of London that September until the following February.

The Booth uprising was one of the most significant rebellions during the period, but was ultimately a failure, due in part to the betrayal of key information to Parliamentarian agents. It's widely believed that Sir Richard Willys (or Willis) was the informant. He was a royalist with an impressive military record and close links to Prince Rupert and Charles I. During the Interregnum he was imprisoned and questioned several times, entering into an agreement to pass secret intelligence to John Thurloe, Oliver Cromwell's infamous spymaster. The circumstances of this agreement and Willys's motives are unclear. Willys's reputation began to crumble in 1659 when rumours of his double-dealing emerged. Some stood by him, unable to believe the accusation of treason. A close look at the evidence suggests plenty of room for doubt but he was found guilty. Charles II eventually issued a pardon in recognition of Willys's previous service to the Crown and he retired to a quiet life. Willys always maintained his innocence.

Whatever the truth of Willys's story, Thomas Fanshawe's involvement in these political intrigues helps us to establish Katherine's likely connections, acquaintances, political influences, and financial circumstances. We know that she had lost her family, her fortune and her home. Her husband was preoccupied, there were money troubles and she had failed to provide an heir. Her husband's imprisonment would have caused an additional burden, not to mention the impact on Katherine's reputation by association. It's not so hard to believe that a woman in such dire straits might have taken matters into her own hands.

The only further mention of Katherine occurs in the memoirs of Anne Fanshawe – a passing reference that Katherine was residing at the Strand when Charles II made his triumphal entry into London in May 1660. Her burial is recorded just two weeks later, on 13th June; it's likely that she was interred in the Fanshawe vault, at St Mary's church, Ware. She was twenty-six years old.

Researchers have suggested that she may have died in childbirth. A record of the burial of Marie Fanshawe, daughter of Thomas Fanshawe, in November 1660, supports this theory. But there is no evidence of Thomas's child elsewhere and Anne Fanshawe does not mention a pregnancy just two weeks prior. It's also worth noting that if Katherine gave birth to a daughter who survived, albeit for only five months, then the child must have been carried to term and conceived the previous September, when Thomas was imprisoned in the Tower.

There is no historical evidence that Katherine was ever involved in highway robbery.

No record of Ralph Chaplin has ever been found.

It's easy to imagine the scenario as legend tells it. The English Revolution really did turn the world upside down for many people, and for more than a decade, aristocratic families who believed they had a right to their inherited status and wealth found their estates taken away, heavy fines and taxes imposed, and in some cases, no choice but to live a life of poverty in exile. Married women, considered the property of their husbands, and with no means of their own, were forced to cope with painfully reduced circumstances that were the very opposite of the life they had been raised to expect. But such women were not necessarily powerless. Many rose to the challenges of war and misfortune, exhibiting great fortitude and strong political views, changing the world around them through a variety of means. Anne Fanshawe is just one example of a woman who suffered great loss, adversity and danger but wielded considerable influence via her husband. Her writing still influences our view of Civil War women today.

In other social spheres, women were prominent in radical political movements, some demanding equal rights with men. Female preachers and prophets played key roles within new religious sects and published their ideas in pamphlets and tracts. Women took over family businesses, defended their homes and even took to the battlefield. Once sampled, these freedoms might have been hard to give up.

The only known portrait of Katherine Ferrers, now owned by Valence House Museum, shows a slight, pretty young woman. We don't know exactly when the portrait was painted or by whom. It was perhaps a wedding gift, executed by a journeyman painter sometime around 1648. Recently restored, the image reveals something of Katherine's character: a direct gaze, a certain mischief in the eyes and a Mona Lisa smile.

The mystery of how this young woman became the Wicked Lady of legend remains obscure. *The Silvered Heart* is one fictional version of events, but I hope, one that gives an insight into what life might have been like for those women and children whose fates were irrevocably altered as a result of the English Civil War.

The question of whether Katherine really was the Wicked Lady, I leave to history, and to my readers, to decide.

© Clare Finn

The only known portrait of Lady Katherine Ferrers, now at
Valence House Museum.

Reading Group Questions

1. Were you familiar with the legend of the Wicked Lady before? If so, did the novel alter your preconceptions of that tale?

2. Katherine struggles with questions of morality in her sexual relationships throughout *The Silvered Heart*. How do you feel the author utilised this as a commentary on gender relations?

3. How do you feel Katherine's political leanings in the Civil War influence her character?

4. Female relationships are arguably stronger than those of romantic ones in the novel; to what extent do you feel this is influenced by the historical setting?

5. Many of the main characters commit an act of betrayal in some form or another. How did these individually alter your sympathies as your reading continued?

6. Many of the relationships in the novel are forged across class boundaries. Discuss the dynamic this introduced to different pairings.

7. How was the use of violence in the novel utilised to comment on social and gender divides?

8. Did you find yourself supportive or concerned by Katherine's relationship with Rafe?

9. What other historical fiction did you find the *The Silvered Heart* reminiscent of?

The Crimson Ribbon

KATHERINE CLEMENTS

May Day 1646: Ruth Flowers finds herself suddenly, brutally, alone. Forced to flee the household of Oliver Cromwell, the only home she has ever known, Ruth takes the road to London, and there is given refuge by Lizzie Poole.

Beautiful and charismatic, Lizzie enthrals the vulnerable Ruth, binding her inextricably to her world. But Ruth is still haunted by fears of her past catching up with her. And as Lizzie's radical ideas escalate, Ruth finds herself carried to the heart of the country's conflict, to the trial of a king.

Based on the real figure of the fascinating Elizabeth Poole, *The Crimson Ribbon* conjures a mesmerising story of two women's obsession, superstition and hope.

Praise for *The Crimson Ribbon*:

'The vibrant new voice of historical fiction' Suzannah Dunn

'Exceptional . . . Deftly written, uncluttered and impassioned, this has to be one of the leading historical debuts of the year' Manda Scott

'Impressive and inspirational' Alison Weir

978 1 4722 0422 6

headline
review

THE RAVEN'S HEAD

KAREN MAITLAND

Never trust your secrets to a Raven,
when you are not its true master . . .

The Raven is waiting.

France, 1224. Vincent stumbles upon a secret that could destroy his master and a naive attempt at blackmail leaves him on the run and in possession of a silver raven's head.

The Raven is coming.

Vincent escapes to England but every attempt to sell the raven's head fails and instead he makes his way from town to town, selling lies and stories to line his purse.

The Raven is here.

He hears of a Baron, a man whose reputation should make him a buyer for the head . . . or a story. Vincent demands an audience with Lord Sylvain, but it might be the last demand he makes. It doesn't pay to deal with an Alchemist.

Some might think the Raven was seeking passage home.

'Dark and woven with the supernatural' *Daily Mail*

'Rich and believable . . . her deftly drawn characters spring vividly to life' *Sunday Express*

978 1 4722 1506 2

headline
review